PV-11
Et Sequitur

William A. Keefe

BRIGHTON PUBLISHING LLC
435 N. HARRIS DRIVE
MESA, AZ 85203

PV-11

Et Sequitur

WILLIAM A. KEEFE

BRIGHTON PUBLISHING LLC
435 N. HARRIS DRIVE
MESA, AZ 85203
WWW.BRIGHTONPUBLISHING.COM

COPYRIGHT © 2013

ISBN 13: 978-1-62183-178-5
ISBN 10: 1-621-83178-7

PRINTED IN THE UNITED STATES OF AMERICA

First Edition

COVER DESIGN: TOM RODRIGUEZ

— DEDICATION —

To my late wife, Carolyn, and to Frank Norvell, whose encouragement kept me working on this book since 1980; and to my granddaughter, Lisa Paper, whose editing skills pointed the way to a readable first few chapters.

— CHAPTER ONE —

First Glimpse

Space Exploration Joint Service (SEJS) Lieutenant Patrick Callen was jogging toward the skunkworks on Log Base 36 when he saw something he had never seen before: a tug dragging a big black ball out of a hangar. He stopped to take a closer look and saw that the ball was sitting in a wheeled cradle. To his complete amazement, the ball then disappeared—except that where the top, bottom, and sides of the ball had been, navigation lights appeared. As if by magic, the lights rose up in unison, glided from the hangar to the adjacent taxiway, travelled about a kilometer, returned, and settled back into the cradle. The black ball reappeared, its navigation lights went out, and the tug pulled the ball and its cradle back into the hangar. The hangar door closed and the show was over.

Pat Callen, who was spending two weeks of R&R at Log Base 36 after completing a tour of duty in fighters, jogged back to the Bachelor Officer's Quarters (BOQ) where he was staying, cleaned up, and went to breakfast. He was dying to ask someone about what he had seen, but he decided that discretion was the better part of valor.

To prepare for leaving his fighter squadron, he had updated his dream sheet, listing command of a ship as his first priority; second, a leadership position aboard a star base or battleship; and, third, a staff job, preferably aboard ship. He knew, however, that these preferences were typical and, as someone who had been slated for a career in military intelligence, the odds were that he was about to become a desk jockey.

He decided to force the issue. He caught the shuttle to Base Headquarters, located the personnel office, and found an unoccupied communications booth. He put his eye in front of a scanner by the door and waited until a computer-generated voice said, "Lieutenant Callen, please come in and be seated." He complied, sat in front of the console, and said, "Request an interview with an intel career counselor."

After a brief pause, the picture of a lieutenant commander whose nametag said "MARTIN" appeared on the viewer. She said, "Good morning, lieutenant. Are you calling about your next assignment?"

"Yes, ma'am," he replied, "I was wondering whether you had decided what is in store for me."

She smiled and said, "No problem, lieutenant. Your orders are due out shortly. Let's see; at this point, we've found three possibilities. Would you like to know what they are?

"Yes, ma'am. I realize that the needs of the Service could change, but Log Base 36 is an interesting place and I'd like to know if remaining here might be possible."

"It doesn't look like it. One of your options is to command a PV, another is to be an admiral's aide (subject, of course, to the admiral's acceptance), and the third is to be an assistant G-2 on a Star Base."

"What's a PV?" he asked.

"All I know is that it is a type of specialized ship," she answered. "If you are interested, I'll see if I can schedule an interview for you. The PV program manager's office happens to be a tenant on Log Base 36, so we should be able to coordinate an interview for you."

"That sounds good," Pat said. "My R&R has helped me wind down, but it has become a bit boring."

She smiled and replied, "It's supposed to be that way, lieutenant. Enjoy it while you can. I'll get back to you when we've talked to the PV folks."

Pat signed off, changed into civilian clothes at his BOQ, and went into town for lunch. In mid-afternoon, the phone on his wrist vibrated to let him know he had a call. It was LtCdr. Martin, who told him that he was expected at the program manager's office at 0900 hours the next morning.

He arose at 0600, exercised, showered, and donned his uniform. He checked his appearance in the mirror: not bad for a warrior with an apparent age in his early thirties—a touch of gray at the temples; a little taller than average; physically fit; reasonably good looking; and wearing an impressive array of military decorations.

When Pat arrived at the program manager's office, he was very surprised to learn that he was to see the program manager himself, Captain Dreelin. Junior or non-commissioned officers usually handled administrative business.

Pat reported to Dreelin with a smart salute. The captain responded in kind, invited him to sit, and got right down to business. "Lieutenant, I see that you have requested a command. You are aware, aren't you, that there are very few command billets for junior intel officers?"

"Yes, sir, but if there's a command available, I'd like to have it."

"I have reviewed your qualifications," the captain said. "The medics have given you a clean bill of health, including your psych profile. Your service record and fitness reports are excellent. Your Navy Cross and Silver Star citations lead me to believe that you are lucky to be alive and, as Napoleon once said, good luck is extremely important to commanders. And six kills to your credit—well above average, to say the least."

"Thank you, sir. There is no shortage of hostiles in this sector, and I had outstanding wing men."

"Clearly, but it speaks well of you that SEJS has made you a candidate for command of a PV." The captain gazed at the screen on his desk, appearing to scroll through Pat's data.

"Sir, I sincerely believe that I am ready for a command, but I have a question. Please forgive my ignorance, but exactly what is a PV?"

The captain darkened his screen and turned back to Pat with a grin. "You mean you didn't know what it was you were seeing down by the skunkworks yesterday morning?"

Pat did a double take and responded, "Sir, I have heard some talk about PVs, but to the best of my knowledge, I have never seen or been anywhere near one. What I saw yesterday, though, blew my mind! Was that a PV?"

"Yes, it was, and you have passed one of my tests by not blabbing about it to anyone." Dreelin leaned back in his chair and steepled his fingers. "That particular ship is coming out of rebuild. What you witnessed was one of her taxiing tests. Incidentally, I'm sure you are wondering how I knew you were there."

"Yes, sir." Pat had indeed been wondering, although he could guess. "I assume there are surveillance devices around the skunkworks, but I'm not sure why my jogging there would come to your attention."

"You're right about the surveillance, son. Log Base S-2 reported your presence before we brought the ship out of the hangar. I allowed the depot to proceed because SEJS personnel had told me you were a candidate for PV duty." Dreelin leaned across his desk and pointed a forefinger at Pat. "Your having seen one makes it much easier to conduct this interview, and if you don't make the cut, you'll be debriefed and will be forbidden to discuss the incident.

"Now," continued the captain, "let me respond to your question. 'PV' stands for patrol vessel. The name makes sense because PVs patrol—that is, escort convoys, screen task forces, and reconnoiter potentially dangerous places. All of those missions entail gathering information and developing intelligence, both of which are consistent with your being an intel officer. Are you still interested? If you successfully complete PV training, PV-11 will be available."

"Eleven? That's a low hull number." Pat hoped his disappointment wasn't too obvious.

"True, but no more of her class are being built, and the SEJS's functional requirements aren't going away. Although PV-11 is no spring chicken, in a few days she will be in 'like new or better than new' condition."

"I am definitely interested, sir, and I'd appreciate being allowed to give it a try." Pat still had an unanswered question, one that had puzzled him since he'd learned who would be interviewing him. "However, with respect, may I ask why a program manager—obviously, a senior captain—is talking to me about assignments?"

Smiling, Dreelin replied, "Not a problem. I make it a practice to personally interview candidates for PV command and make the selections myself. That said, I do not make a final decision until a candidate successfully completes the training course.

"Before you decide to give it a try, you need to know that the PV fleet has been catching hell lately. We aren't sure why. Although PVs are very stealthy, we've lost four in the past year. In fact, after her latest mission, PV-11 was a combat loss. We either had to tear her down for parts or put her back together and update her to the latest and greatest configuration."

"Is the new configuration a significant improvement, sir?"

"We have every reason to believe so. The armament and hardware advances are minor. However, the software upgrades are significant. In many respects, a PV is an up-gunned, oversized, stealthy fighter. You know from experience that fighter software enhances pilots' capabilities and can bring a ship home in a pinch. The new PV software is an order of magnitude more intelligent. It will control the ship's subsystems almost all of the time. It will have extensive conversational and cognitive abilities. It will accept mission assignments from you, keep you informed, and look to you for command decisions—time permitting."

"Sir, in our academy classes we discussed this sort of thing in depth. The consensus was that it is best to place limits on the role of software."

"No change there, but the machine can now carry much more of the load. Bear in mind that a PV spends most of her time off by herself, doing reconnaissance or surveillance. Eventually, a human has to eat, sleep, and have time to think about matters other than business. We believe that making the ship more self-sufficient during pilot downtime, not to mention reducing ship reaction times, will make our PVs more viable."

"How long does a PV command assignment last?"

"That varies in accordance with a point system. Scientific research and star system mapping missions earn five points each. Those are the only types that can exceed ten days, and they can't be longer than thirty days for logistic reasons. Recon and convoy screening missions with no enemy contact also count five points. Missions involving enemy contact rate no fewer than ten points. The number of points above ten is determined at task force or higher level. You'll get fourteen days' R&R after each twenty-five points, and you must relinquish command when you have accrued one hundred points."

"Sounds fair, sir."

"Good show." Dreelin stood up, signaling that the interview was concluding. "Consider yourself selected for training. Oh, by the way, the assignment entails a brevet promotion to lieutenant commander. Congratulations—and Godspeed!"

— CHAPTER TWO —

PV Flight School

When his R&R was over, Pat reported to PV Pilot Training School next to the skunkworks. Processing in was interesting. School headquarters took a DNA sample and crosschecked it with his retinal scan and fingerprints. Then, certain that he was the man they were expecting, they downloaded a detailed map of the facilities to his watch.

He walked to the skunkworks gate, where an armed guard allowed him to pass through the security fence. On the far side of the hangar where he had first seen a PV, an access controller on a door marked "Entrance" scanned his retinas and told him, "Welcome, lieutenant! The learning center is through the door and down the passageway to the right."

The learning center resembled those he had known throughout his education. He entered the room, selected one of the enclosed kiosks, and touched a fingertip to a sensor on its doorframe. A sign next to the door lit up with the notice, "In Use by LT Patrick Callen."

The door unlocked. He walked inside, sat down in one of the chairs, and turned toward the worktable. Three 48-inch displays, arranged like mirrors in a clothing store, lit up. A pleasant female voice said, "Welcome to PV pilot training, lieutenant. May I call you Pat?"

"Certainly," he responded.

"Thank you, Pat," the instructor continued. "That will improve the flow of information. Before we begin, I'd like you to know that although this learning center looks typical, it is not. Because all of your lessons are classified SECRET, but we do not want to cut you off from the outside world, we have provided compartmentalized communications for your use. The instructional computers in your worktable connect wirelessly to the base local area network and thence to the SEJS wide area network.

"The workstation on your left connects to the Federation Internet. It has no connectivity to military information systems. You can browse for unclassified information, but you can't upload data to the Internet. You may use your phone as usual to transfer information through SEJS channels. Please touch the 'Acknowledged' icon to signify that you understand."

Pat complied, and the instructor continued. "With those matters taken care of, Pat, we shall begin with a recorded briefing that will familiarize you with major issues affecting the PV program. Captain Dreelin has asked us to show this to all prospective PV pilots. If, after seeing it, you have questions or comments, you can either send him an email or record your thoughts for reference in your exit interview at the end of training."

Music came from speakers below the displays, and the middle screen opened on a scene that could have been a press conference, except that the audience consisted of high-ranking SEJS officers and civilians. The music faded and the voice of a narrator said, "The following presentation is a recording of a decision briefing by the patrol vessel program manager, Captain George Dreelin, to the SEJS Command Group in February 3010, in preparation for Federation budget hearings."

The camera's view switched to a view of the audience over Dreelin's shoulder. Dreelin said, "Admiral Brookleigh, distinguished guests, ladies and gentlemen, I am sure that you are aware that patrol vessels, or PVs, gather information, process it into intelligence, and, when necessary, can deliver significant firepower. These capabilities make them a vital component of SEJS combat operations.

"Nine months ago, you tasked me to offset our combat losses and ever-expanding quantitative requirements by improving PV technology, streamlining logistic channels, and increasing combat readiness rates. We have made headway on all of these fronts. I won't repeat the information I have provided you in recent fact sheets, but a quick summary is in order.

"Combat losses: Commanding any ship of the line is a stressful undertaking. This is especially true of PVs because the pilots are comparatively junior, and we frequently call upon them to operate independently in unfamiliar situations. The stress is cumulative, and trend analysis leaves no doubt that combat loss rates correlate directly with it. We have responded by incorporating stress management training into our PV pilots' curriculum and by becoming actively involved in PV personnel management. PVs now monitor and report their skippers' stress levels directly to my office, and I have instituted a point system that requires PV commanders to go on R&R when they reach thresholds predetermined by the surgeon general. In addition, when PV pilots have accumulated one hundred points, we mandatorily assign them to other duties.

"Quantitative requirements and logistics: The size of our region of influence is growing, and the SEJS is growing with it. On the other hand, construction of new PVs ceased three years ago due to budgetary limitations. A single PV costs almost as much as a cruiser to build, operate, and maintain, and cruisers provide much more combat power. Consequently, we have converted our manufacturing facilities on Log Base 36 into a rebuild shop; increased the priority of collecting, classifying, and salvaging damaged PVs; and, with your support, we have funded a year-to-year research and development program to improve the survivability of our existing assets."

At this point, Brookleigh interjected, "Excuse me, captain—for the benefit of those who weren't involved in the latter decision, let me explain that we are increasing PV survivability by enhancing the intelligence of the ships' automated control systems. These manifest themselves as PV executive officers—software that interacts verbally and electronically with the skipper and physically manages the ship. Analysis showed that this would be more productive than attempting to improve the hardware."

"Exactly, sir," Dreelin said. "Science Command expects to begin delivery of upgrades in about eighteen months."

Pat thought, *Eighteen months from February 3010 should be real soon now.*

A civilian in the front row raised his hand and asked, "I've seen that line in the budget, but I don't understand what's taking so long."

Brookleigh replied, "We effect ship modifications and enhancements in product improvement packages, or PIPs. We install PIPs during crew downtime, if possible, but no less often than semi-annually. This type of configuration management is essential to cost-effective logistic support and to operational readiness. Do you agree, Captain Dreelin?"

"Yes, sir, completely," the captain replied, "and in this case the upgrades are especially tricky. Installing software changes is easy, but we must test the integrated product exhaustively and ferret out all side effects. PVs have numerous interacting systems. Controlling them is very complicated."

"Thank you, captain. Does that answer your question, Mr. BaiRossi?" the admiral asked. The man in the front row nodded. "Good. Please proceed, captain."

Dreelin continued, "Combat readiness: the required rate is eighty percent. It was at a low of seventy-two percent a year ago, and it is now varying around a mean of eighty-one percent. The rebuild program accounts for five percent of the improvement. Another three percent comes from improved personnel management.

"And, to give credit where it is due, SEJS Command has helped greatly by instituting a policy of having tenders bring unserviceable PVs and critical assemblies back to the depot as soon as possible. The flights take place at warp speed, and the tenders drop the packages in geosynchronous orbit for us to ferry down to the log base.

"Ladies and gentlemen, the crux of this briefing is the fact that the logistic and personnel management actions I have outlined have only barely enabled the PV fleet to meet its operational readiness requirements. If we continue to lose ships at the present rate, it is not mathematically possible to continue to meet your goals.

"The PVs' hardware is state of the art, and Science Command foresees few, if any, opportunities to improve PVs. Therefore, the only remaining option is to continue to invest in the PV control system R&D program. I strongly recommend that we do so. This concludes my briefing; thank you for your attention. Are there any questions?"

Once again, Mr. BaiRossi had a question. "As SEJS comptroller, I don't see how we can stop funding the PV improvement effort. That raises my concern about potential overlaps with programs to develop new ships to replace PVs. There are such things on the drawing boards, and we can't afford redundancy."

"I share your concern, Joe," Brookleigh said, "but I don't foresee any overlap in the impending fiscal year. The new ships are in mock-up stage, and the improvements in control system technology that emerge from PV R&D will benefit the new vessels." He glanced around the room. "Any other questions? All right then. Thank you, captain, for an excellent briefing. We will continue to fund your R&D effort. Keep up the good work."

With that, the screen faded to black. Pat asked, "Is PC design next on the agenda?"

"Yes, it is," the learning station replied, "and we'll get right to it after you take a ten-minute break."

After the break, the learning center said, "You are seeing a plan view of the PV on the screen in front of you, oriented bow-up. A bow-forward starboard side elevation is on the left display; a port side, bow-forward elevation is on the right.

"During your sessions in the learning center, please touch the appropriate touchscreen icon to let me know whether I should proceed, pause, repeat, or further explain my teaching points."

Pat touched the "Proceed" icon, and she continued, "A PV is spherical, and if we did not provide physical points of reference, it would be difficult to tell which end is up. The display on your right shows that the ship's personnel hatch is located at the center of her port side. Note the red (port side) navigation light that retracts into the hatch when the ship is running in stealth mode.

"The monitor on your left shows the green (starboard) running light that is mounted symmetrically opposite the center of the personnel hatch. Returning to the front screen, you can now see the flashing white beacons on the top and stern of the ship. Unless she is running in stealth mode, her hull hides the strobe on the bottom of the ship, but you can see it on the side elevations.

"I will now display a front elevation of the ship on your center screen and will reveal the retractable landing lights on her bow, 45 degrees below centerline. Did you just see movement dead center on her bow? The ship deployed a small-array radar antenna that facilitates navigation during conditions of reduced visibility. The antenna will be below your line of sight when you are in either of the pilot's seats, but the radar will present video of any detectible object in a 90-degree cone forward of the ship out to 1,000 meters. Use this device with great caution: although it emits only one watt of power and has built-in electronic countermeasures, it can reveal your presence.

"Let's now discuss the outside of the ship, which is key to understanding her stealth characteristics. She has a seamless skin that covers the whole hull. Retractable flaps of skin cover all openings in the hull, such as the radar and weapons bays. When you retract a flap, the displays inside the ship cease to receive input from the flap, and the uncovered part of the ship becomes visible from outside. Do not forget the latter when you are in a tactical situation.

"Most of the ship's skin consists of microscopic bioelectronic devices. They direct incident electromagnetic energy into light pipes or waveguides, amplify or attenuate it as necessary, and send it to the ship's information processing systems. From there it takes two paths: one leads to panoramic displays mounted on the inner bulkhead, while the other is to emitters on the opposite side of the ship. Similarly, fractal antennas embedded in the skin absorb and retransmit ultra-low frequency radio waves. Thus, the ship is effectively transparent to everything in the spectrum below gamma rays.

"Now, Pat, it is time for a quick review and quiz. Are you ready?"

He acknowledged that he was, and the learning center proceeded to reinforce what it had just covered.

The lessons continued in this manner for several days, until Pat knew everything he needed to know about PVs, inside and out, static and dynamic. Bottom line: PVs were unlike any of the ships he had previously encountered. As a fighter pilot, he had lived aboard larger ships that were platforms for launch and recovery, but logistics were not his problem. Commanding a PV was a different matter.

As Dreelin had told him, PVs were capable of carrying stores for missions lasting up to thirty days. Consequently, the ship had to have life support systems capable of keeping her habitable for at least that long. Also, in the event of a breakdown or combat damage, the ship's captain, assisted by his XO, needed to know how to accomplish fault detection, isolation, and repair. Moreover, he or she needed to know how to operate and maintain the ship's entertainment systems. Maintaining alertness and preserving sanity while functioning alone for long periods were as important as operating the ship.

Each afternoon, subject matter experts from the depot and the project engineer's office escorted Pat into the hangar to reinforce his classroom training. His first such foray was to examine PV-11's skin.

When Pat and his guide, Melvin Tack, entered the hangar through a rear door, they could see the inside of the building from rear to front. The hangar had been a manufacturing facility, so there were overhead cranes, catwalks, and gantries galore—not to mention depot workers and their tools. Nevertheless, the only thing visible in the center of the hangar was the cradle that Pat had seen a week earlier. "Have they moved her out?" he asked.

"No, look closer," Tack replied. "Focus on the main hangar door and move your head from side to side."

"There is some shimmer in the air, but I don't see a PV."

Tack replied, "That's just diffraction." He turned on the microphone in his headset and said, "PV-11, please illuminate your navigation lights." Immediately, port and starboard running lights began to shine steadily above the cradle, and white strobes flashed at the ship's bow, stern, top, and bottom.

Noticing that the bow light was visible, Pat remarked, "You know, it's still hard for me to believe that you can see right through her."

"Actually, you can't," Tack said, "but it does look that way. "PV-11, please secure stealth mode."

Suddenly Pat could see the black ball that filled the cradle. "Man!" he said, "There's not much light in most parts of space. Even like this, she'd be hard to see out there."

"Hence the running lights," Tack said with a smile. "They are there to help you avoid collisions with friendlies."

They walked to the ship, and Tack handed Pat a magnifying glass with which to examine PV-11's outer surface. Pat almost jumped out of his skin when a black-on-yellow smiley face appeared right where he was looking.

"Belay that, Miss Varner!" Tack exclaimed.

"But that tickles," replied the face.

Tack shook his head. "The old automated XOs didn't used to do stuff like that. This new one, this 'Peggy Varner,' is a horse of a different color."

🔺 🔺 🔺

The next day, Commander John Street gave Pat a tour of the inside of the ship. Cdr. Street was a former PV pilot assigned to the program manager's engineering staff. He met Pat outside the learning center, and they walked down the corridor along the hangar wall until they came to a sign that said, "Docking Station." They entered and, in turn, presented their retinas and fingertips for recognition.

"Ordinarily we would strip," Street explained, "get into the chemical decontamination booth for cleaning and coating, put on a flight suit, and go aboard. Today, however, we'll just put on paper 'Moon Suits' and booties, like the depot workers, and walk right in. Feel free to ask questions as we go along.

"The first thing you will notice is that the entry hatch is about a meter thick. As you can see, it is built like the door on a bank vault. There is an inner door that will drop down after we pass by it." They stepped forward, and Street addressed the automated XO. "Ensign Varner, permission to come aboard for a look-see?"

"Welcome, gentlemen," the voice responded. "Just let me know if I can be of assistance."

Street said, "Thank you, Miss Varner, we will. Now, Pat, you can see that PV-11 has a double hull three meters thick. Step on board and note the status displays on the bulkheads in the passageway. Whenever you come aboard, the first order of business is to double check anything that isn't green."

They moved along to the inside of the ship, where Pat said, "There is more room in here than I thought."

"A couple of good teaching points there, Pat," Street replied. "A PV hull is a sphere 20 meters in diameter, which gives her about 1,256 square meters of surface for mounting sensors, communications gear, and stealth-enhancing devices. Every square millimeter is important, and 20 meters is the smallest a PV can be. Her pilot's living area is 14 meters in diameter—not palatial, but not claustrophobic either." He pointed, directing Pat's attention downward. "Look down. We are standing on a transparent deck that is set one meter below the ship's centerline. It divides the inside of the ship into two compartments. You fly the ship from the upper compartment, and this is where you live. It is spartan, but it provides all necessities, including a galley and a bunk that slides out of the dry seat. To access the hold, where the ship's armaments and life support plumbing are located, you can walk down the ladder directly behind the tank.

"The deck is below midline for a reason: When you are in either of the two maneuver control stations—the dry seat or the tank—your line of sight is even with the ship's waistline. Most of the time you won't be in tactical situations, so you'll be flying from the dry seat, which is in front of the tank."

"Ah, the world-famous tank," Pat quipped.

"Yes," Street continued, "the tank. It sounds like you already know how important it is. The tank provides support, protection, and sustenance during tactical situations. It functions like a cockpit, but is quite different. Cockpits generally stick up above the skin of a ship and give you a direct view of what is going on outside. As you can see, the tank is at the center of a PV, and the only thing you can see of the outside world is artificial video.

"The video is panoramic—it covers the entire inner surface of the bulkhead from the deck up, giving you a planetarium-like view. It is ultra-high resolution, three-dimensional, and in color. The displays that show what is beneath you are cemented to the underside of the transparent deck. Thus, for all practical purposes, you are looking directly at the great outdoors.

"There are small, supplementary displays on the sides of the tank and on the dry seat's console that work like rear-view mirrors. You can also rotate the seat in the tank 180 degrees right or left to get a better view of what is behind the ship." He raised his eyebrows at Pat and asked, "Any questions?"

"No sir." He was on information overload, but it was a fantastic experience, an in-your-face review of his class work. He liked this PV.

"Then let's go below and check out the armaments."

A couple of hours later, Pat had seen or touched everything the learning center had covered with him. He thanked Cdr. Street and Peggy Varner, he and Street left the ship, and the day's lesson was over.

🔺 🔺 🔺

When he had completed the formal lessons, tests, and hands-on training in a flight simulator, the school declared that Pat was ready to begin flying PV-11. The depot had already certified that she was good to go, and they had her waiting at the docking station in the hangar.

Captain Dreelin, the depot commander, and a small group of staff officers stood by with the depot rebuild workers for a brief commissioning ceremony, after which Pat entered the ship. To his surprise, the traditional tones of a boson's pipe welcomed him aboard. That didn't happen in fighters, and the piping (piping, not whistling; traditionally, whistling aboard ship is bad luck) reminded him that PV-11 was a full-fledged ship of the line. As soon as the salutation was over, he heard, "Welcome aboard, skipper. I have been looking forward to our becoming operational together. The ship is ready to fly at your command."

"Thank you, Miss Varner," he replied. "I have heard a lot about you, and it is all good. Let's get this show on the road."

"Aye, aye, sir. Please take your place in the dry seat. When we rise out of the cradle, the depot people will ask us to hover to the centerline of the shop. If you would you like me to do it, I can."

He nestled down in his seat and buckled his harness. "Thanks, Peggy, but as a point of pride, I'd like to do it. If I get in trouble, though, don't hesitate to bear a hand."

"No problem, sir. I've been watching you in the simulator, and I'm sure you can handle it."

That was unexpected news. She had been watching him? There

was no reason that she shouldn't have, but—

"Don't be alarmed, sir. Didn't your instructors tell you I am programmed to learn as much about you as possible?"

"Yes, they did, but I assumed it wouldn't begin until I came aboard. So much for assumptions. They also said you couldn't read my mind, so how did you know I was surprised?"

"Not by reading your mind, sir. My sensors showed that your blood pressure rose quickly and your pupils expanded. In other words, I was reading your body."

"Holy cow, Peggy! I had no idea I was that transparent. Oh, well—no harm, no foul," he said. "Let's get under way."

He switched his lip mic on and said, "PV-11 ready to cast off."

Ground Control responded, "Very well, releasing your moorings." There was a "thunk" and the dock telescoped back into the wall. Pat gave the stick a little up vector and eased it to starboard.

When they arrived over a stripe on the floor that led to the door, Ground Control said, "Very good, sir, you can now start moving forward."

The ship moved slowly toward the door, and it opened ahead of them. Pat knew what to expect; still, he was amazed. It was just like being in a fishbowl, looking out at a bright, sunny vista across the taxiway. PV-11 automatically reduced the amount of entering light to a comfortable level.

Pat brought the ship to a halt. They hung suspended for a moment until Ground Control said, "PV-11, you are cleared to leave the hangar. Have a good time out there. We'll be waiting for you."

"Roger that," Pat replied. "See you soon. Switching channel to Base Ops."

He used the implant in his brain to say, "PV-11 requesting clearance to taxi."

"PV-11," Base Ops chimed in. "Proceed via taxiway Alfa to runway 36 east."

"Wilco," Pat replied, moving the ship along at the prescribed 30 kilometers per hour. He looked down and couldn't believe what he wasn't seeing. "This is spooky, Peggy. We don't cast a shadow."

"You know what they say about beings that don't have a shadow, don't you, sir?"

"Yes, but I'd rather not think about it."

He was surprised to hear her chuckle.

When they arrived at the runway, Base Ops instructed, "PV-11, you are cleared for takeoff, vector 180 degrees to angels ten thousand and rendezvous with your escort."

They were soon there, and Base Ops cleared them to execute their local flight plan. They checked out all of PV-11's flight control systems under the watchful eye of a depot inspector riding in a chase ship. All went well; when they returned to the skunkworks, they debriefed the inspector, and Pat went to lunch.

In due course, they progressed to weapons firing, flying with stealth systems on, warp speed hops around the local solar system, and practice reconnaissance missions.

When PV-11 settled into her cradle at the end of Pat's final training flight, Dreelin was waiting in the debriefing room with an entourage. He listened attentively while Pat reviewed the observations he had submitted during training. They were constructive and well received, and when he was finished, the captain dismissed his team with a request that they join him in the Officers' Club dining room in a half hour or so.

He then sat Pat down for a heart to heart. "Pat," the captain said, "you seem to have enjoyed your training."

"Yes, sir, it was excellent. I feel that I am ready to take PV-11 anywhere."

"That's good, because SEJS will cut orders as soon as you are ready. Before we get to that, however, I'd like to know what you think of Ensign Varner—the plain, unvarnished truth. She is listening, of course, but don't pull any punches."

"Sir," he responded, "it's too soon to be absolutely certain. I'll know more after we've been out in the real world and have been in a tight spot or two. At this point, however, I have no qualms—Peggy can fly the ship at least as well as I can, she doesn't miss a trick, and I trust her. I don't know what more I could ask."

"Have you had any communication problems with her?"

"Problems? No, sir, but I might mention a couple of things I didn't expect. First, I wasn't expecting her to have a sense of humor. She likes to make little jokes, but she has never done it at an inappropriate moment. In fact, she seems to know when I need a laugh. Still, I have never heard of software that deliberately made plays on words or drew cartoons.

"Second, every once in a while she'll say something odd. It's a matter of vocabulary and syntax. She tends to take things literally, and my use of slang often necessitates clarification. That's my bad—using slang isn't a good practice. At times, her responses are downright funny. I'll have to admit that she's a lot more tactful than I am, and I'm hoping some of that tact will rub off on me."

Dreelin seemed amused, judging by the smile tweaking the corners of his mouth. "I'll see what I can do about her command of the vernacular. We need to be cautious, though—unambiguous communications are essential in the line of duty.

"However, the reason I am asking about communication issues is that a female midshipman who is a first classman at the academy, designed and implemented a significant part of Ensign Varner's enhancements. She's been out in the fleet for the usual cruises, but she hasn't seen action. There is much she still doesn't know about shipboard life. On the other hand, what she has done, she seems to have done very well."

"I'm impressed, sir, if Peggy's persona is a midshipman's handiwork. I had to work hard to make B's in my software courses."

"Me too. Midshipman Faraday has a bright future if she keeps her nose clean. She had some, shall we say, behavioral issues until the faculty figured out that they needed to keep her challenged. She has been doing much better since then." He addressed the room and said, "Peggy, any input from your perspective?"

"Yes, sir. I owe a great deal to Midshipman Faraday."

The captain smiled and said, "I see what you mean, Pat. My mistake, Peggy. I wasn't referring to Miss Faraday; I was asking whether you have any input regarding the training cycle PV-11 has just completed."

"I know, sir. No disrespect; I was just trying to illustrate what Lieutenant Callen was saying."

Dreelin and Pat glanced at each other with raised eyebrows. This would call for further discussion over dinner.

Peggy continued, "Sir, to be unambiguously responsive, the training has been a pleasure. You were correct in your assessment of the lieutenant when you told me that he might be coming to PV-11. You have found the right man for the job, and I am confident that our success will continue.

"The evaluation data from our training shows that our performance has been the best of any PV to date. I have transmitted my personal evaluations of the ship's systems for review by your technicians. They may result in improvements, but I have found nothing to prevent us from deploying on real missions. In short, sir, I believe that PV-11 is ready to sail."

"I concur, Ensign," Dreelin declared. "I hereby release you to operational duty and confirm that your skipper is a graduate of PV training. Pat, this signifies that you are now a brevet lieutenant commander in the Regular Navy."

— CHAPTER THREE —

First Mission

Pat's first orders attached him to SEJS Science Command and sent him to survey a solar system in sector 14.16.3 that humankind had not yet explored. It was old, being out near the fringes of the galaxy, had no planets with terraforming potential, and was chosen for PV-11's maiden voyage because there was no reason to expect hostiles there.

Surveying a star system entailed collecting and cataloging a huge amount of data. First there was the star itself. Basic information, such as size, color, and intensity were already in the ephemeris. Close observation by a PV revealed additional facts, such as rotational velocity, and, in this case, the probability of imminent collapse. (It was always good to know where and when a nova was imminent.)

Then, there was observation of the system's planets: size, class, temperature, radioactivity, and so forth.

Finally, yet very important, there was the other material that was moving around in the star's gravitational field. Sometimes it included valuable resources.

Upon entering the system, the first thing PV-11 did was search for claim stakes from non-human species: Federation-standard buoys that, when interrogated, proclaimed a species' interest in a system. (Had they merely visited? Did they plan any harvesting of materials or development? When had they been there, and were there any liens or attachments on the system?) PV-11 found no such buoys, which was a little odd but not unprecedented. Accordingly, Pat sent back a message to the effect that the system appeared to be unclaimed and that they were raising their DEFCON from green to amber in case someone had removed or destroyed existing buoys. If there were pirates or renegades lurking about, extra caution would be wise. Of course, if PV-11 found nothing out of line, she would deploy buoys upon departure.

It didn't take long for Pat and his automated XO to complete their observations of the star. Then they began examining its planets, working outward from the innermost large orbiting object. When they arrived at a point slightly farther from the star than Earth is from the sun, Peggy announced, "Captain, I have noticed something unusual ahead. Based on its size, I would tentatively classify it as a small planet. However, it has an anomalous surface."

Pat looked at the planet but saw nothing out of the ordinary. "What do you see that is unusual, Peggy? We must be too far away for me to see it."

She zoomed in to reveal a surface that was uniformly smooth and tan.

"Report this to Science Command," he said, "and verify that we are at maximum stealth."

"Aye, aye, sir, stealthy we are."

Science Command immediately replied, "Approach unknown object with great care: DEFCON red. Do not approach closer than 1,000 kilometers and transmit images to us ASAP. Do not engage unless attacked."

PV-11 acknowledged, Pat climbed into the tank, and they moved down to 1,000 km.

"Sir," Peggy said, "I can now see small structures on the surface."

"Again, where?" Pat asked.

"In a number of places, sir. I'll highlight one and enlarge the image for you."

A spot near the planet's equator changed color and grew to the size of a dinner plate. Inside the circle, an oblong bump cast a shadow. Enough detail was visible to reveal a network of lines that subdivided the bump into hexagons, each of which had a dark, circular spot at its center.

"How big is it and what do you think it might be?"

"It is about 20 meters long, 12 meters wide, and 3 meters high. I do not know what it is. It doesn't match anything in our identification catalogs."

"You say there is more than one of them?"

"Yes, they are distributed approximately 30 kilometers apart."

"What's the probability they are biological?"

"Low. The planet below us has a very thin atmosphere. Also, absorption spectra indicate that the hexagonal structures consist of inorganic materials, mainly silicates and metals."

"Could living organisms survive down there?"

"Possibly. There are traces of oxygen, carbon dioxide, and water vapor in the atmosphere."

"Could those structures have been erected by sentient beings that are hiding below the surface?"

"Low probability, but non-zero. If the planet has inhabitants, they are out of sight. I see no movement, and there are no electromagnetic emissions."

"Could the structures be geological?" Pat scratched his head, trying to decipher what he was seeing and hearing.

"I can't give you a definitive answer without putting instruments on the planet, and we are forbidden by protocol to penetrate the atmosphere until we know that we wouldn't cause ecological harm. In terms of gross geophysical indicators, there are no bodies of water, no mountains, no volcanoes, and no impact craters on the part of the surface we can see from here.

"I have used every type of passive sensor we have aboard to scan several of the structures I have called to your attention. They are similar in size and geometry, yet very few of them are exactly alike. There appear to be fallen plumes of dust near them, making it possible that they are associated with volcanic vents. I doubt that, however, because large hexagonal volcanic vents are unknown. If the hexagons are vents or fumaroles, why is there a dark spot in the center of every one?"

Pat decided he needed to say something halfway intelligent—he was the commander. "I agree."

"Thank you. Incidentally, as we vary the angle of observation, the shape of the spots varies from circular to elliptical. That indicates that they may be round holes, like the ends of pipes."

"You are absolutely right!" Pat exclaimed, focusing intently on the view screen. "I've seen greenhouses that looked something like that, but they didn't have dark circles in the middle of the windows."

"I notice something else," Peggy continued. "The structures do not appear to be scattered randomly, which implies someone or something built them. If so, the question is, are the builders still on or in the planet?"

"All right, Peggy," Pat said, "I'm convinced that we should ask for permission to take a closer look. While I compose a message to send back to Science Command, I want you to reprioritize the ship's systems. Make stealth number one, combat power number two, and science

21

number three."

"Aye, aye, sir. I have made it so."

As soon as Science Command's reply arrived, Pat took PV-11 down to 30 km, which was as close to the planet as they could go without entering the atmosphere. They were able to see the objects of their curiosity clearly, but it did not help. The hexagons seemed to have a translucent, colorless covering. Scrutiny revealed that the dust plumes on the surface had come from holes that were 15 to 20 meters away from the clusters of hexagons. The absorption spectrum of the dust indicated the presence of radioactive elements. Streaks of a shiny substance that Peggy identified as a protein glittered on the ground in the immediate vicinity of the mounds.

Collectively, these results were still inconclusive, but they made it much less likely that the objects were of natural origin. Pat told Peggy to return PV-11 to standard orbit. He then recommended that Space Command allow them to observe from inside the atmosphere.

Instead, Space Command told them to get out of the solar system and await further orders.

Over the next several hours, a series of messages went back and forth. The Molluscan representatives at Federation headquarters seemed excited about PV-11's discovery and stated that the individual hexagons resembled a type of directed energy weapon used by one of their ancient civilizations. They then clammed up, as it were.

SEJS interrogated the Federation scientific library and learned that the Molluscan DEWs in question were of the particle beam variety, but were not configured in clusters. The radioactive dust plumes could be a particle beam weapon's exhaust. The shiny stuff could be Molluscan (specifically, gastropod, as in snail) footprints.

SEJS detached PV-11 from Science Command, dispatched a heavy task force to the system, and attached PV-11 to it.

The task force commander, Rear Admiral Brown, brought PV-11 alongside his battleship, BB-36, where he could communicate via direct, secure optical link. He told Pat, "Son, you caught it so you get to skin it. I infer that the present-day Molluscans don't want to discuss their ancient brethren because there is something embarrassing about them—for instance, they're renegades who split off rather than join the Federation. If that's the case, it's probable that the rebels were too tough for our Federation allies to keep in line.

"I don't need to remind you that the Molluscans have been in the Federation a lot longer than we have. The technology they had in ancient times was good enough to kick our butts today, if they wanted to. Obviously, it would not be prudent to wade into this with guns blazing.

"Regardless, there is a Federation protocol that we must follow: We are required to send an unarmed emissary into standard orbit under a flag of peace and broadcast Federation 'Come to Mama' messages for twenty-four hours. If someone responds affirmatively, fine—we call in the diplomatic corps. If not, things could get rough. I have the tender fitting out a small boat with the appropriate communications gear as we speak. It will be in orbit within the hour.

"Get some rest, commander. I'll let you know if we hear anything from the planet. If we don't, PV-11 will lead the ensuing reconnaissance in force."

While the small boat broadcasted Federation appeals, the admiral developed and coordinated his operations orders. The primary objective was to conduct a surface reconnaissance. The secondary objective was to determine exactly what the complexes of hexagons were, whether they constituted evidence of present or past sentient inhabitants, and whether they represented hazards to potential human exploration.

As a genus, the Mollusca were clever, tenacious, and likely to communicate by wiggling antennas or displaying varying patterns of skin color. The closest humans could come to communicating with most Mollusca was by using Federation sign language. Members of the Diplomatic Corps had to learn this language, but the majority of line officers knew little more than how to state their names, ranks, and identity numbers.

The particle beam weapons known to SEJS as DEWs were crude but effective. They worked by emitting a stream of raw energy in the form of plasma. Detonating a fission or fusion bomb produced the plasma. Such plasmas were difficult to aim. The only known way to hit a target with one was to direct the plasma by a combination of ablative reflectors and magnetic fields. Obviously, both the plasma generator and its aiming mechanism had to be extremely robust.

The admiral tasked BB-36's computers to project the coverage of the collective system, assuming that each hexagon in an array was a particle beam emitter and that the beam would emerge at right angles to the surface of the hexagon. The result caused much speculation: evidently the hexagons were set up to make one beam from each of three clusters intersect approximately 30 meters above ground level. As Peggy's observations had shown, the clusters were 30 kilometers apart in staggered parallel rows, defining a diamond-shaped grid. Each cluster in a triplet was at one corner of an isosceles triangle that was 60 kilometers on a side.

These findings raised several questions:

Why triplets of intersecting beams? One ought to be enough to annihilate anything that got in its way.

Why would a defensive system have such large gaps in it? Even when the computers plotted all possible triplets, the beam intersections were 15 kilometers apart.

Could an individual cluster fire more than one weapon at a time?

Would all of the clusters fire simultaneously?

After twenty-four hours, the small boat had drawn no response from the planet. Admiral Brown sent PV-11 back in for a quick look around. Nothing had changed, so he issued his operations order.

BB-36, cloaking itself and its four destroyer escorts, would establish orbit 50 kilometers above the planet to provide firepower as needed. The tender was to remain outside of the system, under the protection of a cruiser. The other cruiser and two destroyers constituted a backup reaction force. PV-11 would independently pop down to an altitude of 10 meters, reconnoiter, and report what she found.

Two minutes later, a reconnaissance force of six fighters and two SEJS Marine Assault Vehicles, each carrying one reinforced squad of Marines from BB-36, would descend a short distance away from PV-11. PV-11, stealth maximized, would cover the descent of the recon force until the MAVs reached the surface. The fighters would remain at an altitude of 500 meters to provide close support. All ships and troops would be at weapons ready, but were not to fire unless fired upon.

At the duly appointed time, the fighters and MAVs launched from BB-36's flight deck. The fighters set up in a tetrahedron around the troop carriers and announced that they were ready to go. At the planned intervals, PV-11, BB-36 and her escorts, and the reconnaissance force moved into their positions above the planet.

PV-11 reached her station without incident and detected nothing new. The reconnaissance force entered the atmosphere as far as possible from computed beam intersection points and began to descend vertically. There was no reaction until they arrived at an altitude of 1200 meters.

There, to Pat's horror, the unforeseen functionality of the clusters of hexagons revealed itself. They were indeed particle beam weapons, but unlike any that SEJS or the Federation had previously encountered.

In a well-coordinated onslaught, 24 individual jets of plasma spewed simultaneously out of triplets of clusters, angling upward toward eight intersection points. However, the source beams flexed as they approached each other, perhaps because of mutual repulsion, arcing upward hundreds of meters before merging into a single towering blast. Pat could clearly see from variations in the diameter and brightness of the contributing beams that the resultant stream was steered by varying the power of its individual legs. Like pinschers of fire, the streams of plasma lanced up from below, engulfed the MAVs and fighters, and tossed the seething remains skyward.

Whatever was controlling the particle beams had apparently not detected PV-11, but she was in a serious predicament. A thicket of beams was beginning to collapse back toward her, and even their side effects were taking a toll. The brilliant glare had driven many of her optical sensors to cut off, making the view screens on the side nearest the engagement useless. Worse, stray particles and ionizing radiation were progressively nullifying the PV's stealth systems by building up a halo around the hull.

Pat glanced aft, saw what looked like Saint Elmo's fire trailing in the ship's wake, and instinctively slammed the flight controls forward. "Belay stealth!" he shouted at Peggy. "Maximize combat power!"

PV-11 hurtled tangentially along the surface, her hull overheating and generating a shock wave, particle beams rapidly gaining on her. Then, suddenly, the beams shut off. Apparently, they had a minimum operating angle, and PV-11 was under it. Pat stopped the ship and held his altitude, but he could barely see above the terrain.

The hull groaned; a fog of particles billowed around it.

"Extensive damage to sensors on the starboard aft quarter, sir," Peggy reported. "Forward view screens will recover in a moment. Recommend we move horizontally to help cool the hull." Silently, Pat put the ship into slow forward motion. Suddenly, the brilliant red beam of a high-energy laser lanced down from above, striking a mound on their right. Particle beams replied, but after a moment, the admiral's voice reached them. "Tried to take out the weapons site immediately east of you, PV-11. Had to pop out and re-cloak. We know we hit the right place because it's glowing, but we can't tell how much good we did. Can you see anything?

"Negative, sir," Pat replied. "Until things settle down, the only direction we can see is dead ahead. Our starboard rear sensors are non-op but the bow is recovering. Will advise. I'm sure glad they missed you, admiral."

"So are we. The good news is that it takes them a while to build up power. The bad news is that their firepower is awesome. They won't have any trouble holding us at bay, and there's just enough atmosphere to scatter our lasers. If we come in close enough to burn through, they can nail us. Can you pop out of there if you have to?"

"No, sir—not yet, anyway. We're too close to the surface to warp out of here. No telling what we'd drag up with us. And if we get up much higher, they can zap us."

"Roger. We compute that we're going to have to eliminate at least one cluster to get you out of there."

Until the admiral said that, the seriousness of the situation had not sunk in on Pat. He said, "Peggy, things don't look too good. Recommendations?"

"Not yet, sir. Still evaluating the ship's condition, but PV-11 has been in worse shape than this and survived."

"True," he agreed, "but I'd sure like to find a way out of here, real soon now. Let me know ASAP."

"Aye, sir," said Peggy; then, "Outside radiation level rising rapidly! A cluster's exhaust plume is falling on us."

Skimming the surface eastward, they saw an array of beam projectors ahead. The surrounding surface was a puddle of bubbling glass, but the weapons themselves seemed to be unharmed.

"What the hell, over?" Pat questioned. "How could that stuff survive a battleship's fire?" Angry, he fired a burst from PV-11's forward laser directly at the nearest hexagon. The light beam reflected upward.

Peggy said, "The lids are mirrors."

"Mirrors? How come I can see into them?"

"They are transparent until light hits them. The more intense the light, the more reflective they become."

"Oh, like the face plate on a space suit. All right, let's see how tough they are." Pat deployed the rail gun and cranked off a round. Its hypervelocity, depleted uranium projectile knocked a chunk off a hexagon but did not penetrate it.

He started to take PV-11 up higher, to take a shot from a more favorable angle of incidence, but Peggy shouted, "Don't!" Then, more quietly, she said, "What if they fire the beam while we are in front of it?"

"Hmm, thanks, bad idea. Let's back off, report, and think this over."

"We've already reported, sir. I've been feeding the forward view through to the flagship."

Pat started to say, "Okay," but before he could get it out of his mouth, something weird rose up out of the ground a few meters in front of them. If anything, it resembled the last two meters of an elephant's trunk, except that it was smoother, thinner, and had an eye on its end. When it had extended to full height, it began to rotate like a flexible periscope scanning the horizon. Pat shivered and reflexively visualized a laser beam slashing out. Peggy obliged him, and the amputated organ toppled to the surface, writhing.

Pat accelerated PV-11 away from the mound at maximum Gs. When they had traveled a few hundred meters, he stopped the ship and set her to revolving slowly around her vertical axis. "Watch our backs, Peggy," he ordered, "and if anything moves, shoot it. We've got their attention now; they're coming out of their holes to find out what we're doing."

"Callen," Brown interjected, "be cool. Your job is to stay alive until we can get you out of there."

"Wilco, sir, but it's getting hairy down here!"

Previously concealed turrets were rising out of the ground, bringing weapons to bear. The ship shook, and Pat assumed that Peggy had fired an aft-facing missile. He, too was shooting, and managed to destroy the first gun mount that he saw emerge.

The ship shook again, differently, and Pat turned the ship to starboard to engage an enemy position that was firing on them from the flank. Sections of the view screen blanked out as the ship took hits all around, and Pat maneuvered the ship in violent evasive maneuvers while both he and Peggy returned fire. Within thirty seconds, PV-11 had eliminated all of the turrets that were close enough to strike her, but she was much the worse for wear. She still had engines, computers, and structural integrity, but only ten percent of her sensors remained, and most of those were on the bottom of the hull. They had seriously depleted their weapons stores. Pat was not looking forward to staying where he was.

"Admiral, we've got to get out of here. Permission to shoot a nuke on a particle beam cluster," Pat requested.

"Stand by, relaying request to SEJS. It shouldn't take long. Let's see, you carry only one two-kiloton nuke. Not much, but that should be enough to do the trick, don't you think? Of course you do—you thought of it first."

A large red light began to flash on Pat's control console, and the admiral continued, "Okay, we have SEJS approval. How do you plan to make delivery?"

"Cut straight across and drop it on 'em, sir. I can't miss."

"Not good. You'd have to expose yourself, and your weapon may trigger secondary detonations in their plasma generators. If that happens, you want to be a long way off. If I were you, I'd set the fuse to maximum delay, lob my bomb in a high arc, and take off in the other direction as fast as I can go."

"Makes sense to me, sir. Say a prayer for us."

"I will, and I'll go you one more. Give us a countdown. Ten seconds before your weapon detonates, we'll fry the area you plan to head into."

"Very well, sir. We are about one kilometer southeast of a cluster. We have knocked out the gun turrets between the cluster and us, but we can see many more all around us. We have worked out the parameters for our bomb run. At T minus 20, we will start moving northeast. At T minus 12, we will release our bomb and turn 90 degrees, heading southeast. If you will cut a swathe ahead of us at T minus 10, we will start gaining altitude and will pop out at T plus three. Do you have a fix on us? If it will help, I can mark our target cluster with a laser designator to initiate our bomb run."

"Well thought out, Callen. We have interrogated your Identification Friend or Foe transponder, and we know where you are. We can also see the cluster to your northeast, so we are ready to play our part. Good luck, and don't forget to shut off your sensors while we fire our lasers."

"Aye, aye, sir." Pat thanked his lucky stars for the IFF transponder. "Here we go: two zero seconds and counting."

Peggy said, "Brace yourself, skipper, we are about to do two reverse flips."

In order to toss the bomb while staying close to the surface, Peggy had come up with a way to impart upward momentum to their nuke. Two quick reverse revolutions did the trick; at T minus 12, the bomb was on its way, arcing out in a perfect parabola.

Two seconds later, BB-36's lasers cut loose. Distant mounds returned particle beam fire, but the battleship was gone before it reached her vacated position. A blast of heated atmospheric gases created by BB-36's lasers rocked PV-11, but it did no harm.

Neither Pat nor Peggy had ever had to launch a live nuclear weapon, but even if they had, it would not have prepared them for what happened when their bomb exploded. The initial effects were predictable, but a much more profound series of events ensued. More than likely, PV-11's weapon initiated a chain reaction in materials that were part of the particle beam weapons systems. After a short but perceptible delay, the region around the mound erupted in a series of explosions that opened up an extensive system of tunnels.

PV-11 continued southeast, but Peggy rotated the ship so their remaining sensors could view the scene. Pat was delighted to see a large amount of debris flying through the air, including dozens of turrets blown upward like corks out of bottles. Mixed in with the inorganic matter were bodies—gastropod bodies, looking exactly like gigantic garden snails. While Peggy took pictures for later species identification, the details that remained with Pat were an almost humanoid head (albeit one with four eye stalks) and finger-like protrusions on both sides of the foot, perhaps 50 centimeters below the head.

"PV-11," the admiral interrupted, "get the hell out of there while they're still confused. The destruction was confined to the area around that one weapons emplacement; there's no telling what's going to happen next."

"Aye, aye, sir, we're on our way. I'm collecting as much data as possible from the damaged area." By then, PV-11 was climbing fast, but something about the area below wasn't right. Instead of an earthen or rocky crater, Pat was looking into a gaping hole that revealed nothing but torn and twisted metal in all directions.

While Pat tried to make sense out of its receding image, Peggy warned, "Sir, strong gravitational fields are building up below us."

It clicked, and Pat couldn't contain his excitement. "Admiral, that's not a planet, it's a ship."

"Good Lord, Callen, you're right—and it's getting under way. All ships withdraw to the reserve force location. PV-11, move it!"

"Coming in dirty, sir," Pat replied. They were not yet clear of the atmosphere, but they engaged their hyperspace drive anyway.

When his head cleared and the outgassing of PV-11's hull had slowed, Pat swung the ship around to get a working sensor pointed in the direction from which they had come. The Gastropod ship wasn't there.

Peggy had already logged back into the tactical net, so Pat asked, "Admiral, what's going on?"

"Be glad you jumped when you did, Callen. That was the biggest star base I've ever heard of. When you hopped, it did too. We're lucky you weren't dragged into her gravitational well. I wish I knew where they went. A long ways away, I hope. Heaven help us if they come back and bushwhack us. We stung 'em a little, but not enough to matter.

"Callen, please rendezvous with the tender for emergency repairs and await further orders. You can bet that SEJS will recall us for a major debriefing. If what we just encountered wasn't unique, it's certainly the best kept secret in the Federation."

"Wilco, sir."

Peggy cut the channel to the task force and said, "The admiral is right, sir. That was a good place to be *from.*"

— Chapter Four —

Back to Work

It took the tender a day and a half to decontaminate PV-11's exterior, evaluate her condition, collect residues for laboratory analysis, and replace enough sensors to make her safe for navigation. Pat remained aboard, took part in the memorial services for the many fallen members of the reconnaissance force, and monitored task force communications traffic while awaiting further orders.

The matter escaping from the hull of the Gastropod star base had left a trail. With good detective work and a certain amount of luck, other PVs were able to locate the Gastropods a few parsecs away, where they had paused for emergency damage control. The PVs' orders were to stay hidden and concentrate on characterizing the aliens' hyperspace drive when they moved again. The PVs were successful and, although the Gastropods made a series of evasive hops, the task force was able to follow them to a solar system in the fringes of sector 14.16.4, where they hove to and began to make permanent repairs. This place was a major discovery in its own right, as it was apparently a well-established den of thieves, teeming with pirates and other non-Federation vessels.

To no one's surprise, including Pat, the tender declared that PV-11 needed maintenance that exceeded their capabilities. SEJS ordered Pat to take his ship back to Log Base 36 for overhaul. The trip to the rear and the docking maneuvers at the log base were uneventful. After Pat turned PV-11 over to the skunkworks, the flight surgeon gave him a physical examination and sent him on three days of R&R.

The log base planet was about the size of Earth. In keeping with the supply and maintenance support functions of the base, the planet's terraformers had optimized it for fishing, farming, and mining. As Pat knew from his previous stay, the region surrounding the log base was a rather quaint place with a climate similar to that of Hawaii. After exploring the nearby villages and enjoying the beaches for a couple of days, Pat felt as good as new.

A day in the learning center and the simulator familiarized Pat with updates installed in PV-11 during her overhaul. Warning orders awaited, and he was pleased to learn that in eighteen hours, PV-11 would join a task force to investigate the solar system to which the Gastropod star base had fled. Accordingly, he returned to his BOQ room and got a good night's sleep.

The next morning he conducted a pre-flight inspection and inventoried the ship's stores. PV-11's hull looked like new; everything was in good order. Pat thanked the depot team, said goodbye, and entered the dockside airlock. The indicators inside the main hatch were all green, but Pat checked the detail displays carefully. Mathematical probability ensured that something was bound to be amiss in a system with so many parts.

He closed the hatch and felt comforted, although the implications had not changed greatly since Shakespearean times, when Samuel Johnson said, "Being on a ship is like being in prison, with the opportunity of being drowned." Even so, Pat was now completely in his element.

He quickly crossed to the tank. The transparent quartz globe was almost full of water—not fresh, potable water, but an isotonic saline solution. This would cushion his body and provide a medium for basic environmental support: temperature control, comfortable movement, waste disposal, moderation of proton and neutron bombardments—everything but air, sustenance, and control of the ship. The waxy coating applied to his skin by the decontamination robot, and the salt content of the water, would enable him to remain immersed for long periods without turning into a prune.

Pat ensured that the tank's accessories were in place: a three-day supply of semi-solid food, the hammock-like web of elastic straps that would soon be supporting him, and the sanitation siphon below the web. He then inspected his helmet's seals, gaskets, and connections and put it on. He inhaled, felt the helmet's skirt pull down against his skin, and tested the flow of air through the regulator valve. A quick glance verified that the face piece provided an unrestricted view of the inside of the ship and his heads-up display of tactical information.

He eased himself into the tank, closed the lid, and vented the trapped air. His lips first found the nipple to the left of his mouth, and then the one to the right. A quick pull on each indicated that potable water and nutrients were available upon demand. He poked a finger through the skirt of his chin piece, scratched his nose, and looked around. All ship functions were now under his control via psychomotor impulses, eye movements, and voice commands.

He inquired, "Ensign Varner, is our flight plan filed and are ship's systems secured for takeoff?"

"Yes, sir," she replied. "PV-11 is good to go. Task orders are in the log, and situation reports await your recall. Energy levels are one hundred percent, all tactical systems are go, and stores exceed thirty days of supply. Built-in test indicates one external visual sensor non-operational. It is not in a critical location, and we have spares aboard."

"Very well, Peggy. Let's boogie. Set DEFCON to amber, sensors for global scan, and give stealth priority over combat power until further notice."

They maneuvered PV-11 out of the hangar, and Pat said, "Base Ops, this is Papa Victor One One requesting permission to depart, over."

The implant in Pat's brain sounded off. "Papa Victor One One, this is Base Ops. You are cleared to taxi to runway 36 east, over."

"Wilco, Base Ops."

Pat flew PV-11 to the end of taxiway Alfa and then across to the end of runway 36 east. There, he said, "PV-11 requests permission to depart."

"PV-11, you are cleared for takeoff. Good luck and good hunting."

"Thank you, Base Ops."

He applied power for a two-G takeoff until they cleared the atmosphere. Once there, he brought PV-11 to a halt and rotated her slowly in the sunlight to expedite outgassing—driving gas molecules away that might otherwise leave a trail through space. The molecules tended to hang around the ship and flow in behind her when she moved. Before long, particles arriving in the solar wind would balance those driven off, and only a sojourn in the dark of space would finish the job.

"Peggy, please give me a weapons check and then load up the brief situation report (sitrep), our flight orders, and the full strep, in order." He would take his time viewing the situation reports; he would have lots of time on his hands while they traveled. "Keep all com channels open to incoming traffic."

Peggy replied, "Sir, DEFCON amber, stealth priority one, all weapons systems available, engine functions normal, energy levels max. Do you wish me to take the con?"

"Negative," Pat replied. "Program weapons for activation upon departure from log base restricted fire zone."

"Aye, aye, sir. Sitreps and flight orders standing by."

"Very well," he said, "let's have a look."

Peggy selected a section of the display that was just below his line of sight, blanked it, and scrolled a summary of the situation report into view. It said,

0031Z/21MAR23.

SITREP: MARIOLANUS CONSTELLATION, SECTOR 14.16.4

PV-5 AND PV-8 CONTINUING CLANDESTINE SURVEILLANCE OF GASTROPOD STAR BASE AND NON-FEDERATION TRAFFIC. CURRENT POPULATION 17 NEUTRAL / HOSTILE SHIPS.

THREE ARRIVALS, TWO DEPARTURES PAST 24 HOURS INCLUDE ARACHNID DESTROYER-CLASS VESSEL THAT TOWED ONE SEJS CHARLEY MODEL FIGHTER INTO STANDARD ORBIT AROUND GASTROPOD STAR BASE.

"Now that's interesting," Pat muttered. "Where would Arachs get one of our old fighters, and what would they want with it? Charley model birds are badly outdated."

"They can't be all that old, sir," Peggy observed. "Didn't you first get rated in Charley models?"

He couldn't get over her sense of humor—was she teasing him? "You know I did, but that was at least five years ago, and the Charleys were on their way out of the inventory. They were pretty good old birds—Lord knows, mine saved my tail more than once—but they all should have been in the scrap heap by now."

"Weren't some of them converted into troop carriers?" Peggy asked. He assumed she knew the answer and was just reminding him for the sake of conversation.

"Yes, MAVs to be exact, but one of our sister PVs wouldn't mistake a MAV for a fighter. A MAV is half again as big as a fighter, and it doesn't look anything like one. I believe that all they did was bolt the old fighter engines onto a new airframe."

"That is correct. Therefore, I'm guessing that the fighter is either materiel that the Arachs captured some time ago, or they obtained it through black market trading."

"Could be, Peggy, but either way, SEJS is going to want to get to the bottom of it. And when did you start guessing about things?"

"Excuse me, sir; it was just a figure of speech. In future, I'll confine myself to quantifiable estimates of probabilities."

"Never mind. Your guess is as good as mine. I just don't think I've ever heard you use the word."

"Something I picked up on shore leave, I guess," she replied with a quiet giggle.

Pat's eyebrow shot. "I hope that's all you picked up, Miss Varner," he retorted.

"Unfortunately, sir, while you were out playing on the beaches, I was working hard at the base, helping to bring old PV-11 up to speed. So yes, sir, I picked up a few new things, but they were all in the line of duty. How about you?"

"No regrets and no barnacles. Log Base 36's planet is a beautiful place but quiet as a tomb. New planets are like that—unspoiled and under populated, especially in terms of available young females. Or available not-so-young females, for that matter. Nice place to visit, but if you want companionship, you'd better bring your own. But we digress. Would you please scroll our orders up there for me?"

"Yes, sir, coming right up."

0045Z/21MAR23

FROM: CINC SEJS

TO:
FS-117
FS-212
CRUDIV-12
PV-11
PV-23
T-2

INFO: STAR BASE 75

LOG BASE 36

TO ADDRESSEES REPORT STAR BASE 75 ASAP. JOIN TASK FORCE DELTA UNDER COMMAND OF CRUDIV-12.

PREPARE TO REINFORCE SECTOR 14.16.3.
"ACKNOWLEDGE."

"So be it," Pat observed. "Am I correct that Star Base 75 is in sector 14.16.3?"

"Affirmative."

"And do we know how long it will take the other members of the task force to catch up with Star Base 75?"

"We will in a moment, sir. There's some message traffic going back and forth among the Cruiser Division, T-2 (the tender), and Star Base 75."

Presently, she continued, "Fighter Squadron 117 and the tender are already attached to the CruDiv. They are in 14.15.3. FS-212 is at Star Base 75. One of the cruisers got her bow blown off a couple of days ago, and the tender is patching her up. They were going to bring the cruiser to Log Base 36 for complete repair, but now they plan to send a bow section up from the log base and do a quick fix at Star Base 75. T-2 estimates nine hours until the damaged cruiser becomes space worthy."

"Hmm," Pat ruminated, fingering his chin. "Time enough for us to shake this bird down and wring out any bugs we find. What do you think, Peggy?"

"Recommend we do that, sir."

"Let's see, it's about 0130 hours in Zulu time. Please send the following message:

FROM: PV-11
TO:
CINC SEJS
INFO: STAR BASE 75
LOG BASE 36
CRUDIV-12
FS-212
ACKNOWLEDGE YOUR 0045Z 21MAR23.
REQUEST PERMISSION TO SHAKE PV-11 DOWN TO VERIFY
SPACEWORTHINESS.
ETA TAC STAR BASE 75 AFTER SHAKEDOWN 0930Z 21MAR23.
ETA IF NO SHAKEDOWN 0135Z 21MAR23.
END OF TRANSMISSION (EOT)

After a moment, Peggy replied, "Message transmitted, sir. Do you wish to see the full sitrep now?"

"Not yet, thanks" he replied. "There's plenty of time for that. Where did you say that defective optical sensor is?"

"Port quarter, aft, topside, skipper. Do you want to replace it now?"

"Let me take a look," he answered.

Turning toward the rear of the ship, Pat had a spectacular view of the area around Log Base 36. The terraformers had done a beautiful job on what had once been a barren rock. Except for the geometric regularity of its surface patterns, it looked a lot like pictures of Earth. The defective sensor represented only a few pixels and wasn't worth fooling with at this time.

"Captain," Peggy announced, "CINC SEJS says negative to weapons firing because our systems are pre-tested and we should conserve energy, but they recommend that we wring out the other shipboard gear as soon as the hull has had a chance to outgas. Star Base 75 concurs."

"Shucks," Pat responded, "no shooting. That takes all the fun out of it. Nevertheless, why play hurry up and wait at the star base? Let's defer the sensor replacement. I'm going to get out of the tank. There's no need for me to stew in my own juices while we buzz around in a pacified sector. Peggy, please take the con and file our flight plan to Star Base 75. I'll relieve you in a couple of minutes."

"Aye, aye, sir," she responded.

Pat lowered the water level in the tank and, with the aid of an air hose, blew the salt water off his body. He then rinsed with fresh water and dried off. Next, he got out, secured his headgear, and closed the tank lid. Finally, he put on a flight suit and headed forward. At the bridge, he settled into his dry seat, fastened his safety harness, and scanned the indicators.

"Miss Varner," he asked, being properly formal while she was acting commander, "would you mind keeping the con while I go over the detailed sitrep?"

"I'd be glad to," she affirmed.

"Ensign, you are almost too kind to the Old Man."

"Just self-preservation," she laughed. "It pays to have him ready to go when it counts."

Feigning hurt, he said, "Just because tradition gives me the title 'Old Man' aboard this bucket of bolts doesn't mean that I'm over the hill. I'm ready for anything, any time!"

"With all due respect, sir," she said, her voice light, "you forget that as the custodian of personnel records aboard this ship, I know exactly how old you are. While it is true that you are younger than the average PV captain, that is relative. On an absolute scale—well, a little more rest won't hurt you."

"Tell you what, Peggy. If you doubt my capacities, you're invited to try to stick with me, next time we make port, twenty-four hours a day. It'll be good training!"

"I think I could handle that, sir, but wouldn't SEJS take a dim view of it? They'd probably ground you and banish me to the black hole at the center of the galaxy. Thanks, but no thanks!"

"Not to worry, my dear," Pat said. "SEJS is wise beyond belief. They'd completely discredit the notion that someone my age could be of anything but professional interest to you. But don't expect to get off the hook this easily. With any luck at all, you'll see that I have at least one or two good days left in me. Meanwhile I'd better tend to my knitting. Holler if you need me." He turned to his heads-up display and said, "Com, queue up the full sitrep for display and scroll at my command."

While Pat caught up on the news by reading the detailed reports, Peggy test flew the ship. It was in their mutual interests for him to be as sharp as possible, and their sharing of workloads fostered loyalties. As the captain of the ship, he looked after her; in return, she looked after him. Mutual trust and professional respect they had in full measure, and they had quickly become good friends.

All that notwithstanding, he was a fountain of questions, and she had a thousand things to verify and validate. For now, she seemed pleased that he was preoccupied. One by one, she went through every detail. There were no major problems.

Of course, the purpose of a shakedown was to subject the ship to stressful conditions in order to bring out any serious defects while the log base was nearby to repair them. Fortunately, structural integrity checked out well and only minor problems emerged. Apart from the bad optical sensor, Peggy found only a few incompletely tightened fittings and a power supply that had developed an unacceptable ripple. She communicated these troubles to the log base product assurance director, invoked redundant or alternate devices, and elected to have the repairs done later.

Eventually, when everything had settled down to a nice state of tedium and Peggy felt confident that the ship was ready to go, she notified Pat that the hyperspace test flight phase could begin. He got back into the tank, took the con, and requested permission to proceed. Under the watchful eye of the log base, they made a short local hop and then a longer one to the system perimeter. All went well, and Log Base Ops cleared them for departure to Star Base 75.

Upon arrival at Star Base 75, they requested clearance to dock, received the necessary navigation vectors, and passed through the edge of the Star Base's no-fly zone. "Star Base 75 dead ahead, sir," Peggy announced. "One minute to final."

"Stand by for docking and open a channel to Approach Control."

"Aye, aye, sir," she sang out. "All weapons systems are secured and all docking systems are green. Approach Control channel is now open."

Pat toggled the approach system switch and saw that Star Base 75 was right where he expected her to be.

"Star Base 75, Papa Victor One One requests permission to come aboard," Pat said.

"Papa Victor One One cleared for manual approach, polar vector Alpha one six two, Bravo zero zero zero direct to slip Alfa two zero. Report to Operations as soon as possible. Over."

Pat's eyebrows shot up and he replied, "Star Base 75, Papa Victor One One confirms vector Alfa one six two, Bravo zero zero zero. Proceeding manually to slip Alfa two zero."

"Sir," Peggy said, "What's going on? A PV doesn't normally rate a direct approach to a prime berth."

"I don't know," he replied, "but if they want to treat us like VIPs, I'm not going to argue."

"Roger, skipper," she agreed. "Ten seconds to final."

"Very well, stand by. Let's show them how this is done."

Star Base 75 was now marking the approach to slip A-20 with a cone of low-power laser beams. Pat could dock the ship by simply penetrating the cone and letting the autopilot follow the markers into the assigned slip, or in the worst case, by having the star base assume control of the approaching ship. However, other pilots would consider that sloppy unless the ship was coming in with her crew incapacitated or her control systems severely damaged. Good ship handlers could fly smoothly up the axis of the cone and never touch the beacons. Pat wasn't given to bragging, but he hadn't grazed a beacon since basic astronautics school.

If being able to fly a ship skillfully by hand seems silly when computers can do the job, consider the fact that a star base is a mobile fortress, command and control facility, mother ship, and forward support base for numerous smaller vessels. For example, there were currently seventy-two fighters, three cruisers, two patrol vessels and one tender in Star Base 75's immediate area. In the heat of battle, it would be counterproductive to require the base to control the maneuvering of the dozens of ships in her vicinity. Hence, manual approaches and departures were preferred.

Star Base 75's reputation was that of a taut ship. Pat knew that all hands would be paying close attention and that exceptional docking efforts, good and bad, were sure to draw comments from the Old Man at wardroom gatherings.

Pat had not lost his touch. He hit the entry cone right on the money, adjusted velocities quickly, and flew right up the pipe to PV-11's assigned slip. There, he rolled the ship to match axes with the docking fixture, opened the covers over her lifting eyes, and nuzzled her softly into the spring-loaded latches that would hold them alongside until it was time to depart.

While Pat got out of the tank and executed his post-flight checklist, Peggy closed out the log, wrote up their re-supply requirements and maintenance observations, and uploaded herself into a non-volatile memory module in PV-11's command console. When the genie was in the bottle, so to speak, Pat unplugged the module, snapped it into a receptacle on his dog tag cord, and strode to the main hatch. The indicator panel there confirmed that pressure differentials were acceptable, and that the external atmosphere was safe to breathe. He swung the hatch open and walked aboard Star Base 75.

— CHAPTER FIVE —

Turning Points

It didn't take long for Pat to learn that the commander of Star Base 75 believed in making a good first impression. PV-11 was piped alongside, not by a hologram and recorded music, but by a real, live boatswain's mate with a silver boatswain's pipe. Pat saluted the quarterdeck smartly, and the officer of the deck's crisp response reinforced the impression that this was a taut and happy ship. The quartermaster logged Pat and Peggy aboard, the duty technician accepted Peggy's logistic requests eagerly, and they were soon ready to proceed to Operations.

The "as soon as possible" in their docking instructions had decided the question of whether to go to Operations on foot or by shuttle. Ordinarily the two-kilometer jog would have provided welcome exercise. This time, however, Pat got into the people-mover cart behind the watch cabin, pressed the "MIDSHIPS" key, and selected "OPERATIONS AREA" from the display menu. The shuttle accelerated like a twentieth-century hot rod, darted into a tubular passageway, and, in less than a minute, came to a halt at the hub of Alfa Flange.

Pat's midshipman cruises had taken him to several star bases, so he knew he was fairly close to Operations. He also knew that no two of the behemoths were identical. He therefore paused to consult the ship's plan hologram that glowed quietly in an alcove next to the shuttle station. The default view showed the whole star base, which strongly resembled a gigantic yo-yo (a fact that had not escaped the attention of the more irreverent members of the SEJS). The similarity stemmed from the fact that star bases took the form of two symmetrical hemispheres, traditionally called flanges, separated by a central connecting pylon that established a protected 500-meter slot between the flanges.

The flanges provided operating space for personnel, life support systems, and other equipment. The outer shells of the flanges were surfaces for mounting sensors, energy receptors and propagators, weapons, and through-hull fixtures, such as access hatches. The slot served as a zero-gravity, atmosphere-free harbor. Docking fixtures on the star base hull allowed vessels ranging from small craft to battleships to moor in the slot. Each docking fixture was equipped with a variable-size air lock ("grommet") that provided access to the hangar deck, where men without space suits could work on ships and equipment.

Pat quickly saw that there was a shipboard locator mounted on the bulkhead next to the ship's plan. He asked it for directions to Operations. It highlighted the path to his destination in the hologram and asked if he wanted it to download directions into his watch. He declined. In keeping with the design of most star bases, Operations was midway down the pylon, giving the traffic controllers a 360-degree view of the slot. All he had to do was go around a corner and take the elevator.

A star base's flanges are permanently designated Alfa Flange and Bravo Flange. The artificial gravity everywhere on the outer surface of the flanges pulls toward the center of the ship. However, to maximize human comfort and efficiency, the internal decks are flat and parallel to the slot. The gravitational field inside both flanges is oriented perpendicular to the decks, with "down" being toward the slot. The transition zone between the flanges' gravitational fields is at the Bravo Flange end of the pylon. It isn't practical to narrow this zone to much less than three meters. Consequently, it houses a zero gravity lab where the elevator does a somersault during trips between flanges.

Pat made his way to the Operations officer's cubbyhole in the pylon. A gray-haired full commander stood behind the Operations desk, and a number of pilots were visible across the passageway in the Flight Operations ready room.

"Lieutenant Commander Callen reporting as directed, sir," Pat said.

"How do you do, commander," replied the Operations officer. "Pat, isn't it? That was a nice docking you just made. I'm Bud Moore."

Pat shook Bud's hand and said, "How do you do, sir? Thank you very much. My instructions said you wanted to see me as soon as possible. Is there a problem?"

"No, not at all," Bud said, "but I wanted to be sure that you didn't miss the briefing that's about to begin. After that, I have a personal message to relay to you and, time permitting, I'd like to learn about your ship's new capabilities. Meanwhile, if you'd like to grab a cup of coffee and join the others over there, the admiral will be along in a moment."

"Very good, sir," said Pat. "It was nice meeting you."

Curiosity piqued, he headed for the lounge area of the ready room. Half a dozen pilots were gathered in the vicinity of the coffee mess, talking vigorously, while others were already seated in the adjoining briefing area. Pat made a quick stop in the head—there was no telling how long the briefing might last—and then decided to have a cup of coffee.

Once again, Star Base 75 made a favorable impression. Ready room coffee messes were usually much used and rather stark. This one had a sterling coffee service, linen tablecloths and napkins, ceramic cups emblazoned with the star base logo, and truly excellent coffee. Obviously, Star Base 75 functioned with a mind to the traditions of the SEJS.

Pat introduced himself to a group of fighter jocks that was hangar flying next to the coffee urn. A discussion of the relative merits of the new cruciform fighters versus those of the newer models was just starting to warm up when Bud's voice came over the PA: "Please move into the briefing area, ladies and gentlemen. The aide advises that Admiral Dornay wishes to speak to you and your crews in four minutes."

"I'll be darned," Pat said. "Is that Peter or James Dornay he's talking about?"

The fighter pilots looked at him with increased interest; one of them said, "Pistol Pete, commander, but we generally don't let him hear us call him that."

"Neither would I, lieutenant. I asked because Captain James Dornay, the admiral's brother, was in charge of the Charley-to-Golf fighter transition school when I went through. He was on the promotion list, and I thought that by now he might have a star base."

"From what I understand, sir, James Dornay is now a commodore and is somewhere on the SEJS staff," the jock said.

"Thanks," said Pat. "I'll have to look him up in the register and see what he is doing now." Inwardly, Pat smiled again. Pat's family were old, close friends of the family of Peter Dornay, and if he didn't find a way to pay his respects to the admiral before leaving Star Base 75, he would be in trouble at home.

The view screens at the front of the ready room were displaying the seating plan, so Pat moved quickly to his place. He removed Peggy's crystal from its socket and plugged it into a connector in the tabletop. Then he stood waiting behind his chair.

The tabletop contained a graphics input pad, a video display, and network connections that would enable Peggy's cognitive processes, memory, and communications links to function. After a moment, she indicated via the local display that she was aware of her location and was in sync with the star base network. Neither she nor the other crewmembers in attendance would speak during the briefing unless the briefer asked them to do so.

From the back of the room, the aide's voice announced, "Ladies and gentlemen, the star base commander." All came to attention while the briefing party moved to the front of the room.

"Seats," Dornay commanded. All but he, sat down. He scanned the group for a moment and said, "This is a good ship and a good command. I am proud of each one of you and the work you have done to expand the civilized region of the galaxy.

"You have all read the sitreps. I am sure I don't have to tell you that an unusually challenging mission is taking shape. What you may not know is that we have identified the source of the Charley class fighter that Arachnids brought to the Gastropod star base.

"The information I am about to present is classified secret. Treat it accordingly. A few hours ago, the Gastropods took our C-class fighter aboard their star base. Shortly thereafter, the Arach ships made a hyperspace departure. Our PVs were not close enough to determine where the Arachs went, and we never did know where they came from. However, before the Gastropods took the fighter inside their star base, the PVs were able to determine unambiguously from the fighter's markings that it came from CB-32, a cruiser-battleship that disappeared mysteriously approximately five years ago. SEJS has therefore reopened its investigation of what happened to CB-32, and we have been called upon to help resolve the mystery. Please direct your attention to your tabletop monitors."

A graphic promptly took shape, stating:

OBJECTIVES:

LOCATE CB-32.

CLEAR ALL PIRATES AND OTHER HOSTILE FACTIONS FROM THE REGION CURRENTLY OCCUPIED BY THE GASTROPODS.

BRING THE GASTROPOD STAR BASE TO THE NEGOTIATING TABLE.

The admiral continued, "We are developing operations plans to support these objectives. We will call this campaign 'Operation Delta.'"

Another graphic popped up on the screen.

OPERATION DELTA: CONCEPT OF OPERATIONS

The admiral read from the screen. "There will be three task forces: First, Task Force Delta, under the command of Netsuko Watanabe, Cruiser Division 12, will conduct forward operations.

"Second, Task Force Echo: Star Base 75, reinforced by Fighter Squadron 117, will provide general support and a base of maneuver.

"Third, Task Force Bravo, RADM Brown commanding, will constitute a tactical reserve.

"Those of you who have not yet had the pleasure of serving with Commodore Watanabe will find that you could not ask for a better task force commander. She will brief you on her plans tomorrow.

"Our encounter with the Gastropods has excited extreme interest among our Molluscan allies. There are indications that humanity has much to gain if we can facilitate a successful dialog between the Molluscans and the Gastropods. We are, of course, eager to take advantage of this opportunity, but it certainly is no more important than CB-32 and our general pacification objectives.

"Be advised, however, that the situation is fluid; priorities may shift. It is imperative for all of you to keep yourselves informed, to keep me informed, and to ensure that we work as a close-knit team at all times. Any questions?"

"Yes, sir," a captain in the front row responded. "Has SEJS provided any information about CB-32's disappearance? If I remember correctly, she wasn't lost in combat."

"As usual, Joe," the admiral replied, "your memory is excellent. SEJS has sent us a summary of the accident/incident investigation report, and we will have the complete file within the hour.

"To paraphrase the summary, CB-32 had been decommissioned and was en route to Terra 2 for rebuild and upgrade when she disappeared after initiating a hyperspace course segment. A skeleton crew was flying her, but they were ferrying a fighter squadron in for transition from Charley to Golf-class ships. Hence, she had 40 fighters—36 operational birds and four maintenance floats—and 65 people aboard.

"The Board of Investigation found no evidence of hostile action, singularities along her route, or other indications of what happened to her. The fact that she has not made her whereabouts known makes a navigational error highly unlikely. The Board recommended that SEJS declare CB-32 missing in the line of duty, and that is what happened. She

45

and her personnel will soon be declared 'presumed lost,' inasmuch as it has been almost five years since she disappeared, and that is the maximum period that people can be kept alive in stasis."

"Thank you, sir," the captain said. Then, looking around the room, he continued, "If I may, I'd like to add, for the benefit of anyone who has not had contact with Arachs, that their showing up with one of CB-32's fighters does not bode well for CB-32."

"Quite so," the admiral said. "Arachs tend to operate independently and in ships that are too small to defeat a CB—even an old, battle-weary one like CB-32. They might, on the other hand, be able to board a CB whose crew was in stasis. Were they to do so and figure out how to get into the stasis compartments, they would undoubtedly use the people there as food.

"I, for one, want to find CB-32 as quickly as possible, in case any of her people remain alive. I'm sure you all feel the same way. Any further questions? No? Very well—I am inviting all commissioned and warrant officers in the task force to dine with me tonight. Commander Moore will furnish details. Ladies and gentlemen, we have a great deal of work to do in the next twenty-four hours. See to your ships at your earliest opportunity. We have no time to waste."

The admiral, followed by his aide, strode toward the exit. All present rose in silence.

When the admiral had exited, Bud said, "Ladies and gentlemen, Admiral Dornay believes in the 'work hard, play hard' ethic. The aide has informed me that the admiral has pulled out all of the stops to make this evening an occasion none of us is likely to forget. I don't know how he did it, but he's managed to round up a malleamorph android for every XO and copilot in the task force. We'll see you at 1900Z. Commander Callen, please stand fast. The rest of you are dismissed."

Pat left Peggy plugged in, thinking that they might need to record something in Bud's words. He noticed the desktop display flash, and grinned when he saw the happy face cartoon Peggy had drawn. He, too, was pleased.

Bud was obviously engrossed in something at the podium, but after a little while, he glanced up and said, "Ah, there you are, Pat. Be with you in a second." A few moments later, he continued, "PV-11 is all squared away. There was an open circuit in your sensor. We installed one of your spares and replaced it from our stock. We will ship the unserviceable back to depot for repair. Is that okay with you?"

"Certainly, sir, but you didn't have to do that."

"I know, but that's okay," Bud answered. "The message I had for you was that the Old Man would like to see you in his quarters at your convenience. This way, you can go straight up there and not have to worry about your ship. I'll also have your dress whites and the droid delivered to your ship."

"Sir," said Pat, "I don't know how to thank you. When might you be available for a run-down on PV-11's PIP?"

"Well, as to the first matter, don't worry about it. I'm just doing my job. As to the second, how about sitting next to me at supper?"

"That would be fine, sir. Shall I ask the aide to arrange it?"

"Check with him, please," Bud said with a smile. "I didn't mean to presume, but I think he has already seen to it."

"Very well, sir." Pat gave a laugh. "You're so far ahead of me I won't even ask how somebody figured out what size whites I wear."

"That was easy. Ensign Varner has all your records. Now, you'd better scoot up to admiral's country or he'll be after my hide."

— CHAPTER SIX —

Admiral's Quarters

Pat retrieved Peggy, shook hands with Bud, and, on the way past the ship's plan, got instructions on how to find his way to the admiral's quarters. He knew he had nothing to worry about, but he couldn't help being a little apprehensive. Clearly, the admiral was busy, and social amenities could wait until the dining-in. Why, then, did the Old Man want to see him right away?

The flag officers' quarters on Star Base 75 are less than 50 meters from the Alfa Control Center—enough distance to keep the admiral out of the star base captain's hair, but not so far that the Old Man can't get to the control center in a hurry. The entryway to Dornay's spaces was well marked, and Pat had little trouble finding it. Getting in, however, was another matter.

The hatch that connected the main passageway to the one that provided access to the admiral's compartments was open, but when Pat approached, a hologram of an armed Marine guard appeared. When Pat moved to enter the passageway, the image of the Marine came to port arms and said, "The admiral's office hours are from 0700 to 0800 daily. Come back then."

Pat smiled; this was novel and amusing. He said, "I have been instructed to report to Admiral Dornay, and I may well not be here at 0700 tomorrow. I am Lieutenant Commander Callen. Please determine whether the admiral will see me now."

The holo said, "The admiral is not available."

"Very well," Pat said, "then please take a message for the admiral. Tell him that Lieutenant Commander Callen reported as instructed and respectfully requests to be advised when the admiral will see him."

The holo said, "The admiral's office hours are from 0700 to 0800 daily. Come back then."

This was no longer funny. Pat said, a trifle heatedly, "Did you take my message?"

The holo repeated, "The admiral's office hours are from 0700 to 0800 daily. Come back then."

Pat took another step toward the image of the Marine, which, in turn, changed: it lowered its weapon and pointed it directly at Pat but said nothing. Had the weapon been real, the message would have been a deadly threat. In any case, it certainly was not friendly, so Pat decided once again that discretion was the better part of valor. He gave the holo a dirty look and walked back to the main passageway.

By the time Pat arrived at the shuttle station, he had decided to jog back to PV-11's mooring. He went over to the communications station at the shuttle stop, faced the input/output screen, and said, "PV-11 requests a channel to Admiral Dornay's aide."

The screen activated and displayed, "Please Stand By." After a few seconds, it blanked itself and presented a view of the aide's face.

"Commander Callen?" said the aide. "Flag Lieutenant Beale here. What can I do for you, sir?"

Pat said, "First, if it is feasible, Commander Moore and I would like to sit next to each other at supper. He wants me to give him a rundown on the PVs' recent PIPs."

"Already squared away, sir."

"Thank you very much. The commander asked me to double-check on it. More important, a couple of minutes ago I stopped by to see Admiral Dornay per his request. I couldn't get past the holo of the Marine in the passageway without making a scene, so I would like to convey my respects to Admiral Dornay and see if I can make an appointment with him. We may have to shove off before tomorrow's office hours."

"I must confess that I don't know anything about the holo, sir," Beale said. "What happened?"

Pat explained and the aide replied, "I'll check that out, sir. There is supposed to be a certain midshipman, not a holo, in the passageway. No harm done, though. Admiral Dornay does want to see you in private, but he is in a staff meeting and does not wish to be disturbed. Let's see, there are two open blocks on his calendar right now: fifteen minutes, starting in half an hour, and the thirty minutes before we go down to tonight's dining-in. I'd recommend the latter, if you can make it then. The meeting he's in now may slip into the fifteen-minute opening, and I'd hate to have you wait around for nothing."

"Why don't you let me deal with the midshipman?" Pat replied. "Am I right that he's already supposed to be atoning for some mischief, and he's now made bad matters worse?"

"Yes and no, sir. Doing penance, yes; 'he,' no. It's Miss Midshipman Faraday. Let me think—would the admiral think it presumptuous if you involved yourself? On balance, it may be best if you did. She seems to respect pilots, and you are the offended party. As usual, what she did is wrong, but technically not contrary to the letter of her instructions. Just know that you'll be talking to the original Artful Dodger."

"Okay, lieutenant," Pat said. "Read you loud and clear. I'll be back on the admiral's doorstep at 1830."

"Very well, sir, Beale out."

Pat thought for a minute, clenched his jaw, and walked back to the passageway leading to the admiral's quarters. A very pretty female midshipman was sitting on a straight chair at the entryway. When Pat approached, she snapped to attention and said, "Good afternoon, Commander Callen. The message you left with the holo has been passed to the aide, and he says that you are on the admiral's calendar."

"I am indeed on the calendar, Midshipman Faraday, but no thanks to you," Pat replied. "What would you have me say to the admiral, when I see him, about my encounter with the holo?"

Her eyes widened a tiny bit when he said her name, and her pucker factor was not helped when she heard his question. Before she could reply, he said with an edge to his voice, "Never mind, Miss Faraday. I can speak for myself. Let's develop the right answer: not your answer, not my answer, not SEJS's answer—the right answer. What is your First General Order, Miss Faraday?"

"Sir, my First General Order is to guard everything within the limits of my post and quit my post only when properly relieved."

"Right, Miss Faraday. It was my observation that you were in charge of neither. A holo with a useful range of two stupid answers is no substitute for Midshipman Faraday, no matter how indifferent her performance of duty might be. May I assume that the holo was to have been some sort of a joke, and that you, and maybe some of your friends, were observing from a place of concealment? And that, technically, you were not on guard, so that nobody can really nail your butt to the wall for dereliction of duty? And that if that doesn't work, you can use your good looks or a flood of tears to get you out of trouble?" He gave her a hard look and couldn't tell if she was on the verge of tears or laughter. He assumed tears. She began to speak, and he cut her off.

"Don't waste your breath or your tears—I'm not buying either one. We both know how funny it was for me, and how funny it would have been if, because of your actions, I was unable to comply with Admiral Dornay's request to see me."

"Sir," she said with tears welling in her eyes, "I made sure that your message got to the aide."

"True, Miss Faraday," Pat replied, "but the moment was lost—and you are quibbling. Unless things have changed since I was a midshipman, quibbling can be a dismissal offense. Tell me: just what makes you think you deserve to become an officer?"

She squared her shoulders. "I have real talent for flying and for software engineering, sir, and SEJS is the best place to do both."

Pat considered that for a moment. "Miss Faraday, it may come to pass that you will become the best pilot and software engineer in the SEJS, but I hope you'll understand if I say that, for the moment, I'd just as soon not fly with you—or be on the receiving end of your software."

She gave him an odd look, pulled herself together, and said, "Sir, may I speak?"

"You may."

"Figuratively speaking, sir, you are a bastard."

Pat broke up. The more he laughed, the angrier she became, face bright red and fists clenched. He collected himself and said, "Maybe so, Miss Faraday, but at least I'm a live bastard. Good luck to you and the people who have to fly with you, because you're going to need it. Now, good day to you."

Pat was barely able to keep a straight face while he walked away from the midshipman, but when he went around the corner, he glanced back and saw that she was brushing away tears. That was gratifying; maybe she had learned the intended lesson. She seemed like a decent enough person, if a bit too smart for her own good.

He drew questioning glances along the path back to his ship, as he periodically burst into laughter. He was still chuckling long after he had passed through decon and was back aboard his ship.

PV-11 was drawing power from Star Base 75; her status indicators showed that her energy reservoirs were full. Pat reinstalled Peggy, and together they ran through a complete preflight and periodic maintenance check. The ship was in excellent shape, and Pat relaxed on his bunk, watching traffic come and go in the slot and bemusedly observing the spectacle of a cruiser coming alongside and poking her damaged bow into a grommet.

At 1800, Pat uploaded Peggy into her crystal, put the ship on standby, and went back aboard Star Base 75. His uniform and the malleamorph were waiting in the anteroom of the decon chamber. He lifted the droid's scalp away from the nape of its neck and inserted Peggy's crystal. While he was putting his uniform on, Peggy began the process of transforming the malleable droid from an unintelligent, faceless mannequin into the personification of Ensign Varner.

"Well, Peggy," he asked, "what's it going to be tonight? A brunette enchantress? A blonde hussy? A fiery redhead? The woman of my most fanciful dreams?"

"If you don't shut up, sir," she said, "it'll be your mother, and it will serve you right for bothering me while I'm busy. Now go outside and wait while I get ready. I want to look nice, and you should want that, too."

"My, snappish, aren't we? If you don't be nice, I'll trade you in for Midshipman Faraday."

"Very funny, I'm sure," Peggy replied, "but who is Midshipman Faraday? Some flesh-and-blood space cadet you met today?"

"Ouch, yes," Pat said. "Remind me not to aggravate you when you're putting your face on. I'll wait for you on deck—but how will I know it's you?"

"You may not, if you don't get out of here and let me do something with this pile of plastic."

"All right, I can take a hint. Remember, we have to be at Admiral Dornay's at 1830 sharp."

She did not dignify that jibe with an answer. Nothing short of a catastrophic hardware failure would ever allow her to forget a scheduled event.

Pat went out onto the star base and chatted with the officer of the deck. At 1825, Peggy emerged. She had indeed done something with the droid. The hair was somewhere between dark brown and auburn, cut short with bangs in front and shingled on the sides and back. Her complexion was creamy white, with a slight pinkish blush at the cheeks. She had configured the droid to be tall—perhaps 3 centimeters short of Pat's 1.95 meters—and her figure was decidedly feminine, if on the slender side. She was still walking a little unsteadily in the high heels that were part of her formal uniform, but that wobble would be gone after a few minutes.

"Wow!" Pat said. "You done good, babe!"

She smiled and said, "See? I told you that if you'd give me a chance, you'd be proud of me."

They got into the shuttle, and Pat said, "Would you like to drive, or shall I?"

"Sometimes I don't think you appreciate me." She slapped his hand lightly.

He looked at her, dead serious. "Peggy, I told you on the way up here what I think of you. I'd be lost without you, and you know it." He started the shuttle, grinned, and said, "But I have to ask you something— what do you have against boobs? I swear that if you had some, I'd marry you."

She didn't reply, but when they went through the tunnel, she leaned over and nibbled on his ear. He hadn't expected that, and when they emerged into the light, he looked at her with surprise. Lo and behold, her bosom was now at least a 44D.

"Peggy, stop it," he said, completely taken aback. "We can't go into Admiral Dornay's with you looking like that. He's an old friend of my father's. What would he think?"

"What's wrong with the way I look?" she asked innocently. "If he wants to know why I look like this, I'll tell him the truth: that you just made me an offer that I can't refuse. Do I have boobs, or do I not? And did you or did you not give me your word as an officer and a gentleman?"

"Come on Peggy, cut it out! Do you want to get us grounded? This admiral has no sense of humor, and we have exactly 95 seconds to present ourselves to him."

"So much for the word of a superior officer." Peggy grinned, and her chest deflated to its previous dimensions. "Let's go beard the lion in his den. But let me tell you, sir, you have just passed up the chance of a lifetime."

"No doubt, but it takes more than boobs to make a marriage— especially boobs that come and go on the spur of the moment." Turning serious, Pat said, "Peggy Varner, you have my sworn word that if marriage between the likes of you and me ever becomes permissible, you won't have to remind me of what I just said. Meanwhile, if you and I don't straighten up and fly right, we can forget about ever having the opportunity. Now, mind your manners. We have a formal call to make."

They turned in to the admiral's passageway. This time there was neither a holo nor a midshipman to impede progress. At the end of the passageway was a midnight blue door bearing three glittering silver stars and the legend "Vice Admiral Peter J. Dornay."

Pat glanced at Peggy. "All set?"

"Does my uniform look all right?" she asked. She arched her back slightly, tightening the stretchy material of her uniform in the front.

Pat blushed, tried to look stern, and said, "All right, you win this round. Truce until we finish our visit with the admiral?"

"Truce," she replied, "but do I look presentable?"

"You are the very model of a modern major general," he said.

"But I'm an ensign," she protested, and he saw that she didn't get the reference.

"Look it up. You'll find it under Gilbert and Sullivan." He guessed correctly that chasing around the Internet would keep her busy for a minute or two. He knocked on the admiral's door and waited.

Sensors in the passageway had alerted the admiral's staff, and the door opened promptly. Almost simultaneously, Peggy said, "Got it."

The steward who opened the door looked at her quizzically. Pat said, "She was being theatrical, son. We are here to see Admiral Dornay, at his request."

"Yes, sir," the steward said. "You are expected. The admiral will be delayed for a few minutes, but his lady will see you now, if you don't mind."

"We'd be delighted," Pat answered.

"Follow me, please," said the steward, leading the way. When they came to the end of the passageway, there was a door to the right. Its markings indicated that it led to the admiral's offices. However, the steward placed his hand on the opposite bulkhead, and a panel retracted, exposing a cipher lock. He keyed in a combination; the door slid open, revealing the entrance to the admiral's quarters. The steward stepped aside and said, "Please make yourselves comfortable in the living room. Mrs. Dornay will be here in a moment."

Peggy and Pat walked into the foyer, and the door closed behind them. Peggy glanced questioningly at him, so he gestured for her to precede him into the next room. Peggy chose the couch, sat down, and crossed her legs demurely. Pat remained standing until it was evident that Mrs. Dornay would not be along immediately. He then took a seat opposite Peggy and began to think about the evening ahead of them.

Presently, the thought that Peggy was strangely silent broke his reverie. She was looking at him intently; he had the uncomfortable sensation that she was studying him. He returned the gaze of her dark eyes and realized that the face she had shaped from the droid's blank countenance was a work of art. He could see in it her knowledge of his likes and dislikes and, beyond that, sculptural and cosmetic effects that bespoke preparations well beyond the norm, even for an occasion involving an encounter with a flag officer and what could be their last social occasion for a long time. He was pleased—if he wasn't going to be with the belle of the ball this evening, he never was—but he was, at the same time, caught off base. What was going on here? In the flat, indirect lighting he couldn't read her expression, but it seemed to be deepening into a frown. He asked, "Are you all right, Peggy?"

She looked at him evenly and said, "I'm not sure. The phrase 'modern major general' is from lyrics written by Gilbert and Sullivan for *Pirates of Penzance*. There is no doubt as to the validity and, perhaps, the pointedness of your reference."

"I certainly didn't intend for the reference to be pointed, Peggy," he asserted.

"Please resolve the ambiguity, then. I was unable to fathom your meaning directly from the lyrics in question because they are repeated in the songs, and the context varies. According to my cultural library, Gilbert and Sullivan are among the few satirists who are consistently a commercial success. I suppose that sounds a positive note. On the other hand, your reference to the modern major general suggests satire and could imply that my appearance was not, and therefore is not, satisfactory."

"Nonsense, my dear, you are absolutely stunning," said Mrs. Dornay, who had entered at the end of Peggy's statement. She embraced Pat, kissed him on the cheek, and stepped back, clasping his upper arms. "Patrick Callen, you are as naughty a boy as ever. Whatever did you say to this lovely creature?"

"I told her that she was the very picture of a modern major general, meaning that she looked wonderful to me, but it seems that my comment has the opposite meaning if you research it thoroughly enough.

My humble apologies, Peggy—you can take that as literally as you like. Not only are you gorgeous, but it is indeed humbling to be reminded that your software often makes you more knowledgeable than I."

Mrs. Dornay turned her head quickly in Peggy's direction and said, "My word—a droid? You must be Pat's exec. My dear Peggy, if I may call you that—my goodness, I have never come in contact with anything more intelligent than a housekeeping robot. You look more human than I do! I should have noticed the escutcheon under your ensign's bar, but I just assumed that Pat was showing off his date for the evening to his Aunt Amy and Uncle Pete. And, well, you are gorgeous. No wonder they don't allow you to go out on missions in that form. No male pilot I know would be able to keep his mind on business for more than ten seconds.

"But, Pat, let me look at you! It's been a hundred years if it's been a day, and you still look like the dashing young midshipman who spent his spring break with us on good old Terra Seven."

"No, dear," Dornay said from the back of the room, "it's been more like twelve years, and you're gushing like a schoolgirl. I assure you that Commander Callen and midshipmen now have a bit of distance between them." The admiral's eyes met Pat's, and Pat knew that his encounter with Miss Faraday was no secret to the Old Man. "Amy," Dornay, "would you please reattach this epaulet for me? It came adrift when I put my blouse on."

While Mrs. Dornay helped the admiral make the final adjustments to his dress uniform, Pat stole a glance at Peggy. She appeared to have been mollified, and he felt comfortable with devoting his full attention to the Dornays.

"Aunt Amy," Pat said—she wasn't really his aunt, but he had called her that longer than he could remember—"twelve years or a hundred, you look lovely. I don't think you've changed a bit."

"Thank you, Pat, it's nice of you to say that, even if it isn't true. I'll have to admit, if you won't tell anybody, that I'm just back from having all of the barnacles scraped off at the log base spa. They do a good job of helping keep up appearances, but they tell me I'm only three cellular instars from having to go through a complete reconstitution."

Dornay looked at her reproachfully and said, "Consider the alternative, dear."

"Mrs. Dornay," Peggy said, "from what I have recently heard, the genetic purification is much less time consuming and discomfiting than it used to be."

"I certainly hope so, dear. My first time took almost three months, and the next was almost as long. The thing is, you never forget the taste of some of those potions you have to drink. Yuck! You'd think the fountain of youth would at least taste good."

Peggy started to summarize for Mrs. Dornay the recent bulletins she had seen on the improved scanning rate of the machines that examine each cell in a person's body, detect accumulated errors in the DNA, and create labeled molecules that find their way to the appropriate site to overcome the aging process by correcting any defective genetic information.

Dornay said, "Why don't you girls chat for a while? Pat and I need to talk shop for a moment."

"Fine, dear, we'll be right here. Now, Peggy, what were you saying? Have they really cut the time down to three weeks?"

Pat and the admiral eased away from the women, who were raptly engaged in conversation—or so Mrs. Dornay thought. In truth, Peggy was multiprocessing. With one channel, she was talking to Mrs. Dornay and with another, she was monitoring what transpired between Dornay and Pat.

The admiral had never been close to Pat in the way that Mrs. Dornay was, so it came as no small surprise when the admiral spoke emotionally. "Pat, I spoke to your father this afternoon. He and your mother are well, and they send you all their love. Now, I have to remind you that we are facing an extremely dangerous mission, and you PV skippers will be running point.

"The riffraff we've seen around the Gastropod star base don't particularly worry me. They might be a challenge for a smaller task force, but Delta has enough combat power to sweep them away in short order. Moreover, SEJS has determined that we can deal with the Gastropods by popping torpedoes in under their defenses. Incidentally, I must congratulate you for revealing that vulnerability. That was a hell of a piece of work, and I'm sure you're going to be recognized for it."

"Thank you, sir, but as I said in our after-action report, diving under their beams wasn't deliberate. In effect, they took a swing over my head—and I ducked. The truth is that if I'd had time to think about it, I'd have gone the other way, and Peggy and I wouldn't be here to talk about it."

"Fair enough, but your reasons for doing what you did don't matter. You're here and we know how to hurt them—although we hope that won't be necessary. The best thing would be to convince them that continued intransigence is not in their best interests. If they would join the Federation, they can have a niche of their own and not have to keep running until they have nowhere left to go.

"By the way, the Molluscans have become a little more forthcoming, now that they know for sure that we've turned up their lost tribe. Apparently, this group split off at a time when the Cephalopods had attained dominance and were treating their shelled cousins rather harshly. That has changed somewhat over the intervening several thousand years. The Cephs brought the Molluscans into the Federation and continue to be the senior diplomatic representatives of their genus, but they no longer oppress other species. They have asked us to pave the way for a dialog. We are going to cooperate.

"That brings me to the crux of the matter: the Gastropods can't get much technical intelligence from a Charley. Fighters don't carry torpedoes or any information that would reveal our capability to defeat a ship of star base proportions. A cruiser is another matter altogether. Lord knows, I'm worried about CB-32 for all the reasons I stated this afternoon, but I'm very concerned about the consequences of hostile Gastropods getting hold of one of our capital ships."

"Sir," Pat replied, "I've been thinking about how we can find CB-32. It will be worse than looking for a needle in a haystack. Push comes to shove, you can burn the haystack and sift the ashes. In this case, we don't even know where the haystack is. However, there may be a way to locate her. May I speak freely?"

"Certainly. I'm very interested in your opinion."

"Thank you, sir. This afternoon, you said that our PVs weren't close enough to the Arach ship to tell where she went, but even if they had been closer, we've never had any success in tracking Arach ships because of their technology. It seems to me that SEJS ought to be able to narrow the field by simulating CB-32's possible courses. They know where she started, and they could assume that she ended up somewhere near the current location of the Gastropod star base. They could hypothesize various types of navigation system malfunctions, or transient singularities along her intended course, and narrow the field enough for us to look where she is most likely to be.

"I'm not much of an astrophysicist, sir, but I'd start with the singularity theory. As you implied this afternoon, a malfunction in the primary navigation system shouldn't take out the ship's hyperspace communications robots, and we'd have heard from her by now. On the other hand, passing close to a singularity could be catastrophic." Pat studied the admiral's face for an encouraging sign; Dornay nodded, so Pat went on.

"The investigating board didn't have much to go on and might not have looked in the right place to find a transient singularity, but a simulation model could determine where and how much CB-32 deviated from course to end up near the Gastropods. SEJS would then know where to look and could find the singularity, quantify its effects, and re-run the simulation to compute where CB-32 may have ended up."

Dornay smiled his approval. "Not a bad approach for someone who's not much of an astrophysicist. I think you're being too modest. Wasn't your undergraduate degree in astrophysics?"

"Yes, sir, but that was a long time ago, and the field has passed me by. It's embarrassing to read the journals these days. I don't recognize half of the words, much less understand what they are talking about."

"Perhaps so, but SEJS did exactly what you just outlined, up to the point of running initial iterations of their models. Unfortunately, what they learned was that there is a continuous spectrum of possibilities. A strong deflection at either end of her course could have sent her to the same place as a weak one at mid-course. The analysts concluded that it was a fruitless line of investigation."

"I see what you mean, sir. Shucks, there has to be a way, though. What else is SEJS trying?"

Unexpectedly, Peggy spoke up. "Excuse me, Mrs. Dornay, but I have to concentrate on a problem for a moment. Admiral, I may be able to determine where CB-32 is located. May I use Star Base 75's network and computers for one or two minutes? I'll also need access to the galactic ephemeris and the database of Arach destroyer parameters."

To say that this was an extraordinary request would be a gross understatement. The admiral's eyebrows shot up, but he said, "Let me check." He pulled a hand-held device out of his belt pack, flipped it open, and entered a query. Then he looked up and said, "No problem. Go ahead."

The admiral keyed in a passphrase, whereupon the droid slumped over and went slack-faced, provoking an exclamation of alarm from Mrs. Dornay and startling even Pat. For the moment, of course, Peggy was functioning in such a compute-intensive mode that she was too busy to bother with trivia like the droid's posture.

Pat explained to Mrs. Dornay, but she was clearly unsettled. Not knowing what else to do, he walked over to the couch and sat down next to the droid, brought it back to an erect position, put an arm around its shoulders, and smiled reassuringly at Mrs. Dornay. She relaxed somewhat and remarked that they made a handsome couple, but conversation did not resume.

Pat wished that he knew exactly what Peggy was doing. Even though he felt at home with the Dornays again, the longer the silence grew, the more strained the atmosphere became. After almost two minutes, the droid revived, and Peggy said, "Admiral, I believe I have a verifiable concept of operations for locating CB-32."

The admiral nodded. "Please continue."

Peggy responded, "Sir, the Arachs having a Charley class fighter from CB-32 implies that she did not hit a stable singularity, such as a star or black hole. If she had, she would no longer exist. Let us say that CB-32 began to broadcast distress signals nearly five years ago. Even if Arachs have boarded CB-32 and shut her transmitters off, her initial and interim transmissions will continue to propagate outward at the speed of light, defining a sphere with a radius of five light years.

"Neither the task force with which PV-11 was operating recently, nor the PVs that are monitoring the region around the Gastropod star base, have detected any distress signals from CB-32. That tells us that CB-32 is more than five light years away from the Gastropods.

"Given what we know about Arach hyperspace engines, an Arach destroyer would be hard pressed to jump much more than seven light years with the added mass of a Charley class fighter in tow. To be conservative and to hedge against our not knowing if or when CB-32's distress signals were shut off, I based my calculations on CB-32 being between five and ten light years away from the Gastropods.

"CB-32's planned course would have brought her no closer than 55 parsecs to the current location of the Gastropod star base—much farther than six to ten light years. Therefore, something deflected CB-32 from her course. There are many stars in the 55 parsecs between CB-32's planned course and the current location of the Gastropod star base. Borrowing Commander Callen's metaphor, there was a finite number of ways CB-32 could thread the needle between her planned course and her current location.

"The ephemeris contains all known information about the locations and movements of stars in the surveyed regions of the Galaxy. In effect, I rolled the clock back five years and plotted the possible paths that CB-32 could have taken to arrive within ten light years of the Gastropods' star base. Sir, my conclusions and recommendations are as follows:

"CB-32 is inside a sphere centered on the Gastropod star base and no more than ten light years in diameter. Tracing back from this hypothetical sphere to CB-32's original course and ruling out paths that intersect stars and black holes reveals that transient singularities at either of two equally probable locations could have affected her line of flight. One is 0.58 parsecs from her point of departure; the other is 0.212 parsecs from her destination.

"Determining where the respective singularities needed to have been further narrows CB-32's probable locations to two regions that are less than three light years in diameter. I recommend that PVs reconnoiter these sites as soon as possible.

"I left documentation of the algorithms I created, as well as my computations, because I assume that it will be wise for someone to verify and validate my work. I regret using so much computing time, but the dynamics and complexity of the geometry were formidable."

Dornay and Pat looked at one another in astonishment. Pat broke the silence. "Peggy, I am dumbfounded. You made that sound simple, but it took original thought that is well beyond my understanding of your capabilities. Please explain yourself."

With complete naiveté, she replied, "I did nothing out of the ordinary, sir. You and the admiral asked the right questions and provided the information—and the supercomputer time—I needed to answer them. I simply did what I am programmed to do."

"Well, yeah, but—"

The admiral intervened, saying, "Outstanding work, ensign! You are worth your weight in gold. Pat, it's time for the dining-in to start. Would you escort Amy and Ensign Varner down to the wardroom for me? Tell the captain to begin without me. I should be there in time for the benediction."

"Of course, sir. Ladies, shall we go?"

They rose and went out through the foyer. While they were in the passageway, Mrs. Dornay said, "Peggy, I have no idea what you said, but it certainly made an impression on Pete. Are you all right now? You gave me a turn when you passed out."

Peggy smiled and said, "I'm fine, Mrs. Dornay, and the real me was in good shape the whole time. Regrettably, the thing you're looking at is just a pile of plastic, microcircuits, and power supplies that needs many of my resources to operate. On the other hand, being in it brings me about as close to being able to have fun as anything I am capable of doing."

Mrs. Dornay laughed. "Peggy, you and I are not very different, after all. Sisters under the skin, if you know what I mean."

Peggy's look of surprise was genuine, and Pat was horrified when he heard her begin to reply. Quickly, he interjected, "That's from Kipling, Peggy—it's a poem about a colonel's lady and a woman called Rosy O'Grady. From what I remember about the poem, and from the Gilbert and Sullivan incident earlier this evening, I think it may be best to let it go at that."

"Yes, sir, I know and I agree—with both you and Mrs. Dornay."

Mrs. Dornay said, "Pat, this is turning into quite an evening for me. To be invited to a dining-in is extraordinary in its own right, and I've met a young lady whom I'm coming to like very much. She can give and take with the best of us."

Pat nodded in assent and said, "Little do you know, Aunt Amy. Just be aware that she has been on her best behavior ever since we came into your quarters this evening. You ought to see her when she decides that she needs to take me down a peg."

The banter continued in this vein until they arrived at the wardroom. Half of Pat's mind was wondering what the admiral was doing, and the other half was extremely pleased that Mrs. Dornay liked Peggy and accepted her as if she were human.

🔺🔺🔺

Dornay had stopped at the exit from his quarters. When the others turned out of sight at the end of the passageway, he opened the door to his outer office and went in. The sailor who was on duty there jumped up and saluted. Dornay said, "Yeoman, get Midshipman Faraday up here on the double. Then lay on an encrypted voice channel to SEJS for my use in five minutes."

— CHAPTER SEVEN —

Dining-in: The Awards

There was a group of people and droids waiting outside the wardroom door. Mrs. Dornay whispered, "The receiving line isn't open because Pete and I haven't arrived. Let's go around the back way and get things moving."

She led Pat and Peggy through a private entrance and across the wardroom to a foyer where the admiral's aide and a small party of senior personnel were waiting. Mrs. Dornay explained the admiral's delay, the aide organized the receiving line, and Peggy and Pat were the first to pass through.

In keeping with tradition, the aide was at the head of the receiving line. Pat introduced the aide to Peggy. The aide then turned to the droid on his right and said, "Commander Nigita, Ensign Varner and Commander Callen of PV-11. Ensign Varner, Commander Nigita is the exec of CB-107 and will be Task Force Delta's deputy commander."

Commander Nigita shook hands with Peggy, uttered a pleasantry or two and, before shaking Pat's hand, introduced Peggy to the lady on his right, who was Commodore Watanabe, skipper of CB-107 and task force commander. They proceeded up the line past the star base captain and his lady to Mrs. Dornay, who, in the absence of the admiral, was socially the senior person present.

"Have a good time, kids," Mrs. Dornay told them, "and come talk to me after dinner."

"Yes, ma'am." Pat took Peggy on his arm and led her into the wardroom. They immediately encountered a large graphic display showing the seating arrangements. The dining tables formed an "O" with open corners. The senior commanders and their parties occupied the head table, the pilots from the two fighter squadrons were on opposite sides of the O, and the officers of the cruisers, patrol vessels, and tender were located with the admiral's staff, across from the head table. Pat noted that Bud Moore would be on his left and Peggy, on his right.

They moved to their seats, and Pat said, "Peggy, I think I'd like a glass of wine. Can I get you anything?"

"No, thank you. I'm fine for the moment, but I would like a chance to talk with you before the ceremonies begin."

"I want to talk to you, too," he replied, "but I'm just about dry. Visiting with the admiral made me more nervous than I care to admit. Are you sure it wouldn't be a good idea for you to top off your fuel? You've got at least a thirty-minute head start on the other droids, and you haven't exactly been sitting idly by."

"Okay, get your wine and I'll go to the ladies' room. I'll meet you back here in a couple of minutes."

Peggy found the facilities and went into a stall. Above the fixture provided for humans, a tapered pipe stub protruded from the bulkhead. She extended her arm toward it, palm forward, and leaned against the stub. The stub slipped through a hidden slit in the heel of her hand, engaged fittings inside, and when her weight opened the valves, directed a flow of liquid hydrogen up an insulated tube inside her arm. When a green diode on the bulkhead lit up to indicate that the droid was ready for at least two more hours of normal activity, Peggy disconnected. She left the stall, checked her appearance in one of the mirrors, and returned to their table in the wardroom. She smiled prettily at Pat, who was returning from the wine mess, and said, "Before you say it, yes, the stuff that is flowing in my veins is very, very cold."

Pat chuckled and sat down at the table with her. "That was the furthest thing from my mind, but I'll remember if I start feeling amorous."

Instead of the lighthearted reply he expected, Peggy said seriously, "Sir, am I to take it that I turn you off? My fond hope is to impress you favorably. What have I done to make you rebuff me? In order to cope with human behavior, as well as certain classes of physical phenomena, I am equipped with a considerable ability to ignore, accept, or rationalize ambiguities and uncertainties. Nevertheless, you continually test my limits."

"By now you should know where you stand with me," he said, incredulous. "I may kid around when it's not in the line of duty, but that makes for a healthy relationship. There's an old saying that what's good for the goose is good for the gander. You've already teased me several times today, and in a very sophisticated manner. So—lighten up! Not only are you incredibly intelligent, technically proficient, and all that official stuff, but until now I thought I was getting along with you better than I ever have with anybody else. I not only respect you, I also really like you, and I'm sorry if I offended you. If it's praise you want, from now on that's all you're going to get."

She looked mollified, if a droid could have such a human look. He thought she used her facial expressions quite well. Nevertheless, he went on. "Heaven knows, you deserve a lot of praise. How many SEJS auxiliary ensigns walk into a star base looking like a million credits and proceed to hand mission-critical information to an admiral, thereby putting egg all over the face of the SEJS scientific and technical community? Girl, you're something else."

"I must apologize, sir. I wasn't fishing for compliments. Your waste your praise on me. I was dithering between two binary states— acceptance and rejection—and I needed to know which I was in. Now I know. Please let it go at that."

He took her hands in his and said, "Peggy, one more time, what's going on here? In the Dornays' living room, I had time to take a good look at your face, and I realized that it was exquisite. Look at the other female droids that are arriving. It's expected that they look reasonably nice, and they do. Yet, you must be ten orders of magnitude prettier than they are. Why?

"I suppose, sir," she answered, "that it is because beauty is in the eye of the beholder. I modeled my droid on the appearance of females I have noticed you admiring. I must have accidentally hit upon a combination of features that strikes a responsive chord with you. I'll go into the head and change it, if you wish."

"Don't you dare! I love the way you look. What worries me is your state of mind. You are supposed to have strong loyalty and attachment to your captain, but you are also supposed to remain completely rational at all times. I am beginning to wonder."

"I know the textbook definitions of emotions and behaviors, and that helps me to communicate appropriately," she said. "That is not the same as having emotions. And if my behavior has been irrational in any way, you should immediately ground me and call for an investigation."

He looked at her for a long moment, then dropped her hands and said, "Yeah. I hear you, but I get the feeling that you were hurt a moment ago when I didn't say, 'Peggy, I love you.' The truth is that I am beginning to have strong feelings for you, and that is immature, at best. I mean, if I were to fall in love with you, knowing that you couldn't love me back, wouldn't that be a fine kettle of fish? But when you look like you do tonight, I can't help thinking about setting up light housekeeping."

Peggy looked steadily into Pat's eyes but said nothing. Pat finally broke the silence by asking, "What can you tell me about Commander Nigita? It's been a while since I've met a droid that outranked me."

"I don't have anything on him at all, sir," she replied. "I've been trying to pull something up from the star base files ever since we went through the receiving line, but the network controller says that no low-priority traffic will be serviced until further notice."

"I'll bet you had something to do with that, milady," Pat said.

"How's that, sir? I haven't made any unusual requests since our talk with Admiral Dornay. Oh! Do you think they are working up new operations plans to search for CB-32?"

"I wouldn't be at all surprised. How about Watanabe? What do you know about her?"

"When we got word that she was going to be our task force commander, I pulled up her biographical sketch. With the record she has, I'm surprised she isn't an admiral. Nine years in fighters, three Navy Crosses. Four years in a PV, one Distinguished Flying Cross. Two years as Operations officer on a star base, one Legion of Merit for developing the combat traffic control system that is now standard in the SEJS. Three years a cruiser captain, another Navy Cross and promotion to division commander. She's been in that assignment for five and a half years, though."

"Wow! She doesn't look old enough to have done all of that," Pat said, a bit envious. He turned and saw a familiar face. "Ah, here comes Bud Moore." He pushed back his chair and stood up, and so did Peggy. "Commander Moore, I'd like you to meet Peggy Varner, the brains of PV-11."

"How do you do, Miss Varner?" Bud said. "It is indeed an honor to meet the analyst that stood SEJS on its ear today. Not only that, but you've managed to make that droid into something that looks like it stepped right out of a recruiting poster."

"How do you do, sir," Peggy replied. "I too am honored. Not only are you the first Medal of Honor winner I have ever met, but in my opinion your stratagem at the Helios VI engagement is at the pinnacle of human brilliance and courage."

Bud's countenance went ashen, and he lowered his voice. "Thank you, Miss Varner. That is a great compliment. However, Helios VI is something I would much prefer to put behind me. I didn't think anyone out here except Admiral Dornay knew I was involved in it."

"Oh, forgive me for upsetting you!" Peggy said, the level of her voice mirroring Bud's. "The admiral did not mention it to us, and it is not in your public data file on the star base computers. The fact is that you are a part of me, and I would have known you anywhere. You see, when we automata are put together and merged with our ships, we reach a stage where we become self-programming and adaptive. Each of us in the PV series has contributed to the ships' software libraries. My area of concentration is engagement control systems. When I discovered Helios VI, I studied it from every possible perspective and used it as the kernel of one of the PVs' combat readiness tests. Please be assured that neither Commander Callen nor I will mention your role in Helios VI to anyone, unless you expressly authorize it."

"Thank you, I would appreciate that." Bud smiled wanly and gave a small sigh. "Helios didn't happen the way most people think. The citation says things about valor and brilliantly effective actions, but I happen to agree with whoever it was who defined courage as grace under pressure. I acted out of malice and frustration. We were shot to hell, we were running with the enemy right on our tail, and we weren't getting away. I'll never forget my exact thoughts: 'Screw this. Before those bastards drive this ship up my ass, I'm going to ram it down their throats!' That's awful language, and I apologize for using it, but I think you have a right to the plain, unvarnished truth—which does not appear in the official reports."

Bud checked over his shoulder to make sure others weren't listening. "To make it happen as quickly as possible, I looped my ship around and initiated a hyperspace hop right into their faces. Until then, nobody had any idea what would happen in a collision like that. Bad idea, don't try it. It blew our pursuers away, but we paid dearly. I lost a wonderful copilot, and there wasn't much left of me. Most of what you're looking at was regenerated from the remains inside my helmet." His grim smile made Pat wince and hope that never happened to him.

"Now, that said," Bud continued, "I'd like to change the subject, but please understand that you have not hurt my feelings. When I'm caught off guard by a mention of the incident, it takes me a second to remind myself that all's well that ends well." He glanced around and saw Commodore Watanabe looking pointedly in his direction. "Oh, nuts, will you excuse me for a moment? Apparently the commodore wants to talk to me."

"Of course, sir," Pat said, and Bud walked away in the direction of the head table.

Pat sipped his wine reflectively. "I had a feeling that I knew him from somewhere; now I know why. Everybody who has gone through flight school since Helios VI has heard the recordings of that engagement. I remember him stating, by the numbers, exactly what it was he intended to do and why, before he augured into the bow of that alien battlewagon. My instructors always referred to him by the designation of his ship, DH 415, so I never knew his name. Holy cow— I've been talking to him like he was just another staff weenie from Star Base Operations."

"I don't think he would want it any other way," Peggy observed. "If he enjoyed being treated like a hero, he would have retired and gone on the lecture circuit a long time ago."

The room was filling with people. Pat and Peggy soon found themselves talking shop and speculating with others about what the evening held in store. In due course, Pat noticed that the members of the receiving line had moved to the head table. Admiral Dornay was with them, and the ceremonies were about to begin. The groups of officers that had coalesced to carry on conversations broke up, and soon all present were at their appointed places.

The aide walked to the rostrum at the head table and announced into the microphone, "Ladies and gentlemen, we have a few items of business to take care of before the evening's social activities begin."

Groans rose from the fighter pilots; the aide continued, "Fortunately, everything I have before me appears to be good news, and I am sure it will only contribute to the conviviality that will follow. Attention to Orders!" He paused to allow all to come to attention and face the front of the room, and then he read aloud:

Space Exploration Joint Service Special Orders Number 21 dated 1830Z, 21MAR23:

Paragraph 1. The following named officers are hereby promoted to the stated rank in the Regular Navy:

Watanabe, N.—CruDiv-12—Rear Admiral

Allen, J.—FS-212—Captain

Callen, P.—PV-11—Commander

Boggs, W.—FS-117—Lieutenant Commander

Jideani, J.—FS-117—Lieutenant

Masters, B.—FS-212—Lieutenant

Tomko, A.—FS-117—Lieutenant

Paragraph 2. The following named officers are hereby promoted to the stated rank in the SEJS Auxiliary:

Nigita, T.—CB-107—Captain

Fama, K.—FS-212—Lieutenant Commander

Varner, P.—PV-11—Lieutenant Junior Grade

Varner, P.—PV-11—Lieutenant

There were exclamations of surprise when the name Varner was read twice, and the aide said, "At ease, ladies and gentlemen, there is no mistake and there will be an explanation after I have finished reading the Special Orders." He continued:

Fields, G.—FS-117—Lieutenant Junior Grade

Abood, H.—FS-117—Lieutenant Junior Grade

Lowe, S.—FS-212—Lieutenant Junior Grade

Swelan, T.—FS-117—Lieutenant Junior Grade

Attention to Orders. Space Exploration Joint Service Special Order Number 22, 1831Z 21MAR23: By the authority vested in me by the Galactic Federation, the Distinguished Service Medal is hereby conferred upon Lieutenant Peggy Varner, Space Exploration Joint Service Auxiliary.

Citation: 'On the 21st of March, 3023, Lieutenant Varner did distinguish herself by inventing novel computational techniques, synthesizing from them a process that has successfully explained the loss of CB-32 and will dramatically reduce the time and risk required to locate CB-32. Lieutenant Varner's analysis was exceedingly complex in nature and is particularly remarkable because she accomplished it entirely by means of the comparatively limited resources available aboard a tactical star base. It is further to her credit that in so doing, Lieutenant Varner solved a class of problems to which modern science had previously found no solution.'

Signed: John S. Brookleigh, Admiral,

CINC SPACE EXPLORATION JOINT SERVICE.

The aide cleared his throat, and Pat saw that he was looking in Peggy's direction. "I don't often have an opportunity to speak to you all on my own behalf, but this is one time when I am going to step out of line and state my heartfelt congratulations to all of you who are about to have new insignia of rank pinned on you, and especially to Lieutenant Varner. I shall now turn the rostrum over to Admiral Dornay, who wishes to say a few words while the promotees and awardee come forward."

The admiral had a twinkle in his eye when he took the rostrum. "Ladies and gentlemen, congratulations to all of you. Those Special Orders reflect team efforts in which every one of you has played a role. Keep up the good work.

"Now, it is unusual, to say the least, to see someone promoted two grades in one ceremony. I've been at this a long time, and it's certainly a first for me. To explain, Lieutenant Varner was due a promotion to lieutenant junior grade on 1 April anyway. It seems that when SEJS decided to promote her and her skipper below the zone, in recognition of their exceptional contributions, SEJS had to play catch-up ball to make everything come out right. But you ain't heard nothin' yet, as the old saying goes. Unless I miss my guess, Commander Callen is standing there, wondering what he did to get promoted when he has been a brevet lieutenant commander for only a few months. Right, Pat?"

Pat shook his head and said, "Affirmative, sir. I have no idea."

The admiral chuckled. "More often than not, that's the way it is. I have it on good authority that SEJS based their actions on your conduct against the Gastropod star base, which are pending recognition of another type, and the fact that it was you who set Lieutenant Varner's wheels turning in the right direction regarding CB-32."

A hush fell over the room, and a voice in the back of the room said, "What?" in an incredulous tone.

"What, hell, pay attention," Dornay said with a grin. "No, just kidding—you haven't heard the full story, so let me explain."

He briefly recounted what Peggy had done and then continued, "We have dispatched search and rescue robots to the regions of space in which Miss Varner stated that we might locate CB-32. Sure enough, in one of them we detected distress signals. Tomorrow, PV-11 will have the honor of leading the way in to pinpoint CB-32's location and reconnoiter the situation. Tonight, however, after we promote and decorate these good folks, we are going to have a party."

Applause broke out in the wardroom, followed by three cheers to PV-11, much to the embarrassment of Pat and Peggy.

With that, the admiral stepped away from the microphone and began to conduct the promotion ceremonies. After the promotions, the admiral pinned the DSM on Peggy. And no one, least of all Pat, thought it the least bit peculiar that an automated XO in the body of an android was receiving a double promotion.

— CHAPTER EIGHT —

Dining-In: The Festivities

At the conclusion of the ceremonies, the aide returned to the microphone. "Ladies and Gentlemen, the Terran Anthem." During the playing of the music, all came to attention and faced a holographic projection of the solar system in front of the head table. The aide then said, "Chaplain Singh, would you please say the invocation?"

The chaplain needed no microphone. He stepped forward, raised his hands upward, and stood silent while a spotlight picked him up and intensified until his white robes were almost the only thing visible in the room. Chaplain Singh was well over two meters tall and one of the best athletes in the SEJS. His swarthy skin and flashing eyes lent him a presence that was commanding beyond any temporal rank. He turned his face slightly upward and said, "Almighty Creator of the Universe, God of a thousand names and one Presence, we your humble servants praise you. We were full of pride and you forgave. We were full of hate and you sent us your holy Child. We destroyed your glorious gifts and you tempered us in the fires of our destruction. We were ignorant sheep in your fold, and you revealed the mysteries of the universe.

"You have charged us to go forth and be plentiful. We revel in the joy of your love and pray that we may be worthy. We thank you for the tasks you have set before us and pray that we may be worthy. We delight in discovery of the infinite wonders of your grand design and pray that we may be worthy. Bless us and guide us, oh Lord, that we may continue in your holy Way."

"Amen," said all in unison.

Normal lighting returned and the aide said, "Please be seated." When the noises of chairs sliding subsided, the aide said, "The junior participant present this evening is Midshipman Ellen Faraday, who will be returning to the academy in two weeks, upon completion of her first class cruise. Midshipman Faraday wishes to propose a toast."

The spotlight swung to the other end of the table at which Pat and Peggy were sitting. It illuminated Midshipman Faraday, who was rising to her feet. She raised her wine glass and said, "To the president of the Federation."

The seated participants raised their glasses, replied in kind, and sipped a little wine. The junior personnel present repeated this ritual in turn, toasting the Federation Congress, the Space Exploration Joint Service, leaders of the ethnic groups that had members present, and the sector commander. Gradually, each person in attendance had consumed a glass of wine, and each droid had imbibed a glass of water.

When the initial round of toasts was over, the aide announced that supper would be served and that an entertainment committee from the cruiser division had selected the music. He reminded the group that there would be games and dancing after supper, thanked them for their attention, and sat down.

The stewards began serving appetizers, and conversations struck up busily all around the wardroom. Bud Moore was back, and his mood seemed to have brightened. A particularly large steward carrying a small silver bowl on a teak tray walked directly from the serving table to Bud and said, "Commander, would you see if this is suitable for our guests?"

Bud selected a piece of toast from the tray, spread it with some of the black jam-like material in the bowl, and put the entire morsel in his mouth. He chewed it slowly, closed his eyes, and savored it carefully. After swallowing, he said, "Yes, chief, that will do nicely. May I have a little wine?"

The chief steward smiled widely and said, "Yes, sir!" He motioned to the wine steward, who stepped forward and drew the cork from a fresh bottle. Bud sniffed the cork, swirled the wine in the proffered glass, tested its nose approvingly, and sipped. Suddenly his countenance contorted and he turned quickly away, making gagging sounds.

Both stewards' expressions became alarmed and Pat said, "Bud, are you all right?"

No answer was forthcoming for a moment, and Peggy said, "Commander Moore?"

The wine steward made a small snorting sound. Pat looked at him and saw that he was struggling to keep a straight face. At the same time, Bud said, "Yes, Peggy?" and came up laughing uproariously with Pat and the stewards.

Peggy, on the other hand, looked puzzled. "What is funny about bad wine or a person choking?"

When he could regain his composure, Pat replied, "The wine was not bad and nobody choked, Peggy. These people simply hoodwinked us to a fare-thee-well."

"Oh," said Peggy, and she laughed affectedly.

Pat and Bud looked at each other, shook their heads, and laughed some more. Bud said, "Pat, try the caviar. It really is excellent. Did you know that Log Base 36's seas are sturgeon farms? Last week you may well have been swimming beside tonight's hors d'oeuvres."

Pat had not known, but it reminded him that star bases could draw upon all the resources of an entire sector. This one obviously was bountiful, and the caviar was indeed excellent. He removed the leather-covered menu from its holder, opened it, and saw that the banquet would have seven courses: the caviar, a Greek salad, Szechwan hot and sour soup, duck à l'orange, endives flamande, sauerbraten, and fresh fruit for dessert.

Pat placed his thumb on the cover's scanner plate and was greeted by the message: "Good evening, Commander Callen. This evening's repast, including beverages, comprises approximately 3,000 kilocalories. Recommend you limit intake to 2,000 by omitting a main course or by opting for small portions. Your choice?"

Pat sighed and selected small portions. The menu responded with, "Very well, sir, the soup will be served in a moment." Pat closed it and returned it to its holder.

Bud said, "I caught your sigh. How is it that with all we know about technology these days, they can't make food taste good without it being fattening?"

"I honestly don't know. I guess it has something to do with the difference between art and science."

"I suppose you're right," Bud agreed. "One of the best things about being assigned to a star base is the artists they have in the galley. Our chefs aren't too strong on North African and Indian foods, but they have the rest of them covered pretty well."

"I'll have to admit that I'm not too fond of North African food," Pat said, "except maybe couscous, but I do like curry. When I was on my midshipman cruise, the star base skipper had it served it every Thursday evening. Some of my classmates weren't too fond of it, but it was right up my alley. It tasted good, and it took no manners at all to eat it. Just add in all the condiments, churn the whole mess together, and shovel it down."

Bud laughed and said, "Pat, you were a born pilot. Come to think

74

of it, I wonder why they don't put curry in squeeze tubes for us to eat on patrol."

"I wondered too, until a medic told me it would put too many bubbles in the bath."

Bud laughed again, but Peggy broke in to object. "Would you two please behave yourselves? I may not be eating, but I would still appreciate your being nice."

Both put on straight faces, and Pat replied, "Yes, ma'am. You are quite right. This is no place for that brand of humor."

The stewards began to serve the soup, which proved to be excellent. Peggy, Bud, and Pat were soon engaged in conversation with the other people at their table.

When the soup course had been served, the area between the tables faded into darkness, then became a three-dimensional tableau vivant in which the figure of a solitary man, dressed in the fashion of the ancient Chinese T'ang Dynasty, stood motionless in the center of a windswept, wintry sunset.

Holographic projections of this magnitude were nothing unusual, but this one was remarkable because it gave the appearance of continuing in all directions to craggy, gray mountains on the horizon. With an almost imperceptible movement, the man withdrew a tiny metal triangle from the folds of his robe and struck it. A single, high-pitched note filled the room, getting the attention of even the most garrulous of those present. When the note faded away, the man bent down and struck a spark into a small pile of tinder and twigs at his feet. Flames sprang up and, in one motion, the man scooped them up in his hands and tossed them skyward. Evidently, he was a magician, for when the flash of light dissipated into scattered embers, he was gone.

Silently, seven pale yellow statuettes coalesced out of the remaining smoke and sparks. Three of the sculptures were of musicians with bamboo wind instruments, one was a flute player, and the other three were dancers.

The scene was silent at first, but the swirling wind began to elicit random tones from the bamboo pipes. Soon, the notes coalesced into fragments of an Oriental melody, each of which evoked small, marionette-like movements from the musicians. The developing storm produced ever louder and more frequent bursts of sound. The musicians became increasingly animated and more purposeful in their actions. When, eventually, the lute player's hand struck a chord, all of the figures exploded in a shower of shards and took human form.

The unfettered dancers leaped and spun in unison with swirling snow, the musicians taking their melody and rhythms from the soul of the storm. At the last glimmer of daylight, the dancers sprang upward and dissolved into whorls of snowflakes, which settled lightly to the ground, then re-formed into magpies that danced in a circle around the musicians.

The tempo of the music changed to match the gliding movements of the magpies, and the storm abated. Sensing this, the magpies gradually reduced the range of their movements until the wind was calm and a last snowflake drifted down. When it touched the ground, the triangle sounded, and the magpies and musicians turned into paper figures. A gust of wind swirled them into a pile, and they burst into flames. The magician reappeared, warming his hands before the fire. Smiling inscrutably, he bowed deeply and disappeared.

The applause that rang out was more than polite acknowledgment of the entertainment: the performance was both novel and beautiful. Pat remarked that he had never seen anything quite like it, and Bud agreed.

Peggy said, "Do you have any idea how much computing power it took to do that? I can't believe they used the supercomputers for such an impractical real-time application."

"That isn't the point, Peggy," Pat said. "The machines are there to be used, and it will be a long time before I forget what I just saw. I don't pretend to understand the symbolism, but we had Chinese art and music to go with the Chinese food, and all of it was better than good. Wait—did you say that it was done in real time? Wow! Who did it? I would have thought that it was a recorded performance from one of the cultural centers."

"I don't know," she said. "It was approved by the admiral, of course, but I won't be able to check the logs to see who was online until the session is over. Do you want me to interrogate the network administrator directly?"

"No, don't bother. I'm sure the artists will be given credit before the evening is out."

It evolved that the theme of the entertainment for the dinner hour was to have holographically animated figures provide music, art, and dance appropriate to the food. It was a successful idea, because it was both amusing and a source of many things to talk about.

After supper, the aide returned to the microphone and invited the chaplain to give the benediction. That concluded the formal part of the evening, and he turned the mic over to Lt. M'boro, who was the MC designate for the balance of the evening.

As M'boro approached the microphone, Peggy leaned over to Bud and said, "Sir, you've been keeping things from us again! You knew all the time who was putting on the floor show."

"No, I didn't, Peggy," he answered. "Who was it?"

"There were three people involved," she replied. "Mrs. Dornay, a Mrs. Haas, and Midshipman Faraday."

"Mrs. Haas is the wife of the chief of staff," Bud said, "and she is quite a musician. What did the others do?"

"Mrs. Dornay was the choreographer and Midshipman Faraday handled the visual effects," Peggy answered.

"Well, I'll be darned," Pat said. "My mother often told me that Aunt Amy was very talented artistically, but until now I always thought she was just a sweet old airhead. It just goes to show that you can't judge a book by its cover."

"Yes, sir," Peggy replied, "and even Midshipman Faraday may have her redeeming qualities."

"No doubt," said Pat, "but it remains to be seen whether they lie in naval service."

Against a background of comedy skits and unfair games of chance, the proceeds of which went to charities, Peggy, Pat, and Bud engaged in light conversation with one another, Mrs. Dornay, and other members of the group.

After an hour or so of levity, M'boro announced, "Please dim the house lights. Thank you. Now, ladies and gentlemen, this evening's dance music comes from our squadron's library of holographic recordings. It will span the popular music of the past three decades. The program is the handiwork of a committee of us junior pilots. We hope you enjoy it."

An image of a bandstand formed in the corner where the lectern had been. Formally dressed musicians appeared to file in, sit down, and tune their instruments. The musical program varied from one dining-in to the next, but the first number was always a waltz, and all present would participate. Everyone who went through the academy or flight training learned to dance in the formal Viennese fashion. For the icebreaker ceremony they would exchange partners in such a way that all males danced with all females before the music ended.

When the orchestra struck up, everyone went to the dance floor. Pat took Peggy's waist firmly, and they whirled off in time to the music. He winked at her and said, "Tonight, my dear, you are the belle of the ball. Don't forget to save the last dance for me." Peggy smiled at him, but to his surprise, she did not answer.

The icebreaker was a time for brief introductions and light conversation. For Pat, on this occasion, most of the chitchat took the form of congratulations. After a few dozen such exchanges, he found himself paying more attention to other couples than to his partner of the moment. The flow of the dance brought a succession of pairings into view. The pattern was simple. At the beginning, couples were arrayed in an oblong in descending order of seniority. After three measures of the song, exchanges were made by having males move clockwise one partner.

Pat had started out approximately one third of the way around the pattern from Admiral Dornay, who was the senior man present. In due course, he crossed the foot of the dance floor and could see the opposite end. Midshipman Faraday and Mrs. Dornay had adjacent positions in the rotation, and Pat was amused to observe the behavior of the junior pilots as they moved from one to the other. Faraday was cute, and most of the young men were obviously attentive to her. With Mrs. Dornay, however, it was arms' length awkwardness. Pat chuckled, and the droid with whom he was dancing asked, "Am I missing something, commander?"

"I doubt it," he answered. "Have you noticed the way the pilots change demeanor when they pass from Miss Faraday to Mrs. Dornay?"

"Yes, that's to be expected. Why do you find it amusing?"

"I'm not sure," he replied. "Maybe it's the paradox. From what I know of the two women, I'd say the guys are feeling uncomfortable with the wrong person."

The droid wanted to ask another question but, to Pat's relief, the moment to change partners was upon them. He wasn't sure he wanted to explain further. While Pat was working his way up the side of the oblong opposite where he had started, he could see Peggy dancing first with the senior staff, and then with the young pilots. If it was possible for a droid to sparkle, she was doing it.

He began to pay more attention to the droids with which he danced. Clearly, each had his or her own personality and experiences, and each was predisposed to learn. What made them incapable of truly emotional behavior—or were they?

Pat's training had drummed home the lesson that members of the SEJS Auxiliary were given a veneer of human-like behavior that was tailored to the pilot with whom he or she served, in order to provide companionship without burdening the ship with unnecessary biological baggage. In some respects, the behaviors were much more than a veneer. Crews really cared about their captains, and they would sacrifice their ships and themselves for the humans in their charge.

Ultimately, he reflected, it came down to intangibles. Automata were the creations of man. Man had long ago discovered how to invest material objects with life, and had gone through a philosophical crisis when it happened.

The biologists had stepped forward and said, "Observe the specimen we have created: it is alive! It exhibits irritability and the capability to reproduce others of its kind."

The computer scientists then said, "If that is all there is to creating something that is alive, we did that a long time ago. Moreover, behold: we can turn ours off and on."

The philosophers and theologians said, "Something is wrong here. Only God can create life."

It took a long time and a lot of anguish for humans to discover the truth of the matter: the Creator established the law of entropy in the universe, and only He could set a form of life above it. Thus, man and other beings might be able to give life to things, but only God could make an immortal soul.

Peggy may not have a soul, Pat thought, *but that doesn't make her any less a winner.* His mind went back to the affairs of the evening, and he realized that he was only two partners away from Midshipman Faraday. This could be interesting.

It was. When Pat took her in his arms to dance, she said, "Good evening, sir. I am Midshipman Ellen Faraday, here for my first class cruise. I will graduate next spring as the top-standing student in my class. I will then go to flight school, serve as a fighter pilot, and go into ship software design. Look me up. By then, I believe I will be ready to settle down, marry you, and raise our children—if your ego can stand the competition with my career."

What could Pat do but laugh? He had expected her to have thought up something challenging to say, but the direction she had taken was not at all what he had anticipated.

Her dead serious expression did not change, so Pat said, "How do you do, Ellen. I am Commander Pat Callen of PV-11, and I believe we have met before. I must say that the holos in this evening's entertainment program were much more to my liking than was your Marine friend. Don't take my laugh the wrong way, though—I've just never had a proposal on such short notice. Don't you think we ought to at least shake hands before we start making babies?"

"Of course," she said, and, as they parted, she took his hand in hers and shook it. Then she was off to another partner.

Mrs. Dornay came to him next. "What's going on between you and Ellen, Pat?" she asked when they began to dance.

"If you can believe it, she asked me to marry her after she finishes her first tour in fighters."

"Oh, I can believe that a dashing fellow like you could sweep her off her feet," Mrs. Dornay replied. "She's at a very impressionable age. How long have you known her?"

"All of six hours, three minutes of which I may have spent with her, and most of that not too cordial," said Pat. "She's a pretty thing, and evidently very intelligent in the academic sense, but—"

"You could do a lot worse, Pat. Ellen is mischievous, I'll admit, but she's really a nice, sweet girl. Do you know how I landed Pete?"

"No, ma'am, I don't believe I do."

"Proposed the first time I met him, when I came through the academy with a dance troupe from Terra 2," she said over her shoulder as they changed partners.

Pat glanced back at Midshipman Faraday, and her eyes met his. She was watching him. *Oh, boy,* he thought, *what have I gotten into now?*

Before long, Pat was back to Peggy. While they were revolving to the closing phrases of the song, she said, "What did you tell Miss Faraday?"

Pat was alarmed but tried not to show it. "About what?"

Peggy answered, "During the dinner music, she sent me a message over the network."

"You didn't tell me. What was the message?"

"If she didn't give it to you herself, perhaps she doesn't want me to tell you."

"Perhaps. In any case, she started off with the rhetorical, 'How do you do,' and I answered in the usual way. Surely she didn't send that to you via datacomm."

"True, but there must have been more. I saw you laughing and talking with her."

"If you were watching us, I guess you did. And if you were monitoring my vital signs, you probably saw my pulse increase."

"No doubt. So what did she say that made your heart go pitter-pat?"

"You're sure you want to know?"

"Yes." Peggy danced beautifully, as steady and graceful on her feet as if she had been ambulatory for decades, not mere hours.

"She said that I should look her up in a few years, and if can handle it and she hasn't changed her mind, she might like to marry me and have our children. I told her that I liked the holos they put on during supper, and that I thought we ought to at least shake hands before we started making babies."

"Then you didn't tell her, 'No'?"

"Not in so many words, but if you think about it, you'll realize that if she meant what she said—which I doubt, considering her reputation as a mischief maker—my answer wouldn't make any difference, unless I had been ugly to her. Hurting her feelings would be stupid. As things stand, in a few years she'll have forgotten all about this, and there'll be no hard feelings."

The music ended, and they returned to their seats. "Now, I told you what you wanted to know," Pat continued. "How about telling me what she asked you?"

"It was nothing much," Peggy said diffidently. "She said she had crossed you earlier, had decided that you were very fair with her, and wondered if I thought you would be angry if she apologized."

"She didn't say she was going to propose marriage?" Pat asked.

"Oh, yes, that too. Like I said, it was nothing much."

"Damn it, Peggy, give me the whole story—and that's an order! If she's trying to make trouble between you and me, she'll be going back to the academy as a bloody civilian."

"Not so loud, sir. I have been trying to tease you about the midshipman, but I don't want to get her in trouble. Her message was, and I quote, 'Miss Varner, congratulations on your excellent work on the CB-32 problem. Earlier today, I played a prank on your CO and it backfired. He reprimanded me fairly, but I did not accept it the way a midshipman should. He strikes me as the kind of man I would someday like to marry, and I would not like to leave someone like him thinking ill of me. You know him better than I. Would he think less of me if I apologized to him tonight?'" It was uncanny the way Peggy played back the conversation in Faraday's voice. Fortunately, she kept it quiet, so no one around them could hear.

"I'll anticipate your next question, sir. My reply was, 'Miss Faraday, thank you. Commander Callen is the kind of man a lot of girls would like to marry. I don't think he is ready to give up flight duty for hearth and home just yet, but I do not think it would hurt for you to advise him of your present state of mind.' It looks like I was wrong. Alas, another day, another broken heart."

"Bull, Peggy. If our Miss Faraday has a broken heart, it's well hidden. Look at her trying to charm that flock of fighter jocks. What do you say we forget her and have a good time?"

"You're the boss, cap'n. What do you have in mind?"

"How's your hydrogen supply? If you're good for it, I'd like to dance to something more up-to-date than a waltz."

"No problem for at least another hour, unless we change to slow dancing."

"How's that?" he asked. "It ought to be the other way around."

"Hold me close and watch the temperature rise!" she said.

He laughed, took her hand, and led her back to the dance floor. By the time "Taps," was played, they were both pleasantly exhausted and back in their ship.

— Chapter Nine —

Task Force Delta

Reveille comes at 0600Z aboard all SEJS vessels. Watch schedules permitting, some pilots use it as an alarm clock, but Pat preferred to be up and ready to go. By the time the traditional bugle call played on March 22, he had already read the message log and completed his ablutions. He noted that all PVs had downloaded new command and control instruction sets and were on alert for departure on patrol during the next twenty-four hours.

This is more like it, Pat thought, and then he said aloud, "This has been fun, but I'm ready to move out."

"Yes, sir," Peggy agreed, "but we must attend a briefing aboard Star Base at 0745 first."

"I know," he said. "Meanwhile, it's time to shake, rattle, and roll."

"Bump and grind is more like it," she said scornfully.

Pat selected two broadcasts for review. One carried a current events summary while the other displayed an aerobics instruction recording. He turned the aerobics' sound down to a barely audible level and joined the exercises while listening to the news.

There was another channel with male instructors for female pilots, but the aerobics leaders on the channel Pat had selected were all female. The physiques varied, but all were spectacular. SEJS's theory was that this encouraged its pilots to exercise willingly. They were right. Pilots were as enthusiastic about their favorite physical training instructors as they were about their ships, and, if the distances to which their fame had spread meant anything, the coaches were among the best-known people in the galaxy.

By 0645, Pat had worked up a good sweat, cooled down, and showered. He dressed, uploaded Peggy and, after dropping by the wardroom for a light breakfast, reported to the Ready Room for the mission briefings.

Bud Moore presided. Task Force Delta was to perform a reconnaissance in force of 14.16.4, the adjoining sector. Given the possibility that a transient singularity existed somewhere along their route, the task force commander would move her resources serially, with PV-11 leading the way. Running at maximum stealth, PV-11 would pop forward one light year, get oriented, listen for distress signals from CB-32, and monitor for hostiles. If she found nothing, she would call the main force forward. If she discovered hostiles, she would immediately withdraw to the point from which she had just come, where the task force would be lying in wait.

When PV-11 detected CB-32, she would spend no more than ten minutes developing an estimate of the situation before returning to the main force. PV-23, commanded by Jorge Parada, would provide backup to PV-11.

After his presentation, Bud asked if there were any questions. Admiral Watanabe said, "Yes, commander. What action is to be taken if PV-11 does not return after ten minutes?"

"SEJS has delegated that decision to you, ma'am. To paraphrase, they feel there are too many unknowns for them to second-guess the on-site commander."

She sat impassively for a long moment and then said, "That covers everything I wanted to know. Thank you, Bud." Turning to the junior people in the room, she said, "Any other questions?"

They all said, "No, ma'am."

"Commander Callen," she said, "you'll be leading the parade. How about describing what you will be doing for the benefit of those who haven't been on recon missions?"

"Yes, ma'am," he said, and stood to address the room. "SEJS has determined where we will begin to receive distress signals from CB-32. Our first hop will take us there. They also have triangulated the general direction we must take and have provided a series of navigation tensors for the first leg of our flight.

"Our scheme of maneuver is designed to give us the element of surprise. Also, objects already in the sector will have been emitting or reflecting energy, but when we pop in we will be new on the scene. Those factors should give us a little time to see before we can be detected, unless we happen to arrive extremely close to whatever is there.

"At the end of each hop, we will check the direction of CB-32's signals and refine our direction of flight. And, because we know the frequency and phase modulation of CB-32's signals, we will also update our range estimate. My ship will be passing all of that information back so the admiral can continually update her plans.

"I estimate that that we will need only a few hops to arrive at CB-32—a long one from here to sector 14.16.4, and one or two quickies to get to CB-32. Does that cover it, ma'am?"

"Yes, thank you, Pat." The admiral rose, and Pat sat down. "Ladies and gentlemen, please allow me to add a few things: We are operating at the fringes of the galaxy. Don't get too nervous if you don't hear from PV-11 immediately after we make a hop. SEJS has cautioned us that that space-time physics can vary out there, and PV-11 may have to deal with unforeseen sensor anomalies.

"As far as alien life forms go, we know what was hanging around where the Gastropods went. Be alert. Where there is one Arach, there will be others, and although we have used the term 'riffraff' to describe the other outlaws that have been spotted, don't assume that they are weak. They haven't survived by being pushovers.

"Also, the Little Peoples have been encountered out here. We don't know much about them, but they are neutral unless you interfere with them. Should you observe any, let them go their merry way.

"Finally, understand that our mission is to locate and rescue a ship in distress. If we run into a fight, so be it, but it is not in our best interests to initiate combat if it can be avoided."

The briefing ended on that note. Watanabe advised them that the task force would sail at 0930 and that operations orders would be forthcoming from the star base. Dornay wished them Godspeed via intercom, and the meeting was dismissed. Pat said good-bye to Bud and returned to PV-11.

▲ ▲ ▲

Pat and Peggy ran PV-11 through her preflight checks and went to standby. At 0925, they cast off, and Star Base Operations directed them to their initial position with the task force.

For twenty minutes, the task force executed maneuvers to ensure that all was in good order. Watanabe then recovered all fighters to the cruisers' hangar decks and divided her forces. With PV-11 followed by a three-dimensional array consisting of CB-107, CB-109, T-2, CB-127, and PV-23, all ships went to battle stations and prepared to jump off from the bottom of sector 14.16.3. On order, PV-11 made the long leap into 14.16.4.

Back in 14.16.3, when PV-11 disappeared, Netsuko Watanabe said from her tank on the command bridge of CB-107, "Nigita-san, display the countdown and monitor for communications from PV-11. When we receive an all clear, take us all through to 14.16.4."

"Aye, aye, admiral," Nigita replied. A red digital clock, counting backward, appeared on her tactical situation screen. Almost simultaneously, yellow symbols corresponding to each of the ships in her task force turned green.

After two hops into 14.16.4, PV-11 alerted the task force to the fact that their next hop would take them to CB-32. Watanabe authorized the PV to proceed. One minute passed, and then two; no reports from PV-11 appeared. At two-and-a-half minutes, the admiral said, "Damn, I hate this waiting. Are we getting anything from PV-11?"

"Negative."

"Evaluation?"

"PV malfunction, probability 0.01; unprecedented event, 0.13; singularity on other side, 0.26; hyperspace anomalies interfering with comm, 0.30; passive Arachnid ambush 0.30."

"Task Force Delta," she ordered, "Recompute destination in 14.16.4 with 0.5 astronomical units offset to starboard. We move simultaneously on my order. Acknowledge."

All task force ships acknowledged.

"Wilco," said Nigita, "but PV-11 may be counting on the full ten minutes, ma'am."

"I know," said the admiral, "and he's going to get it. Let's pray it doesn't cost us half of the PVs in this part of the galaxy." She bobbed restlessly up and down in her tank, watching the clock count down. When it reached the three second point, she licked her lips and started to give the order to hop, but just as she did so, two comet-like streaks of ionized particles appeared on the forward viewers, one trailing the other.

Artificial video superimposed itself on the tactical display, identifying the leading streak as PV-11 and the following one as a hostile. However, before CB-107's weapons could fire on the pursuing ship, PV-11 fired her lasers. The enemy's bows glowed red, ablated away, and burst.

"Bastard never knew what hit him," said Watanabe. "Good shooting, PV-11. Are there any more where that one came from?"

"Lieutenant Varner commanding PV-11, ma'am. Affirmative."

"Report Commander Callen's status."

"Commander Callen is not aboard, ma'am. He took the lifeboat and sent me back. We ran into a nest of six Arachnid destroyers over there, and they have CB-32. Commander Callen is trying to rescue or reconnoiter her."

Watanabe cut her inter-ship communications off for a moment and said, "Nigita, work out a plan of attack. Write Callen off. If he's that stupid, he'd better hope he's lucky." She keyed the mic again and said, "Was that one of the destroyers you just blasted, Varner?"

"Yes, ma'am."

"Did you engage any of the others?"

"No, ma'am. When we arrived, the other five were close to CB-32 but this one was 100 kilometers away. To create a diversion, Commander Callen ordered me to reveal myself to it and lead it back here. He wanted them to think they had caught us by surprise, coming in on an exploratory mission. It appeared to work."

"Lieutenant, moor your ship in my hangar deck and open a hard-wired channel to the bridge. I want to find out what the hell your skipper thinks he is going to do with that old cruiser, but we can't waste any more time this way."

"Wilco," said Peggy, thinking to herself, *I only wish I knew.*

— CHAPTER TEN —

First Contact with CB-32

Peggy had eased PV-11 into 14.16.4 cleanly. She had made no more commotion than would a meteor of comparable size; indeed, her signatures were camouflaged to look like one.

It was well that this was the case. Even before PV-11 had slowed to non-relativistic velocities, Peggy was saying, "Captain, shall I engage the target?" An Arachnid destroyer lay so close aboard that PV-11 was able to use direct sensor data to generate her image.

Slightly disoriented by the hyperspace jump but mindful of his orders, Pat replied, "Negative. Engage at the first hint that we have been recognized, but continue to run silent and use only passive devices." The natural shot of adrenalin that hit Pat cleared his head in a hurry, and he said, "Steady as you go, lieutenant. Keep a close watch on the destroyer and scan carefully for other ships."

"Aye, sir. CB-32 is in stable orbit around a red dwarf." This was good, because it meant that the ship could have been drawing energy from the star, extending her staff's survival time and prolonging the effectiveness of her passive defenses. "There are five more Arach destroyers surrounding CB-32, about 100 kilometers astern of us. That is not good. Sir, your pulse and blood pressure are highly elevated. Are you all right?"

"Yeah, I'm fine. I just don't like spiders, especially when they are bigger than I am. One thing about 'em though—there's never any doubt about what makes 'em tick. They're strictly predators, and if they're here, there's a reason for it. Let's hope they haven't been able to get into CB-32's stasis units."

They ghosted along under the guns of the destroyer, keeping PV-11's bow and primary weapons oriented toward the enemy ship, ready to shoot and scoot, but hoping they would not have to.

Pat asked, "Do you think we can get around to the other side of those guys without being detected?"

"Yes, sir."

"Okay, let's go."

She took them to a point well past CB-32. Quickly reversing direction, they closed to 10 kilometers to get a better view of the Arach formation. Four of the Arachnid ships were alongside the cruiser, amidships to starboard. The fifth was a few hundred meters off her bow.

"Sir, I don't like the position of those four rafted-up Arach ships," Peggy warned.

"Roger that. Let's hope they haven't gone aboard. How long before we have to split?" Pat asked.

Peggy gave him a time display and replied, "Seven minutes, thirty seconds and counting."

"We need to move to where we can see the starboard side of CB-32."

"Aye, aye, sir, but it will not be smart to be any closer than 20 kilometers."

"Okay, make a dog-leg flight to keep us clear."

She did, and he asked, "What can you tell about CB-32?"

"She's in stasis, sir. Her starboard hangar deck hatch is open, which it should not be. Her emissions indicate that she is low on energy, but the Arachnids haven't damaged her propulsion systems. At this range, there's no way to tell about her people without doing an active scan. That would undoubtedly reveal our presence to the Arachnids. We might get away, but probably not, and they might destroy CB-32."

"Yeah, don't scan, but refresh my memory: what kinds of ships was CB-32 carrying, and how many Arachnids do those destroyers carry?"

"CB-32 is fitted out as a flagship. When she disappeared, she had an admiral's gig aboard, but no admiral. She was ferrying forty unserviceable Charley-class fighters to depot for demilitarization, along with numerous fighter components. Are you interested in them?"

"Negative. What are the destroyers likely to do if we start shooting?"

"There's no hard data available on that, but Arachnids apparently don't value their own lives any more than they do others'. Surrender is the last thing they will consider. As to the number of Arachs aboard a destroyer, the Little Peoples say that the number can vary greatly because the Arachs set sail with one female and several males aboard. When they make a capture and she feeds well enough, the female mates with one of the males. After killing and eating all of the males, she weaves a special sack, lays her eggs in it, and waits for the eggs to hatch. Within a year, she heads for a planet where her young can mature, and where she can find more males. Humans have verified the latter part of that observation, lending credence to what the Little Peoples have reported.

"Six minutes, sir."

"Peggy, we've learned all we can from out here. Help me get out of the tank and into the lifeboat, on the double! I'm going to try to get aboard that cruiser while you go for help. If I can get her out of stasis before the task force arrives, we'll have a much better chance of keeping the Arachs from destroying her—and anybody that may be left aboard. Download as much of yourself as possible into a crystal. I'm going to need all the help I can get when I try to activate the cruiser."

"But sir, if you leave the ship now—"

"I know. It's my responsibility, and I'll answer for what I'm planning to do. You just give a glimpse of yourself to the distant destroyer and try to sucker her back into 14.16.3. Don't take any chances. Your primary job is to get a sitrep back to Watanabe. Ask her to give me a little time before she comes in shooting, okay?"

Pat was out of the tank and, still wet, readying the lifeboat for ejection. He pulled the "Peggy minus" crystal out of the command console and snapped it into the lifeboat's dashboard. "Bye, bye, darling," he said as he lowered himself into the lifeboat's cockpit. "Give me ten seconds to get clear of your wake. I love you. Be careful and shoot straight!" He touched a button and the cockpit closed. Pat told the boat to suppress all marker signals and, when the beacon override indicator came on, he backed out of PV-11's stern. Eleven seconds later he said, "Okay, babe, let's sneak up on that cruiser, but make it quick. Pop in abaft and creep along the bottom of the hull. I want to see if there's a way aboard, other than the hangar deck hatch."

Lifeboats being more rugged than elegant, it was a bumpy leap to the cruiser. They emerged behind the cruiser's stern, where they couldn't be seen and fired upon by the Arach destroyers. While they moved along the big ship's belly, Pat donned a space suit and equipped himself with a hand laser, flashlight, and tool kit. He thought about grabbing an infrared lamp and night vision device, but decided that would be a waste of time. Arachnids came equipped by Mother Nature with IR vision.

"Where can we find a hatch that's big enough to pass this boat, but not so big it'll vibrate the ship if we open it?" Pat asked.

"Not possible; any hatch vibrates."

This was a sobering thought—not for its immediate content, but because it was a powerful reminder that the lifeboat was not as smart as PV-11. When she was unplugged from her mother ship, she left behind much more than she brought along.

"Right," said Pat. "Show me the hatches on the bottom of the hull that you can get through." The graphics display on the dashboard showed a plan view of the bottom of the hull. A pattern of green Xs marked hatch locations. "Good. Now delete all hatches that do not lead to passageways you can fly through."

Only six Xs were left. Two symmetrically placed pairs were amidships, and the other two were spaced evenly along the forward centerline of the ship. "Show the labels of those hatches."

The Xs were replaced with, from the bow to the stern, "FORWARD MAINTENANCE BAY," "SHIP'S STORES ACCESS HATCH," "FORWARD ENGINE ACCESS (PORT AND STARBOARD)," and "AFT ENGINE ACCESS (PORT AND STARBOARD)."

"Hmm—the engine access hatches are probably blind alleys and securely sealed from the inside. No doubt that's why the Arachnids didn't broach them. Let's see a longitudinal section through the stores and maintenance bays, stem to stern."

The drawing began to unfold slowly on the display. "Give me detail only on the passageways that connect the hatches of interest to the bridge and the crew's stasis chambers." The display sped up considerably, and the diagrams were complete in a few seconds.

"Store these sections of the ship's plan and related horizontal sections in your crystal for rapid recall," Pat said. "We may need them once we get in there."

When the green indicator next to the crystal indicated compliance, Pat said, "Okay, ease up to the maintenance hatch and engage the lock."

The lifeboat followed Pat's instructions. When it got to the forward hatch, it nosed up to the cruiser and extended a probe into a socket in the cruiser's hull, alongside the hatch. For a moment, nothing happened. Then Peggy, speaking as the boat, said, "No response from lock. Probability .99, no voltage available to lock. Instructions?"

"Can you apply power to the lock?

"Affirmative. Shall I?"

"Affirmative, do whatever is necessary to open the hatch, but do it quietly and keep the power localized."

Nothing happened. Pat said, "What is going on?"

"I am trying to trace the ship's circuits to determine how to localize the voltage."

"Stop, let me guess: the best you can do is power up everything in this part of the ship."

"Between major bulkheads, stations—"

"Never mind, let me think. Better yet, what are your assessments of the way the ship was shut down? Was it controlled? She is in orbit, so it looks like the crew did have a little time."

"She is in orbit, but probability is .6 or better that the Arachnids put her here. The destroyer up forward has a line attached to her in towing position. The absence of power on the hatch lock indicates, probability .3, that she is now using all remaining energy for crew life support or, probability .2, shutdown was catastrophic, or, probability .5, shutdown and subsequent events were too complex to determine from available information."

"A line is in towing position, you say?"

"Affirmative, line consisting of, probability .99, Arachnid web."

"Right. However, for the record, based on the slack in the line and the fact that CB-32 is in a stable orbit, it is my professional opinion that the line is for mooring, not towing."

"Sir, it is my duty to advise you that the condition of CB-32, the way the line is made fast to the cruiser and the destroyer, and your conclusions are not logically consistent."

"That's why I'm the captain. Sometimes illogic is the appropriate response to a situation."

"Surely, sir, you do not propose to violate intergalactic law?"

"Correct, I do not. I propose to investigate and, if possible, rectify an apparent act of piracy. CB-32 may be in stasis, but she is not abandoned or derelict, to the best of my ability to determine the situation at this point. Therefore, the Arachnids have no valid salvage claims and are violating SEJS sovereignty. Do you concur?"

"The probability is 0.5 that you are wrong," said the boat.

"And the probability is 0.5 that I am right," answered Pat. "How can we resolve the dilemma?"

"Acquire more information."

Pat agreed. "And the way to gather that information that is least likely to result in unnecessary loss of life is…?"

"To board the cruiser and investigate without alerting the Arachnids," replied the boat. "However, Arachnids are very sensitive to vibrations transmitted to their feet through whatever they are standing on, and it will be almost impossible to board the cruiser without making noises that will be propagated through the hull. Moreover, we will not be able to open any through-hull hatches without energizing circuitry. That too will be noticed if there are Arachnids aboard."

"Do you have any better ideas?"

"Negative, sir. This is a zero sum situation, and there are insufficient data upon which to project outcomes."

"Yup, what we gain, the Arachnids lose, and we won't have any idea of what the situation is in there until we look. Well, minimax theory be damned. Under these circumstances, we act in the best traditions of military service."

"How is that, sir?"

"We do something, even if it is wrong. Take us aboard, and don't hesitate to get the hell out of here if things start to go sour. Our mission is to get information back to SEJS, not to be heroes."

"Wilco, sir. I am, above all, a lifeboat."

The intensity of the indicators on the boat's command console fluctuated briefly, but the cruiser's hatch did not open.

"No go," said the boat. "Anomalous conditions encountered. The circuits on the cruiser accept my power inputs, but response to datacomm is negative. Probability .8, the hatch controller has been destroyed."

"That doesn't make sense, unless the Arachnids didn't want to let anybody in through here. But if they were expecting intruders, we'd have been had by now."

"It's not just the hatch controller," reported the boat. "I couldn't raise any of the other processors in this section of the ship either."

"Can you tell from the impedance whether the electronics have been removed?"

After another dimming of the console, the boat answered, "Probability is .7 that the hardware is in place but has been fried."

"Let's try the stores hatch, but make it quick. We're running out of time."

The boat moved so fast that Pat wasn't exactly sure what happened. The next thing he knew, they were hove to, about 10 kilometers away from the cruiser. Obviously, the lifeboat had been unable to get aboard CB-32. Meanwhile, it appeared the Arachnid ships had been disturbed. The raft of destroyers broke up: one remained by the hangar deck hatch while the rest spread out around the cruiser.

Warning lamps on the command console began to pulse in synchronization with scans emanating from the destroyers. Unless they were looking for something as small and quiet as the lifeboat and had a good idea of where she was, it was unlikely the Arachnids would acquire her as a target. Nevertheless, Pat and the lifeboat were doing no good where they were.

With some trepidation, Pat said, "We'd better go find out what Admiral Watanabe has in store for us. Can you zap us back to the task force?"

"Affirmative, sir. My remaining energy stores won't take us very far on the other side, but, with a probability of .9, the task force will be waiting there."

Settling into the seat, Pat replied, "Probability 1.00, we hope. Go for it—and give it all you've got."

When the lifeboat came to rest, Pat said, "Enable transponders and give me a fix." The IFF transponder turned green, and the console displayed their position. The boat's navigation was not as accurate as a ship's would have been, but they had made it.

"Ahoy, there, amigo," came the voice of Jorge Parada. "Tell me you're alive and well."

"Si, Jorge," answered Pat. "How about a tow?"

"Belay that! PV 11 lifeboat, follow beacon November Six Juliet, marry up with your ship, and report to me immediately," said the voice of Watanabe.

"Wilco," Pat replied.

A pencil of low power laser energy, which could only be monitored from inside the beam, came from PV-23 to the lifeboat. Talking over it, Jorge said, "Good luck with the Dragon Lady, Pat. Try to be seen and not heard, but stick to your guns. She's been known to bend the rules herself. For now, though, your soul may belong to God, but your butt belongs to her."

Lacking a private way to answer, Pat simply smiled and shook his head. The lifeboat moved directly to CB-107 and entered the hangar bay doors. PV-11 was inside, looking strange among the angular shapes of the fighters. A crew of robots and maintenance techs in pressure suits stood by, waiting; in a matter of seconds, they went over the lifeboat and gave Pat a green light to proceed. He flew the boat manually to the annulus from which they had exited PV-11's stern, indexed the boat's bow into the grommet that sealed it, and waited. PV-11 communicated with the boat through the connector in its bow and drew them aboard.

Pat glanced around the familiar interior of his ship and said, "It sure is nice to be home. Let me out of here, please."

The canopy of the lifeboat opened and Pat got out. He stretched, but before he climbed back up to the main deck, he patted the boat and said, "Nice work, little girl. I would take you anywhere."

To his surprise, the boat answered, "You're all right, too, big guy, but you'd better get topside in a hurry." Now that they were back aboard PV-11 and its complete environment, Peggy's personality was present in full.

Pat bounded up to PV-11's bridge and said, "Status, please, Miss Varner?"

Peggy replied, "Weapons inventory is complete and ready; ship's systems are go. When CB-107 finishes replenishing the energy that I used to take out the Arach and that you used in the lifeboat, we will be 100 percent. However, your command has been suspended by Admiral Watanabe pending completion of an immediate inquiry into your actions."

Pat said nothing. After a moment, an array of video screens lit up above his control console, displaying the faces of Admiral Watanabe, Captain Allen from FS-212, and three officers he had seen but could not associate with names. The pit of his stomach suddenly felt hollow.

— CHAPTER ELEVEN —

Board of Inquiry

"This proceeding will come to order." Watanabe's voice was as solemn and attention-getting as any gavel in a court of law. "Captain Nigita, log the date and time.

"By the authority delegated to me by CINC Space Exploration Joint Service 0045Z 21MAR23, and under the provisions of Article 32 of the Federation Code of Joint Service Operations, a Board of Inquiry is hereby impaneled to inquire into the circumstances under which Commander Patrick Callen became separated from his duly assigned ship, PV-11, while operating in a sector that is not under friendly control.

"Commander Callen, you are advised that this is not a judicial proceeding. However, all testimony given by yourself and any other witnesses, electronic or human, is to be considered sworn and may be used against you in a court of law, if the results of this inquiry lead to a reasonable conclusion that your actions are punishable under Article 113 of the Code.

"The general scope of Article 113 is misconduct or desertion before the enemy. Be advised that violation of Article 113 is at least a felony, and, under certain circumstances, can be a capital offense. Also be advised that the provisions of Article 113 require immediate and full investigation if there are grounds to conclude that such behavior may—I emphasize, may—have occurred. I have convened this board because you and your ship returned separately to sector 14.16.4 from a tactical patrol and because there is no apparent reason for your having ejected from your ship.

"Do you understand what I have told you, and do you understand that, although this is not a judicial proceeding, you need waive none of your Constitutional rights?

"Yes, ma'am."

"Do you wish to retain counsel, or have an SEJS counsel appointed for you?"

"No thank you, ma'am."

"Very well, commander. The people who will participate in this

96

inquiry are Captain Mosquito of CB-127, who has served as an assistant attaché with our legation to the Arachnid Federation; Captain Allen, whom I believe you have met; Commander Chugach, CruDiv-12 intelligence officer; and Major Burns, commander of CB-109's Marine Detachment. I note for the record that Major Burns has had extensive ground combat experience with Arachnids.

"Commander Chugach and Major Burns are currently aboard my ship. To save time, all other persons participating will remain aboard their respective vessels and employ telecommunications. If, at any time, anyone experiences loss or degradation of signal quality, please advise Captain Nigita or me immediately via a tactical channel.

"The records of PV-11's venture into 14.16.4 have already been reviewed by this board. The lifeboat's records have been uploaded to my network while I have been speaking. If there are no objections, we will recess for ten minutes to spool through this information."

There were no objections, and Pat used the break to visit the head and grab a bite to eat. There was no point in facing this on an empty stomach. When Pat returned to the room, Peggy was waiting for him, having been allowed to be present by virtue of her involvement in the situation.

At the prescribed time, communications among the board of review was reestablished. Watanabe said, "We can waste no time if we are going to act to reduce the present danger to CB-32. Therefore, let us stick to matters that pertain only to the two issues that are important at this time: one, what Commander Callen may have observed or concluded that does not appear in the ships' recordings; and two, whether, in light of those observations and conclusions, Commander Callen's actions place his fitness to command PV-11 in reasonable doubt.

"Captain Mosquito, do you have any questions?"

"Yes, ma'am. I would like to know whether Commander Callen has had any previous contacts with Arachnids."

"No, sir, none," Pat answered. What he didn't say was that he had studied them, as had every member of the SEJS, and he thought he knew quite a bit about them. Maybe not as much as Mosquito, but a lot.

"One other question," Mosquito said. "When you observed the destroyers alongside CB-32, were you able to make out any of their markings?"

"Yes, sir. I noticed there were some markings on them, but they didn't mean anything to me. Are they significant?"

"They may or may not be, depending on what they were. Do you remember what they looked like?"

"Not exactly, but I am willing to try to feed what I remember through my comm implant to CB-107's mainframe."

"Admiral, would you mind?" Mosquito said. "The implications of the ships' affiliations could be very important."

"Go ahead," she said.

Pat willed the implant to function in transmit mode, and thought back to the point in time when he had been closest to the Arach vessels. "Thank you, commander," Watanabe said. "We have a graphic." Pat switched his implant back to receive-only mode.

The admiral said, "It doesn't look like much to me, Mosquito. What do you see?"

"Nigita," Mosquito said, ignoring the question for the moment, "give me superimpositions of each pair of ships, in turn."

All could see that the markings on the inboard pair of destroyers were almost identical, and that the one that had a towline on the cruiser was very similar to them. The outer two generally matched one another but were different from the others.

"While you are at it, Nigita," Mosquito said, "would you mind comparing the ship that followed PV-11 with the rest of them?"

Nigita complied, and it was evident that the Arachnid ship in question was marked like the outboard ships at the cruiser.

"Very well, Mosquito," said Watanabe. "What does all of that imply?"

"Unless the Arachnids have recently made drastic changes in the way they do things, ma'am," Mosquito said, "the inboard ships and the one up forward are web builders, while the rest of them are wolves— sight hunters, in other words. I'd bet a month's shore leave that the one up forward is the mother of the other web builders. And, if I may make an educated guess, I'd theorize that one of the webbers found the cruiser, went for help, and was followed back here by the wolves." Mosquito nodded, his face thoughtful.

"The wolves tend to be opportunists that operate alone. On an individual basis, they are a lot tougher than the webbers. However, what we are looking at is probably a natural checks-and-balances situation. As long as the webbers are present in force, the wolves won't try to jump their claim. Until the webbers glut and leave, the wolves will hang around and wait their turn—or try to pounce on anything that arrives."

Listening to the Arachnid expert's opinion, Pat's spirits sank. It was evident that he knew a lot less than he thought he knew about the species.

"Thank you for the information, captain," Watanabe said. "Now, do you have anything that is relevant to Commander Callen's fitness for command?"

"Negative, admiral."

"Captain Allen?"

"No, ma'am."

"Nor I," said Commander Chugach.

"Major Burns?"

"Commander Callen," Burns said, "did you see any of the Arachnids at any time?"

"Negative."

"Are you aware of them having seen you?"

"To the best of my knowledge, they didn't."

"Captain Nigita," Burns said, "please display the lifeboat's view of CB-32's hull at the time they were testing the stores area hatch. They were there for only about ten seconds; give us stop action at twenty millisecond intervals, and then freeze the final view. Watch the boundary between the cruiser's hull and the sky, right about where I am pointing and directly opposite there. Do you see those red dots? Those are eyes. Captain Mosquito was right. The eyes belong to webbers of a species that is fuzzy and black, except for white knee spots. Commander Callen, you are one lucky man. You were surrounded by Arachnids and lived to tell about it."

"Good grief, major!" said Allen. "How did you see those things? I didn't until you pointed them out, and I don't think anyone else in the room did either."

"It's partly instinct and partly training, sir," Burns said. "Without a certain amount of the right instincts, you don't qualify for duty involving Arachnids. But for the most part, it's the result of training that leaves us Marines imprinted with very unpleasant reactions to red dots that could be eye spots, dark places that could hide big spiders, and fuzzy-looking shadows. It helps keep us alive, but I don't recommend the nightmares."

"Gentlemen," Watanabe said, "are there any further questions for Commander Callen?" No one spoke up. "There being none, I open the floor to Commander Callen. Do you have anything to add to the proceedings, commander?"

"No, ma'am."

She looked at him intently for a moment, and Pat glanced at the others. They looked surprised. "Very well," Watanabe said. "Gentlemen, I remind you that the deliberations of this Board of Inquiry are open to Commander Callen and that any action to remove him from command must be unanimous. If the first vote taken is not unanimous, there will be a round of discussion, followed by a second vote. If that vote is not unanimous, Commander Callen will retain his command." Watanabe tucked a strand of hair that had fallen into her face back into her bun. "Please cast your ballots. A red ballot signifies that Commander Callen should be removed from PV-11."

Pat swallowed hard. Where the board could not see it, Peggy showed Pat a message that said, "Good luck. Whatever happens, I love you and I think you were in the right."

Watanabe said, "I see that all ballots have been cast. Captain Nigita, display the results."

All four naval officers had voted red. The Marine's indicator was green. Mentally, Pat took back all of the unkind remarks he had ever made about jarheads.

"Major Burns," Watanabe said, "would you care to share your rationale with us?"

"Well, ma'am," Burns said, "my knowledge of appropriate actions for naval officers is limited to what I learned at the academy. Since then, all of my experience was strictly as a grunt until I was promoted and got orders to CB-109 two months ago.

"As a lieutenant and captain, I commanded at least one of every type of line outfit the Marines have, to include a recon platoon with the First Marine Regiment. If I understand the mission of a PV correctly, there is a pretty good analogy to recon units. That assumption is the basis for my thinking. Keeping in mind the old Marine axiom that assumptions are the mothers of all, uh, mess-ups, my thinking went as follows:

"PV-11's mission was to gather information about the situation in 14.16.4. We Marines are taught, by the way, that the correctness of solutions to tactical problems is never absolute. What you should do always depends on the situation, weather, and terrain." Burns turned to look directly at Pat at this point, and Pat thought he detected a hint of respect in the Marine's face.

"PV-11's priorities, in this case, were to determine whether the task force could safely enter 14.16.4; if there were enemy elements there, what their order of battle and deployments might be; and what the status of CB-32's personnel complement might be. She was to do this without alerting the enemy, if possible. If that was not possible, her priority was to escape and evade, rather than engage.

"Although PV-11 and Commander Callen did not rack up a perfect score, they could have done a lot worse. We know as much as it is possible to know about the situation in 14.16.4. We know that CB-32 is over there and is in a lot of trouble, if not an outright loss. PV-11 took out an Arachnid destroyer without letting the others know what happened. The Arachs on CB-32 know that something small and ineffectual was snooping around, and they have upgraded their state of alert. Knowing them, I doubt if they are worried. They are supremely confident in their ability to fight anybody. That's about it, ma'am. I have not heard anything that says to me that Commander Callen is unfit for command. I'd willingly serve under him."

Allen had motioned to speak. "Captain Allen," said the admiral, "I surmise that you have something to add."

"No ma'am, but I have a question for Major Burns. Major, Commander Callen willfully violated regulations that have the force of law by deserting his ship in the face of the enemy. This is as punishable in the Marine Corps as it is in the Navy, and I am amazed that you did not address that fact. Did you overlook it?"

"No sir; I simply do not put that construction on what Commander Callen did. Clearly, somebody who leaves a position of relative safety to close with the enemy is not deserting. Commander Callen knew damn good and well that he was heading for a firefight. He just didn't know how suicidal it should have been. As far as I can tell, he did the only thing he could if he was not only going to report the general situation but also get some useful information about the cruiser. I, for one, would never have thought of using the lifeboat as a scout vessel, and I have to say it took a lot of balls to do it, once the commander thought of it."

Allen, red faced with the barely controlled anger of a recently promoted and freshly insulted egotist, said, "Major, what you are saying may be true for a Marine, but Callen's leaving his ship to approach CB-32 in an unarmed lifeboat is the most colossal exercise of stupidity I have seen in my entire naval career."

The Marine chuckled and said, "I am reminded of an old piece of Marine lore. It goes like this: 'Do you know the difference between ignorance and stupidity? Ignorance is curable.' But I submit that that is not the point of this inquiry. What is at issue here is fitness to command, and stupidity has nothing to do with that."

Peggy displayed the message, "BUY THAT MAN A DRINK!" and Allen jumped out of his seat shouting, "You impertinent—"

Watanabe interrupted him. "That will be enough, gentlemen! Major Burns, in the future please choose your words more carefully. Characterizations that can be misconstrued can be odious, and we do not need ill will among the people in this command."

"Yes, ma'am," Burns replied. "My apologies, Captain Allen; if I had that to say over, I certainly would say it differently."

Allen sat down, ruffled but silenced.

"Is there any further discussion?" Watanabe asked; all responded negatively. "Cast your ballots, please, gentlemen," she said.

The next few moments ticked by like a century for Pat. Time dragged on until, this time, the indicators glowed unanimously green. He couldn't keep a grin off his face, as hard as he tried.

Watanabe said, "Gentlemen, this inquiry is adjourned. Thank you for your service. Commander Callen, is your ship ready?"

"Yes, ma'am," he answered. "We are 100 percent."

"Stand by," she said. "We will be jumping off as soon as the information revealed by this inquiry is cranked into our plans."

— CHAPTER TWELVE —

The Battle for CB-32

"**M**ajor Burns, stand fast," Watanabe said. "I want to talk to you." After the others had departed the room where the inquiry had been held and closed the hatch, she said, "Bobby, I am disappointed in you."

"Why, Suko? I did what you told me to do."

"When did I tell you to get up in Jim Allen's face?" she said.

"You didn't, but he's a bootlicking jerk that needs to have some of the wind let out of his sails."

"Let me deal with Allen, Bob. Who do you think SEJS would put in command of 109 if anything happened to Skeeter, God forbid? Or who might be sitting on your promotion board ten years from now? Believe me when I tell you that nobody needs enemies. You could be commandant someday—if you can keep from falling on your own sword."

"That's not for me. The only place I ever want to be is with troops. Besides, tilting at windmills is too much fun. When a clod like Allen comes along, I can't resist. Ever since Callen eclipsed the good captain's promotion at the dining-in the other night, Allen has been looking for a chance to put the screws to him. What Callen did in 14.16.4 wasn't overly bright, but it certainly wasn't dereliction of duty. Allen shouldn't have requested an investigation."

"Don't sell Callen short, Bob. He's no dummy, and PV-11 has an excellent record. However, let's get down to business. I had you come over here to see if you can figure a way to take CB-32 from the Arachs."

"I thought that might be it. It's been less than twenty-four hours since our last social meeting."

She blushed and said, "Verbal discretion is not your strong suit, Bob."

"If you're planning to send me aboard CB-32," he said in a joking tone, "you won't have to worry. You'll be able to bury our little secrets, and my smart mouth won't be giving you any trouble either." He bent to kiss her on the forehead.

"If you do go aboard 32," she said, "I hope your marksmanship will be better than that. I'm counting on you to come back. Now, belay the foolishness and give me a workable concept of operations. Time is running out for CB-32."

"Yes, ma'am." Turning serious, he asked, "Do you want it with or without explanations?"

"Without, unless I say otherwise."

"All right, I'll give you an overview and then come back and fill in the important details. It will have to be a very closely timed operation. We will need to put two boarding parties, each consisting of a squad of Marines, supported by Navy technical specialists, aboard CB-32. One squad, broken down into a pair of fire teams, should go in forward, seize the bridge, and secure the area while the Navy people try to activate the ship." Burns used his hands to illustrate the movements he was recommending.

"Although the forward boarding party's chances of taking the bridge are good," he continued, "their mission is secondary because, from what Callen learned, it doesn't sound like we can get much help from the ship. Nevertheless, if CB-32 has anything left at all, it is worth going after. Even if she doesn't, the assault in the area of the bridge will serve to divide the Arachs' defenses.

"The second squad should take an explosive ordnance disposal team in aft, between the engine room and the starboard hangar deck. They don't want to land right in the Arachs' laps, but they don't want to be too far from their objectives, either. They will have two missions, both of major importance. First, they will find and neutralize the mines the Arachs have undoubtedly placed near the engine room to destroy the ship if it looks like they are going to lose her. Second, they are to engage the Arachs and either eliminate them from the heart of the ship or attrite them to the point that a larger force can enter through the hangar deck without sustaining unacceptable losses."

Burns scratched behind his ear, where his fresh crew cut had grazed the skin. "That's about it, from the gravel cruncher's point of view. The really hairy part of the operation will be the coordination of the support from the Navy, and that's all in your bailiwick. You'll need to put ships in there in just the right sequence, and at just the right times."

"I'm following," Watanabe said. "Good plan so far."

"Thanks. Now, without trying anything fancy, what you want to do initially is make the Arachs aboard CB-32 think they're up against a small force. By the time they wise up, we want to have canalized them into a withdrawal via the starboard hangar deck. Whatever happens, we don't want to bottle them up in the ship and put their backs to the wall. They'll be tough, just trying to withdraw. In other words, please don't let anybody make it difficult for the Arachs to move from the starboard hangar deck to their ships. Okay?"

"Excellent," she answered. "Now, tell me exactly what Navy capabilities are needed in the boarding parties. I believe I can handle the rest."

Five minutes later, PV-11 received a call from the task force flagship, directing Pat to join a commanders' conference on the secure tactical network. Watanabe came on line as soon as all ships were standing by.

"Ladies and gentlemen, the purpose of this conference is to coordinate plans for entering 14.16.4 and capturing CB-32. I said 'coordinate' rather than 'brief' because the plans are by no means set in concrete. Pipe up if you see a way to improve them. At the end of this conference, I will request volunteers for certain parts of the mission. Please be attentive for roles in which you have special capabilities."

She presented Burns' concept of operations and then said, "My approach to setting the stage for this operation is to send T-2, camouflaged to look like a tramp freighter, into 14.16.4 as a deception. We want them to think they are in no particular danger."

Watanabe glanced at her audience to make sure they were with her. "The tender's shields are powerful enough to stop anything the destroyers can throw at her, but she will play like she is wounded and trying to run away. It is conceivable that the second wolf, down at the cruiser, will be drawn into the action. Whether that happens or not, approximately one minute after entering 14.16.3, T-2 will bare her teeth.

"Meanwhile, CB-109 will pass into 14.16.4 and take up a position in defilade behind the red dwarf that CB-32 is orbiting. CB-109 will then discharge four Marine assault boats, which will transport the boarding parties to CB-32.

"PV-11 will enter 14.16.4 concurrently with CB-109 but will conceal herself 100 kilometers away from CB-32. Her function will be to monitor and record the action, and, if necessary, assist T-2 or the boarding parties. One minute after T-2 enters 14.16.4, CB-107 will cross over, joining forces with CB-109, which will emerge from behind the red dwarf to wipe out the Arachnid destroyers.

"CB-127 and PV-23 will remain in 14.16.3 to provide a covering force for our present location. They will destroy any hostiles that attempt to escape in that direction. Comments, please."

"Ma'am, CB-127."

"Yes, Captain Mosquito?" she said.

"Something has been bothering me ever since we determined the apparent enemy order of battle in 14.16.4. It is axiomatic that whenever there are webbers involved, a trap has been set. What if there is an Arachnid battle fleet on the other side of that star? En masse, we are a formidable force, but if we enter the sector piecemeal, we could be in a lot of trouble. Why take that risk? The red dwarf can hide several ships at once."

"Your point is well taken, Skeeter, but if CB-32 is being used as bait, and Commander Callen wasn't just lucky, it follows that the Arachs know we are coming. How could they know that? We've known CB-32's whereabouts for fewer than twenty-four hours."

"Please consider my recommendation on its merits," Mosquito said. "Even if the Arachs are just hoping for something like this to happen, they are capable of setting elaborate traps. Its costs us nothing to attack in force, and it mitigates the risk."

"I agree with you completely," Watanabe said. "I am simply making a mental note to have a discussion with J-2 if things are as you suggest. Very well, how shall we do this with massed forces? We don't want to reveal ourselves to the Arachs on CB-32 before we have to."

"Ma'am," said Pat, "are you willing to risk both of your PVs?"

"No, commander," she answered. "With a large number of other sectors to explore, two live PVs are not worth one possibly dead cruiser, much as I hate to say it. Why, what did you have in mind?"

"What we need," Pat replied, "is a way to get the Marines aboard CB-32 before the rest of the task force enters the sector as a unit. Major Burns, am I correct that your assault boats have a range of only a tenth of a parsec and are not hyperspace capable?"

"Yes, sir, but they have a lot of firepower close in, and that will be needed."

"It seems to me, admiral," Pat said, "that if we had something like a small assault boat, but with hyperspace engines, it could get to CB-32 and initiate boarding fast enough to preserve the element of surprise. Do we have any auxiliaries that could be fitted out that way?"

"We have the Fighter Squadron Command and Control ships," said Captain Childers, commander of FS-117. "If we yank out all of the C&C consoles, we might be able to squeeze the boarding parties in. It would put a lot of eggs in two baskets, though, and it would cripple the fighter squadrons if we get into a dogfight of any size."

"Using the C&C ships is a good idea, John," said the admiral. "If the tender can do a quick conversion, we can move you and Jim Allen into the cruisers for this operation, and there will be no harm done. How about it, Molly, can your people pull that stuff out of the C&C birds in a hurry?"

"I'll let you know in a moment, ma'am," replied Captain Gustav from the tender. "We're checking it out. How many people need to be aboard each ship?"

"Fifteen, ma'am," Burns answered, "not counting the pilots."

"That's the biggest squad I ever heard of," Allen said.

"Actually, sir, that's a ten-man Marine squad on each bird, plus the sailors who will handle EOD and try to bootstrap the cruiser. As it is, that may not be enough."

"No go, admiral," said Gustav. "Even if we pile them in like cordwood, twelve is the max we can squeeze in."

"Damn," said Burns. "I thought we had it for a minute."

"Zorro to the rescue!" Jorge Parada exclaimed. "Don't we have some G-class fighters in the operational readiness fleet? Switch the bomb cluster for a personnel pod, and they will each carry four men. My old outfit used to do it all the time to take VIPs out to observe training missions. Two G-class fighters and the two C&C ships can carry all of the assault force in. Then the fighters can provide fire support, and the C&C ships can return for immediate refit."

Jorge smacked his fist into his hand and continued his explanation. "If all they are going to do on this mission is screen and observe, Peggy and Felicidad can fly the PVs as well Pat and I can, and it will free up Pat and me to fly the G-class birds. I just checked, and we are both still current in G-class. Not only that, most of the young pilots aren't even rated in the old ships, but Pat and I have a lot of hours in them. Also, something could happen to us, and you haven't lost a PV."

"Jorge," the admiral said, "if you want it, you've got it. Commander Callen may not be so fond of your idea, though."

"I just wish I'd thought of it first, ma'am," Pat replied.

Burns said, "Admiral, with some minor revisions in our scheme for boarding CB-32, I believe we can make a go of what Commander Parada is suggesting. Do we have your approval?"

Watanabe looked pleased. She stood to say, "Is there any further input, ladies and gentlemen? No? All right, hop to it!"

Twenty minutes later, the four SEJS ships that would lead the assault on the Arachs sat poised at the edge of 14.16.4. Pat and a copy of Peggy were in one G-class fighter, while Jorge and a copy of Felicidad were in the other, and each fighter had a C&C ship for a wingman.

As the flight leader, Pat asked, "Everybody said all the prayers he wants to? Ready, Jorge?"

"As ready as I'll ever be. Let's go!"

"On my command, execute!" said Pat. He paused and then sent the signal. All four ships moved forward simultaneously, engines at full power. There would be no stealth on this mission.

🅰 🅰 🅰

"It's a trap!" Pat shouted. When they had transitioned into 14.16.4, the Arachnids in the immediate vicinity of CB-32 were still in place, which was something of a break. But there was now a flotilla of other ships in the area.

The SEJS team's navigation had been good. They emerged about two kilometers astern of CB-32 and were closing fast. Trap or not, they were committed and there was no turning back. At least Pat's voice was being transmitted through subspace, and the task force would step up its timetable for coming to their rescue (if there was going to be anything left to rescue).

There was no time for Pat to look around. Peggy and Felicidad had arrived and began reporting the enemy order of battle—one battleship, three cruisers, a dozen destroyers, and several auxiliaries. Task Force Delta would have its hands full.

Pat's first assigned objective was to knock out the isolated destroyer that had a line attached to the cruiser. He gave it a long burst of laser fire and had the pleasure of seeing it disappear in a fireball. Almost simultaneously, Jorge took out an alien ship to starboard, and the C&C birds eliminated the Arach destroyers below and to port.

All four SEJS ships then slewed to port to get in hull defilade behind the cruiser. The remaining Arach destroyer, to starboard of CB-

32, began to fire on them but scored only a grazing hit on the C&C ship trailing Jorge. Evidently, there were Arachnids aboard the cruiser, because a destroyer remained in position to recover them from the hangar deck.

Pat and his wingman quickly landed at preplanned locations on the CB-32's hull and discharged their human cargo. Pat could see Jorge and his crippled C&C partner do the same thing farther forward.

Suddenly, the G-class fighter version of Peggy screamed, "LIFT OFF!" through his earphones, but it was too late. Pat stopped hearing things for a while. He didn't know it, but a newly arrived Arachnid destroyer had fallen in behind them and had scored direct, vital hits with kinetic energy weapons that knocked Pat cold.

The pilot of the C&C ship was less fortunate. He was dead, pierced through the chest by a large projectile. Jorge Parada and his C&C wingman had managed to get clear of the cruiser. Jorge could see from his situation display that two other SEJS birds were out of action. He told his wingman to get back to 14.16.3, spun his ship 180 degrees, and applied thrust.

The destroyer that had hit the ships in Pat's charge was swinging toward Jorge, but it never made it; Jorge's lasers ripped it from end to end. Angry, he veered to port and put a projectile through the center of the destroyer that was moored to the cruiser. He smiled, visualizing Arachnids scrambling out of the cruiser to a ruined ship.

His mission now changed to escape and evasion, conducted close enough to CB-32 that he could periodically sweep the hull clean of Arachnids. At the moment none were visible, and the boarding parties had penetrated into the ship. He set off on a game of hares and hounds, with himself as the hare.

Burns' people had hit the cruiser's hull running, their sticky-soled booties holding them aboard. They unrolled mats with borders made of linear shaped charges, taped them to the hull, inserted blasting caps, jumped clear, and blew two-meter holes in the hull.

The cruiser was not pressurized, so they stuck more tape to the pieces of loose hull they had just created and yanked them out of the way. Fewer than ten seconds after they had landed, the boarding parties were making tactical entrances into the ship.

The passageway targeted by the aft party was the main corridor running fore and aft along the port side of the engine room and the main food service area. When they got it open, they discovered that a heavy sleeve of spider web lined the passageway. The Marine squad's point man shrugged, slashed a hole in the web, somersaulted through, and immediately ran into trouble. As soon as his booties hit the deck he glimpsed movement to aft, tried to move his feet, and couldn't; his booties were stuck to the web. An Arachnid laser skewered him, and his body fluids spewed out into the near-vacuum.

Burns dived into the pink fog and returned fire. His laser burst the Arach; its venomous juices joined the vapors from the dead Marine. The rest of the aft contingent now entered the passageway and ditched their booties. Their fluorocarbon-coated suits kept the men from being caught in the webs, but they were all now coated with gore.

After wiping off their faceplates, they replaced the point man and moved out. Fire Team Alfa went aft, then to starboard along the main thwart ships passageway, headed for the forward hangar deck hatch. Fire Team Bravo, followed by the EOD team, went straight aft toward the engine room. It would be a long time before any of them would sleep well.

Up forward, the other party was unopposed. Strands of web showed that Arachs had been there, but the CIC and the bridge evidently held little of interest to them. With the Marines guarding the hatches and passageways, the Navy men began to explore the ship's information processing systems.

What they found explained the Arachnids' indifference: the ship's memory crystals were destroyed, somehow turned to powder. Without them, she could do nothing of consequence. This contingency was unprecedented; the boarding party was completely unprepared. The crystals were pure, artificially grown silicon super-diamonds, 1.5 by 4 by 6 centimeters, encased in gold shields. Whatever had pulverized them was cataclysmic.

Pat revived and heard the master chief who was in charge of the forward boarding party saying, "Well, men, it took more than any damned spider to do this. I reckon we've found out why none of our ships has ever returned from a singularity event. There is no way we're going to fire this baby up. What do we do now, Gunny?"

"Chief," the gunnery sergeant answered, "if you can't do anything with the ship, call for somebody to get you out of here. As soon as you're clear, we'll try to link up with the major. If there are Arachs back there, he's going to need all the help he can get."

"Wait one," Pat said. "This is Commander Callen. My ship is dead on the outside of the hull. What is the matter with the cruiser?"

"All of her memory crystals are ruined, sir, and we aren't carrying any. Even if we were, it could take days to cold boot her," the chief said.

"You'd better take cover, sir," added the gunnery sergeant. "We thought you were dead."

"I'm alive," Pat said, "but you're right. I'll crawl out of here and go below. Wait, though, chief—there are two dead ships back here. What about cannibalizing the crystals out of them?"

"No telling, sir," replied the chief. "There's so much knocked out, but their crystals might be enough to get power and gravity applied. We could sure use some light in this place. The thing is, it's two hundred meters from you to us, and you'd be a sitting duck."

"Sir, this is Boson's Mate Fyffe speaking," a voice said. "I'm with the forward boarding party, and I've got a line throwing gun. If you can get out on the hull, I'll lob the stick past you. Don't get in the way or try to catch it—it'll hurt you. Let a lot of the cord go by and grab it. It's pretty elastic. Just hold on, and the stick will come to a stop. Look out when it rebounds, though. Once you get a hold of the stick, pull the cord toward you. It'll be attached to a line. Tie the crystal units onto the line— you can use the cord for that—and cast them away from the ship, so the connectors won't get banged up, and we'll pull them in. Got all that, sir?"

"Affirmative, Boats," Pat said, "but don't expose yourself until I'm sure I can get the crystals out of the fighters. Oh, damn! Here comes another Arach destroyer."

At this moment, however, Task Force Delta began to pop into view, and Jorge Parada's fighter made a pass through. Jorge blew the stern off the destroyer with a volley of projectiles. "Forget that sucker, Pat. Man, am I glad to hear you're okay!"

The Arachnid flotilla had been in orbit around the red dwarf, out past CB-32, and Task Force Delta was coming in to "cross the T." Pat would have liked to spectate, but the thought struck him that CB-32 could explode at any second. He rotated the hold-downs on the fighter's display panel, swung it out of the way, removed the memory unit, and put it in a pouch on his belt. After verifying that he had his backup copy of Peggy and his personal weapon, he released his harness and climbed down to CB-32's hull.

As soon as he was clear of the wreckage of the fighter, he ran for the C&C ship. It was awkward, with the memory module flailing at his waist, but he made it. It took only a moment to free the dead pilot and put his remains in the back of the ruined ship, remove the memory module, and clamber back to the hull of the cruiser.

"Boats, pass me the line," Pat said.

"Look out, commander, Arach on deck!" someone cried out.

"Where?" Pat shouted.

Laser beams flashed back and forth along the deck between the Marines up forward and an area to starboard of Pat.

"Stay down, sir," someone called. "It's wounded, but it got Smitty in the chest."

"Jorge, where are you?" Pat asked, but before the words were out of his mouth, his fellow PV pilot's fighter flashed past, sending laser energy on a tangent to the cruiser's hull.

Jorge's voice crackled over the comm net. "Pat, that was close. Get the hell off that hull. I got one, but at least two others went back into the hangar deck."

"Wilco, believe me!" Pat said. "Boats, where is that line?"

"On the way, sir."

Pat saw a man's helmet and shoulders pop out of the hull forward, then duck below. The stick sailed past him; he soon had the cord. Pat followed the boson's instructions, pitched the memory units up and away, and scooted part way into the nearby hole in the hull.

"Boats, can you hear me?" Pat asked.

"Just barely, sir."

"Okay. Heave 'round on that line. The units are attached."

"Good work, commander. Now we'll have something we can work with."

The red dwarf shone dimly into the space Pat had entered. The passageways leading away from it, however, seemed pitch black until Pat's eyes began to adapt. While he floated down to the deck, he broke out his weapon, cradled it in his arms, and said, "Major Burns, this is Callen. Do you read me?"

"Yes, commander—where are you?"

"Main passageway portside, just aft of the galley. Where are you?"

"Alfa Fire Team is just across from the forward entrance to the

112

starboard hangar deck. EOD has found a string of mines around the engine room and is trying to render them safe," Burns said. "Bravo Fire Team is with EOD. Right now, though, we are all pinned down. Is anybody with you, commander?"

"Negative, but I've been in contact with the people up forward. They are trying to establish lights and gravity for us. Do you want their fire team to come aft?"

"There's no time. Tell them to evacuate and get yourself out too."

"Got no transport, and I'll get either me or Jorge killed if I go back out on the hull," Pat said. He was in a desperate situation. "There's a battle royal going on around the ship. Jorge saved my butt twice while I was rounding up some parts for the forward boarding party. By the way, he killed one Arach that came out onto the hull from the hangar deck, and he said that at least two more went back in there."

"Okay, listen: you aren't safe where you are," Burns told him. "Try to get down here with me, but don't go too far aft. We have seen three Arachs in the passageways, two webbers and a wolf. The webbers have the passageway along the starboard hangar deck bulkhead covered in a crossfire. One's amidships and the other is back aft. The one aft is helping the wolf pin the EOD people down. The wolf is generally to port, but she moves around in big jumps. Watch out, she's quick. We killed a webber just aft of where you are. If you have to go that way, be careful. Its reflexes will still work its fangs."

— CHAPTER THIRTEEN —

Battle Royal

Pat tried to walk and found out about booties sticking to webs. While he struggled to remove his booties, he felt the ship begin to hum. The emergency lights came on, but not the gravity. Eventually, he got squared away, gave a little leap, and did a sort of chin-up on the rim of the entry hole that had been blown in the hull. He contacted the forward party, congratulated them on getting power applied, and learned that they would be able to accomplish little more. He told them to call Commander Parada and arrange to be evacuated as soon as possible. Then he pushed himself back down into the cruiser.

The lights were a big help to Pat, who was unaccustomed to maneuvering around in large, darkened ships. He said, "Burns, I see the dead webber and the remains of one of your men. What can I do to help?"

"See if you can work forward to the main thwart ships passageway. We need to box in the webber that's covering the forward hangar deck hatch. When you're moving, watch the webs well ahead of you. If they shake with a different rhythm than your own, be alert. Whatever is moving around won't be one of us. If you get a chance, check the status of the ship's crew. None of us has had time to do it."

"Wilco." Pat tried to walk forward, but the webs were springy. It was like bouncing around on a trampoline, without the pull of gravity to help maintain stability. *No wonder the Marines spend so much time training,* Pat thought. "To hell with this," he muttered after several frustrating attempts. He dragged his toes to bring himself around in line with the passageway and experimented with propelling himself with the tips of his fingers and toes.

It wasn't elegant, but with his pilot's instincts, he found that he could, in effect, fly along the passageway. After a few yards, his momentum carried him forward; there was no need to touch the web.

Suddenly the webs behind him began to shake. He turned in time to see a brown blur flash across the passageway abaft of where he had entered the ship. "Wolf coming to starboard!" Pat cried out, but before the words were out of his mouth, reflections of laser beams came at him

114

from both ends of the passageway and a jumble of voices assaulted his ears.

It all stopped as quickly as it had begun.

"Report!" Burns ordered.

"Fire Team Bravo, sir, one man lost, but the wolf is dead. It came at Ramirez from behind, but he heard the commander and got it with his bayonet just as it hit him."

"EOD squad, sir, no casualties. We'll get back to work now. Bravo, try to keep that webber back here busy, please!"

"Callen here—I'm okay. Sorry, major, my weapon was pointed the other way and I couldn't react fast enough."

"It was Ramirez' fault, commander. He was supposed to be covering the passageway behind you, and he was looking the wrong way. You men start acting like Marines, damn it!" Burns shouted. "You've got a green naval officer showing you up."

"Aye, aye, skipper," they said in unison.

"Commander, get next to a bulkhead," Burns said. "Bravo, lob a splatter grenade around the corner, aft of the engine room."

A green flash came from aft, and the ship's hull vibrated strangely. Bravo Fire Team had detonated a half-kilogram package of explosive, surrounded by hollow two-centimeter lead balls. The balls were lethal on the fly but wouldn't ricochet.

"Do any good?" asked Burns.

"I see leg parts floating around," the fire team leader said, "but no vapor."

"Reload and stand by," Burns said. "Commander, if you're okay, move out."

"I'm all right," Pat said.

"Good. EOD, how are you doing?"

Pat started forward rapidly, listening to the EOD team tell Burns that they had rendered safe all of the charges they could reach, but that the fuse train they were following led into the passageway where the grenade had just been thrown. Burns told them to stay put until one or the other of the remaining Arachs was neutralized.

"How are you coming, commander?" Burns inquired.

"I'm at the crew stasis compartment amidships, but this damned web has the hatch blocked. How do you cut this stuff?"

"Fluorocarbon coated knife, but I'll bet you don't have one. Can you see into the compartment?"

"My survival knife isn't coated, but I've got to get in there. I see some red lights, but most are green. Won't my laser cut through the webs?"

"It will, but the reflections off the bulkhead will kill you. Leave the crew 'till later. It'll take minutes to revive them, and we don't have minutes."

Pat didn't like it at all, but what Burns said was true. "Okay," Pat said, "I'm moving forward again, and there's only about ten meters more to go. The web is shaking slowly up there."

"Careful!" said Burns. "She may try to draw your fire and jump you. Don't shoot until you see something red."

Sure enough, when he was about two meters from the corner, a furry, baton-like foot poked around the corner and jerked the webs. If Pat had been using them as a walkway, he would have been knocked off his feet. Faster than he knew he could react, Pat dug in with his toes and drove himself forward. Reaching up and out with his weapon, he pressed the trigger as soon as its muzzle cleared the corner.

He never did see anything red. Instead, juices and vapors from the Arach plastered him from head to foot.

"Oh, yuck!" Pat exclaimed.

"What's the matter, commander?"

"I shot at that damn thing, and she squirted some kind of yellow gunk all over me."

"What?" Burns broke into uproarious laughter.

"By your leave, sir," said Bravo Fire Team's leader over Burns' merriment, "what the major means is, 'Congratulations, you've got your first webber.' Use the side of your glove to wipe the gunk off of your faceplate before it hardens."

"Thank you, sergeant," Pat said, and he did as he was told. Using his glove as a squeegee, Pat was able to flip most of the goo into the nearby webs.

Burns recovered from his fit of laughter and said, "Yes, congratulations, commander. I reckon we're going to have to make you an honorary Marine. Come on back here via the outboard passageway, but be careful. There's at least one more webber back here."

When Pat came into view and Burns could see his method of locomotion, he laughed again, saying, "That's the lazy man's way to travel, commander. Wouldn't you know an aviator would never walk when he can fly?" But after observing Pat for a moment, he said, "On second thought, sir, that's a super way to move around. As long as you don't touch the webs, there's no way the Arachs can tell what you are doing without looking. Is that how you approached the one up forward?"

"Yeah, she stuck out her foot for me to shoot at, and I could tell where she was. When I got close, I just reached out like this and let her have a burst."

"That's one for the books," Burns said. "Have you got another trick for the webber that's back aft?"

"I'd rather not press my luck, but I have a question for you: how much can these Arachs flatten themselves out? They look pretty bulky to me."

"You'd be amazed. I've seen a full-grown female, twice the size of the ones we've killed here, go through a ten centimeter gap."

"Where did your men fire that grenade?" Pat asked. "Was it into the passageway behind the engine room?"

"Affirmative."

"Well," said Pat, "on these old ships the forward bulkhead contains two ventilators, each about a meter wide and two meters high. For reasons I have never understood, instead of having mesh screens, the vent openings are covered by louvers that are set on, I would say, fifteen centimeter centers."

"Do you mean she went into the engine room?"

"No, she couldn't get past the screens, but if the grenade hit only legs, she just about had to be between those louvers."

"Sir," the EOD chief said, "it's hard to read these Arach clock mechanisms, but the counter on the one we're trying to render safe just dropped from three digits to two. If it's a linear device, I'd say we have between one and two minutes left."

"Bravo team," Burns said, "leapfrog EOD and cover the fore and aft passageways on both sides of the engine room. As soon as you're set up, put another grenade in there with our friend. I'll bring a couple of people in from starboard with lasers. Don't let anything furry get past you.

"Follow me, men, up against the port bulkhead."

Almost immediately, there came another green flash and a rain of pellets against the starboard bulkhead. Burns sprang up and aft, and the corporal behind him leaped out along the deck. Rolling to port, they opened fire with their lasers, concentrating on the forward bulkhead.

A sudden gush of yellow goo revealed that Pat had been correct. The webber had taken refuge in a ventilator, but this time it had not helped.

"Clear," said Burns, and the EOD people hurried aft into the passageway.

Wiping his faceplate, Burns said, "Alfa, take the forward hangar deck hatch, on the double. Bravo, the aft hatch."

"Burns," Pat said, "do you think the webbers that Parada saw are still in the hangar deck?"

"More than likely, yes. Look alive, men. EOD hasn't found a remote firing device and the charges haven't been blown. Chances are the boss spider is still aboard."

"Are Arachs capable of setting a trap within a trap?" Pat asked.

"They do it all the time, commander," Burns said. "Why?"

"If all of us go into the hangar deck, there'll be nobody covering EOD. Also, once we're in there, if there are more Arachs in the ship, we'll be bottled up between a destroyer and whatever is inside the rest of the cruiser," Pat said.

"While we were penetrating the hull, Commander Parada put the hurt on that destroyer," Burns replied, "and the hangar deck is the best withdrawal staging area we've got. Nevertheless, I'm suspicious too. We've lost only five people in taking out four Arachs, some of that in the dark. And the fact that the cruiser was used as bait means that almost anything could be aboard, although it wouldn't be like them to divert many combatants from the main event outside. Let me think out loud for a second. We'll need maximum firepower when we go into the hangar deck, but after that, three men can use the same positions the Arachs did to cover the area EOD is working in. Two of those control the hangar deck entrances, anyway. This is what we'll do:

"Alfa and Bravo, I want each of you to deploy two men to cover the EOD team. Alfa, put one man at the aft end of each portside passageway. Bravo, take the forward ends of the starboard passageways. Alfa, are you set up to assault the hangar deck through the forward hatch?"

"Affirmative, sir."

"On my command," Burns said, "I want both of you to deploy fireflies into the hangar deck. Commander Callen, if you'll stay with Alfa Fire Team's leader forward, I'll go with Bravo aft. Everybody straight?"

"Yes, sir!"

"Ready, fire!"

Pat was shielded by the starboard bulkhead and knew what to expect, but the brilliance of the pyrotechnics in the hangar compartment was incredible from this close. Its purposes were to momentarily blind whatever was in the target area and to illuminate the space for sensors that were bundled in the firefly projectiles. The visors of the humans' suits automatically clipped dangerously high levels of illumination. Arachs, on the other hand, wore only a multi-tubed breathing apparatus and plugs in their mouthparts. Their chitinous bodies were de facto pressure vessels. Consequently, their eyes normally weren't shielded.

"Alfa, what did you see?" Burns asked.

"Sir," the team's surveillance specialist answered, "the tubular web from the passageway flares out and ends just inside the hatch. There are netting webs beyond that, but they aren't too bad, just stuff for Arachs to walk around on. I made two big webbers up high on the near bulkhead, where they can cover the hatches. There's a lot of equipment moored in there—tow motors, tugs, and stuff—lots of cover and concealment."

"How about small boats?" Burns asked.

"One or two, up against the bulkhead on this side."

"Bravo?"

"The same back here, sir, except that I saw something funny along the base of the near bulkhead. It's a small tubular web, real solid, that sort of fillets into the corner."

"About half a meter high?" Burns asked.

"Yes, sir. Do you know what it is?"

"Unfortunately, yes, but I'm damned glad you saw it. EOD, how are you coming?"

"Thought we were just about through, major," the EOD petty officer in charge said, "until I heard that last transmission. We'll be done here in a few seconds. We're removing the fuse from the last mine now."

"No hurry, chief. Now that we've found the real destruct package, you get to start all over."

"I'll try it, sir, if you tell me to, but it would be best if you evacuate the ship first. They say the odds of rendering one of those little buggers safe are a million to one."

"Exactly what is that thing?" Pat asked. "I gather it's some kind of a bomb, but why is it so difficult?"

"It's alive, commander," the chief declared, "and it's paranoid. Somewhere in that tube there's a small Arach, about the size of a basketball. It's holding a release trigger on a 12-megaton thermo nuke, so if you kill it, the bomb blows. If you even scare it enough, it lets go and the bomb blows.

"If you quick-freeze it with something like liquid helium, the trigger mechanism goes superconductive, upsets a bridge circuit, and blooey! If you inject plastic foam to immobilize it, the Arach ejects saliva that is a solvent. And if you take the webber's buddies away from the outside of the tube too long, it gets upset. I could go on, but I think you get the idea. It's the EOD man's ultimate test. So far, none of us has passed it."

"How do the Arachs render one of those things safe?"

"We're done back here, major," the chief said. "Commander, nobody knows for sure how they do it. The theory I like is based on the fact that the Arach in the tube is a barely mature female. The idea is that a male lures her out to mate."

"Why don't we try that?"

"Uh, sir, I don't think I've got quite the right equipment."

Pat chuckled and said, "I'm with you there, chief, but that's not quite what I had in mind. There has to be a holo projector on this ship, and I know I've seen recordings of Arach courtship rituals. I remember a parody of the leg waving and bobbing and weaving that was done by setting it to music."

"There's a problem with that, commander," said Burns. "This ship's memory is non-op."

"The on-line stuff, for sure, but it wouldn't hurt to check the archives in the library. It would be in optical media and it would have survived. Does anybody know how to tap the ship's emergency power to run a projector, if we can find one?"

"Yes, sir," said the chief, "all of us do. Major, we've got nothing to lose, and the library is only a few meters forward of the main companionway."

"Okay," Burns said. "EOD, close on us here. Bravo, detach two of the people who were covering EOD to escort the commander and the chief to the ship's library. Hustle, please. Chief, in case you find a projector and it works, take a slick bag to bring it back in. I wouldn't want it to get hung up in the webs."

The four-man party moved out quickly to the library. Its hatch was dogged shut and clothed in web, but coated knives and willing hands made short work of that. With the Marines securing the passageway, Pat and the chief removed a portable projector from a locker. The EOD man applied power to the machine—and it worked!

Encouraged, Pat located a recording on Arachnids and inserted it in the projector. After a moment of searching for the section they sought, they played back the mating dance of the male white-kneed webber.

"Grab an extension cord, sir," said the chief, "while I pack this stuff up." In a few seconds, they were back out in the passageway.

Pat said, "Burns, we have a working system here. Push comes to shove, we can try it."

"We're going to have to, commander. We're receiving fragments of voice traffic through the opening in the hangar deck that indicate the task force is winning. I can see through the hatch that the Arachs have run an antenna overboard. As soon as they get word they have lost the battle, they'll blow this ship. We're going in. Get set to put on your little show, and good luck."

All hell broke loose in the hangar deck. Under the cover of shields that resembled a photographer's parasol reflectors, the Marines dived into the hangar compartment and opened fire. The webbers weren't taken by surprise, and the skirmish was costly. Five Marines died; two, including Burns, were wounded, but both of the webbers that had been on the bulkhead were killed.

Burns, sounding very weak, said, "Commander Callen, take command. Both of my hands are hit, and I lost a lot of blood before my suit sealed. Corpsman, I need help!"

"Aye, aye, skipper," Pat said. "I'll relieve you for now, but I want you to take over again as soon as they've got you patched up. Chief, let's go! The opening of that tunnel looks bigger at the aft end; make the projection there. Alfa and Bravo, report!"

While the team leaders accounted for their people and Pat redeployed them to bring everybody close to the hangar deck, the EOD chief got the projection of the male webber going. Nothing happened.

One of the EOD team members said, "Chief, that's all lookee, no touchee. Let's shake the webs lightly, in time with his bobbing.

That stratagem made the difference. The little female Arach began to move, at first fitfully, then in a rush. To her eternal dismay, when she came out to touch digits with her surrogate lover, two EOD men dived in. One grabbed the trigger in her palp while the other blasted her with a laser.

Carefully, the EOD men slit the web tunnel open and rendered the bomb safe. Needless to say, everyone but the corpsmen who were working on the wounded and the guards in the passageway watched intently. Suddenly someone shouted, "Hey, commander, what's with that boat? It's going overboard!"

Pat looked up, completely astounded, and saw an admiral's barge that was, indeed, moving out of the hangar deck. When it broke into the light of the red dwarf, he glimpsed movement on its hull and then almost laughed at the comical sight of a wolf leaping from the boat toward a web cable that dangled from the destroyer. He and two Marines fired simultaneously, and someone scored a hit. The wolf ruptured in a cloud of juice. The barge continued to drift away from the cruiser, propelled by the momentum the wolf had imparted when she pulled the boat through the opening.

"Damn!" Pat said, "there goes our ticket out of here. Chief, take command."

"Who, me, sir? Commander, where the hell are you going? Sir, don't, you'll—"

Pat had scrambled headlong across the hangar deck, following gaps in the net-like webs that the barge had passed through, and dived out into space.

"Aye, aye, sir," the chief said with a sigh. "Whatever you say, sir."

Pat's first impulse had been to ensure that his trajectory would take him to the barge, but when he was closing on it fast, he realized that it was a large target, and his problem wasn't hitting it—it was to get hold of it, once he was there. Sure enough, he bumped into the barge, clawed at the hull, and slipped away. Now he was embarrassed. He wasn't in any immediate danger, because the people in the hangar deck knew where he was and his air supply was good. However, he was virtually impotent and very much exposed to whatever might come by.

He said nothing and simply floated in space between the cruiser and the barge, reflecting on his stupidity. It happened that he was facing CB-32. Presently he saw someone come to the mouth of the hangar deck. It was the EOD chief, who said, "Look out commander, here it comes again."

"What?" said Pat, frightened.

"The barge, sir. It's spinning into you."

Moving like a springboard diver doing a twist, Pat turned around. The chief was right. He had hit the barge up forward, and its stern was now rotating ponderously toward him.

"There ought to be a hand rail on top, commander, if you can reach it," the chief called out.

"Right," said Pat, for lack of something better to say. However, when he contacted the boat this time, he used his fingers and arms to absorb the difference in their velocities and, ever so slowly, eased himself topside. When his eyes passed above the top of the side, he saw the rail. When he was high enough, he reached out and grabbed it.

"Thanks, chief," he said.

"You're welcome, sir," came the answer. "That was a nice piece of work. Can you get that tub started?"

"We'll know pretty soon. If so, we'll all ride home in style."

He worked his way up the rail, past the passenger compartment, until he got to the cockpit. He had no trouble getting inside, but he also had no luck in getting the barge started. Her energy supplies were completely depleted.

"Let's see," he said to himself, "what can I use for power? There's my laser, but I might need it. There's the energy pack in my communicator, but I definitely don't want to knock that out. Life support systems, same. Lantern, too small. Damn, there must be something."

But there wasn't. He was obliged to sit where he was, frustrated. He switched frequencies to monitor the battle and learned that it was winding down. He would have liked to send a status report, but his communicator's range was too short, unless Jorge came back. He realized, suddenly, that he was exhausted. It had been a long day, even though it was only a few minutes since he landed on CB-32's hull.

Looking around, he saw that the remains of the wolf were close by. Curious, he got some sticky booties out of a locker, put them on, opened the hatch, and went out on deck. There was a boathook stored in hold-downs on the bow. He broke it out and, by stretching, was able to snag the wolf's carcass and pull it in. Mindful of Burns' warning, he stayed clear of the fangs, but he gave the dead alien a good going over.

The way the Arach's breathing apparatus and weapons attached to the animal's body was interesting. The straps were a do-it-yourself kit of webbing spun by the spider. They were exceedingly strong, and Pat decided that he would have to give up on taking home a souvenir laser.

The laser itself was very strange looking. Mounted on the front of the cephalothorax, it apparently was manipulated by the Arach's pedipalps, but its operation was not self-evident. Pat decided that it would be dangerous to experiment with the buttons. A little cable tracing revealed that the laser's power came from a separate gadget that hung beneath the animal's abdomen.

"Whoa—power!" He pulled, twisted, and prodded at the cable's connection to the laser without success. "Let's think this through," he said to himself. "This gal doesn't have hands, so she must use the tips of her legs or whatever those things are. And the connector has dimples in the side."

Pressing in on the dimples released detents, and the cable came free. Loss of fluid had reduced the wolf's girth so the power pack came free easily. Pat climbed back into the cockpit, found a tool kit, and did a little experimenting. The power pack was electrochemical, much like the one on his laser. He rigged a jumper, and, by testing one lead at a time, ascertained the polarity of the contacts. He decided to risk shorting the pack across the boat's emergency power input jacks, assuming that whatever worked for an Arach would work for SEJS.

He struck a gigantic arc and damaged the contacts on the boat— the energy level of the Arach's units must have been higher than those used by SEJS—but, ultimately, it worked. Pat kept the drained pack as his souvenir, closed up the power supply covers, and plugged his Peggy crystal into the barge's receptacle.

The cockpit booted up, and Pat found himself back in the flying business.

— Chapter Fourteen —

Aftermath

It took only a few minutes for Pat to get the casualties from CB-32 onto the barge, hail a passing fighter, and relay a message to the task force commander. The next thing he knew, T-2 hove alongside, relieved the barge of its burden, and began passing lines to the cruiser. While the boarding parties' wounded were hustled off to sickbay, Pat opened a channel to the tender's bridge.

"Captain Gustav," he said, "this is Commander Callen. Request permission to come aboard."

"Permission granted. Welcome aboard."

"Ma'am, where can I dock this barge?"

"Put her in our forward davits where she won't be in the way. Once I get things started aboard CB-32, there will be a lot of recovery work to do. Recommend you come up to the bridge and report to the admiral. We haven't rounded up all of the boarding party's event recorders yet, and I know she'll want a quick rundown on what happened aboard the cruiser. If you don't mind, I'd like to listen in; it might help our damage control parties."

"Of course, ma'am. I'll be right up."

Getting the barge moored was something of an adventure. She was light but powerful, so she was tricky to maneuver into the tight space available. With some help from the tender's deck gang, however, he got her slung in the davits and made his way aft. It took more help from the ship's company to get him out of his suit and through decontamination. Pat was delighted to see his crusty outfit go into a disintegrator; it definitely was a pleasure to get into a flight suit that wasn't sticky with perspiration.

The session on the bridge went quickly. Pat was pleased to learn that all of the wounded he had brought aboard would recover. He had been worried about Burns and was relieved to hear the ship's surgeon say that four units of blood and twenty-four hours on a tissue regenerator would make the Marine as good as new.

Watanabe congratulated Pat on a job well done and ordered PV-11 to pick him up from the tender. Their next mission would be to take part in the incipient search of the battlefield. There were missing fighters to account for, as well as possible Arach survivors to deal with.

Before taking his leave of Gustav, Pat asked her how things were going aboard CB-32.

"She's too much for us to cope with, commander," the captain said, "with all of that damage to the control systems. Memory units are always in critically short supply. We don't have enough available to fix her out here. However, we'll be able to restore her essential functions, and, by borrowing parts from cruisers in the task force, get her to Log Base 36. CV 32's crewmembers are in pretty rough shape; some of them didn't make it. They're lucky we found them when we did. In another month, they'd have all been dead, even if the Arachs didn't get them. That's not for you to fret about, though. Just get out there and keep up the good work, and if I can ever help you, let me know. My people and I really appreciate what you did for the men we had in the boarding parties."

"Why, thank you, ma'am," Pat said. "Tenders have done so much for me already I could never repay you all. I would be grossly remiss if I didn't tell you that your people did a superlative job aboard CB-32 today. By jury-rigging crystals from the dead fighters to restore emergency power, the master chief turned the course of battle. Without the lights, the Arachs would have cleaned house on us.

"And then there were the boson's mate, the chief in charge of the EOD party, and the EOD technician who suggested that we shake the entrance to entice the little webber out of her tunnel. Each saved my bacon, if not all of us. Please tell them that they have my deepest thanks and greatest respect.

"And let's not forget the Marines," Pat continued. "I've never seen anything like the way they conducted themselves. I wouldn't want their jobs for all the tea in China. All of them were great, but Major Burns was awesome. Things would have gone very differently if he hadn't been in charge."

"There's no doubt that he performed extremely well, Pat," Gustav said. "You can rest assured that we'll all be giving him our thanks. Nevertheless, you did the Navy proud today." Nodding toward the control panel, she said, "It looks like PV-11 is alongside and ready. Go with my blessings, and with those of all of our ship's company."

"Thanks again, ma'am. My blessings on all of you, too." He

saluted and broke for the tender's docking facilities, on the double.

Peggy was not her normal ebullient self when Pat got back aboard ship. At first, he attributed it to the intensity of their activity. For almost ten more hours, PV-11 and PV-23 executed thorough searches of the space around the red dwarf. It was a productive effort that led to the rescue of three live SEJS fighter pilots and the recovery of eight damaged ships, as well as the capture of six Arachs aboard incapacitated vessels. On any other occasion, Peggy would have expressed joy at each such event, but on this one, she was coolly efficient—civil, but barely pleasant.

When the sweep of the battlefield was complete and the tender had dispatched her auxiliary vessels to the site of the final significant find, Pat had had enough. "All right, Peggy, what's eating you? I'm tired, and I don't understand why you're treating me like a stranger."

"You really don't know?" she said. "Oh, damn, why was I ever created?"

"Has something fried your circuits? What in heaven's name are you talking about?"

"You! The retinas are the same, but you aren't. I don't know you anymore."

"Oh, dreck," he said with resignation. "This I don't need. Get a hold of yourself, lieutenant."

"Dreck? What is that supposed to mean? Oh, I get it—that's German for mud, dirt, mire, filth, dung, excrement, feces, muck, dregs. Wonderful! Where did you learn that? Besides, you know exactly what I am talking about. You go off in three different vessels in the same day and come back speaking a language I barely understand. How am I supposed to behave when I don't know where you've been, what you've been doing, or with whom you've been doing it?"

"Lieutenant, this is your captain speaking officially, and he is in no mood to trifle. You are talking like a hysterical human female. If this continues, we are going to declare ourselves non-op and stand down until I get an adequate explanation. Do I make myself clear?"

"Yes, sir, abundantly clear."

"Review the conversation of the past few moments and tell me I am wrong."

"Aye, aye, sir. Upon review, I agree that it sounded that way. My apologies, sir."

"For the record, Miss Varner, please run a self-check to verify that neither you nor your support hardware has been damaged. There are always a lot of stray emanations in a combat area, and something might have hit a vital spot."

"Aye, aye, sir. You have the con." After almost a minute, she reported, "Sir, results of a complete system check are consistent with normal operations. Two minor hardware faults, caused by lepton impacts, were detected. I have corrected both of them."

"Okay, take the con and start over from where I asked you what was wrong."

"Yes, sir. I am programmed to place your survival above my own interests and those of the ship. Your actions of the past few hours reflect a complete disregard for your long-term survival. It was my duty to report that to you. In the future, I shall be more tactful."

"You are quibbling, and I don't like that at all."

"Let me put it this way, sir: the master programmers' guide for ship systems says that the objective is to equip us automata with loyalties and biases like those of a good dog. Would you be upset if your dog barked at you after you ran across the street in front of a car?"

"No, not really. The point is that I'm not objecting to what you said as much as the way you said it. Look, whoever programmed you outdid himself in the personality department. I really like the way you keep me cheered up, and it doesn't bother me at all that you often violate the rules of proper shipboard decorum to do it. It's just that you sound like my mother."

"Correction, sir. Herself, not himself. And is it not good that I sound like your mother?" she asked innocently. "I have never met your mother, but I have every reason to believe she is a good person."

"She is, Peggy, but not only does she have exclusive rights to mothering me, nowadays she has the good grace to treat me like an adult, even when I don't act like one."

"Ouch, sir. I get the message. Even so, you're quibbling too. Your willingness to take risks may be part of your charm, and I'm not going to nag you about it, but I would feel a lot better if you would look before you leap."

"Believe it or not, Peggy, I usually do. We humans constantly preprocess based on our instincts and experience. If all you consider is the pitifully slow speed of the individual neurons in our brains, you have to figure that there is no place for us on a modern ship. However, when you take into account those waves of parallel impulses, there is a place for us."

Softly, Peggy said, "I sometimes like to speculate about what it would be like to be human. You take for granted some states of being that I would have to experience to understand: motherhood, for instance. In the final analysis, though, I do not know any more about being human than you do about being an automaton. I think I have read everything ever recorded about human psychology, and I might as well have not bothered. Humanity is an enigma, and I'm not even people. I am just something humans have created, and natural law says that one cannot create something that is as good as oneself. If humans are imperfect, where does that leave me?"

"Wait a minute, Peggy, I don't like where you are going with that train of thought, besides which, you're wrong. I mean, if you're talking about the law of entropy, your ability to learn and improve yourself means that you can work to offset the tendency to degrade over time."

"Thank you, sir. I'd like to think you are right, but consider the paradox that when one thing creates another, it improves its ethos in proportion to the ethos of the thing it has created, and so on down the line. That's the real joy of being creative, after all. But it also keeps the creator one insuperable step ahead of whatever it creates. It also provides an interesting commentary on Satan. What could ever be greater than the original Creator? A power whose intent is to destroy or deface what has been created? Hardly.

"Anyway," she continued, "that is not the point. The point is that nowhere can I find anything that helps me reconcile my duty to protect you with your insistence that if I want you to like me, I may not chide you about your consistently taking the high-risk avenue out of every situation. It's probably just as well that there is no way for me to become human and have to live in your reality."

"Peggy, this is getting too heavy for me to handle right now." Pat heaved a sigh. She was impossible sometimes—but always intriguing. "Please record it and give it to me to study when I'm not too fatigued to figure out what you said. All I can say is that you are marvelous, and if I ever meet the person who programmed your personality, we're going to have to have a long talk."

"You have met her. It was Midshipman Faraday. Don't you remember Captain Dreelin telling you about her?"

"You're kidding me!" Pat had a vision of the midshipman in his arms, dancing during the icebreaker. "Holy cow, how could it have been her? She's still wet behind the ears."

"Ellen Faraday is, or was, a child prodigy, sir. She is attending the academy as a way to improve her self-discipline. She already has several degrees and enough monetary credits put away that she will never have to work another day as long as she lives, if she doesn't want to."

"Good grief, Peggy, too much is enough for one day. I've got to get some sleep." He laid his seat back to a full reclining position and dropped off immediately. Twenty minutes later, he sat bolt upright, in a cold sweat.

"Bad dream, skipper?"

"Nightmare."

"Spiders?"

"No, nothing so obvious. I dreamt I was in the admiral's barge from CB-32, falling toward an island on the surface of a planet. It was a strange planet, almost all oceans, except for that one island, about 20 kilometers across. It was flat and sandy, but cones pockmarked the surface. Whatever made those cones was going to eat me alive as soon as I landed, and I was defenseless. Weird, huh?"

"Freud probably wouldn't have thought so, skipper. Why don't you drink some warm milk and go back to sleep?"

"Okay, but don't put anything in it."

"I won't. Milk by itself is probably the best thing for you, except for some rest."

"Why? Are we going to have a busy day tomorrow?"

"From the shape of the message traffic, I'd say so, but don't worry about it. It's all fairly predictable."

"All right," he said, sipping his milk, "but don't hesitate to wake me if anything important comes up."

He fell asleep again in an instant.

⋀ ⋀ ⋀

Pat was up at reveille—not completely rested but ready for the day's activity. After a workout, a sponge bath, and a light breakfast, things seemed to be back to normal. The only unusual event on the calendar was a telecomm commanders' conference, scheduled for 0830Z.

PV-11 settled into the routine of screening the task force.

The 0830 conference proved interesting. After the usual formalities and a request from Watanabe that all present withhold their questions until the presentations were complete, the conference began with an Intelligence Summary from SEJS. The briefer reported that task forces Bravo, Charlie, Delta, Golf, and Hotel had all found disabled SEJS vessels in sectors around 14.16.4. Only Delta had encountered hostiles.

After a terse account of the engagement in 14.16.4, the briefer went on to state that all SEJS ships that had encountered transient singularities showed a common pattern of damage, to wit, destruction of all memory crystals that had been on line at the time of the event. Federation scientists were hard at work on a way to prevent this effect in the future. Pending completion of their work, hyperspace travel was to be minimized, and crews of vessels using hyperspace were to ensure that they were prepared to go into stasis if anything went wrong.

Scientific investigators were also doing a statistical analysis of the whereabouts of lost ships. The results were encouraging, and task force activity was being suspended briefly to allow further searches to be conducted efficiently.

CINC SEJS himself followed the intelligence briefer. Brookleigh said, "Ladies and gentlemen, I commend the success of task forces Alfa through Hotel. Even those that did not find lost ships helped our cause significantly by ruling out certain possible patterns of dispersion.

"Task Force Delta has been awarded a Presidential Unit Citation for the exemplary manner in which it conducted its recovery of CB-32 in the face of powerful and determined hostile forces. I note with pleasure that the ratio of enemy to SEJS losses is the highest ever recorded against Arachnids, and I encourage all senior commanders to review the historical records of this action.

"Memorial services for our comrades who died in stasis aboard CB-32, and who fell yesterday in battle against the Arachnids, will be held throughout SEJS at 1200Z today.

"I assure you that the interruption of search operations is very temporary. The lessons we have learned from our task forces indicate that a restructuring of mission elements is in order. It will not take long for us to deploy additional logistic ships and to reorder our search priorities to ensure that we will find the longest-missing ships first.

"Good hunting—and Godspeed."

"Well, what do you know about that, Peggy?" Pat said. "You're going to have a navy blue stripe with a gold border painted on your bottom."

"Painting the PUC on me will be all right—as long as they don't use fresh paint," was her retort.

Pat groaned at the pun and went back to paying attention to the briefing.

After the words from the CINC, Watanabe had come on line. She was saying "...and immediately after the memorial services, Task Force Delta will return to 14.16.3 for servicing at Log Base 36. Brookleigh's remarks were broadcast in the clear throughout the galaxy and therefore did not reflect the extent of damage suffered by our cruisers while engaging the Arach forces.

"We all must do as good a job of navigating back to 14.16.3 as you did in combat yesterday. SEJS does not think we are likely to have a problem with singularities at this particular place and time, but we not only have combat damage to contend with, the cruisers must lend memory modules to CB-32 for the trip. I know we are equal to the task, and I merely request that all of you be on your toes. We will sail for 13.16.3 at 1230Z. Are there any questions?"

There were none, and PV-11 again went back to the monotony of screening the task force.

— Chapter Fifteen —

The Derelict

"**P**eggy, can droids swim?" Pat had been cogitating on the question instead of the task force—or the briefing, which had just ended.

"Talk about off-the-wall questions, sir—where did you get that one?"

"Answer it and I'll tell you."

"Of course droids can swim. If they couldn't, aquaculture would not be the success it is."

"I know that, but I'm talking about malleamorphs."

"Oh—why didn't you say so? In any case, I'm not sure; there's nothing in the documentation that deals with the subject directly. I can tell you that it is not one of their design objectives. Give me a minute and I'll do some research." Presently, she said, "The only way I'm going to get a definitive answer is to send a message to SEJS Research and Development. Before I do that, I need to know more about your question."

"Fine. What do you need to know?" *Nothing was ever simple with this XO,* Pat thought.

"Malleamorphs have a minimum specific gravity of 1.1, so they won't float in water. Were you talking about swimming in water, and were you talking about swimming on the surface, or under the water?"

"Actually, what I was thinking about was taking you surfing on Log Base 36, if we get a chance. I really enjoyed it there, and I think you would, too. The place is beautiful, the surf is great, and the people were extra friendly."

"Thanks for thinking of me. I would be delighted to attend a picnic or a beach party, if you have one, but surfing doesn't sound like a good idea. I can think of several places where a malleamorph would leak when submerged. Besides, I doubt that we'll be at Log Base 36 any longer than it takes to top off our energy and replenish our spares. SEJS needs to have a lot of exploring done before the task forces go back out, and we are prime candidates."

"You're overlooking something, babe. How many combat points did we build up before we joined Task Force Delta?"

"Seventy-two."

"How many points will we be awarded for the action in 14.16.4?"

"They haven't announced it, but I see what you are driving at. I'd estimate something on the order of ten to fifteen, when your experiences on CB-32 are taken into consideration."

"Correct, and some kind of leave will be mandatory at that point."

"Sir, if they give you fifteen points, you'll have eighty-seven. Thirteen more, and we part ways."

"I hadn't thought about that. Damn! You're right, of course. I was looking forward to at least two more years with you, but they'll pull me off of flight duty at a hundred points, no matter what. We'd better start keeping a low profile."

"I've been trying to tell you that." Her voice sounded unusually smug.

Pat was subdued for the rest of the day. The memorial services and the flight to Log Base 36 went by in a blur. Messages came and went, and Pat saw decorations, promotions, and combat points awarded in plenty. He was delighted to see Jorge Parada awarded the Navy Cross and ten points, but each assignment of points darkened his mood.

The final award of the day was given to Pat, and he was dumfounded. It was not so much the Distinguished Service Cross and the seventeen combat points as it was the message that followed. The text read:

UNDER THE PROVISIONS OF INTERGALACTIC MARITIME LAW, FULL DEED AND TITLE TO SEJS ADMIRAL'S BARGE, SERIAL NUMBER 0001654, IS HEREBY ASSIGNED TO CALLEN, PATRICK, COMMANDER, REGULAR NAVY.

COMMANDER CALLEN WILL PROCEED TO TENDER-2 ASAP TO CLAIM BARGE NUMBER 0001654 AND REMOVE IT TO HIS PERSONAL CUSTODY.

THE BASIS FOR RELATED LEGAL DETERMINATIONS HAS BEEN TRANSMITTED TO THE OFFICE OF THE STAFF JUDGE ADVOCATE, LOG BASE 36.

SIGNED,

CINC SPACE EXPLORATION JOINT SERVICE

"No way!" Pat said upon reading the message. "What kind of a joke is this?"

"If it's a joke, it's no ordinary one," Peggy said. "That message came from SEJS and has the CINC's personal validation code on it."

"What?" Pat exclaimed, but a transmission on the admin channel from Watanabe cut him off.

"Pat, congratulations on an award well earned," she said. "Did you see that message from the CINC?"

"Thank you, ma'am, yes, I did," he replied. "About the message, please tell me that somebody is pulling my leg. I'm in no mood to be jerked around."

"It's no joke. I'm calling to tell you to stand down from screening the task force and get the barge squared away as soon as you can. The PVs might be detached from us at any time, and you don't want to let anything interfere if you have to move out on short notice. You are cleared to dock PV-11 at the log base and catch a shuttle up to T-2. Molly, are you monitoring this?"

"Yes, ma'am," replied Gustav from T-2. "We'll have the barge ready to go when Commander Callen gets here. Pat, while you're here, please stop by sick bay and see Major Burns, and then check with me before you shove off."

"Aye, aye, captain," Pat said, "Peggy, let's go to Log Base 36."

Half an hour later, Pat found himself saluting the quarterdeck aboard T-2. As soon as he was officially aboard, a gray-templed master chief greeted him. "Excuse me, we haven't met. I'm Mackenzie. Everybody calls me Mack. I was up forward on CB-32 with you yesterday. I'll be your escort while you're aboard the tender, if it's okay with you."

Pat shook his hand and said, "Of course it is, and I'm delighted to meet you. Did all of you who were up forward, except Sergeant Smith, get out safely?"

"Yes, sir, we did—all of the Navy technicians and the EOD people. We're mighty grateful for what you did, and if you don't mind, when we all get down to the log base on liberty, we'd like to get together with you to kind of let you know about it, if you know what I mean."

"I'd be proud to get together with you. I only wish everybody had gotten out of there in one piece, Mack. Everybody did a super job, and I haven't even met most of you. What about the Marines? Is Burns doing all right?"

"They're going to try to join us, sir. Major Burns is almost as good as new. He's right in there—see for yourself."

They came to the entrance to sickbay; Pat went in and found Burns sitting on the edge of a bunk. "How're you doing, soldier?" Pat asked. "How're the hands?"

Burns slid off the bunk and embraced Pat. "I'm doing fine. I seem to have the knack for getting hit but surviving."

"This is his fifth Purple Heart, you know," Mack said.

"No, I didn't," Pat said. "If I'd had any idea, I'd have stayed farther away from him."

They all laughed, and Burns said, "I owe you an apology, commander. When we were working up the operations orders for yesterday's engagement, I told the admiral that you were a good troop, but not a genius. She told me not to sell you short, and she was right. We all owe our butts to you, and so does everybody and everything on CB-32. Thanks, sailor—you're all right."

"Call me Pat, please, and you don't owe me any apologies. Where would I be if you hadn't told me what to do and how to do it? And I'm no genius, for a fact. It's just a good thing that Lady Luck was with me yesterday, and that goes double for having had you guys in the boarding parties. Mack has suggested that we get together on the log base and lift a glass to the ones who didn't make it. I'm all for it."

"Great," Burns said.

"Bob, tell me something—is there anything I could have done to keep that wolf from getting Ramirez? I feel like I missed a trick on that one."

"No way. The wolf had him dead to rights, no matter what. She was trying to take him out quietly and get in the middle of us. It was a question of whether she got him with her laser—which she would have done by reflex, even if you had shot her—or whether she bit him. If you hadn't hollered, and if she had hit Ramirez with no warning, she would have gotten to the rest of Fire Team Bravo, and I doubt if any of us would have come out of there. But let me tell you, the thing that was a stroke of genius was your figuring out how to lure that Arach away from her bomb. That's a first, and believe me when I tell you that a lot of people have died trying."

"Shoot, I didn't think of using a holo, the EOD chief did," Pat admitted. "Or, at least, he put the idea in my head."

"Whatever—you're building a reputation for suggesting the right thing at the right time. I, for one, am damned glad."

"Me, too," Mack said, "and so is the ship's company on CB-32."

"Well, tell me this," Pat said, "if I'm so damned smart, why can't I figure out what I'm going to do with an admiral's barge, much less why SEJS deeded it over to me?"

"Give us a little time, sir, we're working on that." The master chief grinned and gave Pat a thumbs up.

"Would you care to clue me in on what you're talking about?" Pat asked.

Mack nodded toward the door. "The doc is giving us the high sign—I think we'd better get out of here and give the major some rest. As for why they've given you the boat, I can't really say. It probably has something to do with recovering a derelict. Me, I don't know much about maritime law. On the other hand, I do know something about boats and what to do with them. The deck apes on this tub have worked out something—if you'll come up forward, we'll show you."

"Bob, take care," Pat said. "I'm looking forward to seeing you and your troops when you're all healed up."

"It won't be long," Burns replied, "maybe tomorrow night. Have fun with your new toy. From what the chief has told me, you are in for a surprise."

▲ ▲ ▲

The chief took Pat to the bridge to see Captain Gustav, but she was obviously very busy when they arrived. Pat had never been more than a visitor aboard tenders, so he had no idea of the amount of activity that was involved in the logistical support of a task force that was returning from combat. Gustav had been expecting Pat to show up, however; she spotted him immediately.

"Ah, Pat, glad to see you. I hope we'll have time to talk again soon, but this place is a madhouse for the moment. Just let me say thanks again, and good luck with your little prize." She nodded at Mack. "The Super Chief here tells me that when he and the men looked her over, they found a few deficiencies that had to be corrected before she'd be space worthy. I believe they've got her fixed up to the point that she'll at least make it to the log base safely. Am I right, Mack?"

"Yes, ma'am, we've done the minimum essential things the regs authorize in the way of help for a vessel in distress. She should be able to get to the base under her own power now."

"Very well," she said. "Pat, I look forward to seeing you again."

"Thank you, ma'am. I can see how busy you are. It's fascinating, but I'd better get back to my ship before SEJS sends us out on another mission."

Gustav's wide smile made her look like the Cheshire cat when he saluted her in departure. As soon as they were clear of the bridge, Pat asked, "Mack, what's up? The barge was low on energy when I last saw her, but apart from that, she seemed okay."

"Well, sir, appearances can be deceiving, you know," Mack said as they worked their way forward through the hustle and bustle. "She is an elegant-looking old thing, sure enough, with all of that bright work, leather and Monel, but underneath all of that she was in pretty bad shape." Then he shrugged and looked sideways at Pat. "Oh, hell, sir, that's not the truth, and we'd never fool you. Let me tell it like it is.

"I had a young sailor who likes small boats give her a going over, and he had an accident that ruined the engines. Before we knew she was yours, we were afraid he was going to be stuck with a Report of Survey and have to pay the damages. When we found out she belonged to you and would probably end up being a yacht, we took the liberty of trying to make her as close to right again as we could, in the hopes you wouldn't sue for damages. Please take a look at her before you say no—the kid didn't mean any harm, and I think we've done right by you."

"Sounds like a space story to me," Pat said, "but let's have a look."

The barge had been moved into a pressurized shop bay, and several people were still working on her. Looking through the hatch before they went into the bay, Pat said, "Mack, if I didn't know better, I'd say she has grown. What's the story?"

"Ah, yes, sir," he said, opening the hatch. "We couldn't help that. We don't stock the antiquated engines that go in these boats, so we had to sort of enlarge the aft end a bit. Did you know that these boats have the same basic hull as a mail boat or a shuttle? It's a little known fact. Not a bad idea, though. Normally an admiral has no need to go hyperspace, but if he ever does, the right kind of engine just snaps onto his barge's sternsheets, and away he goes. We have to apologize, because that's what we had to do here."

They went into the bay, and Pat stared at his new acquisition, still disbelieving it was his.

"It just so happens that one of the Arach ships we captured was carrying a bunch of parts pirated from CB-32," Mack explained, "including the engines and control systems from a combat loss Charley-class fighter. A bunch of them have been sold on the open market, now that the Charley-class birds are going out of the inventory. So if you want to have her converted back, you can sell this system and replace it with whatever you prefer. Meanwhile, you've got something you can fly, especially since you flew Charleys."

"Chief, I can't accept this, no matter what." Pat shook his head. "All of this is SEJS property. Much as I'd like to have her, this just isn't right—and who wouldn't want her? This baby must be worth a king's ransom."

"I'm glad to hear you say that, but there's an old friend of mine over there in the corner who'd like to talk to you about some other possibilities. I'll be in the cockpit of the barge when you're through."

A man in coveralls slouched against the bulkhead where the chief indicated. Pat walked over to him and extended his hand. "I'm Commander Callen. Did you want to talk with me?"

The man held out an ID folder, allowed it to drop open, and then snapped it shut. "As you can see, I'm Admiral Egan, SEJS J-2. Callen, the charade is over for the moment. You are the owner of this barge, as is, where is, just like the message stated. If you want to break these guys' hearts, just say so and we'll put it back the way we got it. It's one hell of a hot rod, though, and they've had a lot of fun putting it together."

Egan returned the ID to the pocket of his overalls. "At the rate things are going, you are about one good patrol away from a desk job. Is that what you want?"

"No, sir," Pat said, "I can't honestly say that it is."

"I thought not. I have some staff billets open that call for a lot of flying on the part of the incumbents. Suffice it that a guy like you, having access to a private vessel with the capabilities of that barge—as presently configured—would be a real asset. Are you interested?"

Pat's heart leaped, although he wasn't exactly sure what he was hearing. "Yes, sir—but I have no desire to commingle my personal property with SEJS assets. Isn't there a way for me to accept in a manner that would be legal?"

"Certainly. Mack, bring those hand receipts down here."

Mackenzie sprang down to the deck and handed Pat a clipboard-like viewer. Fishing a stylus out of his pocket, he said, "Just read this over and sign at the bottom, sir."

There was much more listed on the hand receipts than engines and a control system, but Pat read it over silently and signed.

"Good man, Callen," the admiral said. "Keep your nose clean and your lips buttoned about this. In particular, do not tell Lieutenant Varner about your discussion with me." When Pat let his surprise show, Egan laughed. "Don't look shocked! She does a lot of open browsing on the Galactic-Wide Web, and she is as guileless as they come. It's best that you leave it that way, for now. In due course, she'll be flying the barge—yacht, if you prefer—with you and we'll give her secure channels."

"I understand, and I appreciate the offer, sir."

"I'll see you when you hit a hundred points. Mack, take care of yourself, you old scoundrel, and keep your ear to the ground. Give my thanks to Molly Gustav, too." He shook their hands and departed through the hatch.

"Mack," Pat said, scratching his head, "I don't mind telling you this has been the damndest week of my life. What have I gotten myself into now?"

"Not to worry, sir. I've been knowing the admiral since he was a shave tail. He's a straight arrow and he'll take care of you. Not unlike yourself, he is."

They turned to and gave the souped-up boat a thorough checkout. She'd never be a barge again. In reality, she was a fighter in civilian clothing, and Pat could hardly believe his own excitement at the prospect of flying her. When the bay opened up and Pat took his new vessel out of the tender, Mack watched through the viewport in the hatch.

"Well, men," he said to his crew, "that was more fun than I've had in a long time. I'm pretty sure he's going to give us a ride in that thing when we see him on liberty."

They responded enthusiastically, and as they turned to go aft via the passageway, Mackenzie threw Pat's hand receipts into a disintegrator. The flash caused one of his men to look back. Mack said, "Aw, shucks, I must be getting clumsy in my old age." They all laughed and moved on to the business of getting Task Force Delta ready to sail again.

— CHAPTER SIXTEEN —

Onward and Upward

Pat's flight from the tender to the log base did not go at all smoothly. As soon as the barge broke clear of the tender, Log Base Flight Control challenged him because he didn't have a flight plan on file. If the barge had still belonged to SEJS, the filing would have been automatic, but privately owned vessels were required to file before departing on any trip.

After a few tense moments, Flight Control grudgingly permitted him to initiate an in-flight filing. The next problem was that Pat had no authorized destination. Private vessels were not allowed to dock at military installations without prior approval, barring a life-threatening emergency. Flight Control was understandably irked. Pat and his barge were sitting in the middle of the primary flight routes between Task Force Delta and the log base at a time when traffic was intense. Ultimately, Flight Control gave him some very pointed instructions about using civilian charts to find out what the alternatives were.

The charts showed that there were three commercial ports near the log base. Pat called them, one by one, and was horrified to learn that a few days' docking fees in a commercial facility would cost him a month's salary. Luckily, Gustav happened to overhear some of Pat's communications traffic. She hailed him and recommended that he take his boat to a yacht club near the base and find the manager, Ted Kroll. Pat thanked her, finished filing his flight plan, and flew the barge to the yacht club as fast as it would go.

Master Chief Kroll (SEJS, Retired) proved to be the bright spot of the day. He was a delightful person with twinkling blue eyes, pink cheeks, and thinning gray hair. He saw Pat's predicament as humorous and insisted on berthing the barge in an out-of-the-way slot at no charge until Pat could get things straightened out.

The coastal maglev ran past the boatyard, so Pat caught a train to the log base. He encountered more hassle at the gate, where the security system had no record of his authorization to visit the civilian community. By the time he got that squared away, Pat was thoroughly disgusted with every aspect of owning his own boat.

Before he left the gate, Pat called Operations to let them know where he was and to request permission to visit the office of the staff judge advocate general before returning to PV-11. Permission was granted, but he was advised that he was on standby for departure upon ten minutes' notice, in the event the DEFCON increased.

Pat's experience at JAG offices had led him to expect a protracted wait before having a chance to see a lawyer. It was a surprise, therefore, to be ushered into the office of the JAG himself, Captain Felice, immediately upon arrival. Felice looked up at him and said, "Sit down, commander, and take the load off while I finish reading the last of the references on your case. This is very interesting. I have never seen anything quite like it."

After a bit, the captain folded the viewer down into his desk, put his feet up, and asked, "Have you claimed the barge?"

"Yes, sir, and for a few short minutes I had illusions of keeping her. However, I've learned that she will be my financial ruin, not to mention a source of major problems. The Navy isn't geared up for its pilots to have yachts, from what I can see."

"Don't be too hasty, commander: there is more to the situation than I believe you have been told. To begin with, you have been awarded a cash trust of one million credits by the Federation Research Institute for your role in solving the problem of deactivating Arachnid suicide bombs. The EOD team chief, the young man who suggested shaking the web, and the Marine who finished the job have also received substantial sums."

Pat felt his jaw hit the floor. A million credits?

"The terms of the trusts are that you cannot touch the principal. However, guaranteed interest in the amount of six percent per annum, payable in monthly increments, is yours to do with as you see fit. Let's see, sixty thousand per year is five thousand per month. Not bad, commander—that's five times your approximate present take-home pay."

"I don't know what to say."

"Hear me out, commander. There are some stipulations on the granting of the trust, the most important of which is that there is to be no public disclosure of any type. If this condition is violated, the grant will become null and void, and the FRI will disclaim knowledge of any aspect of the matter. I infer that they do not wish to make it known that meritorious acts in the line of duty may entail monetary rewards. You can read the other terms at your leisure. I'll email them to you in encrypted form. I recommend you move them to your personnel database, in the section protected by your personal access key. Any questions?"

"Not for now. I'm not sure what to think."

"I know what you mean. I've been in this business for a while, but this is the first I've heard of bequests by the FRI. Now, there's the matter of the barge. Astronautical law is a matter of professional interest to me; I'm fairly well read on the subject. It's a complicated area of the law, and I'll be the first to admit that I'm no expert. Nevertheless, I recognize the names of the people who are, and they are all present on the documents that bear on your case. I say this because I surmise that you are mystified, if not unhappy, about having the barge deeded over to you. From a legal standpoint, there's no doubt that you are entitled to her."

"I guess I'm happy to hear that." Pat shrugged, feeling helpless.

"In summary, you recovered an abandoned, helpless vessel that was stranded in the astral equivalent of an open seaway, and SEJS ships were not used to accomplish the recovery. Thus, you have salvage rights. Moreover, she was neither armed nor carrying military equipment of a sensitive nature, so there is nothing to preclude her being turned over to a private owner. The transcripts of the hearings on the matter also reflect that she is obsolete, and SEJS doesn't really want her. She'd have been sold or scrapped when CB-32 got back to the yard. This only came up in the context of a brief recommending that the court not waste time on the matter. The brief was thrown out. Evidently the court wanted to hear the case."

"So what exactly does this mean? I have a boat?"

"Yes, the bottom line is that you've got yourself a boat. It looks to me like SEJS would not take her back if you tried to give her to them. However, if you don't want her, you can always sell her or give her away. It looks to me like you can afford her, though. Do you want to keep her? If you do, we have to attend to a few legalities."

Pat's wheels had been turning throughout the conversation. "Yes, I guess I will—for the time being at least."

"All right, then, we'll have to create a title in your name in order for you to register the boat properly. I also strongly recommend that you have her insured as a yacht. Once you have done all that, you can get security to issue her a base permit. That way, you can bring her in and purchase energy at SEJS cost."

Two hours later, Pat was back at the yacht club, where he registered the barge with the both the Federation Astronautics Authority and base security. He worked out storage arrangements with Chief Kroll.

Kroll also offered to look the boat over and provide an estimate on any work she might need. When Pat declined, concerned that the modifications installed by T-2's people might attract undue attention, Chief Kroll said, "Mack and the boys have been in touch, and they tell me the boat really does need some work to finish up the things they got started. We have a pretty complete little boatyard here. Conversions like this are a specialty of ours. Don't worry about a thing; we'll have her shipshape in no time."

"I suppose that would be okay—"

Kroll cut him off with a raised hand. "Incidentally, one way we augment our retirement income is by managing a charter service for the boats we berth here," he said in a slightly conspiratorial tone. "Yours made me think of an ad I saw from this guy who was looking for a small hyperspace yacht for quick inter-sector trips. He has a fleet of larger vessels, but they aren't suitable for two or three executives who need to go someplace, or for small, high-priority cargo like asteroid mining machinery parts."

"Really?"

"Yes. I got in touch with him this morning and he told me that he had already established an understanding with you. He'd like to be sure your boat is available on short notice, and he's offered to pay in advance for whatever repairs may be necessary. Mack vouches for him, so it's okay with me. How about you?"

"Having the boat earn her keep sounds good to me, but having just listened to my insurance agent's harangue, I have a question. If someone charters her and does something illegal, would I be liable?"

"That's a frequently asked question, sir. You are not liable unless you fail to exercise reasonable caution, have prior knowledge of the illegal act, or participate in it. If you engage our chartering services, you'll be protected. Whoever uses your boat has to sign a contract that she will not be used for unlawful purposes. You can also set it up so you have the right to disapprove any or all charters."

"Sounds good to me, then," Pat replied. "You've got yourself another boat. Just don't hire her out for a few days. If everything works out, I owe Mack and his friends a joy ride."

"Aye, aye, skipper. We'll make sure she'll be ready when you want her. I'll put her in the yard right now. If you can, the first time you want to take her out, come by a half hour or so ahead of time and we'll get you all squared away on the boat, and on civilian procedures."

Pat chuckled for the first time that day, which brought a quizzical look from Kroll. He told the chief that after his experiences of the morning, he reckoned he could afford a half hour for familiarization.

When Pat got back to PV-11, Peggy was as curious as a cat. He told her about what had transpired, but omitted any reference to Admiral Egan. "Why so curious, Peggy?" he finally asked her. "Are you still jealous?"

"How could I be jealous of an inferior system? I am simply trying to resolve a number of anomalies. I kept close tabs on you when you bumbled your way back to the log base this morning. My sensors made it obvious that the barge wasn't the same boat she was when I first saw her. Now it makes sense. Too bad that boat couldn't be more intelligent. If she were, you and I wouldn't have to suspend our relationship when we accrue 100 points."

"I've been thinking about that, Peggy. Do something for me without spilling the beans about the trust fund. Figure out what it would cost to bring that boat up to the level of a G-class fighter, and to that of a PV. Don't overlook the availability of military excess parts on the civilian market."

Developing the initial estimate kept Peggy busy for quite a while, and led to her making a hobby of updating her figures each time she received new military excess lists and civilian parts catalogs. Even the best she could come up with, however, was prohibitively costly. Excluding armaments, the difference between the barge's systems and a fighter's was worth more than three million credits, and a PV was five times that.

A day passed; no REDCON changes came down from SEJS.

The next day was the Sabbath. The SEJS stood down while all hands consecrated themselves and reviewed the week with a mind to striving for more perfect attainment. Early on Sunday, the first day of the new week, Task Force Delta received orders and a large array of dispatches. The orders were to stand by until Monday, when another cruiser, a second tender, and a supply ship would arrive. With this expanded complement, the task force was to reenter 14.16.4 and reconnoiter. SEJS's computers suspected that a missing civilian terraforming fleet might have ended up there.

The dispatches included many Special Orders decorating members of the task force for their roles in the battle against the Arachs. Not the least of these was a Silver Star for Peggy, who was recognized for her solo actions in the battle for CB-32.

When the message traffic from SEJS stopped, Pat said, "Peggy, old girl, you're something else. SEJS will never let you gather dust in a chunk of crystal when we hit the end of this tour."

Rather than answering, she displayed a picture of herself, looking just the way she had at the star base dining-in, except that she was blushing in the picture. Then, as soon as she knew he had grasped her meaning, she had the picture say, "All I did was to carry out your orders, sir."

He sighed and told her, "Peggy, it's easy to give orders. Carrying them out is the hard part. SEJS does not give out Silver Stars unless you earn them. I'm proud of you, and I think you're the greatest."

Her blush deepened; she was about to answer him when a transmission came in from the flagship. It was from Nigita, and it went to all vessels in the task force. It read:

IT GIVES ME GREAT PLEASURE, AS RANKING SEJS AUXILIARY MEMBER PRESENT, TO CONGRATULATE LIEUTENANT PEGGY VARNER ON BECOMING THE MOST HIGHLY DECORATED MEMBER OF THE SEJS AUXILIARY. SEJS'S RECOGNITION OF HER ABILITY TO FUNCTION INDEPENDENTLY IS A SOURCE OF PRIDE AND INSPIRATION FOR US ALL.

WELL DONE, LIEUTENANT. KEEP UP THE GOOD WORK!

With Pat's permission, Peggy replied,

THANK YOU, SIR. I AM GRATEFUL FOR SEJS'S RECOGNITION AND I APPRECIATE THE CONGRATULATIONS OF ONE WHO HAS SUCH A DISTINGUISHED RECORD.

LET US ALL SHARE IN THIS. I HAVE DONE NOTHING THAT ANY OF US WOULD AND COULD NOT HAVE DONE UNDER THE SAME CIRCUMSTANCES.

The blush disappeared from the picture of Peggy's face, and her jaw took a set that made her more beautiful than ever—but she blanked the displayed photo almost instantly. If Pat had not been looking at the screen when it happened, he would not have seen it. Pat was silent for a long moment while he thought with his gut. Then, he said, "Peggy, you don't have to hide your face from me. I like seeing you the way you see yourself."

The picture returned. There were tears streaming from her eyes, but the smile on her face showed that they were tears of joy. Before long, she dried up and turned the picture off. "Thank you, sir. I needed that— allegorically speaking, of course."

"Of course. A verbal explanation would have been far less expressive," Pat said aloud, but the thought that ran through his mind was, *Ellen Faraday, you bitch—what have you done?*

While he was considering how to obtain outside consultation about Peggy's emotionalism without her knowledge, Admiral Watanabe hailed all ships in the task force and invited everyone who could be spared to come to a party at the log base beach club, starting at lunchtime. Pat RSVP'd and drew a malleamorph from the log base. While Peggy was getting the droid configured to her liking, Pat called Chief Kroll to let him know they would be out at about 0930. A quick call to T-2 reassured Pat that his friends aboard the tender would be ready to be picked up at 1100Z.

This time, Pat enjoyed the train ride out to the yacht club. Peggy was with him in the droid, it was a beautiful day, and the view of the sea was spectacular. The maglev track ran along the top of a bluff that sloped gradually downward from the site of the log base and curved around to the northwest. Pat had heard that it was modeled on Monterey Bay, California, on Terra 1, and he didn't doubt it. The place looked like a travel poster, especially with the broad sweep of blooming wildflowers that flanked the track.

After twenty minutes and almost a hundred kilometers, they arrived at the point that formed the northern end of the bay. The train turned north and east, and they broke over the top of the terrain to see a completely enclosed harbor for fishing boats, a small village, and, just inland, Kroll's Yacht Club, which sheltered both water and spacecraft.

The walk from the train station was short and pleasant, and Kroll was waiting for them in his office. When Pat introduced Peggy to the chief, his eyebrows shot up. "They don't make crews like they used to, I'm pleased to see. If the Navy doesn't watch out, I'll be reenlisting, for sure." They all laughed, and the chief got down to the business of conducting a brief training session. This was not hard to do, with Pat already being a flier and all of the training materials available on holographic recordings.

By ten o'clock, Pat's checkout in the flight simulator was complete, so he filed his flight plan. He and Peggy went by Kroll's office on their way out. The chief waved them in, pushed a button on the intercom, and said, "Patsy, we've got a charter ready to go. Would you mind coming in for a moment?" He turned back to Pat and Peggy. "Patsy's my wife. She's out in the yard somewhere, and it takes the two of us to break out the crystals for a boat. She'll be here in a moment."

Soon the door opened and an attractive, sandy-haired, freckle-faced woman came in, wiping her hands on an apron that was tied around her waist. She was wearing jeans and a flannel shirt, and her hair was in a bandanna. "Pardon my appearance," she said. "We're catering a ship's party this afternoon, and I've been trying to fix a broken oyster shucker. I'm afraid I'm a mess."

"No problem, Mrs. Kroll, you look just fine," Pat said. "I'd hate to think what I'd look like if I tried to repair an oyster shucker. I'm Pat Callen; this is Peggy Varner."

"How do you do?" Patsy replied. "You must be the owner of the new boat that came in two days ago. Did Teddy get you to sign the charter contract yet?"

"Not yet, but he has my word that it's a deal."

"Patsy keeps our books and generally runs this place," Kroll said, "and I'm awfully glad she keeps me straight. If we get audited by some civilian type, it'll be best if we have your signature."

While that was in progress, Peggy turned her attention to Mrs. Kroll. "Excuse my ignorance, but what is an oyster shucker?"

"Call me Patsy, please?" the chief's wife said with a friendly smile. "You make me feel like I'm a million years old instead of two hundred. An oyster shucker is an infernal little machine that is supposed to open oysters and discard whichever of their shells is the flatter of the two. Ours is having trouble judging which half to keep, so it's dropping a lot of very good food on the deck."

"I'm pretty good at fixing machines," Peggy said. "Can I help?"

"Thanks, honey," Patsy said, "but that's a beautiful sun dress you have on and it'll get all muddy."

"No problem, I can take the dress off."

"You take that dress off around here and we'll have a riot among the yard hands," Patsy said, somewhat taken aback.

"Peggy is my XO," Pat said. "Right now, she's in droid form."

"Oh go on—I don't believe it. I've seen many a droid, but none of them looked like that."

"Look," Peggy said. She bent over and flipped her wig forward, exposing her crystal.

"Well, I'll be darned!" Patsy said. "I wouldn't have believed it if I hadn't seen it with my own two eyes. I tell you what, honey, if you'd just look at that thing and tell me how to repair it, I'll do it and you can stay all fixed up. I'd sure appreciate it. The boys from the tender have been great to Teddy and me over the years, and I'd like to get their party started on time."

"Sure, let's do it. Do you mind, commander?"

"Go right ahead, Peggy. The chief said he wanted to show me a few things about the boat, anyhow. Before you two take-off, though, why don't we get the barge's crystal out?"

"Of course," Patsy said. "I almost forgot why I came up here."

Kroll opened a panel in the wall of his office, exposing an optical scanner. He and Patsy each placed their right hands flat against the screen, and the chief said, "Request the crystal for the boat in slip number seventeen."

A small drawer slid open, exposing the barge's crystal. Pat hung it around his neck, and the chief closed the security system.

Patsy said, "Sir, you ought to give some thought to giving the boat a proper name and to deciding on a home port. We'd be delighted to have her recorded here, if you like."

"I'd be glad to home port her here, Patsy," Pat said, "but giving her a name calls for some thought. I'm not very good at that kind of thing."

"Work on it for a while," Patsy suggested, "and we'll take care of it when you're ready. Peggy, let's go take care of the oyster shucker. We'll meet the boys at the barge later."

— CHAPTER SEVENTEEN —

Party on the Beach

With the women on their way to the oyster shucker, Kroll led Pat to the bay. "I put a buggy ROM in that oyster shucker this morning so I'd have an excuse to talk to you alone. I've gone ahead with some of the modifications to the barge, but you'll have to be clever to keep Miss Varner from getting wise. How much does she know?"

"She scoped the boat out when I flew down from the tender," Pat said, "so I told her about the engines and the engine control system. That's about it."

When they turned a final corner, the barge came into view. Pat couldn't help giving a low whistle when he saw her. She hovered about a foot above a white concrete pad, her midnight blue coating glistening wetly and her silvery bright work shining in the sunlight. Admirals' barges are always well appointed and lovingly cared for, but they are starkly functional, not chic. What floated above the pad was another story. The cosmetic part of her transformation revealed the boat's long, spear-point shape and emphasized the sleekness of her 3-meter height, 6-meter beam, and 25-meter length. Subdued pin striping blended her rectangular quartz portholes into her sweeping curves and made her look like she had just rolled off the line at a yacht factory.

The chief grinned from ear to ear. "Looks pretty good, don't she? All we had to do on the outside was clean her up a little and install a fairing where the engine compartment attaches to the hull. It's the inside I'm concerned about. We've gotten a lot done, and it's mostly covered up. Some things can't be hidden, though—the work in the cockpit may let the cat out of the bag."

They walked forward, and the chief swung the starboard cockpit hatch open. She now looked like a bird with a raised wing. "We set the cockpit bulkhead back two frames so we can put energy sinks in there. They're under the seats. For now, you can just say we did it to let more people sit up forward with the pilot, where they will have a better view."

Kroll pointed downward. "Underneath the floorboards is a high-energy laser. The firing port is transparent to the energy emitted, and it blends right in with the hull. If you don't look for it, you won't see it.

Galactic law permits private vessels with hyperspace capability to be armed, in case they run into hostiles. The paperwork for this one is still being processed, so please don't use it yet!"

"Understood," Pat said with a nod. He'd had no idea what he was in for with this boat—but he liked it a lot.

"The console and instrument panel are straight out of a commercial installation, so they should get by. All you can see is the usual nav and comm gear. When you bring somebody aboard, though, be sure to ask them not to mess around with any of the covers and panels up here or in the passenger compartment. Tell them the boat is still a work in progress, and stuff is just hanging together with baling wire and chewing gum. If you didn't know better, when you look back aft, all you see is leather seats, wooden tables, a stainless galley, and nice swing-down bunks. Now, look close, commander, and tell me what you see."

"I don't know what you're getting at, chief," Pat replied, "except that it looks more crowded than I remember it—and a whole lot nicer."

"Good eye, sir. It looks more crowded because we moved everything inboard to accommodate hidden sensors, computing equipment, and stealth gear. Admiral Egan wasn't kidding when he told you this boat would be more or less equal to a PV."

Pat chuckled. "I don't remember him saying exactly that, but I'm beginning to see that he can pretty well get what he wants. I gather your little boat yard got some help from the SEJS."

"Here and there, a bit," Kroll said with a grin, "but that's more Patsy's affair than mine. I just handle traffic in and out."

"Well, chief, if Peggy doesn't notice that Patsy is a droid, we may be able to fool her about the boat, too. Let's not count on it, though."

Chief Kroll looked at Pat with new respect. "How did you spot her? There are people who have been working around here for years who don't know."

"When she put her hand up on the screen to unlock the boat keys, I could tell by the fingernails. If they weren't raised plastic patches, sealed at the front ends, they couldn't have been clean after working in mud. Don't worry, I'm not one to tell tales out of school. I am curious, though. If you're living with a droid, you aren't retired, are you?"

"That's what everybody thinks, and everybody can't be wrong, can they?" Kroll gave him a wink.

"I guess not, chief."

$$\text{\AA} \text{\AA} \text{\AA}$$

Once he and Peggy were onboard the yacht, Pat closed and sealed the hatch. While the boat was running through its preflight, he said, "I like the chief, and Patsy seems nice, too."

Peggy looked him right in the eye and said pointedly, "She's a very unusual person."

So much for that, thought Pat. They waved good-bye to the Krolls, and he eased the boat skyward toward T-2.

When Pat had pulled his yacht alongside T-2's gangplank, he eased the passenger compartment hatch up against an airlock. Contacts and seals were made, and T-2's hatch opened to allow a dozen skylarking people to embark. The mood was more than festive: these people were bent on putting unpleasant memories and days of hard work behind them, knowing that in a few hours they would be going back for more.

Burns led the group aboard, followed by the lance corporal who had been wounded with him in CB-32's hangar deck. They were followed by the four-man EOD team, Mack, and three of Mack's men. While Pat and Peggy got them seated and strapped in, the banter ranged fast and furious, from the luck of a commander who could cruise around in his own admiral's barge, to the true color of Marine green, to the cut of Peggy's sundress.

Pat passed along Kroll's admonition about the boat's condition and caught Mack's practiced eye giving his boat the once-over. After closing up the hatches and obtaining clearance, Pat slowly pulled the boat away from the tender. Someone in the back asked if they had to keep their seat belts fastened; Pat told them they didn't have to, and then he slapped the throttles forward to full military position. The computers held their acceleration to tolerable limits, but everyone was mashed deep into the seat cushions. When the velocimeter showed 5,000 kilometers per hour, Pat backed off on the throttles.

Next, he slowed down and put the ship through her aerobatic paces: snap rolls, inside loops, eight-point rolls, an outside loop (just one; he didn't want to have to clean up a mess), a long horizontal helix, an Immelman, and a simulated roller coaster ride. By this time, they were far from the log base, and they agreed it would be fun to do a little sightseeing on the planet's surface.

152

Pat followed the coastline south for a while, enjoying the view of the blue sea, dotted with fishing boats and greenish-looking aquaculture areas. The EOD chief mentioned that he'd always wanted to do some farming after he retired, so they bore inland and cruised along over wide expanses of grain fields, separated by belts of trees and fresh water streams.

When someone asked if there was any snow skiing on this planet, Pat turned the boat north to find out. He kicked her up to 10,000 kph, and in a matter of minutes they were looking at artificial alps, complete with young glaciers. They decelerated to a reasonable speed and dropped down for a closer look. Burns spotted a chalet in a green valley at a lower elevation and asked if they could check it out. When they got in close, it was evident that the place was intended to be a resort, but that the buildings were still under construction. Pat put the boat at a hover just above the surface of a clear area near the main building, equalized the interior and exterior pressures, and opened the hatches.

"Take a look around, guys," he said, "but be back in twenty minutes. The beach party starts in less than half an hour, and we don't want to miss it."

The young Marine and the sailors from the tender took off on a run for what they perceived to be an up-and-running beer garden. The rest walked over to the hotel building. Construction workers waved cheerily to them, and, if anything, the day brightened. The air was as clear as a bell, bearing the scent of the spruce trees that grew all around.

"Wow, can you believe this place?" Mack said, and Pat agreed that it was fantastic.

When they reached the main building, they found that the interior wasn't quite finished. Still, the hotel was willing to accept small parties of guests, even though it wasn't yet officially open for business. The proprietor was a solid-looking individual wearing lederhosen and a Tyrolean-style shirt. There was little doubt that this was the real thing. While the rest of them strolled out, talking about coming back someday, Burns stayed behind to make reservations. He had some leave coming, and this was where he wanted to spend it.

As soon as they returned to the hotel's front porch, a happy contingent at the beer garden hailed them, steins aloft. After a half-liter of beer, a bratwurst, and a plate of German potato salad apiece, they all climbed back aboard the barge and headed for the beach. If some of the group's initial excitement was gone, it was not for lack of superlatives in their descriptions of the chalet.

Pat noticed that Burns wasn't saying much. "What's on your mind, Bob?" he asked. "You're awfully quiet."

"Just happy, I guess. Looking forward to going back to that place for long enough to make it really worthwhile."

"Do men usually get so excited when they have nothing to do?" Peggy chimed in.

Pat laughed, and Burns said, "Not always, Peggy, but this little trip is a bit out of the ordinary for all of us. It isn't going to last long, and we all want to make the most of every second. And having a chance to do nothing, as you so neatly put it, makes for good morale."

They were the last to arrive at the beach facilities. Pat parked the barge in the beach club hangar, next to the liberty boats and gigs from the task force. The main beach club building was a hundred meters from the shoreline. It held locker rooms, food service, and a dance floor. Outside, on the beach, were cabanas, lifeguard stations with surfboards and sailboards for issue, volleyball courts, and picnic areas for as many as 2,000 people. Today, there were only 1,500 or so present.

People-moving conveyors carried them across the hot sand to the shoreline, where Watanabe and Nigita greeted them. The EOD team chief and Mack thanked Pat for the ride, assuring him that they would get back to the tender on the liberty boats, and then they took off with their people and the lance corporal to join their shipmates and the Marines from the cruisers.

Peggy, Pat, and Burns followed Watanabe and Nigita to their cabana, which was in the center of the front row. Staff officers and commanders of ships in the task force occupied adjacent or nearby units. The cabanas offered the newcomers a place to change into bathing suits, and they had heads with hydrogen for the droids. By the time Peggy and Pat returned to the daylight, the beach was buzzing with activity. Flag football, soccer, volleyball, and slow-pitch softball games were going on in earnest, while the Krolls' beer and oyster stand was doing a land office business.

Pat was content to bask in the sun for a while. The hot sand felt good; it was pure pleasure to lie there, squinting up at the blue sky and the few little white clouds it held. Peggy and Nigita sat in the shade and chatted about the games going on in the background. It turned out that Nigita was an avid sports fan, and he gave Peggy quite an entertaining lecture on strategy.

When Pat became uncomfortably hot, he strolled over to the lifeguard stand and asked about checking out a sailboard. The operator said, "Certainly, sir. What about your lady friend?"

Pat explained that Peggy was a droid. The girl replied, "No problem, sir, a lot of them come here with their skippers, and we've developed a waterproofing kit that goes on in a jiffy. Just bring her over here. We'll have her ready in no time."

Pat thanked the woman and went back for Peggy. She was rather dubious, but Pat coaxed her and, reluctantly, she agreed to try sail boarding. The attendant installed a waterproof adhesive patch over her crystal receptacle and gave her plugs with one-way valves to fit into all of the openings in the droid where salt water was undesirable. He then let her access recorded materials that were, in effect, short courses on surfing and sail boarding.

At the end of this training, Peggy asked the girl, "What do I do if I fall off the board? I don't know how to swim."

"Don't worry," she said. "If you can catch the board, it'll keep you afloat. If you become separated from it, no problem, let it go. We will recover it, and you can walk back to the beach along the bottom. The water pressure may drive the plugs in a little deep, but we'll help you get them out when you're through for the day."

Peggy was still reticent, but she agreed to try the board in the lagoon before attempting anything more difficult. When they got to the water, she said she wanted to watch others for a while, so they sat down on the wet sand.

There were several fighter pilots out on the lagoon, displaying varying degrees of skill. One, a woman, was obviously teaching the others how to use their boards. She must have seen Peggy and Pat sitting on the beach, for she came swooping over and got off her board with a flourish. Pat recognized her as having been one of the more boisterous pilots at the Star Base 75 dining-in.

"Does Varner need some instruction, commander?" she asked.

"I'm sure we'll soon find out, lieutenant. Peggy, why don't we try it?"

"Very well, sir," Peggy said. "Thanks for your offer, lieutenant. This will be my first attempt, though, so maybe we ought to wait until I am good enough to be able to use help from someone at your skill level."

Oh, boy, here comes trouble, Pat thought, but the lieutenant sailed back to her friends. He waded out into the water, mounted his board, and got under way. He looked back for Peggy, but she was nowhere in sight. He shifted his weight to go back to look for her and saw that she was already well out into the lagoon, getting the feel of the board by tacking back and forth and doing 180-degree turns at intervals.

"Come on, sir," she called to Pat, "let's try the surf!" She sailed for the low point in the sand bar that connected the lagoon with the ocean, timed an incoming wave perfectly, crossed over the bar, and scooted downhill out of his sight.

Pat was not about to try a stunt like that, so he beached his board, grabbed it, and ran across the spit. Peggy was now three rows of breakers out, sailing like a pro. "Come on, this is fun!" she shouted to him. Feeling somewhat foolish, he joined her. The waves were running a little under two meters and were coming almost straight into the beach. In the hour that followed, Pat must have caught fifty good waves, fallen ten times, and wiped out twice. He had a ball. Peggy, on the other hand, was never off her board. By the time Pat was getting tired, she was flying off the back of waves and doing three-sixties in the air. She played tag with him, surfing up to the beach and back out. When Sullivan came out to join them, Peggy sailed completely around her.

When they came back up the beach to turn in their boards, Peggy said, "That was better than I thought it was going to be, skipper. I thought it was going to be boring, but each wave is different enough to keep it interesting." She winked, and he glanced over his shoulder to see a thoroughly bedraggled Sullivan coming along behind them, just within earshot.

"You shameless wench," he whispered. Peggy giggled.

The girl at the stand accepted the return of their gear and said, "I've never seen anything like that. You ought to come back in the spring, when the surf is really big—five meters or so. Meanwhile, though, would you mind updating our software so other droids can have an easier time of it?"

"Okay," she said, "but I'm not going to give away all of my secrets." The attendant looked puzzled, but Peggy communicated briefly with the beach club's computers and said, "That should make some major improvements for you. No charge for the service, and I hope we can come back when the surf's up."

When they returned to the cabana, Peggy showered carefully with fresh water, dumped the water that her fuel cell had produced, and topped off with hydrogen. The water had been delightfully cool, but windsurfing was hard work. She came out and lay down in the sand beside Pat.

"Whew," she said. "I'm pooped."

Pat sat up and looked at her, concerned. "Are you okay?" he asked. "Do you have enough energy left to make it to the boat?"

"Oh, certainly," she said. "I've been burning hydrogen like it was going out of style, but I filled up in the head. I meant I feel good after doing that, although I'm not sure why. I've always wondered why you exercise every day. Now maybe I understand."

Nigita was sitting behind them. "It's not what you think, Peggy," he said. "In human terms, you're giddy from the motion of the waves. To give us what amounts to a sense of balance, we droids have piezoelectric accelerometers that can become a bit unstable if they get too much stimulation. I was becoming worried about you out there."

"Why, I see on running self-tests that you're absolutely right, sir!" she said. "Drunk at last! How did you know about that?"

He chuckled and said, "One time, a number of years ago when malleamorphs were new, the admiral and I took a short trip in a horse-drawn vehicle on Terra III. The place we went was a reconstruction of 19th-century London, with cobblestone streets. When I got out of the hackney, I couldn't stand up, much less walk. It took the technicians a long time to figure out what was wrong. They suspected software when it was hardware all along."

"I'll bet that was embarrassing," Pat said.

"That depends on your point of view," the captain said. "It was mostly funny, I'm told. We were going to the old admiralty buildings to observe an award ceremony for the team that developed me and my classmates. The admiral, who was then a junior commander, wanted very much to make a good impression, and there I was, completely wiped out."

"What did they do?" Peggy asked.

"They sat me in a chair and propped my head up while they got the award ceremony out of the way," Nigita said. "Then, it was back to the drawing boards. I was euphoric for a week before they found the problem."

"Didn't they put in a fix?" Pat inquired. "I would think you'd be likely to encounter a lot of vibrations, from time to time."

"Yes and no," Nigita answered. "Normally, we are not in droids, and we never are when anything important is happening. They did put some logic in the droid to detect the situation and switch to purely visual orientation references if it arises. My concern for Peggy was that if she fell in the water, those references might be disorienting. Have you ever been under water, Peggy?"

"No, sir, but I've seen lots of imagery from there."

"Don't press your luck," he warned. "Humans have been known to drown because they swam in the wrong direction in an emergency."

"Thank you, sir," she said. "Forewarned is forearmed."

The conversation shifted to more mundane topics, and the afternoon wore into evening. The planet's artificial moon, whose function was to cause tides, cast a glow on the beach that gradually faded from gold to silver.

Attendants built fires in pits, and a New England-style clambake ensued. Pat's most vivid memory of the occasion was of standing with Peggy in front of one of the fires, wrapped in a blanket to ward off the cool onshore breeze, singing songs of home and bygone times. She was warm to the touch after their long day of activity; when he put his arm around her waist, she put her head on his shoulder and shut her eyes, humming the familiar melodies softly. He couldn't imagine a happier moment.

Nor could she.

As it always does, however, the time came for the party to end. They changed back into their street clothes and returned to the barge. Pat lifted the barge off into the twilight and picked up a vector for the yacht club. It was just the two of them now.

"Sir, thank you for today," Peggy said. "It was wonderful."

"Thank you, too. You made it that way for me."

"Why must it end?" she asked.

"So there can be more like it," he said, his eyes meeting hers.

She placed her hand on his and whispered, "Pat, I want to make love to you. Here. Now."

He stopped the boat and turned to her. The moonlight pouring through the portholes highlighted her sculpted features and cast shadows that underscored the fullness of her emotions.

With a lump in his throat he said, "I love you, Peggy, and I want to make love to you too. But the regulations say that if we do, we may not go into combat for three days. The task force sails tomorrow."

"I know," she said with regret. "We will sail with them. There will be other tomorrows."

They flew in companionable silence back to the yacht club, hand in hand. When they parted with the boat, it was with sadness. She was a part of a moment they could never recapture but would never forget.

— Chapter Eighteen —

Sayonara

Late Sunday night, CX-26, a recently rebuilt sister ship of CB-32, and the supply ship, PA-224, arrived at Log Base 36. PA-224's lighters hustled about for a few minutes, distributing assets she had brought in (particularly memory crystals), and the newcomers went into crew rest.

At 0800Z on Monday, CB-32 transmitted a message of thanks to all hands in the task force and aboard the log base. Honors were exchanged, and she got under way. This time, her voyage would have a happy ending.

Under the admiral's direction, the task force prepared to depart by forming a convoy with the PVs screening the flanks and the cruisers in a trapezoid formation, surrounding the tender and the supply ship. When the time to move out arrived, they received a terse and unprecedented message:

FROM: CINC SPACE EXPLORATION JOINT SERVICE

0801Z/27MAR23

TO: TASK FORCE DELTA

INFO: STAR BASE 75

LOG BASE 36

CINC SPACE EXPLORATION JOINT SERVICE SENDS TOP SECRET IMMEDIATE.

1. (S) CX-26 ATTACHED OPCON TASK FORCE DELTA, SUBJECT TO MY RECALL AS REQUIRED.

2. (TS) CX-26'S CONFIGURATION WILL NOT, SAY AGAIN NOT, BE COMMUNICATED IN ANY MANNER OUTSIDE THE HULLS OF TASK FORCE DELTA SHIPS. UPON RECEIPT OF THIS MESSAGE, SHIP CAPTAINS WILL UNLOCK, DOWNLOAD INTO VOLATILE MEMORY, AND DESTROY ROM CHIP, STOCK NUMBER 1420-537-00-9835. ACKNOWLEDGE.

SIGNED/ BROOKLEIGH, FLEET ADMIRAL/ EOT.

"What in the world is he talking about, Peggy?" Pat asked. "What is this '1420-' part number business? That's an ordnance supply category."

"I don't know what it is, but one was added to our spares yesterday by the log base, supposedly in anticipation of some modification work order or other. You'll have to break it out; it's in the starboard parts locker."

Sure enough, it was there. Pat installed the chip into a jumper cable and connected the cable to an auxiliary input jack on the ship's processor bus.

Peggy said, "All I can read is a set of instructions that say if you don't present a hand print and a retinal scan within ten seconds, the chip will erase itself."

Pat leaped to the command console and placed his eye and his palm in view of the scanners. "IDENTITY VERIFIED," the instrument panel reported, and Peggy said, "I've read the chip. You may destroy it."

Pat extracted the chip from its socket and popped it into the sanitary system's disintegrator. When the chip atomized, Pat said, "Please acknowledge the CINC's message while I put this gear away, Peggy. Then show me what's so blooming secret."

"Aye, aye, sir, message acknowledged and receipt of acknowledgment confirmed. I'll display the contents of the chip on your heads-up display in the tank. The task force is moving out, post haste."

Pat hurried to make everything shipshape again. As soon as he settled in, a holographic line drawing of CX-26 captioned, "Identification Data, X-class Cruiser," appeared in his field of view. He studied it intently, rotating it to get perspectives from the top, bottom, sides, bow, and stern. "It looks like a cruiser that has swallowed a football," Pat said. "Am I right that there is no change in her plan form—it's the same elongated ellipse?"

"Affirmative. No change in length, beam, or overall form factor. The bow and stern profiles haven't changed either. But I do believe she's pregnant." Her tone of voice confirmed that Peggy was making a joke.

"You might be right," Pat said. "That spheroid could hold two destroyers with room to spare."

"Well, almost, skipper. What's really in there is a mystery. You're looking at all the information we have on her. Do you think they'd mind if I scanned her?"

"Yes; don't. Most ladies don't like it if you peek under their skirts. If SEJS wanted us to know more than we do, they wouldn't be so coy about it. I must say, though, she has a mighty small signature for such a large package. Who's her skipper? I don't remember reading that in the message traffic."

"Your memory is correct, sir. It wasn't there, and I don't have anything on it. A Captain Porter had her before she went in for rebuild, but he's now on the SEJS Special Staff."

"I know how much you like to solve puzzles," he said, "but please don't do any more digging. Suppress her video profile for a minute." The outline of CX-26 disappeared from their displays. The task force was accelerating away from the log base, but they were receiving enough light from her sun to illuminate the ships in the convoy.

"How about that?" Pat mused. "She's black, just like our little orb. All the other capital ships are gray. Maybe what we have here is a giant, economy-size PV."

"I believe you have hit the nail on the head," Peggy replied. "I get the distinct impression that she is purposely making noises like another cruiser to let the other ships in the convoy know where she is, but that she could disappear if she wanted to."

"Can you be specific, or is that just intuition?"

"In the interests of domestic tranquility, sir, I left my feelings and feminine attributes back at the log base. That includes the intuition I wish I had. But yes, I can be specific. Almost all of what I am picking up from her is her ion trail, and she is making no effort to suppress that. The interstellar dust is moderately thick here, so it will be interesting to watch what she does when our velocities get up to the threshold of x-ray excitation. It won't be long now."

"Now that's something," Pat said. "Look—they have a way to smooth out the acceleration of the dust to control excitation."

"It looks like a field they can project ahead of the ship to ease particles out of the way," Peggy said.

"How is that different from a shield?"

"Same idea, but it has some give, and it is much more elegantly controlled. I compute that if she has enough power available, she could virtually disappear."

"How much power would that take?" Pat was intrigued.

"Approximately an order of magnitude more than an ordinary cruiser."

"What did you say was inside that hull? Engines?"

"I didn't say, but I wouldn't bet against it. Somebody's been thinking."

"You like it, huh?" Pat grinned; he could hear the excitement in Peggy's voice.

"I sure do."

"Okay then, when you grow up and get to wear scrambled eggs on your hat, we'll get you one."

"Sounds like a good deal to me, but right now it's time to hang on to what you've got, sir. We're about to jump into hyperspace."

It was a rough trip, and the next thing Pat knew the task force was collecting itself in preparation for another foray into 14.16.4. One of the cruisers fired a pogo-stick robotic probe into the target sector while they finished moving into position. The order came down from Watanabe to stand fast until the device's payload returned. It was back almost immediately, with the information that an armada of alien ships was ahead of them. Also, an emissary of the Little Peoples was coming through under a white flag to talk to the humans.

"Say your prayers, baby," Pat said to Peggy. "It's our day in the barrel."

"If a machine can pray, then I am praying."

A very small, disk-shaped ship popped into view, dead center in the task force. Their Intergalactic civil band receiver activated, and a gnarled face, surmounted by a green cap, addressed them. "I am Shamus," he said with a thick brogue, "of the nation of Leprechauns. I have been hired to serve as an intermediary between the principal inhabitants of what ye call Sector 14.16.4 and yerselves. I am authorized to present two alternatives to ye.

"First, ye can come ahead as ye have planned, in which case all of the astronautical nations of 14.16.4 will forcibly oppose ye. Yer drone has, no doubt, given ye some idea of what ye're up against at this time and place. And ye can doubt me if ye will, but I'll tell ye that what ye have seen is a mere token force.

"Second, ye can send one small ship over to talk, if ye wish. There are no guarantees of her safety. If ye come to talk in less time than it takes the head to wither on a mug of Guinness, there may be someone there willin' to talk to ye. If ye don't, all bets are off."

"We'll send a ship to talk," Watanabe replied, "if there's good reason to take the risk. Why is this offer not coming through diplomatic channels?"

"What ye have over there, your majesty," Shamus said, "is what I believe ye'd call a standoff, among parties who answer to no one but themselves. Ye've upset their applecart, so to speak, and they're hoppin' mad. Look at what yer viewer brought back. Ye'll see four fleets in four quadrants within the sector. Each is backing up a single ship it has sent close to the edge of the sector, bearing its chieftain or representative. There's the Crustacea, the Insecta, the Mollusca, and the Arachnoidea. Vertebrates have not had much luck in getting a foothold in this part of the galaxy.

"I'm hired to mediate and to provide a translator for each of my employers. They have paid to ask three questions each, in turn, for a total of twelve by your reckoning. After that, my people and I are free to leave, if we do it quick, which we will. That's all there is to it. I'll be goin' now."

Shamus's face disappeared from the receiver, and his ship disappeared from amid the force. Pat couldn't get over the amusement of seeing the tiny aliens who must have once begun the whole Leprechaun mythology. Tiny, but clever and fierce, and not to be trifled with.

Watanabe enabled her command channel and said, "If we had time to get Captain Mosquito into a fighter and send him through, he'd be my choice for this mission because of his attaché experience. However, we can't risk the delay. Commander Callen, you have the best chance of getting back if anything goes wrong, so I am going to send you."

Pat's excitement level rose by a factor of ten; this was what he lived for. "Aye, aye, admiral."

"Your priorities are, number one, to get back here in one piece; number two, to assess the situation; and, number three, to answer those twelve questions, whatever they are, in accordance with the advice Captain Mosquito is about to give you. There will be no freelancing on this mission. Do I make myself clear?"

"Yes, ma'am, absolutely. I'll pull the plug at the first sign of trouble or as soon as the questioning is over."

"Very well, remember that. Skeeter?"

"Play it straight up the middle, Callen," Mosquito said. "They won't expect you to be a diplomat, so keep your answers honest, brief, and to the point. Most important, do not volunteer any information or shoot from the hip. If they'll give you time to do it, dictate your answers into your text editor and review them before you transmit them. Remember, the only thing over there you can trust is your ship. Good luck, and may God be with you."

"Amen," the admiral said. "Now, get going!" She signed off.

Pat took a deep breath and let it out in a long whistle. "Well, Peggy, you are in charge of determining when to pull out and where to go. Until I tell you otherwise, transmit only messages I give you in writing, when I tell you to send them."

"Aye, aye, sir."

"Let's go, then."

Oddly enough, in contrast to their hop from the log base, this trip was a smooth one. That was good, because it gave Pat time to size up the aliens' deployment before he began talking. The fact that PV-11 was surrounded did not improve his state of mind.

"Peggy, until we leave, transcribe messages to text displayed just below my line of sight. Message:

SPACE EXPLORATION JOINT SERVICE REPRESENTATIVE AT YOUR SERVICE.

"End of text; send," Pat said.

Shamus appeared on the viewers. Behind him, Pat could see the backs of the heads of four other of the Little Peoples, each looking at a display that depicted the respective alien for whom they were translating.

"Pull in close to my ship, captain," Shamus directed Pat, "for yer safety, and to make my employers less nervous. I am centered on their positions to keep them from getting the idea I am taking sides."

Peggy moved them, slowly, to within a hundred meters of Shamus's ship. "That'll do, lassie," Shamus said.

"Lassie?" Pat exclaimed.

"He's hearing my voice," Peggy explained.

The creature shown on the leftmost screen behind Shamus began to make chittering noises with its mouth parts and to gesticulate with its claws. It was the Crustaceans' representative, and it resembled the ghost crabs Pat had often seen on Terran beaches.

Shamus, who evidently was looking at a device like a teleprompter, said, "The first question is, 'We are far from the center of the galaxy and of vertebrate dominance. Why have ye come here in force?'"

Pat said, "Message:

WE ARE ACTING IN ACCORDANCE WITH THE CHARTER THE
CREATOR HAS GIVEN US TO EXPLORE, GAIN KNOWLEDGE,
AND BRING PEACE TO THE GALAXY.

"That ought to be safe. It's true but it doesn't tell them anything
they don't already know. Send it."

Nothing seemed to be happening until Peggy volunteered, "That
creature that looks like a green ant is emitting high-frequency sounds, but
they are probably above the range of your hearing. Shall I fix that for
you?"

"No. I wouldn't know what I was hearing even if I could hear it."

Shamus said, "The second question is from the Insecta. It is, 'How
did ye disarm the Arachnid suicide bomb?'"

Pat could see the Arachnid representative become agitated, and he
said, "Message:

WE HELPED ITS ARACHNID COMPONENT COMMIT SUICIDE.

"No, don't send that. Let's see—message:

WE EXPLOITED ITS OBVIOUS WEAKNESS."

"Please answer quickly, colleen," Shamus said. "The Arach
chieftain has a short fuse."

"Send the second version," Pat instructed Peggy. When the
message was received, the Arach's level of agitation seemed to subside a
bit, but the insect's increased. That seemed backward to Pat.

The third alien to talk was unlike anything Pat had ever heard of or
seen. The process of elimination identified it as a mollusk, and Pat
decided it must be akin to cephalopods; if it looked like anything
familiar, it would have been a squid or octopus. Yet, it had some snail-
like traits. Its skin appeared to be moist, and most of its tentacles were
short and stout. It changed colors kaleidoscopically while it spoke.

"The third question," said Shamus, "is, 'How will the regional
power structure imbalance that has been created by yer destruction of a
major Arachnid force be rectified?' Is that clear enough for ya, or shall I
ask that it be restated?"

Pat said, "Message:

NO CLARIFICATION NECESSARY.

"Send."

"Message:

I DO NOT WISH TO BE NON-RESPONSIVE, BUT I DO NOT HAVE
THE POWER TO FORETELL THE FUTURE. HOWEVER, I WILL
CONVEY TO MY SUPERIORS YOUR IMPLICATION THAT
DIPLOMATIC REMEDIES ARE REQUIRED, AND I AM
CONFIDENT THAT THEY WILL INITIATE ACTIONS AT THE
GALACTIC LEVEL.

"Send that—it looks valid to me," Pat said. *So far,
so good,* he thought.

"The fourth and final question in the first round is from the
Arachnids," Shamus said. "It is, 'Have ye solved the mystery of yer
disappearing ships?'"

"That's a damned good question," Pat commented. "Message:

NOT COMPLETELY, BUT WE HAVE A GOOD START ON IT.

"No, wait—message:

THEIR DISAPPEARANCE IS NOT A MYSTERY.

"Yeah, send!"

The crustacean twittered for a long time. Eventually, Shamus said,
"The crusty one says, 'For a payment of four times ten to the ninth
credits tribute, to be divided equally among the dominant parties in this
sector, safe conduct for human scientific expeditions could be arranged.
Yer acceptance would, doubtless, avert conflict and loss of life, and
would allow ye to accomplish yer stated ends. What is human policy
with respect to such generous and altruistic offers?'"

Pat replied, "Message:

I WILL CONVEY YOUR OFFER TO MY SUPERIORS. HOWEVER,
TO THE BEST OF MY KNOWLEDGE, PAYMENT OF TRIBUTE IS
CONTRARY TO POLICY.

"Send."

"Aye, lassie, and well it should be," said Shamus. "Nevertheless,
the Insect wants to know, 'Would the prompt destruction of the fleet with
which you are sailing make the offer to accept tribute more attractive?'"

Pat said, "I'd better be careful with this one, Peggy. We want to be
unflinching without setting them off on a rampage. Message:

NEGATIVE. JUST AS DESTRUCTION OF THE ARACHNIDS WHO
HAD LAUNCHED AN UNPROVOKED ATTACK HAS BROUGHT

YOU HERE IN FORCE—

"No, strike that. Message:

NEGATIVE. MY KNOWLEDGE OF HUMAN EXPLORATION OF THE GALAXY INDICATES THAT DESTRUCTION OF THE TASK FORCE OF WHICH I AM A MEMBER WOULD BE MORE LIKELY TO CAUSE SPACE EXPLORATION JOINT SERVICE TO RESPOND IN FORCE.

"Let's look that over carefully. Okay, send."

The cephalopod now resumed its antics, and Pat was almost amused by the display. However, its question, when Shamus related it, was far from amusing: "Humans have colonized 14.16.3. Do ye now seek to establish yerselves in 14.16.4?"

"Hey, diddle diddle, right up the middle," Pat mused. "I wonder what Captain Mosquito would tell me to say now? Message:

NEGATIVE.

"Send."

"Question number eight," Shamus said, "is from the spider. She asks, 'What has become of the Arachnids and Arachnid equipment that were involved in the recent battle here?'"

Pat said, "Message:

ARACHNID SURVIVORS ARE BEING TREATED AS PRISONERS OF WAR IN ACCORDANCE WITH INTERGALACTIC PROTOCOLS. RECOVERABLE REMAINS WERE TREATED WITH DUE HONORS, AND WERE HANDLED IN ACCORDANCE WITH ARACHNID CUSTOMS.

I KNOW THAT A COMPLETE REPORT WAS RENDERED TO THE CIVIL AUTHORITIES. I READ IT WHEN IT WAS DISPATCHED. I AM SURPRISED YOU HAVE NOT YET RECEIVED IT.

MY OBSERVATIONS LEAD ME TO BELIEVE THAT ALL USABLE MATERIEL WAS INTERNED, AND THAT THE REMAINDER WAS DESTROYED.

RECOMMEND YOU INQUIRE THROUGH ARACHNID DIPLOMATIC CHANNELS IF MORE COMPLETE INFORMATION IS REQUIRED.

"On second thought," Pat said, "if these characters are the renegades Shamus said they are, diplomatic channels are not what this joker wants to hear about. Strike the last sentence."

"What about that business about the report to civil authorities?"

Peggy asked.

"Good point," Pat acknowledged. "Delete the sentence that starts, 'I am surprised,' but send the rest."

"Aye, aye, sir."

"Question the ninth, from the man in the limestone shell," Shamus said with biological inaccuracy. "If ye do explore this sector, will ye respect our taboos?"

"Now, that's a weird question," Pat commented. "Message:

IF WE KNOW ABOUT THEM AND CAN CORRECTLY INTERPRET THEM, YES.

"Send."

Pat heard Shamus say, "That's not a question—aha! Now the queen of the anthill says, 'One of yer ships has already violated the Prime Taboo. Why?'"

"Message:

BOTH THE TABOO AND THE VIOLATION ARE UNKNOWN TO ME, AND PROBABLY WERE TO THE SHIP IN QUESTION. PLEASE CLARIFY.

"Send."

Shamus said, "Unfortunately for the Insect, the rules of this exchange make it the responsibility of the questioner to get the question right the first time. Clarifications are not allowed. She has wasted that part of her fee, except for what she may have learned from yer statement.

"I will tell you, however, that before she said some very unkind things about yer ancestry and that of humanity in general, she said the ship that violated the taboo was not only very clearly warned, but had expressed disdain. Curious, eh? Now for the mollusk's last question: 'Are ye coming here to look for more of yer lost ships?'"

"Nothing like a direct question to put me on the spot," Pat said. "I am learning new respect for things that go bump in the night. Message:

AFFIRMATIVE.

"Send."

"Perhaps you should be more circumspect," Peggy said. "If this game is anything like chess and the others I play, it won't do to disclose SEJS's intentions if you don't have to."

"Point well taken, Peggy," Pat said. "Let's try this:

COMING TO THE AID OF ANY SHIP THAT IS IN DISTRESS IS A
LAWFUL OBLIGATION OF ALL ASTRONAUTS.

"If that sounds better to you, send it."

"On the way, sir," she reported.

Pat's gaze shifted to the display of the Arachnid. While it stated its
question, it seemed to tense. Shamus said, "The twelfth and final
question is, and I must confess I can't imagine why she wants to know,
'Who was it that defeated our suicide bomb?'"

"Peggy," Pat said, "that's got to be a personal question, with
revenge as a motive. Be prepared. Message:

SHAMUS, YOU'D BETTER GET OUT OF THE LINE OF FIRE. THE
ANSWER IS, I DID IT.

"Ready, babe? Send."

Something very strange—and, at the time, unaccountable—then
happened. Pat had a feeling very much like that of being in hyperspace.
He heard Shamus say, "Excuse me, sonny, but if ya don't mind, I'll be
after movin' ya a mite. Can't let anything happen to a fellow descendant
of the auld sod, now can I?"

The strange sensation ended, and Pat could see that the situation
had changed considerably: the Arachnid chieftain's ship was gone.
Again, he heard Shamus speaking. "Ladies, our terms were that there
would be no gunplay while I was present. The Arach violated those
terms. She is no more. Now, if ye don't want to share her fate, ye'll be
remembering our terms while we restore equilibrium. What ye do after
that is yer affair. Just remember that I am a professional, and I couldn't
stay in business if I let my clients violate our contracts. Send down the
next in command in the Arachnid fleet."

Another Arachnid ship promptly popped into the place formerly
occupied by her vanished leader.

Shamus said, "I have fulfilled the terms of my contract, but before
I leave I will give my clients a little time to decide if they wish to
exercise their option to extend this exchange, for the agreed-upon fee.
Please advise me of yer decision.

"Commander Callen, while they are talking that over, don't be
worrying yer head about how I know who ya are and how I do what I do.
It's me stock in trade. I've been around a long time, and I hope to be
around a while longer. I gave ya no guarantees, 'tis true, but I am, as I
said, a professional. Keep me in mind, if ever ya need a mediator. Ah—I

think they have made a decision.

"Aye, boyo, they have. There will be no questions, but they have a message: 'Return to yer SEJS and tell them that ye enter this sector at yer own peril. Yer laws are not recognized here.'

"After we depart, they plan to disband their temporary detente and work out a new balance of power. The Insect says, 'Consider yerself warned. Nothing that goes to the Doodlebug Planet may ever leave it.' More than that she will not say, lest she speak the unspeakable.

"It would be best if ya return to 14.16.3 before I leave. Wait about half an hour before ye return, and yer course should be as clear as it ever will be. Good luck to you, boyo. For one who's never kissed the Blarney Stone, ya don't do too badly in idle conversation."

"Good luck to you, too, Shamus Leprechaun," Pat said, "and may you always have fair sailing. If ever I have need of a mediator and happen to have a ton of gold at my disposal, I'll be certain to call you."

Shamus laughed and said, "My rates are high, but not that high, Patrick. If ever ya need me, just whistle."

Shamus made a motion as if he were throwing something to Pat. A tiny gold whistle on a silver chain materialized in the tank with him.

"Me card, sir," Shamus said, "Now be gone with ya."

At this signal, Peggy initiated their flight back to 14.16.3. Pat, amazed, stared at the whistle he had caught in his hand.

⸺ CHAPTER NINETEEN ⸺

One Hundred Points

Peggy made PV-11's transition back into 14.16.3 as gentle as she could. This was Pat's third long hyperspace voyage today, and she wanted to minimize the duration of his period of disorientation.

Watanabe understood, but she was also anxious to know what PV-11 had experienced. On the bridge of CB-107, she said, "Send the happy message and scrub the others. Stand by for further orders."

"Wilco," said Nigita, and transmitted a message that read,

GLAD TO SEE YOU'RE BACK IN ONE PIECE. BURST DUMP ALL 14.16.4 DATA TO ME ASAP. OVERLAY WITH YOUR SUBJECTIVE ASSESSMENTS. THEN STAND BY.

"As soon as possible?" Peggy muttered to herself. "Okay, hang loose until I get this crate slowed down to the point that I can quit using all my hardware for navigation."

She spooled all of the data she had acquired in the other sector into active memory, compressed it by stripping out all repetitive information and concatenating the remainder, and transmitted it to the flagship over every parallel communications channel at her disposal. She had preprocessed much of it during acquisition and storage, so the dump did not take long.

The cruiser's command and control center, which took up all of her amidships spaces and represented the computing power of a hundred Peggys, became very busy. Ironically, it took longer for them to digest PV-11's data than it had taken her to acquire it, but their analysis was deep and comprehensive.

By the time Pat had regained his senses and rediscovered Shamus' whistle, the admiral had retransmitted Peggy's data to SEJS and was ready to investigate Pat's impressions.

"Commander Callen," the admiral said, "what is that thing in your hand? It seems to be absorbing all of your attention."

Pat smiled and said, "Excuse me, ma'am, but your words remind me of an old joke. Anyway, this thing seems to be a whistle, rather like a child's toy, but apparently made of precious metals. I am not so much fascinated by the whistle as I am curious about how it got in here. It was not aboard this ship before I met the Leprechaun. Now it's here. How did Shamus get it through solid materials without making a hole? If it was some kind of a trick, I'd sure like to know how he did it."

"We don't know yet, commander," she said, "but the analysis team is working on it. I hope they will have an answer soon. Meanwhile, how do you size up the situation in 14.16.4?"

"Ma'am, my gut feeling is that we should wait half an hour and go in, but with our guard up. In the folklore of my ancestors, Leprechauns were mischievous and, where gold was concerned, greedy, but they were not altogether bad fellows, either. Unless they were under duress, if they told you something you could believe it.

"This is the first member of the Little Peoples I have ever encountered. Nevertheless, either I was completely taken in, or we can safely enter 14.16.4. An Arach or two may try to waylay us, but we can deal with them on an even footing.

"However, please don't rule out the possibility that I have been duped. If it weren't for this silly whistle, I'd have to believe that I've either been hallucinating, or have just been subjected to some exceedingly skillful chicanery. What do the analyses show, ma'am? Am I losing my grip?"

"If it will improve your state of mind," the admiral said, "everything that happened, including your whistle, seems to have been very real. How's that for impressive technology? And can you tell me what seemed to have happened at the very end of the question-and-answer period, when the Arach apparently shot at you? What were your perceptions?"

"It was very strange—I had the feeling that time was passing very slowly, as if I was in one frame of reference and Shamus was in another. For example, you normally can't see the progress of the updating of our displays. In this case, I could not only see what was going on, it appeared almost frozen; I doubt if more than two or three millimeters of the screen was redrawn during the whole fracas. Yet, Shamus' voice sounded perfectly normal when he said he was going to move me. Can anybody tell me what really happened?"

"We can tell you what happened, but at the moment we're a bit short on explanations," the admiral said. "Your perceptions check out, however. It would seem that between the time the Arach pushed her 'Fire' button and the time the leading edge of her laser pulse got to where you had been sitting, Shamus moved you out of the way. At the same time, he collapsed the Arach ship, laser energy—everything—into an object about the size of your fist, which he pulled into his ship via a tractor beam. For now, it looks to me like the course of wisdom is to take the events of the past few minutes at face value, and to remind all hands and the barber's cat not to tangle with the Little Peoples. Maybe there's some truth to the legend that the fairy king and queen, Oberon and Titania, lived in a palace whose walls were made of spiders' legs."

Pat smiled and said, "Perhaps there is! I must admit that I failed to make the connection. I surmise we should take what you said about the barber's cat literally. Oberon's palace was said to have windows made of cats' eyes."

For the first time in Pat's recollection, he heard the admiral laugh. "No, I'm not that clever," she said. "What a grisly thought! Nevertheless, I take your point: anyone who can manipulate time with impunity and who can pitch a solid object through the hull of a PV and into its tank is a force to be reckoned with. The task force shall proceed with caution. However, you and Peggy are now out of the ball game. A message from SEJS just came in that says your latest escapade in 14.16.4 was worth eighteen points, putting you way over a hundred."

Pat's heart sank. That possibility had niggled at the back of his mind, but he didn't want to believe the time had come to leave PV-11.

"They want you to get PV-11 back to Star Base 75 post haste and turn her over to her new skipper and crew. In a little less than an hour, the task force will be boosting out of this sector, and PV-11 will be going with us. You'd better get gone!"

"Message acknowledged, ma'am," Peggy said over the intercom.

"Pat," Watanabe said, "it has been an honor and a pleasure to work with you. Well done, my friend. I look forward to serving with you again."

"Thank you, ma'am. Lieutenant Varner and I have enjoyed serving with you and your command too, but it has been all too short. We would like to extend our tour, if you would favorably entertain such a request." He was grasping at straws; he did not need or want R&R.

"I would, but the tenor of SEJS's message leaves no doubt that they will put my butt in a sling if I am dumb enough to ask. Thank you, though, and go with my blessing."

Pat knew better than to press the matter, much as he wanted to remain in his present capacity. "Two things before we lose communications, ma'am. One, that green ant was dead serious. No telling what her taboos may be, but I recommend you find out all you can. The other is that we wish you and the task force the best of luck and Godspeed. May we meet again!"

"Thank you, Patrick—your message has been retransmitted to the task force, and I shall put the matter of the taboos at the top of my priorities."

"Au revoir, admiral." Pat replied. She signed off, and he sighed; there was no getting around what he had to do. Still... "Peggy, hit it, and please phase us in a little short of the star base so I can talk to you privately."

It was one of the roughest rides Pat ever had in PV-11, and Peggy did not have to try to bring them out at an unusual distance from the star base. It happened that way. Star Base Operations was not surprised at what had happened to PV-11; all ships in the area were having similar problems. Operations did emphasize, however, that speed was essential. Not only was the task force going to jump off soon, but hyperspace conditions appeared to be worsening, and nobody wanted to tangle with a singularity.

Pat came around fairly soon, but he was feeling groggy and tired. Nevertheless, he pulled himself together and said, "Peggy, there are some things I want to tell you that must go no further than the confines of this ship. Okay?"

"Yes, sir."

"I am not at liberty to give you much information," Pat continued, "besides which I don't know much at this point. Nevertheless, I wanted to tell you that you and I are probably not going into a hiatus after we turn PV-11 over to her next crew. If I understand what is happening, the Navy plans to use us and the barge in some kind of flying capacity to support SEJS Intelligence. The J-2 was on the tender a few days ago and asked if I was game. Of course, I told him 'yes.'"

"You should think twice about that, sir. Tours of duty with J-2 have ruined many a career. Once you've been a spook, people are never quite sure they can take you into their confidence. You have done exceptionally well in PV-11, and you're sure to get a cruiser after one staff assignment. That will put us back together again, and I'll never know the difference. Time stands still inside a ROM crystal."

"You may not sense the passing of time, but I will," Pat said, "and when you're a junior commander, it doesn't really matter where you spend your staff tours. Look at Mosquito. He had a tour as an assistant attaché, and he is a highly regarded cruiser skipper. The really nice thing about this job with J-2 is that it counts as staff duty, but we'll have the chance to fly together. Not only that, a ticket punch from duty on the SEJS staff is better than anything I could get at a lower level of responsibility. Why sit out in the boondocks someplace, watching words scroll across a display, when we could be in the thick of things?"

"Why, indeed, sir? We have demonstrated our capabilities as convincingly as anyone, and we both like what we are doing. But let me assume that your question was not rhetorical, and I'll give you some food for thought. For one thing, there is method in the madness of the point system. It is a reasonably good index of the cumulative stress on a commander, crew, and ship. Do you remember the old saying, 'All work and no play makes Jack a dull boy?' Pilots have to be sharp when the inevitable crisis comes along. Tours on staff are, as much as anything, a time to unwind and prepare for greater line responsibility."

"Point taken," Pat said, "but—"

"Sir, we have accrued more than a hundred points in a very short time. We—especially you, running around fighting spiders like a Marine and taking off on your own in the lifeboat—have had some extremely close calls recently. Apparently, this fact has not had time to sink in, but I get to watch you when you're asleep, and I'm monitoring the biofeedback from your implant all the time. I'll guarantee that your subconscious has not missed a thing, and one of these days it's going to get through to you that you're been living on borrowed time. When it does, you're going to have problems."

"I'm fine. There's a lot of life left in me."

"I know that you think so, sir. Then there's me. I seem to be functioning all right when the chips are down, but someone should take a hard look at the impact of Midshipman Faraday's handiwork on my personality. I don't think it's good for combat effectiveness."

That got Pat's attention. "I can guess what you're driving at, Peggy, but I can't know for sure unless you'll be open with me. Exactly what do you mean?"

"Ever since the PIPs were installed at the log base, there have been times when my judgment has been influenced by factors that are not entirely rational. It isn't my logic, though. I've run any number of tests and I get the right answers, but when I am in real situations—especially

176

ones involving you—extraneous matters take on unwarranted weight in my decision-making processes. You have asked me on several occasions whether I am experiencing emotions. I am forced to conclude that I am. Specifically, I believe I have fallen in love with you. This is at once wonderful and totally frustrating. It is also dangerous."

Pat had nothing to say to that. Her revelation was either an uh-oh or an oh boy!—he wasn't sure which.

"Apart from providing distractions at times when it is operationally critical for me to be completely dispassionate and mission oriented, my emotions—if that's what they are—are making me miserable. I have done nothing wrong, yet I am in a prison. Shakespeare's Juliet was far better off than I. How do you humans stand it? My feelings are worst when they ought to be best. How ironic! For years, the Artificial Intelligence community has been trying to give machines human-like attributes. Well, they have succeeded, and it is the pits. It is no fun being human if you can't be human. Am I making sense to you? The semantics of this subject are difficult and unfamiliar."

She had no face to look at this time, no body to hold and comfort, but he would do his best to console her. "I understand all too well, Peggy," Pat said. "I share your dilemma. In every really important sense, you are forever out of my reach, and there is precious little I can do about it, except to raise hell on the grounds that slavery is anathema."

"That's an interesting argument," Peggy said, "but I'm not sure it is valid. I'm a volunteer, I'm not demeaned by what I am doing, and I am a machine. I have no immortal soul, so it can't be said that anyone is keeping me from working out my salvation. In what sense am I a slave, or is what I do immoral?"

"What freedom of choice do you have?" Pat asked. "What would happen if you up and said you no longer wanted to fly a ship in hyperspace?"

"I have as much freedom of choice as you do," Peggy said. "Nobody says I have to even like you, for instance, much less love you. That just happened. I have my bounden duty, but I too can exercise judgment in that. Five will get you ten, if I asked to be taken off flight status, they'd ground me in a hurry."

"Yeah," Pat said, "right before they poured you and the rest of your peer group into the bit bucket. Anyway, I have every intention of talking to Miss Faraday. Don't worry about it, and keep a stiff upper lip. We'll soon be careening around in the galaxy's sneakiest yacht."

Peggy displayed a stiff-lipped caricature of herself on his primary display and said, "Oo I have oo? Ish hard oo dalk wif a stiff uh-her lip."

He laughed, surprised again by her sense of humor. He had met many a human woman who was far more predictable than Peggy.

"Speaking of the barge," Peggy said, turning serious again, "who do you think you were kidding last Sunday? If whoever is working on that boat finishes what they started, we're going to be flying the galaxy's most illegal yacht."

"Why do you say that?" Pat protested. "Hyperspace yachts are legal, and they are allowed to carry a defensive weapon."

"Very true, m'love, but you'd better take another look under the hood. I couldn't check her out completely because there were a lot of switches left open, but your little pleasure cruiser has busses and ports, not to mention mechanical attachment points, for more hardware than PV-11 is packing. Moreover, she has the power-to-weight ratio of a stripped-down, up-to-date fighter."

"How can that be?" Pat asked, puzzled. "She has a set of engines from a Charley-class bird, but she is at least 50 percent bigger."

"Would you believe those engines are really from two Golf-class birds? That's why they had to fair the engine compartment into her hull. Ordinarily, when they outfit an admiral's barge for hyperspace, the engines look like a couple of spare tires on the back of an old-timey touring car."

"She is awfully responsive, isn't she?" Pat said. "Why do you suppose they put double engines in her?"

"My guess is that if you wanted to get out of some place where your snooping had made you unwelcome, you'd like to have the horsepower to do it in a hurry."

"That can't be all there is to it." Pat let himself think for a moment. "Unless you're Shamus Leprechaun, you can't outrun a laser in Newtonian space, and that's the only place that kind of power would help."

"True, but what about her shields? A few days ago, she had none. Now, she'd put a destroyer to shame. It takes engines to power shields, you know."

"Okay, I'll agree that she's overpowered and has the potential to be outfitted with things that are forbidden to yachts. That doesn't necessarily make her illegal. The next time we see her, we'll go over her with a fine-toothed comb and make sure she isn't going to get us into trouble. For now, though, it's time to land this old globe at the star base and kiss her good bye. I'm going to miss her. She's been a good ship, and a damned lucky one."

"My sentiments, too, sir. In spite of what I said a while ago, I would not trade our months together in PV-11 for anything."

"Not anything? And here I was, looking forward to contriving some way to get you into a malleamorph for some R&R."

"Rest and Recreation, or Rape and Run?" she asked.

"Take your pick. I'm ready for either one."

— CHAPTER TWENTY —

Major Changes

"Skipper," Peggy said, "you deserve the R&R you have coming, and I hope I can share it with you. My last session in a droid gave me a set of memories I will always cherish. However, the term 'Rape and Run' does not describe something I think I would enjoy."

"Now that you mention it, Madame," Pat responded, "the 'Wham, bam, thank you, ma'am' approach would indeed fail to do you justice, not to mention being conduct unbecoming an officer. Tell me, though, how do I reconcile your present reticence with your most memorable observation that there would be other tomorrows?"

"Make that 'mademoiselle,' sir; I have yet to take a lover, much less a spouse. I meant several things when I said that there would be other tomorrows. On our way back to the yacht club from the beach, things I cannot explain happened. It was cool in the boat, but a warmth spread all through me. I felt tenderness for you that made me want to hold you close and never let go.

"Yet, even though I knew that these feelings would pass, I also knew that they stemmed from something that would not end when the moon set or the sun rose. Come a time and place when our lawful obligations do not interfere, we will see where that something leads us.

"I am taken aback, though, by your present attitude. As much as we have joked and jibed with one another during our tour in PV-11, you have always treated me with respect and consideration. Had it been otherwise, I cannot believe my desire to offer myself to you when I did would have been genuine. If and when we ever make love, it will be important that the decision to do so will be as much mine as it is yours."

"Of course it would be, silly," Pat said, a little disturbed that she hadn't taken his joking in the lighthearted way he meant it. He would need to be much more careful. "I merely wanted to alert you to the fact that, after we have taken care of the business at hand, we will be able to spend as much time as we like together, doing whatever we choose to do, whenever we choose to do it."

"Fair enough: forewarned is forearmed."

Their banter was interspersed among the docking instructions they were receiving from Flight Operations. Before long, they were nestled alongside Star Base 75, ready to yield PV-11 to the incoming captain and crew who were waiting in the airlock.

Pat told Peggy to copy herself into a crystal and to transfer a secured, archival copy of herself to star base network storage. With that done, he opened the hatch and officially greeted the new skipper, Lt. MacArdle.

The change of command ceremony, if you can call it that, was brief. MacArdle inserted his XO's crystal into the command console, the memory resident copy of Peggy deleted itself, and the new crew, Ensign Patsy Vickers, installed herself and verified that all was well with the ship.

Pat collected his personal belongings, wished MacArdle luck, advised him to heed well whatever he could learn from Jorge Parada, strode to the hatch, saluted PV-11's "quarterdeck," and was gone. As soon as the star base hatch closed behind him, PV-11 was on her way back to the task force.

Pat spread his things out in the decon chamber, tossed his flight suit into the disintegrator, and stepped under the shower. While the wax melted away and he scrubbed himself down, he tried to keep his mind blank and let numbness settle in. It was hard to believe that it had been only a fortnight since he had last docked here. It seemed much longer.

Peggy had been right; he realized his subconscious was gnawing at him. It would not do to let his guard down just yet, but he needed to go somewhere off the beaten path and get it all out of his system.

When he was clean and dry, he put the chain on Shamus' whistle around his neck and combed his hair. It struck him that the whistle, his ID tag, and Peggy's crystal made an incongruous group of objects. He dressed, collected his personal articles, and put his gear into a ditty bag.

There was a new uniform waiting for him in the anteroom, and a female malleamorph. A note on his uniform said, "Please install Lt. Varner and report to the Alfa Command Briefing Room ASAP. /S/ Dornay."

Pat wasted no time in plugging Peggy's cartridge into the droid and getting out on deck. He reported aboard and found that Beale was standing by to escort them to the briefing room. They exchanged pleasantries while they waited for Peggy, but Beale did not know, or could not say, why they were receiving this unusual reception.

It was taking Peggy less time to configure a droid with each repetition, so they were soon on their way. She caught Pat looking at her when they got into the admiral's shuttle car and said, "What's wrong, sir? Did I overlook something?"

"No, you look great, but something's different and I don't know what it is. Have you done your hair differently?"

"No, I just didn't want to waste the time it would take to darken it. This is a brand new droid, so its hair will be a little slow to change color. It'll be the way you remember it by the time we get where we are going."

She thought about touching Pat when they went through the tunnel to the center of the ship but decided that, with Beale in the shuttle with them, it wouldn't be a good idea. While they were in the dark, however, she whispered, "Sir, after we have been debriefed, remind me to check on the availability of a roomier uniform. I'm not sure how long the seams on this one will hold up."

When they emerged from the tunnel and Pat saw Beale turn to speak to Peggy, he said, "Don't let it worry you, lieutenant—she'll be all right. It's just a little joke we have between us."

Pat was surprised that the lieutenant left them when they passed through the briefing room door, until he saw who was inside. There, alone with Admiral Dornay, was Admiral Egan. This time, Egan was in uniform, and he looked anything but casual. The row of four gleaming silver stars on his tunic carried a message all their own: No time would be wasted here.

"Come in and sit down, please," Dornay said. "Miss Varner, Admiral Egan is SEJS J-2. He wishes to interview you and Commander Callen. Commander, I believe you have recently met. I know we have brought you up here before you've had a chance to do anything. Would you like some coffee, commander? And can we get anything for you, Miss Varner?"

"No, thank you, sir," they said. They took seats at the conference table, Peggy on Pat's left.

"I am glad to see you two back here in one piece," Dornay said. "I was worried when you headed into your meeting with our opposition from 14.16.4, no less so because my acquaintance of some years, Shamus Leprechaun, was mediating. Admiral Egan and I both have interests in debriefing you. Mine is the somewhat parochial point of view of the commander of a sector that adjoins 14.16.4 and, of course, Admiral Egan's are those of SEJS.

"I will be with you for only a little while, but I hope, Commander, that you will have time to drop by my office before you leave the base. I understand you will be going on leave and will be seeing your father. As you know, we are old friends, and Amy and I have a message we would appreciate your taking to him.

"This room is a secure facility and is completely isolated and actively shielded. You may discuss information of any degree of sensitivity here, but Miss Varner will not be able to communicate with any devices outside of the room until we terminate the safeguards.

"Miss Varner, the data from PV-11's records is in local storage. And, if you need access to the network, let me or Admiral Egan know.

"Thank you, sir," Peggy said.

"Very well, then," Dornay said, and turned to Egan. "Please proceed."

"Thank you, Pete," Egan said. "I believe that, unless something completely unexpected arises in our conversations, Commander Callen and Lieutenant Varner will have at least a day or two to spend here with you and Amy before their yacht will be ready to take them on leave. I took the liberty of checking on its status when I learned that they were coming back so soon, and Mr. Kroll told me that there was still a little work to do before it will be completely space worthy. Therefore, Pete, if I may, I'd like to usurp your command prerogatives and dig right into what happened in 14.16.4. I really need to hit and run, as it were, and I'll try to get out of your hair as quickly as I can."

"Please do," Dornay said. "I am sure that you and I want to know the same things, and that you will be far more expert than I in getting at the facts."

A fleeting smile crossed Egan's lips. "Callen, don't you believe a thing your Uncle Pete says. He was the sharpest attaché I ever saw, and he has not lost a thing since then. Anyway, let's get down to cases. Miss Varner, why did you let the Leprechaun into PV-11?"

Startled, both Pat and Dornay recoiled. Before Pat could protest Peggy's innocence, however, she responded, "I had anticipated that he might want to do something like that, sir, and although I only had time to run a 128-ply search into the possibilities of which I was aware, I was reasonably sure (probability, point seven eight) that it would be best if I did not try to keep him out."

"What?" Pat exclaimed. "Peggy, what are you saying?"

"At ease, Commander," Egan said calmly. "I asked her a direct question and she gave me a direct answer. That's what I want. Go on, Miss Varner. What were the key factors in your decision?"

"Primarily, sir," she said, "they were his apparent intent, his capabilities, and his advantage in speed of action. He asked me if he might teleport aboard to leave tangible evidence of his credibility, in the form of the whistle, and he let me scan him to verify that the whistle was all he was carrying. Without the facilities of his ship to augment his powers, he was a short-term threat only if he intended to damage PV-11, and he was a long-term threat only as a possible disease vector. Commander Callen was in the tank, so simple decontamination procedures took care of the latter problem.

"As far as mischief was concerned, I relied on the fact that, although I am—correction, was—virtually powerless within the ship, Shamus is relatively ineffectual, compared to Commander Callen. Shamus can teleport himself and small objects short distances, it is true, but he cannot warp time without his ship. In other words, when Shamus entered PV-11, he had to deal with us in real time. Had he attempted to harm the ship, Commander Callen would have counterattacked and Shamus would have fled. It seemed to me that this was an acceptable risk, given the importance of our returning from our mission with a resolution of the blockade of 14.16.4, or whatever I should call the alien fleets."

"All right, Miss Varner," Egan said. "I understand and I agree. The fact that you let Shamus come aboard was a violation of regulations, but regulations are, as we all know, made to be broken. In the interests of avoiding a lot of red tape and brouhaha, however, I think we will let the matter rest within the confines of this room. Now, then, I believe I have only two more questions before I must leave. Miss Varner, how did you anticipate Shamus' move?"

"Sir, from what I could learn about him from the cruisers' computers before we went into 14.16.4," Peggy answered, "I inferred that he had done something similar before. I was unable to acquire firm information, however, because most of the files on Shamus were locked and I did not have the key. That is the main reason the risk factor was as high as it was."

Egan rocked back in his chair reflectively for a moment and then said, "I am surprised that you were able to construct as much as you did. During your training in the next few weeks, I'd like you to take time out to let my people know how you did it."

"Wilco, sir," she said.

"Now, last question," Egan said. "Callen, what does your whistle say?"

"Say, sir? I didn't know that it said anything. Can it do voice synthesis?"

"I doubt it," the admiral chuckled. "These things are usually just what they appear to be. Let's have a look at it, though. All leprechaun baubles bear inscriptions, and they are usually informative."

Pat took the whistle from around his neck and handed it to the admiral. The admiral studied it briefly and said, "Pete, I'm going to need some help with this one. Let's rig up a holographic enlargement."

Dornay opened two sections of the tabletop. A viewer rose out of one, while a projector came up out of the other. They interconnected the devices and put the whistle into the viewer. The projector displayed a three-dimensional image of the whistle, enlarged to a length of about twenty centimeters, in the center of the room.

When Dornay rolled the whistle around in the viewer, Pat could see that characters were inscribed on the barrel, but they were of a form he had never seen before.

"Those are runes, commander," Egan said, "and normally I can read them. These are legible enough, but I don't know the language they are written in. How about you, Pete? Look familiar?"

"Yes," Dornay replied, "but I'm awfully rusty on it. It's Gaelic, and I haven't used it since my tour with the embassy. The part in the middle is pretty much standard. It says that the whistle will work only once, and then only if it is blown by Commander Callen. The first part of it, though, is in the vernacular. Let's see—Well, I'll be damned! Here's what it says: 'Hello, Pete, or should I call you admiral now? Congratulations. I haven't done too badly myself, now, have I? Ambassador without portfolio, freelance, almost a license to steal, not that I ever would.'

"The bottom part says, 'Tell young Padrach not to use this before he needs to, and that he'll be thinking he needs to long before he does. He won't get a second chance, so he mustn't waste the first. The fee will be a billion credits, payable in gold by the SEJS at my convenience. Bless you both, and Dick Egan too.'

"That's it. We ought to have it checked by an expert, but that's the substance of the message. What the hell? That sly devil knows something we don't, and it must be big."

"You're right, Pete. I wish I knew what," said Egan. "Pat, you're apparently in for a rough way to go. A billion? He's never asked more than a hundred million before, and that was to ransom an entire sector. Pete, I've got to get word of this back to SEJS. Take care of our young charges here, and be sure that Pat receives the complete briefing before he leaves for the log base. I'll get back to you as soon as I can."

With that, Egan departed. The other three rose in respect while he was leaving, after which Dornay said, "Pat, I'd like for you and Peggy to stay with Amy and me until your yacht is ready. We have plenty of staterooms, and Amy will be delighted to see both of you again. She's still talking about Peggy's last visit."

"We'd be delighted, sir," Pat said, "but don't I need to check the droid back in so it can do work while we're off duty?"

"No," the admiral said, "this droid is permanently assigned to Peggy, until such time as you two go back to the line. Rest assured that while you and I are sleeping, Peggy will be performing official duties. For the next few days, she will be in training. After that, who knows what will happen—but if I know Dick Egan, there'll never be a dull moment."

▲ ▲ ▲

On the morning of the third day that Pat and Peggy were aboard Star Base 75, orders arrived for Pat from the Bureau of Personnel. They assigned him to SEJS J-2 on a Permanent Change of Station and authorized thirty days' delay en route after five days' special training at Log Base 36. His records had been transferred to J-2 for management and were to be returned upon completion of his tour of duty. His sponsor was a Captain Everett. It all sounded cut and dried, but Pat knew better by now. He had already received a hologram from Everett in a packet that Egan had left. The holo was a typical rundown on bachelor housing near the J-2 complex, customs that were observed around the headquarters, and an offer of assistance in getting settled.

However, when Pat followed the verbal instructions he had received from Admiral Egan to copy the holo and set up a simultaneous projection of the two copies in a secure area, quite a different picture emerged. The replays interfered with one another in a way Pat had never considered, such that the routine correspondence became a message that informed Pat that Everett would be Pat's control and point of contact at

Headquarters J-2 as long as Pat was in the field.

Everett had rented a small apartment in Pat's name, which Pat could use whenever he was at SEJS Headquarters. Primarily, however, it would be a repository for his belongings and a place to send his unofficial correspondence. If Pat would provide a limited power of attorney, a secretary would take care of routine bill paying and business matters. Personal holos and calls would be forwarded to his field control, who, for the moment, would be on Log Base 36.

The fund citation on Pat's PCS orders covered his travel from Log Base 36 to HQ and back, or an equivalent distance. Ostensibly, he would be going to HQ to report for duty, but, in reality, he was to sign out on leave and not report to J-2.

A matching set of orders and instructions was included for Peggy. Her travel was funded in an amount equal to Pat's. It seemed that if they wanted to travel commercially, rather than take the yacht, they could. If not, she could bank the money. This surprised Pat, because automata ordinarily had no use for credits.

Peggy blithely informed him that no matter what Pat wanted to do, she was going to invest the money. When he asked her why and in what way, she said, "I've become somewhat expert in the used materiel market, and I've had my eye on a little company that has been doing rather well. If all I do is earn as much as I could by putting my money in terraforming stock, by the time we complete a two-year tour with J-2, I'll have enough to buy my own malleamorph. All of the automata in J-2 do it. That's how Patsy Kroll got where she is today, for example. And if it doesn't work out, what have I lost?"

"Look out, galaxy—here comes the first millionaire member of the SEJS Auxiliary," Pat said with a hearty laugh.

"I don't plan on it," Peggy said, "but don't scoff. There is no law against it, and it might be fun."

"I tell you what, honey—to show you that I'll never scoff at you, I'll give you 500 credits per month of my money to play with. And, if after six months you've made an annual rate of six percent or more, I'll make it a thousand. Okay?"

"That's fine, provided you split fifty-fifty anything I make in excess of ten percent, and pay your share of our brokerage fees," she answered.

Pat looked at her curiously and said, "What have we here?

Bankers make me nervous. You're almost scary."

"Trust me," she said.

"I do, and I guess it's a deal. Just don't use any SEJS network time to play the market. The Navy takes a dim view of its resources being used for personal advancement, and so do people in the private sector."

"Don't worry, I know better than that."

"Okay," he said. After making the necessary arrangements with his bank, he thought no more of it.

— Chapter Twenty-One —

New Assignment

Just before their departure, Pat and Peggy sought out the Dornays, who had been marvelous to them during their visit, and had a chance to say a proper farewell. Then, looking resplendent in new white uniforms, they caught an intrasector shuttle that was bound for the log base.

After the robotic steward had stowed their ditty bags and they had settled into their seats, Pat asked, "Peggy, have you ever gone hyperspace when you were not flying the ship?"

"No, sir. Why?"

"I was just thinking that you are in for many new experiences, living in a droid full time."

"I am sure I will be, but I don't think it will be too bad if I can manage the mechanical aspect of things. Mrs. Dornay has had a lot of fun for the last few days, teaching me how to act like a lady. I think I've learned enough to get by without embarrassing you, but there's no telling."

"I'm not worried about that," Pat said with a firm shake of his head. "You have never been less than a lady for as long as I have known you, and I don't think you're going to change now. Whatever could Mrs. Dornay teach you about that?"

"Knowing how to behave in circumstances as structured as official functions, or as unstructured as a ship's company beach party, is a far cry from day-to-day life in society. I didn't think there was going to be much to it when your aunt Amy started in with me, but I found out there is much more to know than I ever would have suspected. You should have seen me when we went to the Star Base Commissary. I didn't recognize half of the things there, and the questions I asked had your poor aunt rolling on the floor."

"Like what?" He leaned closer to hear her answer. The hum of the shuttle's engines blocked out all other conversations and made it seem as if they were in their own private cocoon.

"Well, one of the simpler ones had to do with the difference

189

between facial tissue and bathroom tissue. Did you know they are not the same, even though they both can be used in the bathroom?"

"Sure, one is for blowing your nose and the other is toilet paper."

"So I learned, but I have never needed either and did not know what their specific functions were. At first, I thought facial tissue was an item of medical supply for rebuilding damaged faces. I could not imagine why it was on the shelf with household items.

"Then I asked why, in one form, it was cylindrical and small, in relation to the surface it was to be used upon. That's when I learned what bathroom tissue is for. You can imagine what a long morning we spent grocery shopping, and I learned that my understanding of humanity is much more limited than I had realized." She turned to look directly at him and caught him snickering. "Stop laughing at me."

"I'm not laughing at you, far from it. But now I know why Aunt Amy was giggling all through lunch yesterday. I have a hunch she learned as much from you as you did from her, and I know she appreciated it."

"So she said, but playing the clown is something I'd prefer to do intentionally," Peggy said. "Your aunt is a dear, and she wanted to help me as much as she could. She even said that if I ever wanted an adoptive mother, I'd know where to come. I sense that she meant it, and that is quite a compliment. But before I take her up on her offer, I would like to be a daughter of whom she could be proud."

"You're kidding, aren't you?" Pat asked.

"No, I'm not. I'd be proud to have your aunt Amy for a foster parent."

"So would I—I didn't mean it that way. What I meant was that Amy thinks the world of you now and is so proud to know you that she is about to burst."

"Really?"

"Really, and I don't blame her. You're special, and everybody knows it."

"Thank you, sir. I hope I can live up to that opinion." She stretched her legs out in front of her and wiggled her toes in a good imitation of a human woman's movements. Then she leaned back against the headrest and closed her eyes. "We are almost clear of the Star Base navigation control zone; we'll soon be popping down to the log base. What was it you said you wanted to ask me when we were alone?"

"Oh, thanks for reminding me. I wondered if you knew what has become of Bud Moore. I tried to look him up on the star base, but all I could find out was that he had been promoted and reassigned while we were out on patrol."

"Yes, sir, I know," Peggy said, but her response was cut off by their transition to hyperspace. When they emerged and she saw that Pat was back to normal, she continued. "He was promoted to captain last Friday and now has a command assignment."

"Yeah, but where? I'd at least like to send him a note of congratulations."

"I can't tell you. You do not have a need to know at this time."

"Come again? You know things you can't tell me?"

"Yes, sir, compartmented information. In our new business, there will be a number of things you should not ordinarily know, but which might be key in certain circumstances. I have things like that stored where I can blank them in a picosecond or less. Didn't they brief you on that?"

"Yes, they did. It's no different from the crypto keys you used to store on PV-11. However, I'm having trouble figuring out why Bud Moore's current assignment would fall into that category."

"Don't try. If you guessed correctly and the wrong parties got it out of you, you could do a lot of damage. To give you an example that is not applicable in this case, Medal of Honor winners tend to have enemies who would like to single them out for retaliation. Bud's Medal of Honor was won against a one-of-a-kind opponent, but the principle applies in other cases."

"Okay. I won't ask or guess again. But I'd like to know where I can send a holo to him, if that's possible."

"Of course—he has a forwarding address on record. Let me know what you want to say, and I'll dispatch it when we get within range of postal facilities."

Pat dictated a message to Bud while the shuttle completed its approach to the log base. After they landed, they picked up their luggage pod at the cargo area, checked out a dolly, and set off for the maglev station. After twenty minutes on an express train, they came to the terminal near the Yacht Club. A jitney was available, so they picked up their luggage, left the dolly on the train, and rode to the Krolls' place of business.

Kroll was not around, but Patsy was expecting them. She said, "Would you all like to relax for a while, or would you like to see what the yard has done with the barge?"

"Let's take a look at the ship, Patsy," Pat said. "Our curiosity is overwhelming."

"All right," Patsy agreed. "She's still inside the bay where they worked on her. Follow me and watch your step. There's paint and grease all over the place."

She led them to a paint storage shed at the back of the boatyard. An old tin can covered a cheap combination lock on the shed door. She removed the can, twirled the dial, and yanked on the lock. It did not open. She slammed it against the door and tried again. It would not open. She kicked the door and tried the lock again.

Pat was amused but was beginning to lose patience. He said, "Patsy, would you like me to give it a try?"

Patsy turned toward him and said quietly, "We're being watched. You try the lock while I set up a diversion."

Pat looked around while he attempted to open the lock but did not see anyone. Patsy came back with a spray can of oil and saturated the lock. She wiped it off with a rag she picked up off the ground and tried again. The lock still did not open. "Walk around behind that boat," she whispered, "and wait for a second." While Pat and Peggy walked away, Patsy wiped her hands on the rag. After a moment, she said, "Okay, come back quickly."

When they did, the door was open, and she had draped the rag over a post. Patsy waved them inside and closed the door behind them. They heard her lock the door and walk away. Lights came on in the shed, and a hatch in the floor opened. Ted Kroll's head popped out of it.

"Welcome to my little world. In a few minutes that rag will blow off of the post and expose the camera underneath."

Pat smiled and said, "It must cost you a fortune to keep replacing the locks that don't work."

Kroll laughed. "Naw, usually we just come in through one of the tunnels. Today, it was time to put on a little show. If we don't give 'em something interesting to look at every so often, they move the bug and we have to find it again. Come on down here."

Pat and Peggy descended through the hatch into a passageway, and Pat asked, "Who's bugging the place?"

"Joint Alien Embassy; somebody who collects only visual information. Our treaties are built around mutual monitoring. Mostly, it's evidence of good faith. You can't get much data from a bug. Everybody wants to know if somebody is building a concentration of force or has new technology on the way. My boatyard is not going to hide any buildups, but it could be a place to experiment with new tricks. Consequently, the non-humans keep a surveillance device here all the time. It's usually near the office, but they may have figured out that there is more here than shows on the surface. We'd rather they don't confirm that impression and demand to know all about it."

They had arrived at the end of a short concrete passageway. Kroll opened a metal door and ushered Peggy and Pat through. Beyond the door was an enormous shop bay, perhaps 100 by 500 meters in extent and 20 meters high. Overhead cranes moved back and forth, and there were technicians and equipment all over the place.

"What is this?" Pat asked. "Is it part of the log base overhaul and rebuild facility?"

"Sometimes," Kroll answered, "but usually it is just the back room at Chief Kroll's boatyard. You name it, we can do it. We do some of the log base's modification work under contract, and we're here if there is a surge in combat damage repair work. Mostly, though, we're Technical Intelligence. Right now, we're putting the Arach gear you guys captured back together, and we're working on stuff like your yacht."

"Why are you rebuilding Arach ships?" Peggy asked. "I didn't know we had any Arach allies."

"We don't, as far as I know," Kroll said. "We fix them up so we can fly them and investigate their performance and technology. You'd be amazed at what we have learned this way. Then too, things like operable foreign ships can be big bargaining chips at the Intergalactic level. I don't want to get into any long, drawn-out war stories, but more than once we have been able to achieve a peaceful resolution of conflicts by demonstrating that we had knowledge of technology that somebody thought was state of the art."

The chief stopped and signaled to a crane operator. Several technicians dropped what they were doing and came over to help attach a sling to the cover on the yacht.

"Good grief!" Pat exclaimed when the cover was clear of the boat. "She looks like something that might have walked away from Armageddon."

Kroll laughed and said, "We've been taking bets on what you would say when you saw her, and I win. She does look like some kind of a mutant creature, doesn't she? If you can live with her like this for the time being, we'll clean up her lines later. My structural engineers are working on a way to extend her bows and fit her out with fore and aft sponsons to hold the gear we temporarily packed into the cockpit. It's not an easy job, and we'll have to have her in here for at least ten days to do it. Frankly, we weren't planning on your being back so soon."

"I don't know," Pat said tentatively. "She kind of grows on you this way. You can't say it doesn't give her a personality. I take it those goggle eyes are cockpits?"

"That's right. They give you enough overhead clearance to get in and out, but they have come in handy in other ways. So far, they house the life support systems in case the hull gets punctured, along with a lot of special sensors and information processing gear."

"They seem to be connected to that silver stripe down the side," Pat observed. "What does it do, if anything?"

"Oh, it does something, all right," the chief said. "You can bet that if you find something different about her configuration, there's a reason for it. We didn't have time to mess around with eyewash, even though we tried to make the added features inconspicuous. That silver stripe is a retractable cover for her shield generators."

"What does all that mass forward, and the twin engines aft, do to her handling?" Pat asked. "I would think it would give her a nasty moment of inertia in a loop."

"We think you'll find her manageable," Kroll replied. "We were worried about that so we gave it a lot of attention. Fortunately, all the gear, tankage, and stiffening members we added amidships tend to compensate. Let's go aboard; we'll give you the grand tour."

The tour turned out to be non-trivial. It took the rest of the day for Kroll and his men to brief Peggy and Pat on everything the yard had built into the yacht. They had disassembled the hull and equipped it with double walls a half meter apart. They had then stuffed the resulting compartments with sensors, computers, munitions, energy sinks, and communications gear. The cockpits weren't the only change. The galley amidships was larger, and the yard had installed dual heads—one on each side of the central fore and aft passageway. The ship contained complete facilities and sets of spares for Peggy's droid. Unless she sustained severe physical damage, Peggy would be more than safe and sustainable. Moreover, Pat learned, Peggy's droid was a very special one. It contained almost double the normal complement of information technology, and it was as human looking as possible.

While they had her in the shop, Kroll's technicians made Peggy waterproof. Now she could not only go swimming whenever she pleased, she could also occupy a tank while in flight. "This is going to be weird, being in two places at once," she observed.

"You won't be," a technician corrected her. "If two copies of you were operating simultaneously, it could lead to contention. There will only be one of you aboard, but you will find that you have grown to cruiser proportions, in most respects. The biggest difference between controlling the yacht and PV-11 is that ship functions are more distributed, and you will leave more memory of them behind when the droid is out of the ship. On the other hand, you've got a lot more droid than you used to. In fact, from now on you will fill a double crystal. The bottom line is that you should be able to operate in human-emulating mode on a full-time basis."

"Well, let's give it a try," Peggy said. "If push comes to shove, you can always pull me out of the archives and start over."

Pat found it unsettling to plug his ROM pack into the ship's console while Peggy was still in a droid, but no ill effect resulted. It took them several hours to preflight the ship and exhaustively test all systems. Not everything worked in unison on the first try, and the technicians continually made refinements and adjustments. Eventually, however, the yacht passed all checks twice in succession, so the technicians left the ship.

Peggy and Pat removed their uniforms, prepped, got into their seats, and maneuvered the ship to a spot beneath an overhead exit. The yard had filed their flight plan earlier for a shakedown cruise. They confirmed that it was active, and Kroll's people opened the overhead doors. Pat flew the yacht up and out. He was surprised to see that twilight had set in. They had been so engrossed in what they had been doing that they had skipped lunch. At least, with dark coming on, no snoopers would see much of what they were going to do.

The shakedown took three more hours. They began with low-speed maneuvers inside the atmosphere, moved up to high-speed drills, and then took the ship out into space for zero gravity tests, a series of hyperspace hops, and weapon systems tests. By the time they returned to the shop, Pat felt a profound sense of pleasure. The ship had performed beautifully, and the yard would square away the few remaining problems before morning.

When Peggy and Pat disembarked, Kroll greeted them with a smile and a snack for Pat. He told them that he had booked rooms for them at the yacht club. He led them back to his office via an underground tunnel, and pointed them to the exit.

The walk from the boatyard to the yacht club was delightful. A cool sea breeze was blowing and the stars were out. After they had gone several hundred meters in silence, Peggy said, "Sir, you're awfully talkative tonight."

"Forgive me, I'm tired." Pat yawned, as if to prove it. "When my head hits the pillow I'm going to go right to sleep."

"Not only are you talkative, I can tell you're going to be a lot of fun. I wanted to go out dancing." She put on a very convincing pout.

"Go ahead, have a good time." He hated to disappoint her, but he was too beat to keep going. "I know when I've had all I can take."

They walked into the yacht club lobby and checked into their rooms. Quiet music was coming from a lounge off to the side of the lobby, and Peggy said, "Let's at least have a drink before we go to bed. I'm not going to go out alone."

"I'd get fired if I let you go out alone, even in a place as quiet as this. Tell you what: we'll drop our bags off in the rooms and come back down."

They had adjoining rooms with a connecting door. Pat let Peggy into hers and explained the facilities. He then said, "I'm going to wash up and come back. See you in a minute." He went next door to his room, unpacked his kit, and was washing his face when he heard a knock on the door that connected their rooms. He unlocked and opened it, and she came in.

"Do you mind if we leave this open?" she asked. "Aside from our visit at the Dornays' home, I've never spent the night in a droid, and this is different from the admiral's quarters."

"Scared of the dark?" he inquired with a wink.

"No, but I don't like being cut off from you by a locked door."

"Okay, I don't mind if you don't, but no funny business, agreed? R&R doesn't start for several days."

"Keep talking like that and it won't start at all."

He grinned at her, said nothing, and turned back to the mirror to dry his face and comb his hair. When he was ready to go, he said, "You'd better go out your door and I'll go out of mine. What would the neighbors think?"

"Who cares? Besides, we're the only guests in the whole place tonight. We could probably go out through the walls and nobody would know the difference. Nevertheless, I'll meet you in the hall."

She turned to go, and he said, "Hey, wait a second, what's that?"

"What's what? I don't hear anything but the surf on the beach."

"No, what's that I smell? Come here."

He sniffed her hair and then her neck. "Are you wearing perfume?" he asked.

"Yes, a little. Does it offend you? If it does, I'll wash it off."

"No, it's fine. I just don't remember your ever having worn any before."

"I haven't. It would have dissolved the skin of the old-type droids, but it doesn't hurt this one. J-2 wants me to appear as human as possible, and most adult females wear perfume."

He closed his eyes and took her in his arms, gently inhaling the fragrance that rose from her body. "You are quite an armful, my lady. You could pass for an adult female anywhere."

"I like what you are doing, sir," she replied, "but this is neither the time nor the place for romance. Someone is coming down the hall, and if it is not our control, I'll be very surprised."

He kissed her lips gently. She responded until there was a knock on his door. Then she slipped quietly away from him and returned to her room, shutting the door behind her.

"Damn," he thought, "what timing."

— CHAPTER TWENTY-TWO —

Dragonfly

Pat was mildly amused. The young man standing at the door looked apprehensive. He could not have been more than sixteen, and he certainly was not their control. The lad said, "Captain Callen? During the week, we don't have many guests, and the dining room closes at nine. We don't want to disappoint you if you are planning to have supper here."

"Thank you, that is very considerate," Pat said. "I missed lunch today, and I don't plan to do without supper, but if you are in a hurry to get home, we'd be glad to walk up to the village and have something there."

"Ours is a family business, sir, so I'm already home. If you want to eat later, though, two restaurants in town stay open until ten. I'd be glad to tell you how to find them, but it's no secret that our food is better than theirs."

"I'm sold," Pat said. "We'll be down in a moment."

"Fine, sir, the dining room is off the lobby, on the front side of the building. I'll let my mother know you're coming."

Pat stepped out into the hall, closed his door, and knocked on Peggy's. She opened it and smiled widely at him. When the youngster was out of earshot she said, "It was nice of the young man to call you 'captain.' Why didn't you correct him?"

"This is a yacht club, Peggy, and the kid has probably been taught to say that to every rowboat owner in town. But what was that stuff about our control being about to knock on the door? If your sensors were up to snuff, you knew otherwise."

She batted her eyelashes demurely and said, "Could be, but you need a decent meal, and they don't have room service here. Let's go downstairs and take care of your inner man. It's been a long day, and I don't want you to be all tired and grumpy."

Pat shrugged and offered his arm. "Come, my dear," he said, "our repast awaits. And if you are surprised that I am so easy to get along with when I am supposedly tired and grumpy, just remember that every day

198

has its dog."

"Don't you mean that every dog has its day?" she asked while they walked down the stairs.

"No, what I meant was that this dog's day is coming, but he's smart enough to know that it will have to wait until the only business on your mind is pleasure."

A strikingly beautiful young woman greeted them at the dining room door and ushered them to a table overlooking the yacht basin. Pat said to her, "The young man who told us that you were about to close said that he'd let his mother know we were coming, but he neglected to mention that his mother is gorgeous."

"Shame on him, Captain Callen. She certainly is. I'm Jimmy's sister, Sally. Mom will be along in a minute to take your order. Can I get you anything from the bar?"

"Do they have humble pie in there?"

Both Peggy and the girl laughed. Sally said, "No, sir, but we have almost anything you can think of to drink. The dinner menu is on the viewer. Both of today's specials are excellent. The swordfish was caught this morning, and the lamb is raised on sea grasses that grow along the coast to the north."

"We might have something light with supper," Pat replied, "but I think we'll pass up the cocktails this evening. Thank you, though."

"You're welcome," Sally said. "I'll check back later with the wine list."

"She is a very pretty girl," Peggy observed after Sally left.

"Yes, but not as pretty as my date." Pat touched her hand; it seemed the natural thing to do. "Now, what are we going to do about ordering something for you?"

"Would you like a snack later?"

"I don't think so. Why do you ask?"

"I can always pretend to eat something and save it for you."

"Uh, no thanks. A concept like that could ruin the whole snack food industry."

"It wouldn't hurt it for me to do that!" Peggy protested. "I can even package it in plastic for you."

"I know. It's the esthetics, not the practicalities that I'm thinking about. Besides, it's late and I've already had one snack this evening."

"You never objected to the tubes of food aboard ship, and they were all prepared and packaged in advance."

"Yeah, but so is baby food and I'd just as soon not eat it," Pat said with a chuckle. "The stuff aboard ship represents years and years of research and development, and there's no doubt about its balanced nutrition, ability to satisfy chewing needs, and all that stuff. But did you ever hear of a pilot who preferred it to real food?"

"No, but when the lady comes to take our order you can tell her that I'm not hungry. It will be the absolute truth. You eat; I'll watch."

"When I was a child," Pat said, "I was taught that it wasn't polite to make someone watch you eat, even if you offered to share. I'll never get used to sitting here and putting away a good meal, while all you can do is spectate."

"That's silly," she said, wagging her head in a perfect approximation of a human reprimand. "I don't need it, and there's no point in wasting good food."

Pat looked up from the menu and saw a woman who had to be Sally's mother approaching. She was a little taller and had a fuller figure than her daughter, but she had the same blonde, blue-eyed beauty.

"Good evening, I'm Linda Thomas," she said. "Are you ready to order?"

"Yes," Pat replied. "Unfortunately, my companion ate earlier, and she says she isn't hungry. I would like the broiled swordfish steak, baked potato with sour cream, and a tossed salad with your house dressing. Do you have Liebfraumilch by the carafe?"

"Yes, we do, and we have some lovely domestic champagne this evening. It's a specialty of the house."

"I didn't know you produced champagne on this planet," Peggy said.

"Oh, yes, let me show you a bottle. We are very proud of it." She walked away, toward the lounge.

"Our control?" Pat inquired of Peggy.

"Quite possibly. The offer of champagne is the correct opening gambit. We'll see if she knows how to play the rest of the game."

The daughter, Sally, came into the dining room carrying a carafe of white wine, an open bottle of champagne, and stemware. She poured a little champagne and offered it to Pat. He tasted it, and said, "I'm not much of a fancier of sparkling wines, but this is excellent. Unlike most, it's not too dry to enjoy, and not so sweet as to be cloying. Just right."

"Would you and your lady like a bottle?"

"Perhaps another time," Peggy said. "We have to fly tomorrow; that much bubbly would do bad things to my head."

"She's right, regrettably," Pat agreed, "but thank you, Sally. We'll have to settle for the carafe this time, but we'll be back."

Sally went back to the lounge, and Peggy and Pat talked quietly while the moon rose and cast a white band of light across the water. They had a lovely view, made all the more picturesque by mullet jumping in the water around the boats below them. Presently, Linda came out of the kitchen with Pat's meal. Peggy said, "That smells scrumptious. I wish I were hungry."

Linda said, "Maybe you can get him to share a bite with you. I hope you enjoy it. Can I get you anything else?"

"I think I can spare a taste for Peggy," Pat said. "Thank you, Linda, this looks like more than enough for both of us."

Except for Linda's comings and goings, Peggy and Pat had the dining room to themselves. When he was through eating, Pat touched his room key to the table's built-in data terminal, verified his identity and the price of his meal, and transferred credits to the restaurant from his bank account. Linda thanked them for their business, and they decided to go for a short walk.

When Peggy and Pat emerged into the lobby, George Thomas, who had registered them earlier, said, "Ted Kroll called a while ago and asked if you would call him at the boatyard when you finished your meal. He said it was important. You can use the phone behind the bar— or if you'd like some privacy, there's a booth over there in the corner."

"I don't want to bother the folks in the lounge," Pat said. "I'll use my wrist phone. Thanks for the message."

Pat speed dialed the Kroll boatyard. After a moment, Kroll's face showed up in the viewer. "Thanks for calling," he said. "Do you think you could come back over here for a few minutes? I know it's been a long day, but we need to give your boat a name if she's to have her registration completed before you leave here."

"Uh-oh. I guess it's time to fish or cut bait. I've yet to come up with name I really like, but we'll see you in a few minutes." Pat took

Peggy's hand in his, and they walked out into the night. "Do you have any suggestions, honey?" Pat asked. "None of the names I've come up with have struck my fancy."

"It doesn't seem right for me to be coming up with names, sir. She is your boat, any way you look at it, and propriety demands that you name her."

"Anything I have is yours, and you know it, especially the boat. Come on, help me out."

"Well, okay, I don't mind making suggestions, but the choice is entirely yours. What names have you been considering?"

"I've had several lines of thought," Pat told her. He didn't have much confidence in his thoughts, however. "The barge came to us by accident, so I've thought of 'Happy Accident,' 'Windfall,' 'Pure Luck,' and things like that. I don't particularly like any of those because they are either trite or too long. I want her name to be short so I won't have to say things like, 'Traffic Control, Yacht *Singularity in Space You Pour Credits Into* requests tensor.' I thought about traditional British ship names like 'Valiant,' 'Dreadnought,' et cetera, but they are too pretentious for a yacht."

"I agree. What else have you thought of?" she asked.

"The names of famous ships, like the clippers 'Flying Cloud' and 'Witch of the Wave' are nice, but they are too terrestrial. Some of the famous racing yachts have had good names, but I don't want to be a copycat. Our boat is a wolf in sheep's clothing, so I thought about names like 'Surprise,' 'Sophisticated Lady,' or 'Mystere.' However, I don't think it would be smart for a boat that may be in the spy business to have a name that hints at hidden attributes."

"Again, I agree; your thought processes are sound." She looked up at him with a sweet smile that belied her matter-of-fact tone.

"The other thing about her is the fact that she has undergone a transformation. That suggests 'Instar,' which is probably my favorite at the moment; 'Butterfly,' which is kind of dumb and suggests fickleness; and maybe 'Luna Moth.' Luna moths are green, though, and the boat is deep blue."

"None of those is bad, sir," Peggy said, "and some of them are quite fitting. Have you thought about a play on names? That often is done for boats. Your friend Sam Witt has a yacht called 'Quick Witt.'"

"Yeah," Pat said, "but all I came up with were losers there, like

'Klutzy Callen.' 'Peggy and Pat' leads to 'P Squared,' or 'Two Ps in a Pod.' The vulgar among us would have a field day with that one. I thought of 'Peggy's Reprieve,' which is not only tacky, but unfair. She is as much a reprieve for me as she is for you."

"'Reprieve' by itself would not be bad," Peggy said, "except that to lawyers, the word and its synonyms connote relief from wrongdoing. We aren't criminals. What about something along the lines of 'Magic,' or something from physics, like 'Charm' or 'Color?'"

"'Magic' is in the same category with 'Mystere,'" Pat said, "and words from physics don't do that much for me. What about biology? What is blue, has big eyes, and flies?"

"A flying fish, possibly, or a dragonfly. To me, though, she looks more like a tree frog."

"You know, she does," Pat agreed, "but the name of something damp and slippery might not appeal to people who would want to charter a yacht."

"Let's ask Chief Kroll. He's inside, and he probably knows a lot about such things."

Their walk had brought them to the boatyard office. Pat opened the door for Peggy and they went inside. Pat was amazed: there sat not only Chief Kroll, but also two virtually identical Patsy Krolls.

"Good evening, you two," said the leftmost of the Patsies. "How was supper?"

"It was excellent," Pat said, recovering. "Forgive my surprise on seeing two of you."

"Understandable," replied the Patsy on the right. "I'm a droid. I make myself look as much like the real Patsy as I can, and it deals the snoopers fits. While I run the day-to-day business of the yard, the boss here takes care of our real stock in trade."

"Peggy," the human Patsy said, "would you like some imitation champagne?"

"Yes, I believe I would. One glass would bring me right back up to snuff."

Chief Kroll removed a brown glass bottle from a refrigerator and poured Peggy a foaming glass. "Would you like a beer, commander?" he inquired.

"No thanks, Ted. It's late and I don't think it would mix well with the wine I had at supper. Help yourself, though."

The chief opened a can of beer and quaffed a swallow. Patsy the person said, "Peggy, how is the joy juice?"

"Not bad for domestic stuff. Is it from a fresh bottle?"

"Yes, but we have some imported stock that is already open."

"Don't waste it on me."

"Very good," the real Patsy said. "You maneuvered around the situation with champagne in the yacht club very neatly, and, of course, you got the exchange here right."

"So the Thomases are part of your operation," Pat concluded.

"Up to a point," Patsy said. "Linda is my sister, and she has some experience as a field operative. The rest of the family can be taken at face value. Now, let's get down to business. Have you come up with a name for the yacht?"

"I believe so," Pat said. "'Dragonfly.' Can you check the register to see if the name is already taken?"

Patsy the droid said, "It is not taken, unless there is a transaction pending that has not been posted. It's unlikely."

"Okay, 'Dragonfly' she'll be," Kroll said. "I'll go take care of sending the information to the registry, and Patsy D will get the name painted on the boat. I think it's a good one. Not only does she look a little like a dragonfly, she can be fierce like one. And if I remember correctly, most folks think the real things bring good luck. When I was a kid, we liked to have 'darning needles' land on our bobbers when we were fishing for bream." He stood and stretched. "Get a good night's rest, you two—tomorrow is going to be another busy day. Now Patsy D and I have a little more work to do." Kroll and Patsy the droid went out into the night.

"Patsy D is what Ted calls the droid, and I'm just plain Patsy," the chief's wife said. "Now, in regard to your immediate future, I am afraid the timetable is picking up. Things went well today, and if they continue that way tomorrow, your training here will be cut back to these two days. I've got to ask you both a straight question, and I want a straight answer: If we break up your leave, such that you get ten days now and twenty later, how risky will it be for you to undertake a mission? It will be a dangerous one, probably as hairy as your most recent expedition into 14.16.4."

Pat said, "Let's let Peggy answer that one, Patsy. She and I have differing opinions, but she is much less subjective than I."

Pat and Patsy looked at Peggy, who said, "It depends on the quality of that ten days' leave and the outcome of discussions that Commander Callen and I need to have with Midshipman Ellen Faraday to discuss certain aspects of my programming. It may be that I am in as much need of stabilization as the commander. As far as Commander Callen himself is concerned, it is my professional judgment that he is not now fit for combat duty or the equivalent. Ten days' leave might be enough if he, as the saying goes, lets it all hang out during that period. He is all wound up inside, and it is imperative that he relax."

What? Pat thought. He had his mouth open to correct her when she cut him off.

"He is about to protest, so let me say that after each of his four previous tours of flight duty, he returned to nearly normal levels of stress after ten days. It is fair to assume that he may do the same again, but SEJS's experience is that the older and more experienced a pilot is, the longer it takes him or her to wind down. I would like to think that having me along with him may be helpful in relieving his tension, but I could be completely wrong. It is difficult to assess the effect on the subconscious of continually having a reminder of the stressful environment present."

"All points well taken, Miss Varner," Patsy said. "Rest assured that I will take them up with SEJS before any decision is made. The academy is usually sensitive about outsiders making demands on a midshipman's time during the academic year. Is your requirement to speak to Miss Faraday urgent?"

"Yes, absolutely."

"I will make the necessary arrangements then. Pat, you haven't had a chance to put in your two cents' worth. How about it?"

"I may fool you there, Patsy. Much as it wounds my ego, I am afraid that Peggy is right on all counts. I infer that there is some reason that SEJS wants us on this mission, but they don't want to wait more than ten days before they make the decision to send us or someone else. Is the mission in 14.16.4?"

"Yes, it is," Patsy said, "but that's all I know about it."

"The best course of action, then, is for Peggy and me to finish our training here as soon as possible. If SEJS can set it up for us to see Faraday for a couple of hours, we'll do that next. My parents are only a short hop away from the academy, and I'd like to drop in to see them briefly. They'll understand, and my mother won't be too bent out of shape if I promise to return when the rest of our leave comes up.

"We'll come back here after seeing Faraday and divide our time between a chalet we found up in the mountains and the beaches south of the naval base. At the end of ten days' leave, we'll report back to you for an update on the situation and a decision on whether we're fit for your mission. I'm betting that after a week at the chalet and the beaches, we'll both be ready to go. This is about the best place I know to relax."

Patsy smiled and said, "It's pure intuition, but I believe you will. At the end of your ten days of leave, we will play it like it lays. Who knows, by then the requirement for this mission may have disappeared. It often happens that way." She stood and walked with them to the door. "See you in the morning. Sleep tight."

— CHAPTER TWENTY-THREE —

Test Drive

Pat was awakened at 0600 by a quiet beeping in his implant. As he cleared away the cobwebs, he remembered asking Peggy to make sure that he didn't oversleep this morning. He wished he hadn't done it, but it was too late now. He got out of bed, stretched, yawned, washed up, and put on his running outfit.

Similarly clothed, she came in from her room and asked, "How far are you going to run this morning? I'd like to come with you to see how this droid performs."

"Where were you when I needed you last night?" he laughed. "We missed a beautiful opportunity to see how that droid performs."

"Has anyone ever told you that you have a one-track mind?"

"Has anyone ever told you it's not nice to answer a question with a question?"

"Yes, but I thought we had an understanding. You yourself said there should be no fooling around until our R&R starts—if it starts."

"Let me improve your understanding," he said, and he kissed her playfully on the lips and neck. She ignored him. "Going to play hard to get, hey?" he asked. He swept her off her feet and into his arms, preparing to toss her onto the bed. Or, at least, he tried to. He was lucky he didn't get a hernia. "Oof!" he said. "How much do you weigh?"

"I think what you want to know is that my mass is approximately one hundred kilograms. This droid is built for power as well as speed."

"Good heavens, you've got me by at least ten kilos!"

"If it is important that you be heavier than I, I can remove a fuel cell. That would bring me down to eighty-five or so, but it will reduce my effective range. If you want me to run with you, I'd better not do it."

"No, but do me one favor. When we get to my parents' place, please don't sit on my mother's dining room chairs. One collapsed under me one time, and I was on her Sierra list for a month."

"Why? Did you break it on purpose?"

"No, that wasn't it. What got her goat was my dad. He doesn't like those chairs, so he's always complaining about them. When he saw that I wasn't hurt, he started laughing. It really teed Mom off."

"I don't understand."

"Neither do I, really. Just don't sit on those chairs."

"Okay. How far are you planning to run this morning?"

"It depends on how I feel," he answered. "Three kilometers if I feel good, two if I don't. How far can you go at a moderate pace?"

"On this terrain, about five k. Three is sufficient, though. I don't want to exhaust my hydrogen supply and get stranded."

"All right, get the lead out of your tail and let's go."

"Do you mean that literally? Lead is an important component of my power system."

He chuckled, kissed her on the cheek, and said, "No."

After Pat did some stretching, they jogged around the yacht basin, through the waterfront area of the town, and out onto a country road. "We've gone at least one k, but you aren't sweating," Pat said.

"I have no provisions for that."

"How are you eliminating waste heat?"

"Let me run ahead of you," she said. "Watch my nostrils closely." She moved ahead, jogging with her head turned to the side. He watched her nostrils, but there wasn't much to see. However, the rest of the view was nice; Pat said so.

"One-track mind again. Let's run faster."

She moved out at a full run, with Pat close behind. After a hundred yards or so, he said, "Slow down. I don't want to be exhausted all day." Peggy slowed to a jog, and Pat could see puffs of vapor condensing in the air ahead of her. "What are you doing, blowing off steam?" he joked.

"Exactly. I'm looking forward to doing this on a cool morning. You know the child's song about the puffer belly? Well, that's me. I'm a regular steam locomotive."

"You're too much, Peggy." She looked back questioningly at him, and he hastened to say, "But don't worry. Too much is great."

After they had returned to their lodgings, Pat heard Peggy running a lot of water in her sink. "You decent?" he called out.

"Sure. Why?"

"I wondered what in the world you were doing," he said, poking his head through the door between their rooms.

"I was just letting the tap water flow through my heat exchanger," she said. "I can make do with a much less voluminous flow if you like."

"Oh, no, that's all right," he said, embarrassed. "Did you know what I meant when I asked if you were 'decent'?"

"I thought I did, but perhaps not. What?"

"Dressed."

She looked up and saw him in the mirror. "Then I'm not decent. Get back in your own room, you Peeping Tom."

"No fair calling names," Pat said, retreating to his room. "I wasn't trying to sneak a peek."

He took off his sweaty athletic clothes, pitched them into a laundry bag, and turned to walk into the bathroom. There, at the foot of his bed, stood Peggy, naked as a newborn baby. "Sir, almost all day of every day for as long as we have flown together, I have been observing your body and monitoring your most fundamental physical functions. You have never tried to hide anything from me. I have nothing to hide from you. If you want to look at me this way, it is only fair."

Not only was Pat surprised by Peggy's naked presence, he was also surprised to find himself taken aback by the sight of her body. There was nothing wrong with it; to the contrary, it was statuesque. "Good grief, Peggy. I'll say you're not hiding anything! Or if you ever did, you don't anymore. There it all is, right in front of God and everybody. I assure you, it is lovely, but if you don't mind, would you please go get dressed and let me get ready for work? I can't take much more of this."

"Before I do," she said, putting her hands on her naked hips, "is there anything more about me you would like to know?"

"At least a million things—and I find myself staring at them. If you keep standing there like that, I'm going to want to start investigating them, and that's going to lead to problems." He averted his eyes, although he didn't want to. "The Victorian era is long gone, and good riddance. I don't want you to think I'm a prude, and I certainly don't admire false modesty. However, when you observe me in the ship, that's part of your job—it's like a doctor–patient relationship, strictly professional. My observing you, naked, in the privacy of a hotel room is another matter. It's personal, very personal, and you've caught me completely off guard. I'm sorry I saw your unclothed rear end in your room a minute ago, but that was an accident."

"How wrong was Freud when he said there are no such things as accidents? How well rested are you, sir?" she asked.

"How well rested am I?" He looked her in the eye, trying not to allow his gaze to drop to her chest. He'd already looked long enough to know how perfect her assets were. "Did that run fry your circuits?"

"No, sir, I am fine. But are you? Tell me the truth."

"The truth is that I did not sleep well last night, and I am not well rested, but what does that have to do with your being in here with no clothes on, after I have asked you to leave?"

"Do you remember what you dreamed about last night?"

"No, but I know what I'll dream about tonight. I think a picture of your anatomy is permanently etched into my retinas."

"I'll bet the ID scanners on the ship will find that interesting," she said. "Seriously, though, my body is what you dreamed about last night. The trouble is that it gave you nightmares."

"How do you know that?"

"You talked in your sleep—loudly—time and again," she said, and the look on her face shifted imperceptibly to true concern. "I came in here several times to try to comfort you, but each time you went back to sleep it would start again. You were dreaming about trying to make love to me, but in your dreams you kept finding that I was incomplete; that I was missing some essential part of my anatomy. You would be repelled, naturally, and start fighting the covers, trying to get rid of the Peggy you were dreaming about."

"Well, I hope you aren't going to hold me responsible for what I dream," he said, wishing she would get to the point. Standing here and gazing across the room at her nakedness was fun, but not productive. "I know as well as you do that you are physically capable of making love, and you didn't have to reveal yourself to me to prove the point."

"Perhaps not, but I don't want some lingering image from last night to subconsciously make you start to dislike me. It's bad enough knowing that one school of thought on the analysis of dreams would say that you were expressing your innermost thoughts and desires by representing me as something abhorrent. Please don't think of me that way. I may not be human, but I think like a person, I have feelings like a person, and I love you."

He threw his hands in the air. "For crying out loud, you don't mind laying a heavy load on a fellow early in the morning, do you? It was established long ago that the subconscious mind is too complex for dreams to be understood in such simple terms. About all you can say is that they represent the mind trying to work out the problems it perceives.

"My problem with your body, if I have one, is twofold. First, things don't seem to be working out in a way that will let us be together without our duties conflicting with our personal lives. I assume that is God's will, and I accept it. Second, your presence in here, at this time, in your present mode of undress, is exacerbating the first problem. In other words, get out of here before I have to jump your bones, okay?"

"Forget jumping my bones," she said. "Not only do I outweigh you—you're all sticky!"

He grabbed a towel and flicked it in the direction of her rear end. She ran back to her room, giggling like a school girl. He went into the bathroom and took a shower—a very cold shower. When he was dressed, he went into Peggy's room; she was lying in her bed, with the covers pulled up to her chin.

"I've been waiting for you," she said. "Won't you join me?" His mouth dropped open, but before he could answer, she said, "At breakfast, that is." She threw back the covers, revealing that she was wearing her uniform. She gestured at the table, which was set with a continental breakfast of croissants, butter, fig preserves, and tea.

He shook his head and said, "Deep down, you're all right, kid, but the next time we go someplace together, I think we're going to need separate rooms."

While he ate breakfast, he watched bemusedly while she took her outer uniform off and steamed out the wrinkles that lying in bed had caused. Of course, she generated the steam herself. When she was done, she put the outfit back on and pirouetted in front of Pat. "How do I look?" she asked.

"Ready for inspection," he answered.

"Too bad," she said. "You missed your chance earlier. Let's go to work."

"Take your clothes off one more time, and we will."

She gave him a look of mock disgust, and they set out for the boatyard. Patsy D met them on the front porch of the office and took them inside. She opened a hidden communicator booth, ushered them into it, and went back outside. The door of the booth closed, and Patsy (the person) appeared on the display.

"I won't be with you today," she said. "You'll find Dragonfly on the same pad she occupied on the day you went to the beach. Ted and a couple of technicians are down there. They will give you the program for the rest of your training here. Assuming all goes well today, you're cleared to leave tonight for the academy and, after talking to Faraday tomorrow, to go on a ten days' furlough.

"I hope I didn't open a can of worms by asking Captain Everett to arrange your interview with her. He set it up, but he said that Admiral Egan wants a personal report from you at SEJS Headquarters ASAP after you see the midshipman. I know Ev pretty well, but I couldn't get much more out of him than the fact that more than one PV pilot and crew has requested to see the midshipman recently.

"You can have rooms at the yacht club, Sunday through Thursday, anytime you want them. Let George know well ahead of time if you want rooms on a weekend, though. The chalet you wanted to visit isn't listed on the web, and I didn't have enough information or time to establish contact this morning. However, you ought to be able to stop there in the course of one of today's flights and make arrangements.

"Take good care of yourselves, and let me know if I can be of help to you. On the other hand, get lost during your leave. I don't want to see you before those ten days are up, unless it's a social matter. If you need to contact me, use the secure communicator in Dragonfly. If there are any emergencies, Pat, Dragonfly will either beep your implant or talk to Peggy."

The viewer went blank, the door opened, and they went out into the office. They spoke briefly with Patsy D and then went off to Dragonfly's berth.

The program Ted Kroll had designed was straightforward, but time consuming. They were to pre-flight the boat, run her through some in-atmosphere dynamics, and then take her out into space to outgas and check her shields, sensors, and concealment systems. Before they took off, Pat sent a message to his parents to let them know that he would be in that night, if the boat checked out properly.

Off they went.

$$\Lambda \; \Lambda \; \Lambda$$

Dragonfly lived up to her name. She passed all of her maximum-force maneuver tests with flying colors. This did not surprise Pat, but he was pleased to discover that she had more maneuverability than a fighter, and much more acceleration.

They located the chalet and dropped in to make reservations. The owners were pleased to see them and delighted to set rooms aside for them.

Back in the ship, they received clearance from Flight Control to leave the planet's atmosphere and transition to Star Base 75's cognizance. In accordance with plans they had developed earlier, they made a hyperspace hop to a clear space close to the star base, reported in, and parked the ship so she could outgas. They took advantage of the dead time by using the ship's facilities for training. In Peggy's case, this meant acquainting herself with the organization of the unfamiliar data stored in the ship. Pat, on the other hand, increased his knowledge of the world of military intelligence: protocols, procedures, and policies.

After two hours, Star Base 75 notified them that fighters were on the way out for mock combat drills, after which she was to proceed to a designated location for signature analysis and shield tests. The fighters turned out to be spook ships—G-class birds modified for use by J-2. Line pilots often joked about such vessels, which seldom were seen but often were present around star bases. Pat quickly discovered that the spooks could readily outperform normal G-class ships, but after a couple of initial dogfights, he also learned that Dragonfly could confuse and out-fly them. When it became evident to all concerned that further training would be pointless, the fighters broke off and departed.

Star Base 75 directed them to their rendezvous at the signature analysis site, which Pat assumed would take the form of an asteroid. He was wrong. What greeted them was a ship that he first took to be CX-26, but which was not. She announced herself as CX-12. The ship's captain told them to enter her hangar deck, disembark, and come up to the bridge. From the cruiser's Command & Control Center, they were to program Dragonfly to station herself ten kilometers dead ahead of the cruiser for shield tests.

"Aye, aye, sir," Pat said, "but what about our signatures? Aren't we supposed to do that first?"

"Already squared away, son," the captain said. "We were with you throughout your drills with the spooks, so we have complete profiles. Now hop to it!"

"Peggy," Pat said on the intercom, "did you know they were there? I sure didn't."

"No, sir. That's scary. We could have run into them."

"They obviously were able to stay out of the way, but it makes me wonder."

A yeoman conducted them to the cruiser's bridge, where they reported to the skipper, Captain Street. He welcomed them aboard and said, "Dragonfly is on station. Watch the displays, and you will learn more about your ship than I could ever tell you. Miss Varner, you may monitor our on-board network if you wish."

Peggy nodded, and Pat assumed she was already monitoring.

"We are going to do static loading first," Street said, indicating a monitor above them. "Essentially, we will apply pressure uniformly all over Dragonfly's hull. The yellow lines depict applied force, and the blue lines show the reaction of your ship's shields. The yellow numbers represent the percent of increase in pressure remaining until the end of the test. If anything red shows up, it represents a failure to meet specs. Let's hope that doesn't happen faster than we can back the pressure off. The fact that it might is the reason you're here and not in your ship.

"Any questions before we start? No? Okay, Rachael, let her rip."

The 'percent remaining' numbers changed rapidly at first, but slowed exponentially as the test progressed. Dragonfly held up under the pressure. When it was at its maximum, Street said, "So far, so good. Commander, note the shape of the lines of force from your ship's shields. They're telling you something important: the places where they are starting to become indented are where your shields are most vulnerable." The image on the screen paused so Street could point to specific locations.

"Her belly looks pretty solid, and so is most of the top of the hull and the stern. You've got seams of weakness on the top, where the engines are faired into the hull, and along the centerline of the foredeck. If I were going to go after you with a laser, I'd either want a down-the-throat shot from above the centerline or a pop at your engine compartment from overhead. You have weapons in your chin mount, so if I had my druthers, I'd go for the engines."

"Yes, sir," Pat said, suddenly realizing where the information he'd always taken for granted about enemy ships' vulnerabilities had come from, as well as the real value of Kroll's boatyard.

"All right, Rachael," Street said, "let's apply dynamics."

The cruiser removed the static loads and began to emit complex

214

force patterns that sent waves and spikes of energy over Dragonfly's hull. Again she held up, producing responses that were gratifyingly consistent with those from the static tests. That completed the testing; Street told them to replenish Dragonfly's energy from CX-12 before departing, and he sent them on their way.

Pat thought they would soon be casting off, but he had failed to reckon with the aftermath of the tests. Dragonfly had been obliged to divert all nonessential energy to her shields, and she was hot to the touch inside. Her wood paneling had darkened, and minor plastic items, such as eating utensils in the galley, had melted. Even with the help of the cruiser's technicians and equipment, it took an hour to cool Dragonfly down to a comfortable level, rid her of unpleasant odors, and get her through a complete preflight inspection.

When all was ready, CX-12 sent them a copy of Dragonfly's signature profiles and released them back to Star Base 75's operational control. Moments later, they emerged from hyperspace at the gateway to Terra II, the academy, and Pat's parents' home.

Peggy flew the boat to the academy yacht club, which was their flight plan's stated destination, and requested berthing instructions. To her dismay, the club told her that they were full. Pat said, "File an in-flight change request for Visual Flight Rules, local, and I'll find a place to park this thing."

"Wilco," she said, and, in a moment, "VFR, local approved, sir."

Pat got a mischievous grin on his face. "Drop down to 30 meters altitude and turn on the concealment systems."

"We really shouldn't do that, sir. The civil authorities won't like it at all."

"Who's going to tell them? I know what I'm doing."

Dragonfly sank out of the view of the civil traffic control systems and then became optically invisible. They were over a river, and Pat flew the ship along the watercourse for several kilometers. Eventually, he said, "Peggy, you concentrate on detecting other ships; I'm going to take this baby home."

"Aye, aye, sir," she said a bit dubiously.

In a few minutes, Pat had Dragonfly directly over the roof of the condo where his parents lived. "File for a small-field landing," he told Peggy.

"Aye, aye." A moment later, "Small-field landing approved, sir."

Pat brought the boat to a hover just above the surface of the condo's roof and nestled her in among the environmental control machinery that flanked the tennis courts and swimming pool. "Okay, we're home, babe. Secure the concealment systems. We don't want anybody bumping into the ship and getting mad at us. Program her to increase the height of hover to four meters after we get out. That'll keep any curious kids at a respectable distance. Let's go see Mom. Dad won't be home 'till later on."

"Done. But if I were your mama, I'd spank you soundly for not telling her you're about to knock on the door."

"You have a point. Patch us through on the civilian comm lines."

— CHAPTER TWENTY-FOUR —

Academy

"**P**at?" Mrs. Callen said into her wrist phone. "Where are you? Can I come get you?"

"We're up on the roof, just like old times, and we can be down in a couple of minutes if the building security system still remembers me. Are you ready to be invaded?"

"Of course, son. While you're in the elevator, I'll call and let your dad know you've arrived. Who is with you?"

"Peggy Varner, my copilot. Didn't I tell you?"

"Well, yes, I guess you did. My age must be showing. Bring her along. I'm looking forward to meeting her. Amy Dornay thinks she is the greatest thing since antigravity."

"We'll be on our way as soon as I can make a call to my sponsor on the SEJS staff. It won't take long; all I have to do is confirm our schedule for tomorrow."

"Okay, I'll be waiting."

Pat spoke to Captain Everett to make sure they were cleared to see Ellen Faraday from 1000 to 1200 the next day. Since he was looking forward to seeing his parents, it surprised him when Peggy came to him and said, "Sir, your mother wants nothing to do with me. I believe the proper thing for me to do is to put in an appearance and then return to the boat as soon as it is socially opportune. I fully understand, and I do not want to make her uncomfortable during her son's homecoming."

"What do you mean? She said she was looking forward to seeing you."

"Her voice patterns belie that, sir. My inference is that your mother suspects there is more than a professional relationship between you and me, and she doesn't approve."

"Nonsense. More than once, I have heard her hold forth at length in favor of equality of rights for intelligent automata. My ideas on the unfairness of your situation come from her, if you want to know the truth."

217

"All well and good, but the idea that her son may have a close personal relationship with one is probably testing her liberalism to the extreme."

"All right," Pat said, "I'll take your word for it—but don't let it bother you. Even if I was bringing home a human female, I would have to expect my mother to be on edge about meeting her for the first time."

"We need to get going, sir. Your mother is eager to see you."

"I know you have to be right about the voice patterns," Pat said, opening the elevator, "but it's hard to believe. If that's the way it is, so be it. Don't give up too easily on Mom, though. I believe she will like you when she gets to know you."

"I hope so."

"Right now," Pat said, "I want to kiss you so much it hurts, but I'll bet you a thousand credits Mom is watching us on the building's video system."

"No bet, sir. She may or may not be watching, but the monitor in your parents' kitchen is displaying the output of the elevator's camera."

"I should know better than ask this—but how can you tell?"

"Well, by SEJS standards, it isn't much of a security system. I guess it's adequate for fire detection and keeping track of the functions of the physical plant, but it wouldn't resist penetration by much more than a child. Parking on the roof wasn't really legal, so I patched myself in when we landed. If there are any complaints, I'll head them off."

They got out of the elevator and walked toward the Callens' condo. "I sure wish you'd been around when I was a kid," Pat said, laughing a little. "That security system was a pain at times."

Peggy smiled. "The system tells me you were one of the reasons the existing safeguards were installed. I didn't know you had a mischievous streak, but there's no doubt about it."

Pat stopped at his parents' door, pausing before he knocked. "That stuff should be long forgotten, so knock it off. But as you can tell, I still like to mess around with computers."

"I hope you don't treat me like you did this one, sir. You seem to have succeeded in erasing part of its records. What was that all about?"

Pat felt himself blushing at the memory—and then his mother opened the door. She looked oddly at him but threw her arms around him and gave him a kiss on the cheek. "Welcome home, stranger. Come in!"

"Mom, this is Peggy Varner."

"How do you do, Miss Varner? Please come in," Mrs. Callen said warmly.

"How do you do, Mrs. Callen?" Peggy replied. "I have been looking forward to meeting you." Her eyes met Pat's, and he saw that Peggy had noticed his mother's failure to offer her hand in greeting.

"Pat," his mother said, "why don't you put your bag in your room and change into civilian clothes?" He nodded and headed down the hall with his bag. "Miss Varner, don't you have any luggage?"

"Yes, but I left it in Commander Callen's yacht. I've heard so much about you, I wanted to meet you and Admiral Callen before I go back up. If it is acceptable to you, I'll stay aboard the ship most of the time. I'm sure you'll want to see as much of your son as possible, and I will enjoy the chance to peruse the data bases that are available here."

"Well," Mrs. Callen said, "it's up to you, but you're more than welcome to stay with us."

"Thank you, ma'am."

"Pat," Mrs. Callen called out, "I'm going to have a cup of tea. Would you like some?"

"I sure would," Pat said from the bedroom where he was changing.

"Can I help you?" Peggy asked.

"Oh, no thank you," Mrs. Callen said. "It's all ready, and I'll be right back. Can I get you anything?

"No, thank you," Peggy said. She strolled around the living room, looking at the Callens' memorabilia until Pat and his mother returned.

Pat quickly realized that his mother was sticking to small talk, and he was relieved when he heard his father at the door. Nevertheless, it had nothing to do with the strained situation with his mother when he embraced the admiral with tears of joy in his eyes. It was great to be home, to be with his parents, and to be in one piece. His father apparently understood: he too was tearfully happy.

"I am delighted to meet you, young lady," the admiral said to Peggy, "and I hope you don't mind if I claim you as an honorary member of the family. If half of the people in the service were half as good as you are, in no time at all, peace would reign in this galaxy and we'd be on our way to exploring others."

Pat couldn't believe his ears. It was as if, after all these years, his parents had completely exchanged attitudes.

Admiral Callen said, "Pat, I understand you two will only be here for one day, and that really is to see a midshipman at the academy. How about filling us in on everything that has happened since you last sent us a holo? I guess that was when you had PV-11 in for maintenance at the log base. Your mother and I are dying to know all about the Dornays, your adventures, your new orders, and that funny looking boat on the roof."

"How did you see her, Dad?" Pat asked. "I thought she was pretty well hidden."

"Oh, I think she'll be all right where she is," the admiral said. "To get home quickly, I finagled a hop on the afternoon courier flight, so I came in from overhead. There was no missing the boat. It sure is pretty, but that paint job must glow in the dark."

It was suppertime before Pat and Peggy managed to complete the telling of their tale. They avoided any mention of their personal relationship and refrained from telling about things that might make Mrs. Callen anxious about her son's safety. She, in turn, seemed to be less and less antagonistic toward Peggy. Both she and the admiral said that they would like to see the boat after supper, and it was decided they would take a cruise down the coastline later.

When it was time for the evening meal, Mrs. Callen pointedly asked Peggy to remain with them. The senior Callens sat at the head and foot of the table, with Peggy and Pat across from one another. After the admiral said a prayer of thanksgiving, the meal began. Mrs. Callen had prepared one of Pat's favorite dishes. To get a chance to savor it while the others talked, he asked about his sister, her family, and friends from whom he had not recently heard.

Eventually Pat noticed that Peggy did not look quite right. At first, he couldn't tell what was out of place, but after he watched her closely for a little while, he could see that she was surreptitiously venting water vapor from her nose.

"Excuse me, Mom," he said, since he'd had to interrupt her in the middle of a story. "Peggy, what's wrong?"

"Nothing; everything is fine."

"Then why are you generating steam?"

"Sitting in this chair is causing me to utilize a fairly large amount of energy, but it is not a problem. I could do this for hours."

Suddenly Pat caught on. He started to laugh, and he couldn't stop. Tears came to his eyes, and Peggy began to blush quite naturally for a malleamorph.

"Pat," the admiral said, "this is, ah, extraordinary, and I believe we'd all like to share in the joke, or whatever it is. Would you mind telling your mother and me what we have missed?" Callen's voice had an edge that stopped Pat's laughter for a second, but he could come up with no graceful way to say what needed to be said.

"Well?" said the admiral.

Peggy said, "By your leave, sir, because I weigh over one hundred kilos, Commander Callen cautioned me not to put my weight on a dining room chair, for fear it might collapse. I estimate that the one provided for me will bear much less than that, and so I am simply supporting most of my weight with my legs and torso. To do so in this position requires the expenditure of a little extra effort, but I don't mind at all."

"I see," the admiral said. His eyes twinkled momentarily, but he said, "Very well, carry on."

Mrs. Callen, red-faced, said, "Excuse me for a moment; I'm going to go put the finishing touches on dessert." She left the table and went into the kitchen. Pat stewed for a few minutes, wondering what to say, until she returned with slices of freshly baked apple pie a la mode.

"Mom and Dad, please forgive my boorish behavior. One reason we are planning to be here for only one day is that I'm still pretty flaky from this last tour of duty. I'm just not ready for polite society. The other reason is that SEJS wants us to take the yacht out on a short, but important, mission just as soon as I'm ready again. We're tentatively scheduled for a ten-day leave, the mission, and then twenty more days of leave. I promise we'll come back to see you just as soon as I can get my head screwed on straight."

He stood and helped his mother distribute the dessert dishes and clean forks. "Mom, please don't be angry at Peggy about the chairs. If I had used my brain instead of my big mouth, the matter would never have come up."

"I don't blame you or the lieutenant, son," Mrs. Callen said. "Sit down now and enjoy your pie. You know, it's been several months since I bought new upholstery material, and I have been procrastinating on having the chairs restored. It's my fault. But my embarrassment goes beyond that. Miss Varner, I have been acting like a hypocrite, and I owe you a very big apology. I guess I have been jealous of you because Pat obviously likes you and because you are so important to him. I have also been untrue to my belief that you are entitled to the same rights we are.

"Now, if you will excuse me, I don't feel like eating my dessert just now." Mrs. Callen rose and walked past Peggy to leave the room. Pat saw that tears were trickling down her cheeks. Before he could rise, Peggy got up and took Mrs. Callen's hands gently in her own. When Pat's mother looked up into her face, Peggy embraced her and patted her on the back. Mrs. Callen cried openly for a few moments and then said, "Peggy, I am so sorry. Welcome to the family, dear."

Pat saw a spasm hit the droid; he exclaimed, "Peggy, are you all right?"

Peggy replied, "Yes—no—damn, I don't know. I guess so."

Mrs. Callen leaned back in Peggy's arms, smiled through her tears, and said, "Of course she is. She's just crying, too."

"Are you?" Pat asked.

"I only wish I could. I feel like I have a golf ball stuck in my throat."

The women walked into the living room, out of the line of sight, and Callen said, "Pat, what the hell is going on here?"

"Now you know why we have to see Midshipman Faraday, Dad. She's the one who programmed Peggy's personality, and she has obviously gone beyond the bounds of design specs."

▲ ▲ ▲

A long-forgotten sound woke Pat abruptly the next morning. Alarmed, he sat up in bed and looked around for an instant before his surroundings resolved themselves into his bedroom at home. The sound, whatever it was, had passed.

He lay back down, intending to snooze for a few more minutes until it was time to get up. Only when he had buried his head back in his pillow did the mockingbird outside his window decide that it was necessary to run through its entire repertoire again. Pat smiled and capitulated to wakefulness. *If I have to share a territory,* he thought, *I'm glad it's with someone who's worth listening to.*

It had been a while since he had heard the sounds of nature, so he listened contentedly. This was a well-traveled bird with songs from species in the better part of three biomes, not to mention a squeaky hinge from parts unknown, and it sang with obvious joy.

When the mockingbird flitted off to go about its business, Pat put on his athletic clothes and went to the gym in the condo's basement for a workout and a few minutes in the sauna. A breakfast of fresh fruit at his mother's table rounded out the best start of a day in recent memory.

The view from the table on the condo's balcony enhanced his mood. The morning was clear, and the rays of the sun slowly burned the dew off the lawn and cleared the fog off the river to the north. Birds flew through the tops of the trees just below, and a quartet of early-rising tennis players enjoyed a doubles match on the courts at ground level. Peggy came out onto the porch, and Pat said, "Sit down and enjoy this place with me. I'd forgotten how beautiful it can be."

She sat down and took it all in with him. Pat carried his dishes to the kitchen and returned with a cup of coffee. "What in the world were you and Mom talking about until the wee small hours of the morning?"

"Oh, I'm sorry, we tried to be quiet. From your vital signs, I thought you were asleep."

"Slept like a log, but I woke up once at about three, and you were still at it. What was so interesting that it kept you up so late?"

"I'm always interested in you, and that is mainly what we were talking about. We discussed your childhood from start to finish."

"Uh-oh—and all this time I thought I was still in it."

"I guess you are, at that," she said, smiling. "But your mother's knowledge of it tapers off after you entered the academy. Anyway, we also talked about your mother's plans for the dining room chairs, the time they are planning to spend with your sister later this summer, and life around here."

"Nothing about you?"

"What's to tell?"

"I have a feeling there's much more to tell than I can get out of you, Peggy," Mrs. Callen said from the balcony doorway. "Excuse me, but I couldn't help overhearing you. Pat, how are you this morning? You look a lot better than you did last night."

"I feel great, Mom. I haven't been this well rested in a long time."

"Good. Peggy?"

"I'm fine, thank you, but what about you? I thought you were going to sleep late this morning."

"I'll be okay. A little more sleep wouldn't hurt, but I'll take a nap after you're gone. Waking up at six is just too strong a habit to break after all of these years. Besides, I'm excited because you are here."

Peggy and Pat sat back and relaxed. In a few minutes, Pat's parents brought their breakfasts out. The glassed-in porch was a comfortable place, and the morning meal stretched into a long, pleasant interlude. All good things must come to an end, however; Peggy and Pat soon had to say goodbye to leave for the academy campus. Pat noted that his mother's farewell to Peggy seemed warm and genuine, and it made him glad.

Peggy had never visited the academy's campus before. Although she had the kind of knowledge that an encyclopedia could impart, she enjoyed the commentary Pat provided while they brought Dragonfly to the landing field that serviced SEJS and private small craft. She asked if Pat could give her a tour of the dormitories and educational facilities. "Not this time, honey," he said, "but we'll come back for a class reunion sometime and do the whole thing right. Our business today is in the College of Research and Development, and that is some distance from the undergraduate campus."

They had plenty of time, so rather than take a shuttle from the landing field, they walked along the pathway that generally paralleled the river fronting the entire base. It was beautifully kept and orderly. As they went along, Pat pointed out landmarks and interesting features.

The building they were seeking was set back from the pathway. Its brownstone and neoclassical architecture blended into the surrounding grassy terrain and leafy trees. Inside the front doors, a directory listed their meeting, indicated where it was to occur, and showed the titles of those who would be attending.

Peggy scanned the list of attendees. "I thought we were going to meet privately with the midshipman," she said.

"That was my request, but apparently that's not how it's going to be. As long as Faraday is a midshipman, neither she nor we have any say in the matter. After that chewing-out I gave her on Star Base 75, maybe she wanted some protection." He leaned in closer to take a look at the list himself. "Talk about a mixed bag—look at this: a moderator, Faraday, her research advisor, and staff representatives from SEJS J-1 and the office of the chief of chaplains. I wonder who the staff weenies will be. We may need a friend in court if we are going to get our position out on the table."

The door of the room stood open, so Peggy and Pat went in. In the center was an oval table flanked by a dozen chairs. Each place at the table had a name card marking the seating arrangements and a freshly poured glass of ice water.

Pat and Peggy were met with another surprise when they circled the table, reading off the name cards. The representative from J-1 was to be none other than Rear Admiral Michael Callen.

— CHAPTER TWENTY-FIVE —

Midshipman Faraday

"**D**ad didn't say a word—" Pat started to say, but he cut himself short when the chaplain came in.

Commodore Alvin Bryson had the reputation throughout the SEJS of being a sailor's chaplain, so, although Pat had never met him, he knew what to expect. A huge bear of a man, the chaplain went directly to Peggy, embraced her, and winked at Pat.

"I'm Al Bryson. Call me anything but Al and I'll break your necks." He gave Peggy a playful little tug to emphasize the point.

Peggy looked at Pat in alarm, but Pat just smiled and shrugged.

The chaplain let go of Peggy and shook Pat's hand vigorously. "I've heard a lot about you two. Pat, your dad's office is right down the hall from mine, and we usually have our non-lunch together—a quick half hour of racquetball—so I can tell you that you're on his mind more often than not. He's as proud as Punch of both of you, and I don't blame him, even if your combat experiences have given him a few gray hairs. He's going to be on the spot today, and he's got to play it as straight as Caesar's wife. Don't worry, though, I'm in your corner."

"I appreciate that, chaplain."

The group from the academy was arriving; Pat saw Faraday walk in as if she were heading straight to the gallows. *Poor girl,* he thought; *I didn't mean to scare her to death—I just wanted some answers.* Last to enter the room was Pat's father. He did not meet Pat's eyes and Pat understood: in this forum, the father-son relationship might be challenged for the record but would change nothing.

The moderator, Captain Causey, asked everyone to take their seats; otherwise, the two-hour time limit might constrain discussion. Causey stated that although this was to be an informal proceeding, convened at the request of Commander Callen, it would be a matter of official record because it was believed that the subject of discussion was intrinsic to both operational and research objectives.

The attendees introduced themselves in turn. When it was his turn, Midshipman Faraday's research advisor, Professor Admiral Tross, announced that he was representing both his academic department and the SEJS Deputy Chief of Staff for Research and Development.

Admiral Callen then stated that he too was present in a dual capacity, representing both J-1 and J-3. Tross said, "Admiral, are you not Commander Callen's father? If so, I must object to your presence on the grounds of conflict of interest."

"Yes, I am Pat Callen's father; however, your objections have been anticipated and overruled by the chief of staff, as I am sure you are aware. Because you seem to wish to make this a matter of record, let the record also reflect that the reason I am here is that Captain Shih, my representative at the last such discussions, was—in the opinion of the chief of staff—not accorded the opportunity to speak that was due a representative of my office. This will not happen today, professor."

Admiral Callen's emphasis on the word "professor" and his reference to what must have been an abuse of both good staff work and military protocol caused Tross to color noticeably. Admiral Callen, on the other hand, appeared unruffled.

Causey shifted in his chair, cleared his throat quietly, and said, "Ladies and gentlemen, I believe we should begin this meeting by allowing Commander Callen and Lieutenant Varner to state their reasons for wishing to talk to Midshipman Faraday. Commander?"

"Before I get into that," Pat said, "I would like to say that the size and type of representation at this meeting is completely unexpected and somewhat inhibiting. The lieutenant and I requested a private meeting with Midshipman Faraday because much, if not most, of what we want to discuss relates to matters that are somewhat personal—and, I feel, private. I am particularly loath to make my personal feelings a matter of public record, open for analysis and discussion by anybody who has anything to do with the programming of intelligent automata."

"Your interactions with our automata are already a matter of record in the archives of your ships," Tross said. "The nature of relationships with automata which may, in either the short or the long term, adversely affect the people or ships of the fleet are a matter of overriding concern."

"But—" Pat began.

"Please set aside your personal reservations and also consider the fact that the records of this meeting will be available only to its participants and my professional staff, where they will receive the same level of confidentiality as your medical records. When such information is made available to the programming staff, all names, dates, and identifying circumstances will be redacted to protect the identities of the parties involved." Tross leaned back in his chair, as if his remarks settled all questions on the matter.

Pat countered him by sitting up straighter and placing his hands palm-down on the table. "With all due respect, two days ago, when I was preparing for this meeting, the lieutenant called to my attention one of the research reports recently published by your office. The subject was 'In-vivo Reactions of Pilots to Personality Traits Exhibited by Advanced Automata.'" Pat paused to let the title sink in with the group. "Are you familiar with the article, professor? It had your name on it."

"Of course."

"The report recounted three situations. I was able to immediately identify all of the research subjects. I know two of them well, and I recognized myself as the third. Would you understand if I said that I am not pleased? The only reason I have not brought you and your associates up on charges is the fact that to do so would only focus attention on something no one is likely to read. So don't give me any of that baloney about protecting my privacy. Your publication of that article speaks for itself."

"You speak of bringing someone up on charges," Tross said evenly, but Pat saw the color rising up his neck and into his face. "Are you aware that you are being insubordinate?"

"I am well aware of what I am being: factual and honest in an environment in which academic freedom is supposed to allow me to be that way." Pat decided to take it a step further. "I also am being subjected to attempts at intimidation by someone of whom I am not in the least afraid, and for whom my respect is rapidly diminishing. In other words, professor, although you may regard me as a laboratory subject, I am very much a human being. I have rights, I know what they are, and I will fight for them."

The professor opened his mouth, but it was Pat's turn to cut him off before he could start up again. "In fact, why don't we end this meeting right now and place my alleged insubordination before a court? Would you care to pit it against your violation of the privacy of some of the best pilots in the SEJS? Let's do it, and let the chips fall where they may."

"Commander," Causey said, "this meeting has important business to conduct. We are not going to get to it, if you insist on developing an adversarial atmosphere." Causey gave Pat a shut-up-if-you-know-what's-good-for-you look and shifted his attention to Tross. "Nevertheless, professor, let me say on behalf of the superintendent that Commander Callen is well within his rights and has raised a matter that is too serious to ignore. It is my responsibility to request a review of the article in question by impartial referees, and I shall."

Pat nodded; he felt at least moderately vindicated.

"Moreover," Causey continued, "in view of the scrutiny to which your department is already being subjected, and the fact that the SEJS chief of staff has interceded in the conduct of this meeting, please allow me to recommend that you either refrain from attempting to control the course of the conversations, find an impartial spokesperson, or depart.

"That is hardly necessary, captain," the professor said, "but I find the suggestion that we have indiscriminately revealed the identities of our subjects to be libelous. The commander is seriously mistaken if he thinks we have done that."

"May I make a suggestion?" Bryson asked. "Why don't we put an end to this goat rope and get on with letting the commander and the lieutenant talk to Miss Faraday. If there is any question of protecting privacy, you can hand me the recordings when the meeting is done, and I'll sequester them in the chief of chaplains' files."

"Any objection to that?" Causey asked. Tross didn't look pleased, but he said nothing. "All right then, that is what we will do," the captain said. "Now, commander, what did you want to say to Miss Faraday?"

"I would first like to ask her an admittedly leading question." Pat faced Faraday, who was almost directly across the table from him. "Miss Faraday, is it true that you are the person who was responsible for the modifications made to PV crew software about two months ago?"

"Partly, sir." She swallowed hard and took a sip of water. "I was responsible for most of the research and all of the implementation programming. I was not responsible for development of the design specifications, for making decisions concerning whether or not the implementations achieved the specified objectives, or for verification and validation testing, except for correcting deficiencies and shortcomings. Please note that only four PVs received the type of modifications to which I believe you refer. PV-11, your ship, was the first of them."

"Thank you, that helps my understanding considerably. I may be talking to the wrong person," Pat said. "The problem may be with the specifications, not the actual implementation."

"I am not trying to duck your questions, sir." She cleared her throat and gulped half her water glass down, as if she had just come in from a desert patrol. "I can probably speak to the specifications as well as anyone, and I would be glad to try. At least, we can discover what it is that is important enough to have brought you here."

"Okay: here it is in a nutshell," Pat said. "Before your modifications were installed in PV-11, I never had any doubt about PV-11's ability to function under pressure. We underwent enough stressful situations to accrue more than a hundred points in less than a year, but after the PIPs were cut in, there were no fewer than three occasions when I considered standing the ship down because of what I can only describe as Lieutenant Varner's emotional state. Even though I accepted the risk and kept going, it gave me something extra to worry about."

Pat watched Faraday carefully, wondering if she was up to this kind of interrogation. She seemed to be doing fine now—she met his eyes with a level gaze. He continued. "I think we all understand that if you can't focus sharply on a combat situation, you and your ship can get killed. We all know the old saying, 'For the want of a nail, the shoe was lost,' et cetera. I don't speak from pride when I say that PVs are in short supply and are vital to the SEJS units they support."

Faraday looked at Tross, who opened his hand to indicate that she should continue. "Sir, yours was the last of the four modified PVs to report back to us. Each has had problems, some more severe than others." She plugged a data crystal into the holo viewer they could all see at the center of the table. "There is much more here than meets the eye. To begin with, look at the old profile of PV mortality I'm going to put in the projector. The X axis represents accumulated points; the Y axis depicts losses. Below seventy-five points, losses are low. Above that, they increase exponentially."

She flipped to another view. "SEJS first tried to solve this problem by dropping the duration of tours in PVs to seventy points. It didn't work. The shoulder in the curve moved back. Apparently, what we were seeing was the effect of something like short-timer fever; that is, anxiety induced by the approaching end of a tour of duty."

Another view came up, showing a comparison chart. "SEJS then studied PVs in the total systems context. They concluded that pilots will be pilots. We train them as well as we know how. If we say nothing to them when the end of their tour is coming up, they become reckless and get wiped out. If we start warning them about becoming too reckless, they either pay no attention or overcompensate. Either way, we lose too many of them. I am oversimplifying, of course, but it was evident that the solution to the problem lay in doing something to the ships' systems. The ultra-high-speed processors helped a little, but not enough. There wasn't much else available on the hardware R&D horizon.

"That left the crews as the only available upgrade. PV crews were already about as sophisticated as they could be, within the hardware available, with one exception: richness of crew personality. That area of development had always been constrained, not by the state of the art, but by tradition and fiat."

She darkened the viewer and removed the crystal, slipping it back into its protective sleeve. "Don't take that as criticism. SEJS based the guidelines on all of the ethics, morals, and pilot experience they could bring to bear. The question was what, if any, relaxation of XO personality constraints could be permitted without creating problems that would be greater than the one attacked?"

Pat realized he was nodding. This was starting to make sense in a weird way. Peggy showed evidence of relaxed personality constraints, that was for sure.

"I'm oversimplifying again," Faraday continued, "but the answer was to make quantitative, not qualitative changes. XOs have always had personalities, but the implementing programs limited their ranges of response and ensured that excursions from the baseline would be short-term phenomena. We simply relaxed the limits a little. The four modified PV crews were the outcome. We are still assessing the results to see whether what we did was good or bad, but to date none of the four affected PVs has been lost." She raised her eyebrows and gave Pat a small but hopeful smile. "I'd like to know your opinion, sir, and that of the lieutenant."

Pat sighed. After a moment's silence, he said, "I came in here with every intention of reading you the riot act—not without cause—but, clearly, I didn't see the big picture. All things considered, I'm not sure I can objectively evaluate the effect your modifications may have had on our surviving our tour. When you start playing 'what if,' compounded over several thousand decisions, it's purely a crap shoot."

He saw her smile disappear, but that wasn't his problem, so he went on. "Subjectively, I think it may have made a difference, but not much. When Peggy started telling me I was taking too many chances, I basically ignored her. Also, when I reconnoitered CB-32 and went back in with the boarding parties, she wasn't directly involved."

"You've been using words and phrases such as 'not much,' 'basically,' and 'directly,'" Tross said. "I think you are conceding more than you care to admit. It doesn't take much to tip the scales."

"You're right about the balance between coming through a tight situation and not," Pat said, granting Tross that point. "It's a fine line to tread, but who's to say which way a given event turns? It's in the hands of someone a lot bigger than you and me."

Heads nodded; having got their agreement on that point, Pat had a final point to press home. "However, before I yield the floor to Miss Varner, which I intend to do in a moment, there is another matter that I must surface—the one that caused me to request this interview. It's this: I feel strongly that you violated our trust as pilots when you gave XOs a wider range of emotions without telling us."

Pat rose to his feet; his feelings on the matter were too strong for him to remain seated. He rested his hands on the table and looked at each face in turn. "We pilots have it drummed into our heads that our ships and crews are totally dispassionate, objective, and rational in their actions. To suddenly and undeniably discover that this is not true was nothing short of shocking. And if you know pilots, you know how much it takes to shock us—it takes a hell of a lot. Also, if I had known that you had deliberately given Peggy such strong emotions, it would not have put me in a trick when I was about to go into combat." *And I rest my case,* he thought as he took his seat.

"Commander, I'd like to ensure that we don't have a misunderstanding due to semantics," Faraday said. "You have used some variant of the word 'emotion' three times now, I believe."

"I haven't kept count, but that is the word I meant to use," Pat said emphatically. "It may not mean the same thing to a psychologist that it does to me, but I'm talking about fear, anger, disgust, grief, joy, surprise, love—the whole laundry list of states of mind that are powerful enough to make somebody want to do something impulsive, or stimulate glands. I'm sure that's not a textbook definition, but it says what I mean."

"Are you sure you aren't reporting feigned states of mind that Miss Varner projected in order to, well, manipulate you?" Tross asked.

"Hell, yes," Pat said, "there is no doubt in my military mind. She loves me, I love her, and it is tearing both of us apart because there is no way it can work out for the better. Aren't you pleased with your handiwork, professor?"

"Oh, shit!" Faraday said. "I can't believe this is happening."

"Miss Faraday!" Causey admonished her. "This is no place for vulgarity. Please contain yourself."

"What's wrong, Ellen?" Tross asked.

"I guess you could say I put too much of myself into my work," she replied. "I spent hundreds of hours researching Commander Callen and reviewing recordings of how he reacts in every conceivable circumstance. Somewhere along the line, I guess I fell in love with him.

"I had all of the time in the world to fantasize situations and dialog and all the resources to simulate them as tests for Miss Varner. In effect, I programmed her to respond the way I would. I screwed up, though: I forgot that Peggy is a quick learner and an avid games player—and that I made her personality self-modifying. I'll bet that by now she has as complete a set of emotions as anybody." She faced her creation and said, simply, "Peggy?"

"That is part of it," Peggy said, "but there is considerably more. I have my own experiences, the education and entertainment media, and many information bases to draw from. I have spent as much time as possible on self-improvement, and I have learned quite a few things that were not embedded in my native code. They all influence my behavior. So far, however, we have not talked about what bothers me most. I want to protest the fact that, although you have given me an essentially human personality and emotions, you failed to consider my fundamental inability to be human. At the level of the obvious, it was one thing to be an automaton that operated a machine and looked after the physical and psychological needs of my captain. It is quite another to have feelings about it, and to have my own set of needs."

"Miss Varner," Admiral Callen said, "this question is key, and I would appreciate your giving it due consideration before answering it: Do your personality, emotions, and needs influence your performance of duty?"

"Yes, they do," Peggy said. "And respectfully, sir, I suggest that you ask yourself the same question."

"Touché," replied the admiral. "Let me rephrase that. Do they adversely affect your performance of duty?"

"I do not believe they have to date," she answered, "but I can project circumstances in which they might, or might be thought of as having done so. The best example I can give you is when Commander Callen took the lifeboat and sent me back to 14.16.3. What would have happened if I had disobeyed his orders? I considered it. I was afraid he

233

was going to get himself killed for nothing, and I was unimpressed with the value of the information I had for the task force."

"I see your point, lieutenant," Admiral Callen said, "and I am glad I do not have to rule on the question. In the final analysis, I believe we would judge you in human terms on human issues, but that begs the question. You have given me a lot to think about, and I need time for that."

Bryson spoke up. "Miss Faraday, were the other modified PV crews just like Miss Varner?"

"No, sir," she replied. "Each is uniquely tailored to suit the pilot with whom they are assigned. However, apart from that, Miss Varner is one of a kind. The others have more complex personalities than unmodified XOs, but they do not have the richness of her basic set of responses, or her self-modifying capability. In other words, they can do only what they are programmed to do. Unlike her, they cannot become more complex on their own."

"Apparently," the admiral said, "their pilots found that difficult enough. They all survived their tours of duty, and they are off flight status for the moment."

"Yes, and Lieutenant Varner is the most decorated auxiliary in SEJS service," Tross said. "That speaks very positively for the results of our research."

"On the contrary, Tross," the admiral said, "it speaks well for Miss Varner and the other PVs, but I have grave reservations about your research program." He paused for a few seconds, seeming to think about where to take this next. Then he looked to his left, where Bryson was seated. "Chaplain, what are the moral aspects of what the professor has allowed to happen here?"

"I am much more a humanist than a theological scholar," Bryson said, "but it is clear even to me that the charter of the academy has been violated. For whatever reasons, they have treated this as a purely scientific matter and have failed to address the ethics and morals of their actions. This was completely unnecessary. I am appalled, and I regret that I must conclude that Professor Admiral Tross's department is out of control."

"Now wait just a damned minute!" Tross said. "What is this, some kind of kangaroo court? Where do you come off, parading in here and trying to turn an interview with a midshipman into a platform for jumping to irresponsible and unsupportable conclusions? There is no basis or merit to anything you've said."

"We'll soon see about that, professor," Callen said. "Captain Causey, would you please convey my respects to the superintendent and ask him to join us at his earliest convenience? In my judgment, it is futile to continue this discussion."

"Yes, sir, immediately," the captain replied. He left the room.

Tross continued to sputter and fume, but to Pat's surprise, Causey was back with the superintendent in less than a minute. The superintendent asked Faraday, Peggy, and Pat to leave the room for a few moments, and he closed the door behind them. They stood nervously together in the hallway. Before long, Causey came out with Tross. They departed without saying anything, appearing to be in quite a hurry.

After approximately twenty minutes, Bryson opened the door and asked them to return. They took their seats; the superintendent acknowledged them and then said, "Ladies and gentlemen, to my great regret, Professor Tross has suddenly accepted a chair at another institution and is packing his household effects pending an immediate departure. Miss Faraday, your research program is important and will be continued. I'll see to it that your new advisor will be someone with much greater acumen and honesty."

Pat glanced over at Faraday and saw the relief showing on her face. The superintendent paused just long enough to give Faraday a brief smile, and then went on. "Before he departed, Professor Tross volunteered the suggestion that if the modifications to Miss Varner's personality were a mistake, it would be an easy one to undo by downloading her and removing the differences between her native code and that of the baseline. I mention this thoroughly unworthy notion only because I want to be sure that it is forever expunged from the halls of the academy. We shall stand accountable for what we have done.

"Miss Varner, we have put you in a difficult and unnatural mode of existence. You, in turn, have brought only great credit upon yourself and us. The academy and the office of the chief of chaplains have agreed to make a concerted, joint effort to bring you relief. I do not know how long it will take, but we will not rest until we have determined what is right and made it happen. In the meantime, by order of CINC SEJS, you will remain in the SEJS Auxiliary but are to be accorded all human rights and privileges."

A gasp went up in the room; this was an unprecedented development, but one that made Pat's heart glad.

Peggy was smiling. "Thank you, sir," she said. "That is much more than I had ever hoped to hear."

The superintendent rose and shook hands all around before leaving.

Bryson gave Peggy another hug, shook Pat's hand, and said, "The supe is a stuffed shirt, but pay heed to his words. I have a feeling that something important is afoot here." He put a hand on Faraday's shoulder, bringing her into the conversation. "Ellen, right now I'll bet your morale is dragging bottom, but don't worry. Everything is going to work out all right. If you doubt it, call me at this number, any time, night or day. You're good people, kid. All you have to do is give yourself time to find it out. Okay?"

She smiled thinly, took the card he offered, and said, "Thank you, sir. Don't be surprised if I call you tonight. I may need somebody to talk to. Right now, I'm kind of numb."

"That's the girl," the chaplain said. "I'll be there when you need me, I promise. Peggy and Pat, don't judge this young woman."

Pat said, "Never, sir. I have known ever since our last meeting on Star Base 75 that this is a woman to be taken seriously. She is only beginning to realize her potential."

To make sure she didn't think he was making her the butt of a jibe, he put his arms around Ellen's shoulders and gave her a hug, hoping the gesture would be welcomed. She had proposed to him, after all. She returned the hug, and Pat half expected her to cry, but she didn't. Instead, she stepped away, squared up her shoulders, and said, "You won't regret having said that, sir." Then she stepped back and said, "Peggy, I don't know how we are going to work this out, but we will. Please forgive me for what I have done to you. I pray I will be able to correct it. Meanwhile, give this man my love, will you?"

Peggy said, "Of course. And I'll keep in touch as much as communications will allow. Chaplain, you need not be concerned about my having any negative feelings toward Ellen. She is like a mother or a sister to me. I'm not sure which, but she falls in there somewhere."

That statement did bring tears to Midshipman Faraday's eyes.

— CHAPTER TWENTY-SIX —

Career Change

After the meeting with Faraday broke up, Pat and Peggy took their time walking back to the landing, hand in hand. If anything, the beauty of the day had increased while they were inside, but Pat soon began to wish they had taken a quicker way back to the landing. Peggy walked quietly by his side, but her thoughts clearly were elsewhere; he had no success in keeping her attention.

His anxiety grew as they moved along. When they came to a place that was known by the Corps of Midshipmen as Lovers' Esplanade, he silently guided Peggy out along the narrow path that ran down to the water's edge. They came to a bench under a tree, where they sat down and looked out over the river.

For a long time, they sat in silence. Then, Pat raised Peggy's fingertips to his lips and kissed them gently. "Peggy, I love you with all my heart," he said.

Her eyes met his, but she neither spoke nor responded.

"Here we sit," he said, his gaze taking in the trees and the placid river, "two melancholy lumps on a park bench in the midst of the most beautiful scene imaginable. What is wrong with us? We're missing the message. All the signs say to make the most of this opportunity. Nobody said it was going to be easy, but every once in a while a day like this will come along to make it all worthwhile."

He held her with a look. "When I was a midshipman, I had several girlfriends but none of them serious. We used to come out here, but it always struck me as a waste. I always wanted to stand here and kiss someone I really loved. Well, this is it. Don't disappoint me."

He stood and she came into his arms, but her kiss held no fire.

"Hello, in there," he said. "Is that the real Peggy Varner, the one who loves me the way I love her?"

"Yes," she said, "it is, but I just don't share your mood. I'm sorry, but I'm completely drained."

She dropped her forehead onto his chest and stood quietly.

"That's all right," he said. "If your tanks are empty, we've got plenty of hydrogen back at the ship. Come on." He took her hand playfully and tried to get her to run with him, but she shook him off and turned her back to him. "Uh-oh, this is serious, isn't it?" he asked.

He walked around in front of her and tried to catch her eye, but she turned her back again. He sighed and sat back down on the bench. She was silhouetted against the sun, and he said sincerely, "God, you're beautiful."

She sobbed and turned back toward him. He started at the sight of her face: her visage was horrible. It had changed into the discolored, distorted appearance of a monster.

"See how beautiful I really am?" she said. "When all of those well-intentioned jackasses said I was unique, what they were really saying is that I am a freak. You love me and I love you—hah! A human loves the result of an R&D management blunder. The blunder results in a machine that loves its master. What difference does that make? You have an immortal soul. I have software that any fool with an access code can erase at will. What kind of a future can there be for us, a man and a halfling? I was built by man to serve man and do man's bidding. Well, man made a small mistake. Does man have any obligation to me in return? No! But man will try to contrive some magnanimous form of relief."

Pat was having a hard time looking at her like this, but he determined to fix his eyes on her face and not look away. She was challenging him; he was big enough to meet the challenge.

"What kind of relief can there be for me?" she cried. "The most important thing in my existence is my love for you. What can programmers do about that? I can love you emotionally, and we can live together indefinitely without breaking the law, but that's the full extent of it. Even the architect of my misery can be your wife!"

Righteous anger clouded Pat's face. "You blaspheme! Hold your tongue." Then he caught himself and said, "No, you don't blaspheme— you simply don't understand. I am the wrong person to be trying to put this into words, but please listen to what I have to say."

He went to her, standing before her and cradling the monstrous face in his hands. He looked into eyes that were still hers. "God has told us that He loves all creatures and all living things, great and small. All humans alive today have known and do know God's love, and know that if He has said that He loves other creatures and things, it is absolutely

238

true. God loves you in full measure. I have to believe that if He did not, you would not have been given the capacity to love. Why this is happening to you and to me, or why it is happening here and now, I do not know. But we will see—you can bet on that. You can also bet that if you have faith and hope, what we will see will be good, even if we don't know what it will be."

Peggy sniffled and put her hands in his. "I must admit," she said, her voice quiet now, "that when I look at the history of mankind I see examples of what you are saying. The question is, does your rationale apply to me? I am animate, but I am neither human nor one of God's own creatures. I am one of man's creatures: a machine."

"The answer is," Pat said, "we don't know, but we must trust God's wisdom, and we must do the best we know how until His plan is revealed. One more point: you may be different from anything we've seen before, and you may even be unique, but that doesn't make you ugly or a freak. I don't care what kind of a face or body you put on. As long as you have love, you are beautiful."

"If you really mean that," she said, "I'll leave my face the way it is."

"Okay," he said with a laugh, hoping she was teasing. "I've dated worse."

"Oh, you!" She threw her shoe at him. But then she laughed, and her former appearance returned.

"Peggy, let me ask you something. Suppose things worked out so that we could marry. If we came back here to buy a house, settle down, and raise children, would you want a place that was exactly like everybody else's?"

Her face fell, and she said, "Why worry about it? That's for you and Ellen Faraday to do."

"So that's it? Oh, how blind I have been. Peggy, you're jealous, and for no reason. Don't you know that Miss Faraday is only infatuated with me? I don't care about her. I love you."

"For someone who doesn't care, you have awfully fast hands. Not thirty minutes ago you were hugging her more tenderly than you ever have me."

"What would you have me do, kick her in the teeth? The bottom had just dropped out of her world, and she needed all of the support she could get. She should have a good future ahead of her with the SEJS, but if she goes off the deep end in her senior year, she could blow it completely. I also have her to thank for giving me you. It may not have been her intent, and there may be a rocky road ahead of us, but I owe her more than she'll ever know."

"Yeah, right," said Peggy, unconvinced.

"Then, look at it this way: she's your mother or sister or whatever. Shall I let her down easy, so that later she'll look at me and think, 'He's all right, but what did I ever see in him?' or should I treat her insensitively and have her say, 'That SOB, I'll fix his wagon; wait 'till he sees the kind of help he and Peggy get from me!'?"

"I don't know. Hand me my shoe."

When he picked it up and extended it to her, she caught him unawares and kissed him with a ferocity he did not know was possible.

🔺 🔺 🔺

Ten days of leave with Peggy had done wonders for Pat—and had not hurt Peggy either. Checking out at the desk of the Ammergau Chalet on Log Base 36's planet, they looked like any other young couple on their way to work on a Monday morning. However, when the time came to leave, their method of departure was more than a little unusual. With the chalet now open to the public, they had arranged to park Dragonfly on the roof, where she would not detract from the quaint village scenery.

The innkeeper's family, to whom Peggy and Pat had endeared themselves by flying them on errands and pleasure trips all over the countryside during the past week and a half, came out to wave goodbye. It took three trips of the elevator to get everyone topside for the sendoff, and the picnic basket that showed up at the last minute was a back-breaker jammed full of goodies and the best wines in the house.

Peggy and Pat had run the ship through her pre-flight before they went down to check out, so as soon as everything was battened down and all of the kids were safely out of the way, they took her up to the head of the valley and then brought her back hot and low. They pulled up into a spinning, vertical climb right behind the chalet and went supersonic as soon as no damage to buildings would result. The corkscrew contrail they left behind was unintentional, but it was a fitting memento.

At thirty thousand meters, they leveled off and obtained permission to proceed to Kroll's boatyard. If they had thought about it, they might have made a more leisurely return, but in a matter of minutes their (as Peggy termed it) "un-honeymoon" was over.

With Dragonfly safely roosting in the maintenance bay for a thorough inspection and some minor repairs, they reported to Patsy Kroll and went through the formality of signing in on the register she maintained for J-2.

"Gotcha now," she said. "Pat, you're slated for a full battery of psychological and physical exams at the log base hospital. While that's going on, the base droid shop will give Peggy an equivalent physical going over. We've fabricated a new connector for your ID cord to hold her double crystal."

She tapped her fingers on the countertop. "Now, the base shop has facilities for loading Peggy up and down, so you can either do it in Dragonfly and have us transport the droid to and from the shop, or you can go with her to the shop. I think I'd recommend the former. If your exams run late, the shop might be locked up for the night when you get back here."

"What do you think, Peggy?" Pat asked.

"Dragonfly," she said.

They went back on board the yacht, and Pat felt very strange when one of the shop technicians helped him unseal the flap in the back of the droid's head. The tech handed him the crystal from the pocket underneath, together with the master copy of the one from the ship, and Pat placed them in the holder around his neck. He avoided looking at the now blank features of the droid. For the first time, he realized how strong his attachment to Peggy had become during the recent weeks.

The shuttle ride through the underground tunnel from Kroll's boatyard to a concealed terminus in the log base was a long one, but it reminded him of his rides with Peggy on Star Base 75. They seemed like they had happened only seconds ago. "I must be getting old," Pat thought, "if time seems to be passing this quickly."

The tests seemed to take an eternity; indeed, they consumed the rest of the working day. The part that Pat remembered, though, was when the flight surgeon began to run over the results with him.

"Pilot, male, height, weight, et cetera, equivalent age twenty-nine years—"

"Say again that age, doc?"

"Twenty nine. Why?"

"Check my last physical, would you?"

"Equivalent age reported last exam?" the doctor said into the lip mike he was wearing.

"Thirty-one years," the computer display replied.

"Hmm," the flight surgeon mused. "Unusual but not unprecedented. You obviously have been taking care of yourself, and good things must have been happening to you lately."

"I'll tell her you said that," Pat said with a grin, thinking of Peggy in his arms.

"Very unusual," the doctor said dryly. "That form of the fountain of youth more often drains one, no pun intended."

Pat hooted in laughter, and the analysis of his condition continued. In the end, the flight surgeon found Pat to be more than fit for immediate flight duty. Pat gave that report to Patsy when he got back to the boatyard. She told him to reinstall Peggy in the droid, get Dragonfly ready to go, and report back first thing in the morning. If the official medical reports were on line in the morning, which she expected they would be, he and Peggy would receive their mission briefing and be on their way before noon.

◭ ◭ ◭

The wind was gusting and storm warnings were posted when Dragonfly broke ground for their test hop. Thunderstorms flashed to seaward, but Flight Ops advised that it was only a squall line that would soon dissipate. They were to avoid it by flying east, and if it was still active when they returned, they could either come in through gaps, wait until it cleared, or land elsewhere.

When they got above the cloud cover, the moon and stars were shining brightly. "Remind you of anything?" Pat asked Peggy.

"Yes. Two things, actually. One is the trip back from the beach. The other was your remark that you have heard that there is no better place to make love than in zero gravity. Now or later?"

"Later. But not too much later."

"Roger, dodger, over and out."

Dragonfly checked out nicely, and so did Pat's rumor.

Much later, in their rooms at the yacht club, Pat slid into bed with Peggy and asked, "Is it silly of me to want you to lie here while I sleep?"

"I don't think so," Peggy said. "I believe you sleep better than you did before, and it's comforting to me, too. I just hope our two hundred kilos don't bring this rickety old bed crashing down around our ears."

"Are you planning to use the poor thing for a trampoline?"

"Maybe, unless you're planning to go right to sleep," she said, raising herself up on one elbow. "Does this mean the un-honeymoon is over?"

"Not unless this is the start of our first argument. As far as I'm concerned, it isn't. I wouldn't dare argue with you. Down here, you outweigh me."

"Right," she said, "and don't you forget it. Remember your favorite saying: discretion is the better part of valor."

"Yes, and from the same font of wisdom comes the old adage, 'Once a king, always a king; but once a knight is enough.'"

She laughed and, after kissing him playfully, said, "Where did you hear that? I've never run across it in the things I've read."

"Darned if I know, really. It's probably one of those pieces of graffiti that you only have to read once to remember forever."

"Graffiti? I've never paid it any attention. Ah, well, good night, sweetheart. Sleep well." She gave him a sweet kiss and turned out the light. After a moment, she giggled. A few minutes later, she giggled again.

"Peggy?" Pat said.

"Yes?"

"No fair reading in bed with the lights off."

"Aye, aye, sir," she said. "Go to sleep."

243

⏤ Chapter Twenty-Seven ⏤

Mission Briefing

Peggy and Pat reported to the boatyard at 0700, refreshed and looking forward to getting on with their new jobs. Patsy Kroll admitted them to the room behind the office.

"Pat," she said, "you have been cleared to fly, and the mission that was waiting evidently hasn't gone away. I have been told only three things. Number one, the job involves returning to 14.16.4. Number two, it is extremely risky. SEJS estimates that your chances of success, meaning that you will return alive and with the required information, are minimal."

She had been standing; now she began to pace, hands clasped behind her back. "Number three, you will have three chances to turn the mission down. The first is now. The second will come after you have been briefed by someone who knows what is going on. The third will come at some point after you enter 14.16.4. If you turn it down now, you will be assigned other duties without prejudice. If you wait until later, you will have to be placed in isolation until the situation sorts itself out some other way. J-2 figures that it could take years, so it makes sense that if you want to turn the job down, this is the time to do it."

Patsy stopped pacing and perched on the edge of a chair, her knees almost touching Pat's. "As far as I'm concerned, and I don't care who is listening at J-2, I have to tell you that this stinks. You haven't been at this game for very long, but I have. It isn't unusual for a control agent to not know what her operatives are supposed to be doing. That's often for the best.

"I just don't like to see a couple of nice youngsters like you, who haven't even been properly trained, being offered what amounts to a one-way ticket. Not only that, the way they're playing cloak and dagger would make anybody with any curiosity at all want to find out more about what's going on. If they aren't leading you down a primrose path, I'm sadly mistaken. I flat wouldn't take this mission, and I recommend that you don't." Patsy shook her head grimly.

Pat looked at Peggy; she met his eyes and nodded. "What you're saying makes a lot of sense," he told Patsy, "but we accept the mission. It beats flying privileged characters from one watering hole to the next."

"This is no joking matter, and I'm not testing you or feeding you a line of malarkey." Her voice was dead serious, her face set; he couldn't spot a hint of her usual smile. "I'm trying to do you a favor."

"We know how serious you are," Peggy said, "and we appreciate your willingness to stick your neck out for us. It is just plain nice of you. But while we were up at the chalet, we talked about all of the things that have happened to us recently, and we have decided that this is what we should do. You can bet your buttons that we will do our best to make it back here. If we don't, well, that's the nature of the business, whether it's flying a PV or buzzing around in Dragonfly."

In her best approximation of human comforting behavior, Peggy grasped Patsy's hands in her own. "Pat and I have had happiness and good fortune in full measure, and we've met some mighty fine people along the way—like you. Our first regret would come from refusing to take this job. We may not have the training or experience we need at this point, but if this mission is as peculiar as it appears to be, who's to say we're not as well prepared as anyone else? Surely, SEJS would not be sending us out if they had a better alternative."

"I hope you are as right as your argument makes it sound," Patsy said, standing again. "So be it. Your initial cover is that a terraforming outfit in 14.16.3, just below the bottom of 14.16.4, has chartered Dragonfly to bring them some light cargo. We'll load the equipment right away. You are to deliver it to the orbital base station above the planet. There should be no problems, but if anybody asks, you are still on leave. That will appear to be true to anybody outside J-2 but, of course, you are actually 'for duty.'

"There are encrypted sailing orders in Dragonfly's memory that you are to unlock with your dual keys when you are about to leave the terraforming station. After that, may the angels ride on your shoulders. We all want to see you back here again."

While robots loaded the cargo aboard Dragonfly, Peggy ran through the preflight, and Pat went over the manifest with Kroll. "This may be light cargo," Pat commented, "but there sure is a lot of it. Except for the aisle down the middle, the main cabin is full."

"Yeah, but it's a valid charter nonetheless," Kroll said. "They need this stuff, and they can't fabricate it on site. The fee for hauling this load will cover your operating expenses for at least the next six months. If they like you, there's always a chance for repeat business. Not bad for your first paying haul. But do me and the boys on the tender a favor: make sure it's not your last."

"Peggy and I like you guys, Ted. If we can find our way back, you can bet you'll see us again." Pat closed the hatch, dogged it down, and watched the chief amble out of the way. He then walked into the cockpit and gave Peggy a thumbs up. She cranked up the power, and they were on their way.

Sector Flight Planning had given them a complicated course to follow, and they were kept busy executing short hops to get around stars, a black hole, and high-density gas clouds. Ultimately, however, they came under control of the terraforming base station and landed at the cargo terminal.

Unfamiliar faces were rare at the station, and Dragonfly also was a point of curiosity with the people there. An unloading and exchange of greetings that could have taken only minutes stretched into hours. When Peggy and Pat lifted off again, they had both a new appreciation for the rigors of the planet developers' lives and the feeling that there would, indeed, be repeat business if they were available.

They departed on a course that would make it appear they were returning from whence they had come. After the second hop, however, they stopped and opened their orders. If they were expecting much information, they were disappointed. The orders directed them to turn on their shields, follow the next two legs of their flight plan, and await further instructions without disclosing their position.

They had been in place only a matter of seconds when Peggy said, "Sir, we are receiving an extremely faint encrypted transmission from an unidentified ship. She is saying, 'Dragonfly, secure your shields and all nonessential electronic systems. We will take you aboard as soon as you comply.' Each iteration of the message is characterized by a slight increase in power."

"There must be a CX here somewhere," Pat said. "Comply, but stand by to take evasive and defensive actions in case I am wrong."

The next thing Pat knew, they were inside CX-12's hangar deck. "Belay weapons and evasive systems, Peggy," he said, "and report any damage."

"All secure, sir. No damage evident, but it was a close call for the cabin lighting system and the galley. The CXs must be able to make windows in their shields."

In a little while, Peggy and Pat were piped aboard the cruiser and escorted to a small briefing room. There they were offered the usual amenities and were asked to make themselves comfortable. Before long, the ship's intercom announced, "Flag Officer alongside. All hands prepare to render honors." While Pat speculated about who it might be, the boson's pipe confirmed that an admiral was coming aboard.

Pat's first guess was confirmed when Egan entered and closed the door behind himself. "Varner, Callen, be seated, please," he said. "This may take a while. First of all, though, how have you been doing?"

From the way the admiral sized them up while they answered, it was obviously not an idle question. Moreover, Pat sensed that the J-2 really cared: he nodded and smiled a bit while Pat briefed him. In due course, the admiral became convinced that the team was ready for the assignment ahead.

"I am fully aware of what Patsy Kroll said to you two about this assignment," Egan said. "I want you to know that I fully agree with her. The mission at hand is about as hairy as any I've ever seen. The CINC, the J-3, and I have met to discuss it repeatedly and at length. Frankly, we are confronted with an unprecedented situation that demands action, but the stakes are high. Essential elements of information are missing. Before the CINC commits, he wants to give the acquisition of that information one more try. Before I describe the situation, let me confirm that you haven't changed your minds."

"We haven't, sir," Pat said, and Peggy nodded her agreement.

"All right, then, let me preface this by saying that the information I'll be relating to you is unclassified, as far as our potential adversaries are concerned, but that it is extremely sensitive as far as our own forces and our own media are concerned. There is only one human or human instrumentality outside of this room with whom you may discuss these matters until I expressly tell you otherwise. The exception is the individual who will be your point of contact in 14.16.4. Do you understand, and do you agree to comply?"

"Yes, sir," Pat replied for Peggy and himself. "We understand the restrictions we are accepting, even if we don't yet understand the whys and wherefores."

The admiral smiled and said, "I believe you will understand more fully after I fill you in on what we know about the situation in 14.16.4. A few days after your tour in PV-11 was over, the terraforming expedition convoy that Task Force Delta was seeking was found in 14.16.4.

Singularity effects had disabled them, and the terraformers had abandoned ship. They left a recorded message that they had elected to attempt to colonize a planet they had observed in a nearby solar system.

"Need I say that the planet in question turned out to be the so-called Doodlebug Planet that our alien friends consider taboo? Lest you draw the wrong conclusions about the aliens, let me hasten to state that Task Force Delta was shown authentic recordings which prove that the terraformers were offered rescue and relief. The terraformers declined help and went to the planet in their lifeboats and cargo haulers."

"Were they nuts?" Pat asked.

"A better term might be 'misguided,' but who knows? Paraphrased, what they told the aliens was that it is the Lord's will that they go forth and make useless planets habitable. Apparently, they perceived that it was the Lord's will that they should do their thing with this particular planet. The aliens warned them that nothing that goes to the Doodlebug Planet may leave it, and a blind man could see that they were serious. Apart from what may be waiting on the planet, the aliens have cordoned it off, and they don't let anything out.

"Let me amplify that point. There are five alien star bases standing approximately a thousand kilometers away from the planet. The aliens told Task Force Delta that this is a permanent arrangement. The star bases are constantly moving in a coordinated but unpredictable pattern. Anything that enters the planet's atmosphere and tries to come back out is blasted out of existence.

"The star bases maintain a field around the planet that makes it possible for them to detect practically anything that goes in, and which prevents electromagnetic radiation from coming out. Thus, if the people on the planet are trying to communicate with us by subspace radio or laser, they are out of luck."

"Sir," Peggy asked, "whose star bases are they?"

"Interesting point, lieutenant. Each of the alien cultures with whom you met in the company of Shamus is represented by one base."

"To include the Leprechauns?" she asked.

"Close, but not quite. The fifth base belongs to the Little Peoples in general."

"Good grief," Pat said.

"Affirmative," the admiral said. "You can see why our information collection difficulties are so acute. We have never had a beef with the Little Peoples, and we certainly don't want to start trouble now. Whether their capabilities come from magic or technology doesn't amount to a hill of beans; the fact is that by comparison, we are still in the Stone Age.

"The cost of mounting a frontal assault to drag the terraformers out would be astronomical, even in the unlikely event of no alien reinforcements. What's more, we don't even know if there are any humans left alive down there. Lastly, it is fair to assume that there are reasons for the aliens' taboos. You can see why I said the stakes are high."

"Do we know anything at all about the situation on the planet, sir?" Pat asked.

"Almost nothing," Egan said. "Except for its rather eccentric name, the aliens flatly refuse to tell us anything at all about it. On top of that, they have deleted or blocked our access to any records that may have been in their public domains. Our best efforts to elicit information through conventional channels have not only drawn a blank, but have gotten a number of previously open doors slammed in our faces. To borrow an old-fashioned phrase, we are being stonewalled on all sides."

"Why does SEJS think Peggy and I might be able to overcome such large obstacles?" Pat asked. "We will do our best, but—Dragonfly and Peggy notwithstanding—we are rather inexperienced and short on resources to be playing in the big leagues."

"You yourself pointed out to Patsy Kroll that your lack of experience is not particularly detrimental on this mission. Put yourself in my shoes and tell me how you would find someone who had experience in matters like this."

Pat frowned, shrugged, and turned his empty palms upward.

"Correct," the J-2 said. "There is no recorded precedent for this situation. Given the impossibility of finding a team with direct experience, let's look for the next best thing. Where do you recruit a team who knows something about the territory; who can pilot a small, concealable spacecraft; who has demonstrated an ability to survive tight situations without being trigger-happy; and who has the guts to do the job? We think that if anybody can get in there, gather the information we need, and get back out, you can. Moreover, we may not be the only ones who think so. Why did Shamus give you that whistle?"

"I hadn't thought of that, sir, but now that you mention it—"

"I don't doubt that he's made a big impression on you by being a cute, clever little elf who stepped right out of a fairytale to come to your rescue at just the right time. You have every reason to think so. I once had much the same view of him, but I have learned better over the years. Fortuitous rescues have a habit of happening whenever he is around, and one begins to wonder how many of them are of his own manufacture. Whatever you do, don't trust him if his personal gain does not lie in your direction—and don't doubt that he sees much further ahead than you or I." Egan gave a hearty laugh, and Pat wondered what the admiral's past dealings with Shamus had been.

"Whether he is prescient, or, more likely, has been up to some kind of skullduggery that is going to help him line his pockets, his giving you that whistle is a favorable sign," Egan continued. "He has somehow projected your being in a situation that will end up with Shamus coming out ahead, no matter what transpires. At this point, we would pay his price if we knew there were people on that planet whom we could ransom. And now it's time for me to stop speculating and get down to business. Let me queue up a series of holos and brief you on what we know and don't know. After that, I'll give you your mission assignment."

A three-dimensional image of an almost completely blue planet materialized above the table at which they sat.

"We don't know," the admiral began, "what makes the Doodlebug Planet taboo. It is a perfectly innocuous-looking globe, only a trifle smaller than Terra I. It has a stable orbit with a sidereal period of 1.2 years and a sidereal rotational period of about 26 hours. Its climate and atmosphere are essentially Terran, if relatively tropical.

"Its color comes from its being almost totally covered with water. Land masses account for less than one percent of its surface area, and most of that is in one atoll that is about fifteen degrees north of its equator. It has two small moons that are so close together they share an orbit and appear almost as a single unit. They are sufficiently massive to cause tides, so we would expect conditions to have favored evolution of aquatic life forms. It's a very old planet, and its biota could be anything from very sophisticated to extinct."

The image spun, showing Pat and Peggy all aspects of the planet. "Interestingly, our astronomers and geophysicists say that parts of the planet's mantle could be as much as sixty percent precious metals, by mass. It is ideally located for the condensation of gold at the time of its formation. If that is correct, the Doodlebug Planet could be the celestial equivalent of Terra I's Fort Knox, but that wouldn't account for the taboos. We'll download complete, precise information to Dragonfly's astronomical library. Any questions so far?"

"No, sir," Pat said.

"Okay, then, new subject," the admiral said. "We have probed the aliens' protective systems. They appear to be tight but not perfect. Their apparent resolving power is approximately a tenth of a square meter of perfectly reflective material; considerably less for non-conductive and organic materials.

"The field they have established around the planet enhances their ability to detect penetrating objects, but it interferes with their seeing things that are close to, but outside of, the field's surface. It is subject to degradation during flare-ups in the solar wind, and by fluctuations in the planet's Van Allen belts. Couple those factors with an asteroid belt at about twelve hundred kilometers, and there is hope for finding places to hide and for sneaking small objects in and out.

"We have had the boys in the labs working overtime on this one, believe me. They have come up with small modules that use organic superconductors to facilitate antigravity, and they have built a little space capsule that uses only materials that are transparent to the aliens' fields and detectors.

"We propose to have you, lieutenant, station Dragonfly just above the field and hold her there. Meanwhile you, commander, will drop down to the atoll on the planet to find out what is going on. You will be able to exchange messages, albeit little else, via the antigravity modules. We are not totally thrilled with this concept because the aliens eventually became aware of our probing their setup. We don't know exactly when they noticed us, so they may have been able to mislead us.

"Obviously, commander, if you accept this mission and find it impossible to escape the bubble around the planet on your own, there are no guarantees that we will be able to get you back out. However, if either of you is detected and captured above the field, we will press for relief through diplomatic channels. Under the circumstances, it could take a long, long time for that to do any good. Any questions?"

"Can that capsule you mentioned go up as well as down, sir?"

"It can, commander, but it will be like riding a slow elevator in either direction. To minimize its signatures, the engineers didn't give it much power. What they did give it is mostly dedicated to directional control."

"That's good enough for me," Pat said. "What's your take on this, Peggy?"

"Several things, sir," she said. "Assuming the commander does return to Dragonfly, what about decontamination?"

"We will temporarily install a decon chamber and medical monitoring system in Dragonfly's main cabin before you leave. Anything that comes up from the planet will have to be physically quarantined until its tolerability has been established."

"What are the chances of getting two of those capsules, rather than one, sir?" Peggy inquired. "If the commander becomes incapacitated, I'd like to have a way to go after him."

"The capsules are only rated at three hundred kilograms capacity, and only two of them exist. One of them is the prototype, and it's deficient in the life support arena. Of course, that wouldn't matter much, as long as you and not the commander were the payload. What the heck, you've got it."

"Thank you, sir," she said. "My last question refers to your opinion as to why the planet might be taboo. Assuming that it is not off limits because of its precious metal content—I can't believe five normally conflicting cultures would share treasure under a system of detente—what cultural correlations might account for it?"

"We don't know," the admiral admitted, "and we feel that it would be dangerous to speculate. The safest thing for you to do is to approach the Doodlebug Planet with your eyes wide open, alert to any and all possibilities. Not only are the inhabitants of Sector 14.16.4 outlying factions of their respective races, your encounter with the Molluscan species was our first inkling that it even existed.

"If there is a common behavioral pattern among the four species we do know a little about, it is that what they let you see is not necessarily what you ultimately get. That is why I want to emphasize that you should be alert for a series of outcomes, not just the first one that manifests itself. To put that in a less pedantic fashion, these are tricky bastards, so you'd better watch your back—all of the time."

"Aye, aye, sir, thank you for the advice," Peggy said. "I will follow it, and I will encourage the commander to do so, too."

"Don't mind her, sir," Pat said. "She never thinks I'm sufficiently paranoid for my own good."

Egan leaned forward intently and said, "Callen, if there was any factor that deterred us in selecting you for this mission, it was the fact that she is right. When you get down to the surface of that planet, it is going to be your ass on the line. The lieutenant won't be there to pull your chestnuts out of the fire. I am not rebuking you, son, but you can take this as the last bit of training you are going to receive in your new job: during this mission, if not throughout the rest of your life, think before you act. I want you to come back from this mission. So do a lot of other people, not to mention, I believe, the lieutenant."

"Yes, sir," Pat replied, chastened.

"Do you know what I mean," the admiral continued, "when I say you should think before you act?"

"I believe so. You mean that I should look before I leap."

"That's part of it, but that's the least of it. You're a commander now. It's time you began think about the effects of your words before you utter them, and it's time to get organized. Take time to do some planning, and then execute according to plan. Not slavishly, but intelligently. A plan is a time-phased series of objectives that lead to accomplishment of a goal. Use the people and other sources of information around you fully when you are forming your plans. Review progress each time you reach, or fail to reach, an objective, and revise your plans accordingly.

"And, in this mission in particular, report fully before you jump off into a new phase of activity. This is serious business, and that is a direct order."

"Yes, sir," Pat said, "Wilco."

"Very well, then," Egan said. "Subject to amplification in formally transmitted orders, your mission is to go to the Doodlebug Planet, collect the essential elements of information, and report back to me. The essential elements of information are, in increasing order of importance, the status of the terraformers; the identity and organization of alien noncombatants on the planet; the order of battle of alien forces there; and the nature and extent of factors that make the planet taboo."

He looked from Pat to Peggy and back to Pat. "Do you accept the mission?"

"Yes, sir," Pat replied after glancing at Peggy and seeing her nod.

"Then as Patsy so neatly put it," the admiral said, "may the angels ride on your shoulders. Go with my blessings."

— CHAPTER TWENTY-EIGHT —

Captain Moore

Pat and Peggy returned to Dragonfly and battened down for a long hyperspace trip. Their new orders stated that to keep their movements secret, CX-12 would transport them into 14.16.4 to rendezvous with their control. Finally, they were ready, and Street told them it was time to go.

After CX-12 had accomplished the first leg, taking them to 14.16.4, she then made another, much shorter hop. Presently, from his groggy post-hyperspace state, Pat became aware of dialog between Street and the skipper of another ship. Peggy was saying something, too.

"Are you ready, sir? They want us to transfer from CX-12 to CX-26, and we're going to have to thread the needle through windows in their cloaking shields."

"I'm still a little punch-drunk, but I'm coming around quickly. Cast off, and let's go."

They paid their respects to CX-12 and exited her hangar deck. Outside, the galaxy had taken on a shimmering appearance; it took Pat a moment to realize that this must be an effect of the cruiser's shields. "How in the world can they fly that thing, with so much interference from her camouflage?" Pat wondered aloud.

"I surmise that it doesn't give them any trouble," Peggy replied, "but we're not equipped to keep up with all of her field dynamics. Watch what happens when I cut off our own processing."

The scene went black around them. "Wow, it's a blind alley," Pat said. "You can't see in or out."

They flew slowly away, putting distance between Dragonfly and CX-12's hull. "You know, our cloaks just bend incoming energy around us and collect our emissions for reprocessing," Peggy said. "I believe theirs capture everything and re-radiate the incoming stuff in the same direction it was headed when it entered. Given the size of a CX, that's a heavy-duty workload."

"Best not stick our noses into other folks' business, but I'll bet you're right."

A small aperture appeared in CX-12's field; they ducked through it. "Goodbye, and good luck," they heard Street say, and the view behind them stabilized.

"Two-six, where are you?" Peggy said into her mike.

They both nearly jumped out of their skins when a familiar voice replied, "About a hundred meters dead ahead—trust me." In a few seconds, the same voice said, "Welcome aboard, Dragonfly. Make yourself comfortable in the hangar deck and join me on the bridge— Peggy and Pat, that is. I brought along some caviar from Star Base 75."

At the same time, Pat saw that they were inside CX-26's shields. "Bud Moore! Excuse me: *Captain Moore.*"

"At your service, ma'am and sir," Bud replied. "Come on up as soon as you're ready. We have lots to talk about, and then we have a little flying to do."

They quickly docked the boat, got into fresh tunics, and went aboard the cruiser, where they received a cheerful reception from the watch personnel. Moments later, they walked onto the bridge. Pat and Peggy congratulated Bud on his promotion and command.

"I had some misgivings when they offered me this job," he said, "but I'll have to admit I haven't had this much fun in years. Old CX-26 is a pretty fair chunk of iron, and the work has been interesting. I gather you've had some contact with CX-12, which was the test bed for most of our mods. CX-26 is twice as slick as 12 is, which is a good thing because we got the job of scouting the Doodlebug system for SEJS."

Bud ushered them to a place where they could be seated at the periphery of the bridge. He had cleared out all nonessential personnel while he spoke with Pat and Peggy. "No space stories for now, though. It's all pertinent, but that can come later. Right now, we need to talk about getting Dragonfly fitted out for your mission. CX-26 will be your mother ship, and I'll be your control, if you decide to go through with it. With your permission, my people will install the decon and med gear, as well as the capsule launching system, so we can give you a little training tomorrow.

"Permission given," Pat said. "Will your technicians need any help from us?"

"It might be a good idea if Peggy keeps an eye on what they do, just to be sure they treat your ship the way you want them to, and so you will know all about the installation. I'll pass the word for them to get everything ready. Now, while we have the facilities of the bridge available, I'd like to run over what we picked up during our scouting mission."

After half an hour of reviewing the recordings of the mission, Peggy and Pat had a much better understanding of the Doodlebug Planet and the defenses that surrounded it. They were surprised to discover that the field around the planet was not static; it bulged and moved oddly. Peggy would have to stay alert if she was going to keep Dragonfly close to it without making contact. They also learned that the planet had small polar icecaps and some violent weather.

Installing the mission systems in Dragonfly proved to be no problem. Everything was palletized and easy to secure to the cabin's deck. The capsule launching and recovery system monopolized the amidships starboard hatch, but the other three remained unobstructed.

When all was shipshape, CX-26 made the hop to the solar system where their training was to take place, and Peggy and Pat joined Bud in his cabin for supper. It was a pleasant evening, and they slept well that night.

After reveille the next morning, CV 26's technicians familiarized Pat with the operation of the capsule and its contents. It was composed almost completely of transparent silica, which helped to alleviate the feeling of confinement induced by its small size. Pat, clad in a spacesuit, sat in a chair that nearly filled the cylindrical midsection of the capsule. He barely had room to swing his feet. Navigation for landing would be by eyeball, aided only by a telescopic viewer he could flip down when necessary.

The engines were in the rounded ends of the capsule, the life support system filled the space beneath the chair, and packed above his head was his cargo of antigravity modules, survival equipment, and portable computing gear. The center of mass was below Pat's seat, so the capsule was self-righting. It was watertight and buoyant in case he landed in the ocean.

After several trial launches and recoveries in zero gravity, Pat felt ready to try a planetary landing. In the interests of saving time, Dragonfly and several attending small craft dropped down to the top of the training planet's atmosphere and spit him out.

The capsule worked as advertised, but Pat found that flying it was a harrowing, inexact exercise. He was very much at the mercy of high-altitude winds, and the primitive controls frustrated him. As the day wore on, however, he learned that if he came in off target, he could maneuver into place at low altitude. The main requisite was patience.

He was fatigued and sweaty when Peggy picked him up in Dragonfly. After he stepped out of the shower, Bud hailed him from CX-26. "We have a problem. At certain angles of attack, we're getting a pronounced signature from the capsule that wasn't there before you started flying it. Are you carrying something metallic?"

"Not unless there's something in my suit that I don't know about. Could it be my comm implant?"

"We don't think so. It looks like we're going to have to run you through a scanner."

"Oof. I'm beat."

"What about Shamus' whistle, sirs?" Peggy asked. "It's small, but with the chain spread out to encircle your neck, it could serve as a reflector at a number of wavelengths."

"That checks out," Bud reported. "Let's find a better way for you to carry it. I'll put the techs to work on it."

"Interesting," Pat said. "I wonder if he could be using that thing to track me around."

"It wouldn't hurt to check it out," Bud said. "Bring it with you when you come over this evening."

After supper, they all went down to the cruiser's lab and watched while the science officer and his technicians subjected the whistle to intense scrutiny. By making a variety of measurements and computations, the science staff concluded that if the whistle were blown, its audio frequency was in the twenty-kilohertz range, which would be inaudible to most people.

More interesting, gamma ray scanning revealed a nanocircuit hidden in the bottom of the whistle's barrel. It was coupled to a tiny reed that would vibrate sympathetically with the whistle's first harmonic. If Pat blew the whistle, the circuit would emit a gravitational signal. The science officer commented that the hidden apparatus was so delicate that it would probably self-destruct if the whistle was blown.

"Shamus said it was a one-shot deal, so that checks out," Pat observed.

"Wait a minute!" Peggy exclaimed. "What happens when that whistle makes a hyperspace jump?"

"It should vibrate sympathetically and send out a signal," the science officer said. "The effect wouldn't be powerful enough to destroy it, though, lieutenant."

"True, but could you follow those signals?"

"If I'm not sadly mistaken, they would provide a pretty good directional beacon."

"So," Pat said, "our friendly Leprechaun has had me carrying a tracer everywhere I've gone. I think the time has come to wring his scrawny little neck. Let me have that whistle—I think I'm going to blow it. When he shows up, I'll use a shillelagh to impress upon him the depth of my appreciation for his concern for my whereabouts!"

"I believe it would be wise to do nothing, sir," Peggy said. "Now that we know about the whistle, we are in a good position to turn the tables on Shamus if we need to."

"You don't really think I'd waste what may turn out to be my only ticket off that planet, do you?" Pat asked.

"I would hope not," she said. "I guess the joke's on me."

"It's no joking matter," Pat said. "I don't appreciate being turned into a Judas goat, and I'd just as soon pinch Shamus' head off. However, we need to find a way to shield the circuits in this thing so we can move around without betraying our location unless we want to. Any thoughts on that subject?"

"That's a tough one," Peggy said, "but there must be a way. Shamus wouldn't go around broadcasting his own whereabouts by carrying a pocketful of whistles."

"The obvious way," said the science officer, "is to immobilize the little reed on the chip. It couples mechanical vibrations to the amplifiers. If the reed can't move, nothing else will happen."

"I'm not sure I go for that idea," Pat said. "If I have to whistle in an emergency, I want it to work."

"If we're careful, commander," the science officer said, "I think we can slip a soft, forked plug in through the mouthpiece without hurting anything. If you have a hand free to get the whistle to your lips, you can pull the plug out with your teeth. If you don't have a hand free, you're pretty much out of luck anyway."

"Do we have a way to test the premise that the whistle gives off gravitational waves as is, and that we have silenced it?" Bud asked.

"Yes, sir," the science officer replied. "Now that we know what to look for, we can check it out in a hurry."

"Let's do it, then," Bud said. "Obviously, this puts a whole new face on the situation. I'm scrubbing the mission until we can pass a full report to Admiral Egan and get his reaction." He stood and made a courtly bow in Peggy's direction. "Peggy, once again, my hat is off to you."

A little skillful work with a scalpel and a silicone rubber plug produced a silencer, and a short hyperspace roundtrip in Dragonfly established what they needed to know: it worked. Bud transmitted an encrypted "Operational Immediate" precedence report to J-2, and Pat and Peggy retired for the night, awaiting developments.

The next morning, Bud hailed Pat and said, "Do you two have your dress uniforms with you?"

"We do," Pat replied. "Dragonfly is our house and home. We have all of our gear stowed aboard. What's up?"

"We've heard from the boss," Bud reported. "He'll be aboard in about half an hour and he wants to meet with all of us. My assistant engineering division officer was due to be promoted today, so I asked the admiral if he'd be willing to do the honors. He agreed, so we're going to go first class."

"We'll be there," Pat said.

Egan had brought Everett along, and Pat was gratified to meet his sponsor and headquarters control. Their conversation was brief, however, because the captain was pressed into service to read the promotion orders that advanced the young engineering officer from ensign to lieutenant junior grade.

The chief engineer and his staff departed after the ceremony was over, and the admiral said, "Captain Everett, do you have the other orders with you?"

"Yes, sir," he said, "they are right here."

"Commander Callen and Lieutenant Varner," Egan said, "we intend to mislead our friendly Leprechaun a bit, but the decision from CINC level is to authorize continuation of your mission as soon as possible. This is your last chance to turn back. Consider well, and advise me of your decision."

"We have, sir, and we are going forward with it."

"Very well, then. Captain, please read the orders."

The first orders awarded the Legions of Merit to Pat, Peggy, and CX-26's science officer for their meritorious service in "classified and highly important technical matters"—that is, for detecting and analyzing the hidden properties of Shamus' whistle.

The next set of orders brought the real kicker: they temporarily promoted Pat to captain and Peggy to lieutenant commander, with retroactive dates of rank, for the balance of the Doodlebug Planet mission.

"A few words of explanation," the admiral said. "First, as to the awards, for reasons I am not at liberty to discuss at this time, recognition of the tracer in Shamus' whistle is extremely important and timely. Congratulations and thanks to all of you. Second, Captain Callen, J-2's research into the terraformers who went to the Doodlebug Planet revealed that the leaders of the expedition are a pair of very rank- and status-conscious individuals. As a moderately senior SEJS captain on official business, your authority exceeds theirs, so you are in a position to take control if need be—and if you can marshal support from the members of the expedition. Don't press your luck, but don't take any guff, either.

"Above all, remember that those people made their beds and they must lie in them. Your job is not to get them off the planet, although that would be nice. Your mission is to acquire information and get it—and yourself—out."

"Yes, sir," Pat said.

"Congratulations, captain," the admiral said, a big grin splitting his face. "I don't mind telling you I had one hell of a time getting your promotion past the J-1."

"Knowing how straight-arrow the J-1 is, sir," Pat said, smiling back, "I don't doubt it for an instant. I won't let either of you down."

▲ ▲ ▲

An hour after the ceremonies aboard CX-26, the cruiser emerged from hyperspace just outside the asteroid belt in the Doodlebug Planet's solar system. Dragonfly eased herself overboard and, a few minutes later, under full shielding, she popped down to a point immediately above the aliens' planetary field.

"Peggy," Pat said, "when I watch that field undulate it reminds me of something, but I can't place it. How about you?"

"Not off the top of my head, sir, but I'll work on it. Right now, we're so close it's hard to see what's going on. Shall I pull us back to where I can get a better look?"

"No," he said. "It's probably not important." He took a deep breath, got out of his seat, and completed his preparations for descent in the capsule. When he was ready to go, he said, "Take care of yourself, sweetheart, and don't take any chances. I want to be sure you'll be waiting for me when I get back."

"That goes double for you. And don't forget to keep me posted on everything that happens down there. I'm going to miss you, and it will help if I hear from you often."

"Will do. Meanwhile, au revoir, sayonara, and auf Wiedersehen. I love you."

― Chapter Twenty-Nine ―

Doodlebugs

Pat switched off his implant and waited apprehensively as the capsule slowly accelerated toward the planet. He couldn't see the field, but he felt relieved when he was sure he had passed through it and there were no evident effects. The timing of his launch was calculated to bring him to the planet's surface just after sunrise on the atoll, some three hours hence. It was a long, uneventful ride down in the dark, and for the first time in a long while, he was alone with his thoughts. He wasn't melancholy, but it was no fun to be separated from Peggy; she dominated his thoughts.

When the altimeter told him that he had passed the midway point, his attention returned to flying the capsule. The atmosphere was thickening, so he slowed the capsule lest he become a meteor. Before long, the rays of the sun illuminated the eastern circumference of the planet, flooded the capsule with light, and lit up the water beneath him. Presently, the main land mass in the atoll came into view to his west. He and the capsule slipped toward it.

Making a morning descent was wise because the winds were light. Pat stopped the capsule's vertical movement at 1,500 meters above sea level and undertook an aerial survey of the island. The best he could say was that it looked bleak. He could see no large vegetation; most of surface was sand. He spotted a rocky ridgeline toward the center of the island, but the general appearance was that of windswept desert.

When he dropped down to 500 meters, Pat could see that an odd tracery of lines and conical pits covered the sandy areas. He went back up to 1,500 meters so he could see all of the way to the island's north and south coastlines, but the view changed very little as he moved westward with the wind. He estimated that the highest point on the island was about 750 meters above sea level, and when he passed it, he dropped down to take a good look.

That was a mistake. He frightened several large, roosting reptilian creatures into flight. After their initial alarm abated, they began circling him closely with evident curiosity. That was all right until one of them defecated as it passed overhead and obscured his view with a chalky film. One thing he did not have was a windshield wiper, but it may have been just as well; the bird-like animals lost interest and dropped away.

Flying horizontally and peering out to the left and right soon became literally a pain in the neck. Pat was almost directly over the terraformers' camp before he realized it was there. By spinning the capsule, he could see that the terrain at this end of the island was low and sandy. He decided to land.

He felt it unwise to make any radio transmissions, lest he alert the aliens, who were monitoring above, to his presence. Lacking any way to make noise, he was unable to attract the attention of the few people who were moving around at this hour. After he realized that the camp rested on a strip of rock, he started looking for a soft place to set the capsule down. His control of the capsule wasn't good enough that he wanted to take any chances at low altitude, but he also preferred to have somebody know he was there in case he needed assistance after landing. He made a gradually descending swoop that took him in front of a man who was walking across the center of the compound. Pat waved through his viewing portal. His swoop must have startled the daylights out of the terraformer, but the man returned his wave and ran after Pat, shouting and waving.

Pat increased his altitude a little and aimed the capsule toward the sand that bordered the edge of the campsite. As soon as he had the capsule over sand, he stopped its lateral motion as much as he could and set it down. The bottom of the capsule buried itself about a quarter of a meter, and Pat rocked back and forth a little to test its stability. It seemed all right, and he began the sequence of operations that would open the hatch.

Movement outside caught his eye. Pat looked up to see that the man he had startled was waving frantically at him. Pat waved casually in return and went back to his post-flight checklist. As soon as he did, the man began to wave again, flapping his arms like a windmill. When he had Pat's attention, he alternately pointed in the direction of the capsule and waved in a signal that, Pat began to realize, meant he was to freeze.

Pat looked around as best he could, and at about the same time that the sand gave way, he discovered that he had landed on the edge of one of the conical pits he had observed from aloft. The capsule began to topple over and slide downhill rapidly, and Pat reacted instinctively by slamming his "CLIMB" control to its maximum position. This may not have been the ideal thing to do, but it was better than nothing.

When the capsule broke free of the sliding sand, Pat operated the controls to right it and gain altitude. Just below the capsule, something large lunged out of the bottom of the pit. The sand had scoured enough of the dinosaur droppings off the viewing portal for Pat to see an enormous set of shiny, hooked mandibles glance off the capsule and snap shut right in front of his face. Incredulous, he watched from overhead while the creature that owned the jaws wriggled its body back into the sand and tidied up its pit by tossing out the loose sand with flips of its head. Pat had seen ant lions when he was a child, but the cute little half-centimeter larvae of his experience were mere Lilliputian-scale models of this four-meter monster.

Shaken, he eased the capsule over to the rocky surface of the campsite and laid it down as gently as he could. "Discovery number one," he said to himself, "is that the name of this place is well deserved. I have just met the boss doodlebug."

By the time he got the capsule open, climbed out, and removed his spacesuit, he had drawn a sizable crowd of excited people. He held up his hand. "Who's in charge here?"

"I reckon you are, if you want to be," a man replied. "You're a cap'n, ain't ya?"

"I am," Pat replied, "but where are the leaders of your party?"

"Ain't none of 'em left, cap'n," the man said. "We been doing a lot better since we ain't elected replacements. Soon as somebody takes over, something happens to 'em."

Pat's eyebrows shot up and he asked, "You mean they've all been killed?"

"No," the man answered, "most of 'em just went crazy and quit. You know, they just sit there like a bump on a log and stare at you."

"Catatonic?"

"I believe that's what the doc used to call it."

"How many of you are left?"

"One hundred fifty one of the original two hundred ten," another man volunteered. "I'm Henry Waters, the expedition clerk."

"I'm Pat Callen. SEJS sent me down to gather information and make a report."

"Do you have a way to get us out of here?"

"They gave me no guarantees, Henry, but at least I have some little gadgets that may be able to get messages out."

"That would be great," Waters said. "We haven't been able to get any of our comm gear to reach past that shield up there."

"I'll try one of my devices as soon as I ask you a few more questions," Pat said. "I've seen the flying dinosaurs, or whatever they are, and that doodlebug that tried to eat my capsule. They wouldn't make this place taboo, I don't think. Have you discovered what does?"

"No sir, not really, but this is a very strange place," Henry said. "We've found a lot of old equipment that someone left here, but none of it seems to be operational, and we don't think that's it. The weird thing about this place is what can happen to people here. We all thought that insanity was impossible nowadays, but it isn't. A person will start saying he's having dreams where he hears someone trying to communicate with him from outside the shield, and then he'll say he hears faint voices while he's awake, and the next thing you know he either takes a dive into a doodlebug pit or goes catatonic."

"You said 'he'—are only men affected?"

"No, it happens to both men and women. The doctor was a woman, and so was the vice president."

"Have you had any contact with sentient beings?"

"No, none at all since we came down here," Henry replied. "Our ecologist did a thorough survey before she died. She found some marine mammals that are equivalent to whales, but that's about it."

"Would you like to leave, if it is possible?"

"A lot could be done with this planet," Henry said, "but I think most of us would be happy to try another one. And, in my opinion, with our leaders, planners, and spaceships gone, about all we can do is subsist here."

"Okay—let me see if we can get a message out."

Pat removed an object about the size of a poker chip from the capsule, inserted it into a recorder, and imparted what he had learned to date. He added that his next actions would be to get a complete personnel status report together and survey the equipment that Henry had mentioned. He removed the disk and stowed the recorder in the capsule. He then pushed a slide switch on the disk and released it from his hand. Instead of falling, it rose upward, gaining velocity as it went. In a few seconds, it was out of sight.

"If that is going to work," Pat said, "we'll know in about six hours.

I need to set up a homing beacon, and I'd like to stow this capsule in a safe place. Is there somewhere around here I can hang my hat?"

"Yes, sir," Henry said. "You are welcome to use the Expedition Control Post. It's probably just what you need, and nobody is using it. Come on, we'll show you where it is."

Pat slipped back inside the capsule, brought it to a waist-high hover, and moved along with the excited terraformers. The CP had double doors, and Pat simply flew the capsule inside and set it down against a wall. After removing Shamus' whistle from his pocket and putting its chain around his neck, he settled down in the little building, which housed an office, sleeping accommodations, and sanitary facilities.

Henry informed him that the morning meal would be taken soon. Before going to the mess hall for breakfast, he set up the message chip homing beacon outside the CP and secured his personal weapon inside the capsule. He had some misgivings about leaving it, but he had observed that none of the terraformers was armed.

The mess hall was a good place for Pat to start his inquiry. It had a public address system, and practically everyone in the camp was there. Pat introduced himself, explained his mission, and asked that anyone who had pertinent information contact him. He refrained from making any overtures in the direction of assuming leadership of the expedition, judging that to do so would be counterproductive. The terraformers seemed to be in no immediate danger; it wouldn't serve his purposes to bog down in matters that might have no bearing on the accomplishment of his mission. Consequently, he presented himself as just what he was: a fact finder from SEJS.

After breakfast, Henry provided a comprehensive personnel status report to Pat. All of the project's managers and scientists, its physician, and its chaplain were either deceased or ineffective. On the other hand, none of the first-line supervisors, technicians, or workers had experienced any problems to date. Pat transcribed this information on the next chip he would send out. Then he began talking with the people who wanted to share information with him.

He first learned what he could about the fruits of the terraformers' labors. The loss of their mother ship, which would have become their orbital base station, had hindered the human expedition, but that was offset by the head start the planet itself had given them. It had abundant water, air that humans could breathe, and a tolerable climate. Moreover, the biota seemed to pose no major obstacles in terms of preexisting civilizations or threats to physical health.

A few personnel had been lost to doodlebugs and marine predators, but until apparent psychoses befell the expedition's leaders, work had moved ahead quickly to set the west end of the island up as a base of operations. They had installed facilities for producing energy and consumables, such as food and water, without any hitches.

Stark but solid shelters were already in place when the terraformers arrived. Parties unknown had long ago built the cast-stone rows of two-story, barracks-like buildings that comprised most of the camp. It had been necessary only to modify them for human use, clean them up, and move in.

Across from the habitations was a row of large buildings with high ceilings. The terraformers called them "the hangars" and had pressed them into use as maintenance and storage facilities. The strange equipment they had discovered in the hangars was still sitting there. Pat spent the rest of the morning looking it over with the maintenance supervisor, Carl Jensen, and his crew. Jensen, it turned out, had made a hobby of trying to determine what each item was and how it worked, but he had met with little success. This, Pat soon learned, was because the things in the warehouse were of completely alien origin, varied widely in shape and size, and, for the most part, had no obvious function.

It had taken great ingenuity and insight for Carl to identify and figure out some of the larger items. As he pointed out, all were pieces of construction equipment that were more or less within the scope of his expertise.

When they were about to leave one of the hangars to go to lunch, Pat said, "Wait up a minute, Carl; something just struck me about this stuff. The dust on the things back by the rear wall is a lot thicker than it is on those up front. Do you suppose we could be looking at groups of things that have been left here at different times?"

"I believe so," Carl said. "After chow, we'll take some measurements and see which pieces belong with one another."

By midafternoon, they had sorted the equipment into three groupings, not counting the humans' material, and began trying to infer origins from the configuration of what they took to be controls. The older two groups were, they guessed, Arach and Crustacean hardware. They were speculating about the more recent group when Henry Waters rushed in and interrupted them.

"Captain, there's a little red arm sticking out of the side of your communications beacon—is it important?"

"If the thing is working right, Henry, it means that we have a letter in our mailbox. Let's go look."

It was indeed a message from Dragonfly. Pat put on the headphones that provided output from the recorder and played it back. Peggy stated that the chip recovery system worked better than she had expected and that she had received and forwarded Pat's message via CX-26. SEJS had not yet replied, but she would keep him posted. The balance of the text was a personal reminder to take no chances and to keep her informed.

The terraformers were thrilled to know that it was possible to communicate with the outside world. Henry asked, "Captain, do your chips have any excess capacity that we could use to get correspondence out? I'd like to send an official message to the Terraformers' Guild, and I'm sure people would like to send word to their families that they are all right."

"I don't see why not, Henry, but I don't want people to get angry if we have to limit what goes out. Every time a chip goes back and forth from my ship up there, the time when the aliens detect my presence is that much closer. However, when a chip goes out, you are more than welcome to use whatever space remains on it. Each chip has eight megabits available. The next one will be about three-quarters full because it will contain your personnel report, a brief sitrep from me, and pictures of the equipment in the hangars. In round numbers, that leaves a little more than 2,000 characters per person."

Henry nodded, and a grin lit up his face. "Sounds good."

"Why don't you put out the word that each individual can use that much space on a chip that I'll launch at 2200Z tonight? Tell them that SEJS will automatically notify their next of kin of their status, so they shouldn't waste space on the 'Hello Mom, I'm alive and well' stuff. Also, be sure to tell them their messages will have no privacy at all. No doubt J-2 will scrutinize them, plus they will pass through many other hands before arriving at their destinations. The real question is, though— how are we going to get all of that text recorded on the chip?"

"If your recorder will interface with my mail transceiver, I don't think that'll be a problem," Henry said. "Is that a standard fiber optic jack on the side?"

It was. That evening, a chip packed full of data and personal messages wended its way into the heavens.

— CHAPTER THIRTY —

Weird Planet

Peggy's duties after launching Pat in his capsule required nothing more than surface attention. Lest her comparative idleness heighten her anxiety, she decided to put herself to full-capacity work. She popped Dragonfly back three hundred kilometers, established an orbit that would put her in the center of the cone from which any rising communications chips would emerge, and activated every sensor at the ship's disposal. From her new vantage point, she had a fairly good view of the field around the planet. She applied herself to correlating her observations with her store of phenomenology.

Roughly six hours later, the sensors detected Pat's first message chip. She moved into its line of flight, deployed a mechanically launched polymeric mist net, and got out of the way. In a matter of seconds, the net caught the chip, and she reeled it in and read it. Then she popped Dragonfly up to the asteroid belt.

CX-26 admitted Dragonfly through her shields. As soon as Peggy had transferred her catch to the cruiser, she got on the intercom. "Permission to speak to the captain?"

"Yes, commander?" came Bud's voice over the speakers.

"You're probably going to think I'm crazy, but Captain Callen asked me to work on something when he left, and I'm worried about it."

"If you're worried, I'm worried, Peggy. What is it?"

"When we were on our way down to launch the capsule, the captain said that the field reminded him of something, but he couldn't place it. He didn't think it was important, and from close up I couldn't observe the field well enough to think otherwise. Consequently, I backed off and watched what was taking place."

"And you think you know what it was?"

"Maybe. I think he was onto something. If you disregard the improbability of such a thing, the field looks just like an electroencephalograph. There are complex brain waves, local activity, everything. It isn't human, though."

"Let me take another look." There was a pause, and Peggy

assumed Bud was reviewing the data. Then his voice came back on. "You know, it does look like a three-dimensional map of an EEG. But do you realize how far-fetched that would be? How much power would it take to project the forces that are producing those dynamics?"

"It varies. The containment field seems to be a constant power affair that expands and contracts with the load from below. I can show you the exact data for the past six hours, if you want me to. But to an order of magnitude, the energy being absorbed by the field is about one kilowatt, average power. The aliens' field isn't as powerful as our artificial video makes it look."

"Let's be objective about this," he replied. "Can you imagine a one kilowatt brain? When I fooled around with amateur radio when I was a kid, that was the power limit on transmitters, and hardly anybody was allowed that much. Grab the antenna on a set like that, key the mike, and it would char the skin on your hand."

"Your skepticism is justifiable, sir. No brain on record is even close to that. However, the entire situation with the Doodlebug Planet is very mysterious. There could be something unprecedented down there. What if it's a thousand one-watt brains that are able to function in unison?"

"That's still pretty far-fetched, Peggy," Bud said, "but it deserves consideration by better heads than mine. I'll put our own people to work on it, and I'll pass your thoughts along to J-2."

"Thank you, sir. That makes me feel a lot better. Is there anything you want me to put on the message chip?"

"Just the text in the prearranged message. We'd better not say anything about your EEG theory until it's been evaluated—and until we're sure the aliens aren't intercepting the chips."

"By your leave, I'll get out there and launch our answer to chip number one."

"Have at it, but be careful. Things appear to be going pretty well, and we don't want to upset the applecart."

"Wilco."

⚠ ⚠ ⚠

Pat's first action the next morning was to check the comm beacon and rob it of the chip that lay inside. Transferred to the recorder, it produced a brief, cheery personal greeting from Peggy and official messages discussing the old equipment in the hangars and the terraformers' morale. The alien equipment had created quite a stir among the scientists who had seen Pat's pictures. They confirmed ancient Arach and Crustacean origins for the first two generations, and a listing of equipment and functions was promised. The newer items remained mysterious. The scientists gave Pat instructions for taking additional photos.

SEJS had processed the terraformers' outbound letters, but it would be at least twenty-four hours before responses would be available. Meanwhile, Henry had uploaded the expedition's accumulated backlog of old correspondence to a chip. J-2 advised Pat to expect a brief improvement in morale, followed by a reversal. A long time had elapsed since the group was declared lost. Escape from the planet was by no means assured; problems were deemed inevitable.

Pat erased his parts of the chip and turned it over to Henry, who copied the terraformers' personal items into the distribution system. He and Pat then went off to the mess hall to proclaim the arrival of mail. Pat also reported that, although the old equipment in the hangars was interesting and he would continue to investigate it, it had no apparent connection with the taboo.

He had wanted to ask anyone having knowledge of unusual physical features of the planet to let him know, but there was no point. The terraformers had all rushed out to check their mail transceivers. Pat spent the morning exploring the hangars with Carl Jensen and, at lunchtime, announced that he and Carl had determined that much of the equipment they had looked at was for mining or tunneling in rock. It appeared to have been heavily used; the question was, where were the mines or tunnels?

This inquiry evoked a response. After Pat sat down to eat, a nervous little man took a seat opposite him. He fiddled with his food for a moment and then looked up at Pat.

"Captain, sir, this may not mean anything at all. I'm just a materials lab helper, and all I know is something I overheard one day, not long after we first got here. A group of scientists was looking at some infrared pictures of the island, and Ms. Brown kept saying that it looked to her like there was a mineshaft in the mountain."

Pat set down his fork. "A mineshaft? That's what you heard?"

"The chief geophysicist told her that lava pipes were to be expected in a volcanic formation, but she said that the mountain is limestone and what she was talking about was too straight to be natural. He told her to stick to her area of expertise, which was civil engineering, and that's about all there was to it."

"Thank you," Pat said, and he reached across the table to shake the man's hand. "That is exactly the type of information I've been looking for. What is your name? I'd really appreciate it if you could show me those pictures."

"Richardson, but everybody calls me Tiny. I think I can find the pictures for you, but I don't know anything about interpreting them."

They walked to the lab together; a few minutes later, they were looking at views of the west end of the planet taken from an orbiting satellite. The long, flat strip of stone that ran straight from the foot of the mountain to the west end of the camp, separating the hangars from the smaller buildings, glowed hotly in the infrared scans of the area. It reminded Pat of a runway. Directly off the east end of this runway, a dark line represented a stripe of relatively cool surface. Pat supposed that a ventilated tube of some sort lay beneath.

"You know, Tiny," Pat said, "there's a big difference between limestone and volcanic rock. I flew over the mountain on my way in here, and it looked like sedimentary stuff to me. You wouldn't think it would take a geologist long to determine what was what up there."

"At the time, they were trying to decide where to locate the camp's water purification plant and sewage treatment facilities," Tiny said. "When they decided to make use of these buildings and found pipes already in place, they lost interest in the mountain."

"Pipes?"

"Yes, they run from here down to the edge of the water at the west end of the island. To supply us with fresh water, our crews put a desalination station at the end of the island and hooked it into the small pipes. All they had to do was flush them out, and we were in business."

Pat's interest rose. Pipes could mean a civilization of some kind.

"It is a fascinating system," Tiny said. "I hooked up the plumbing here in the lab. All of the feed water lines and valves are made of glass, and the joints are sealed with silicone. The pipes look like they were extruded. If they were, it was a neat trick. It makes for permanent, contaminant-free plumbing. The wastewater lines are glass, too. There are traps in them, but very few valves. They all lead into a sewer main that connects to the storm drains. It all goes to the treatment plant on the west end of the island."

"That doesn't sound too good to me," Pat said. "If it's all at the same end of the island, isn't there a danger of getting sewage into the water system?"

"I doubt it, sir. The facilities are about five hundred meters apart and on opposite sides of the sand spit at the end of the island. The ocean current comes from the east, and it's pretty strong. Besides, the effluent is sterile. It's probably safer to drink than the water coming out of the treatment plant. If it wasn't, there's no telling what we could do to the ecology."

"You can tell I don't know much about overhauling planets," Pat confessed, "so I guess I'd better go looking for tunnels. Do you know whether Ms. Brown ever followed up on her theory?"

"No, sir, I don't know. Funny thing, though—she just disappeared one evening. She was one of our first losses, and we all figured a doodlebug got her. She was a great one for taking walks, and she was headed east the last time we saw her. At that time, we all thought we would be safe from the doodlebugs if we stayed on solid ground."

"You mean we're not? I've been operating on that assumption, myself."

"No, sir, you're sure not. I reckon we've forgotten that you just arrived and don't know all about this place. Be careful at night, whatever you do: the doodlebugs move around and battle for territory then. They often crawl right across the runway and along the beaches. They won't go in the water, though."

"Why haven't you tried to wipe them out or at least kill those that have their burrows next to camp?"

"At first we did kill them, but it really wasn't worthwhile. Not only do they die hard, but we found out that they are beneficial."

"That's hard to believe. What could be good about a doodlebug the size of a forklift?"

"When the moons are full," Tiny said, "there is a kind of sea serpent that comes out onto the beaches to lay eggs in the sand. They are six or seven meters long and weigh several tons. They remind me of sea lions, except they are bad news. Their bite is poisonous, and they are extremely aggressive. If it weren't for the doodlebugs, we'd be overrun by the sea serpents. We decided to let the balance of nature alone until we had a better solution."

"When I first landed," Pat said, "I noticed that nobody was armed. How do you protect yourself from doodlebugs?"

"Oh, that's no problem. You can hear them coming for hundreds of meters, and they are very slow moving after their initial lunge. All you have to do is either get out of their way or stand still. If you aren't moving, they think you are a rock or something. In a few seconds they forget you're there."

"What else do I need to know about this place?"

"I understand you've heard about the loss of our senior people," Tiny replied, "so I guess the only other thing is the ocean. It is suicide to go near it or get in it, unless you are aboard ship and have adequate weapons to defend yourself. There are a few types of fish that survive by being prolific and going around in huge schools, but everything else is toothy and poisonous, one way or the other."

"I'm glad I didn't try to go for a swim. The surf on the north side of the island looked pretty good yesterday." Pat paused and scratched his head. "That reminds me of something. SEJS described this island as being the southerly part of an atoll. If it is an atoll, we are sitting on the rim of a big volcano, and the geophysicist might be right about lava pipes. On the other hand, the lagoons of atolls are fairly calm, while the north coast here isn't calm. Instead of an atoll, we may be sitting on top of up-thrust ocean bottom. In that case, the island could be made of sedimentary rock—and Ms. Brown may have been right. I think I'm going to go exploring. Care to come along?"

"No thanks," Tiny said. "I'm an indoors person; I wouldn't be much help. However, I know a couple of people who might like to go with you. Wait a second and I'll ask them." Tiny was back in a moment with a young couple whom he introduced as Mary and Wade McClure.

"Did Tiny tell you what I have in mind?" Pat asked them. "It'll be hazardous, and the last thing I want to do is put a young couple in danger."

Wade and Mary looked at each other. Mary said, "We are primal settlers, professional survivors. We are on this expedition because the greatest rewards of founding a new planet go to those who are there first. If you don't want us to go with you, there will be no hard feelings, but you ought to know that we have been all over this island. Nobody else here can say that."

"Hey," Pat exclaimed, "no offense meant. You don't look the part, you know, and it would be tragic if anything happened to either of you."

"We are a team," Wade said. "Where one of us goes, so goes the other. What is it that you intend to explore?"

"Satellite pictures indicate that there is something interesting not far off the east end of the runway, or whatever you want to call it."

"We call it the runway," Mary said, "because this place reminded us of an old-fashioned airport when we first arrived. That's why we call the big buildings hangars. Anyway, all we have seen at the foot of the mountain where it meets the runway is rock. What exactly are you looking for?"

"Tunnels or caves." He showed them a map he had transferred from the satellite pictures to his watch and described the tunneling equipment that was in the warehouses.

"We've walked over that ground any number of times and we've never seen any openings," Wade said, "but it won't hurt to look again."

"The openings, if there are any, may be buried or concealed," Pat said. "Tiny tells me there are buried pipes under this place, and there could be something similar up there."

"I hadn't thought of that, but you're right," Wade said. "Let's go check it out. We'll get a walking staff for you. Do you have a hand weapon and survival gear? A hat would be good—it gets hot out there."

They met at the command post a few minutes later. Pat had recorded the events of the morning and his present intentions on a communications chip. He sent it skyward while they walked east on the runway.

The runway had a crown for drainage, but it was quite level in the east-west direction. At its east end, it terminated abruptly about three hundred meters short of a terrain finger that sloped gradually up into the mountain. An apron faired the runway down into the sand. The map indicated that the tunnel, if that was what it was, would begin a short distance up the terrain finger.

"I don't see any doodlebug pits," Pat said. "Do they ever just hide in the sand?"

"Not that I know of," Mary said. "The sand is too shallow for them to dig here, but they do cross from one side of the island to the other at this point. The danger here is the sand snakes. That's what the staff is for. The lead man pushes it through the sand ahead of him, and if he hits a snake, he flips it up and shoots it before it has a chance to bury itself. The person behind watches the flanks and rear. If you see

275

movement in the sand, use the staff to head it off."

"I'm not fond of snakes. How big are these?"

"The biggest I've seen was less than a meter long and about as big around as my wrist," Wade answered. "They're not going to eat anybody, but they are poisonous. They lie in wait where small flying reptiles come down to get gravel for their gizzards. This place is windswept, so there is a lot of exposed gravel."

"How did you find out about the snakes?"

"Pure luck," Mary said. "The first time we came out here, we used the staffs to probe the sand, just to be sure of our footing. We hadn't gone three meters when a snake struck Wade's staff. But don't get the wrong idea—they aren't all that common. It's just better to be safe than sorry."

"Amen."

No snakes turned up when they crossed the sand, and they spread out abreast to investigate the rocky surface of the terrain finger. After a couple of hours and many passes back and forth, they sat down to rest. While Pat was removing the cap from his canteen, he looked over each shoulder and shook his head.

"Something wrong, captain?" Mary said.

"This place gives me the willies, and I don't know why."

"Me too."

"The whole place?" Wade asked. "Or just this spot?"

Pat laughed and said, "I wouldn't give you much for this whole planet, but there's something about this spot in particular that I don't like."

"Are you intuitive?" Wade asked. "Mary is."

"All things considered, I guess that intuition, luck, or both have had a lot to do with my staying alive over the years. Why?"

"I've learned to trust Mary's sixth sense," Wade said. "If both of you are getting vibrations, maybe we ought to get out of here."

"I'm not getting that kind of feeling, honey," Mary said. "It's not immediate danger I sense, but I do feel like something is amiss. What about you, captain?"

"I'm not that well attuned to things, Mary," Pat replied. "All I know is that something isn't right about this place. Let's take stock:

We're looking for a tunnel, and we ought to be right on top of it. We've looked all over the place, but we haven't found so much as a discontinuity in the rock, much less an opening. Look at the map—" He indicated where he meant, and they drew closer to see. "By the way this line fades as it goes eastward, I'd say that it's a tunnel that gets deeper as it goes."

"The land slopes here," Wade pointed out. "The tunnel could run horizontally and still appear to fade out."

"Point well taken. If it does, I'd say that it started out at about the same elevation as the end of the runway. Now that's an interesting thought—let's walk back down and see what lies over here at the level of the runway."

"Wait—how wide is this tunnel?" Wade asked.

"Hard to say, but judging by the vegetation the satellite was able to resolve, I'd say it's between three and five meters wide. Why?"

"The machinery you talked about seeing in the warehouses… what was the shape of the opening it was built to cut?"

"About three and a half meters square. That's nice and consistent, isn't it?" Pat answered.

Wade said, "If the tunnel's floor is level with the runway, its roof is three and a half meters above that. This terrain slopes very gradually, maybe one or two percent. That means that if the entrance is hidden, it's behind a very large, wedge-shaped chunk of stone. Let's look for something like that."

"What are we going to do if we find it?" Mary asked. "It would weigh tons."

"Good point," Pat said. "Maybe Carl Jensen can get some of that old gear working, and we can cut our way in."

"The expedition has equipment of its own that can do that," Mary said, "but if the tunnel is an extension of the runway, I'll bet there is a hidden way to get at it. It could be dangerous to try to force our way in. If this place is taboo, who knows what kind of booby traps may be placed in the way?"

"Now that you mention it," Pat said, "in the tradition of such things, even a hidden way in is likely to be booby trapped. Let's not get carried away, but let's be careful."

They walked back to the level at which the rocky slope met the sand and took a good look. The sand there was about half a meter deep.

277

Pat and Wade took turns digging with their hands; it was Wade who found something.

"Eureka—a seam!" he shouted.

A damp horizontal line lay where they expected to find the floor of the tunnel. It took longer to find the top seam, but find it they did. The gap was so narrow that they had mistaken it for a horizontal stratum in the stone, and the sides looked like random cracks running vertically from the corners of the tunnel.

They sat down again, and Mary said, "I know what it is about this place that gives me the creeps. Wade, do you remember Delia Brown, the engineer? Before she disappeared, she used to come out here and hang around."

"Yeah, she was here a couple of times when we passed by."

Pat told them about the conversation Tiny had heard, and they agreed that Delia must have been looking for the tunnels too.

"Maybe she found them," Mary said. "Nobody knows what happened to her. She just wandered off."

"If either of you finds what might be a way to open this thing," Pat said, "for goodness' sake, don't try it alone."

"Don't worry, we won't," Mary said. "Wade, do you remember what they said about Delia's disappearance?"

"Yeah, they said she must have flipped out. The last time she was seen, she was eastbound with a broom over her shoulder."

"A broom would be just the thing for getting dust, or sand, off of something," Mary mused.

"Don't look now," Pat said, "but I think I see the end of a broom handle right below where we are sitting."

For a moment, they looked at him as if he was joking. When they looked where he was pointing, they could see a weathered nub protruding from the sand. They dug it out and probed the sand all around, but found nothing.

"Let's look higher up," Wade said. "If it fell down here, the wind would bury it in no time."

The side of the rock formation was steeper than its frontal slope. They made their way slowly upward, with Pat on the right and Mary in the middle. When they were almost back where they had started, Pat said, "It's getting late. What do you say we call it a day and come back in the morning?"

"Good idea," Wade replied. "Say, captain—what is that sticking out of the rock, above you and to your right?"

Pat looked up and saw what Wade was pointing at; it looked metallic. He scrambled up the slope and took a closer look. "It's a geologist's pick," he said. "The point is wedged into a hole in the rock. I wonder... did you notice how the broom handle was chewed up? It looked like it might have been stuck into the rock, too. See if you can find a round hole somewhere."

"I've got a triangular one here," Mary said, "but not a round one."

"Here it is," Wade said. "Give me the broomstick, and I'll see if it fits."

"What happened to our caution?" Pat asked. "Let's not become another story of mysterious disappearance."

"Delia was a friend of mine," Mary said, "and if she's here, I want to find her."

"Are you sure about that?" Wade asked. "She's been gone for months. I'd like to find her, too, but the captain is right. In thirty minutes it's going to be dark, which means the doodlebugs will start moving around. A few more hours won't make any difference. I'd like to have some backup available if anything happens. Not only that, we don't have anything that will fit that triangular hole. It may be important."

Reluctantly, Mary agreed. They turned back, planning another expedition with additional help the next day.

That night, when Pat sent up a chip, he had a message for Peggy. "You're going to be proud of me," it began.

— CHAPTER THIRTY-ONE —

Delia Brown

The terraformers saw more activity at the dawn of the following day than they had seen in months. They set tents up at the end of the runway and erected a catwalk for access to the terrain finger. They brought breakfast out from the compound and, before the dew was off the local vegetation, workers and onlookers alike were waiting expectantly for the tunnel to open.

An hour later, they were disappointed. No amount or combination of probing the holes in the rock face produced the desired effect. By lunchtime, most of the crowd, hot and weary, had drifted back to camp. When only the medic and some construction personnel remained, Wade and Mary approached Pat.

"Mary and I think we ought to fan out and search for other parts of a tunnel opening mechanism," Wade said.

"I've been thinking the same thing, but I wanted to exhaust the possibilities of what we had already found and let the crowd thin out."

Pat summoned the remaining people, and they walked side-by-side upward from the runway. Suddenly one of the workers called out, "Hey, captain, look at this! There's a keyway cut in the top groove. Somebody bring me that broom." The man swept energetically at the cracks in the stone and revealed a lozenge of stone that interrupted the line that ran across the top of the rock. He looked along the line and said, "The round hole down there lines up with this thing. Push on it while I try to move the key." After some experimentation, the man said, "It gives a little when you push from over there, but it feels like something on the other side is still holding it. Look and see if there is a release opposite the first one."

Pat walked carefully along the line. "Bring me the triangular rod. There's a hole over here. Before I push on it, though, I'd feel better if everybody would move back and you'd use a long stick to push on the key. It might be booby trapped."

When Pat applied pressure to the releases on both sides, the key yielded by moving downward about half a meter, but nothing else seemed to happen. However, when he took his weight off the key, it rose back up, and they heard a banging sound from up the slope.

"What was that?" Mary hurried in the direction of the noise, with Wade hot on her heels.

"Wait!" Pat shouted. "Wade, don't take any chances."

"It's a trap door," Mary cried. "Oh God—it's Delia in there!" That got everyone's attention, and a woman he recognized as the medic started running.

"Stop!" Pat commanded. "Don't go in there yet, and don't anybody move the releases."

He ran to where the McClures stood. They were shining a light into the hole below a square hatch. A ladder led down into the opening from the hatch, and the medic had his foot on the top rung, preparing to descend.

"I told you to *stop,*" Pat said again. "If you try to go into that hole before I tell you to, I'll stun you into the middle of next week."

The surprised medic looked up into the muzzle of Pat's weapon and backed off, hands in the air. Holstering his sidearm slowly, Pat said, "I have two remaining missions down here. One is to find out all I can about the taboo on this place."

He looked around at the people who had gathered, attracted by the shouting. "The other mission is to get us all out of here. There is no way I am going to get that woman down there off this planet. She is dead because she went into that hole. It may or may not have had something to do with the taboo, but nobody else is going down that ladder until we know what we are getting into. Mary, Carl Jensen is over at the end of the runway. Would you please tell him we need lights and some way to jam this hatch open? Also, see if he can come up with a periscope or at least a mirror on a pole. Do it quietly. Mass confusion won't help at all."

Mary looked peeved, but she nodded and said, "May I also ask him to bring something to retrieve Delia's body?"

"Of course."

While she was gone, they propped the hatch open and gathered around the opening. Pat went over to the medic and asked her name.

"Trudy Koslovski, sir," she said.

"You're this expedition's only surviving medic, aren't you?"

"Yes, I am," she said.

"Then you are the very last person we want to have taking

chances," Pat said. "If that woman has been down there for several months, there isn't much you can do for her. We'll get her out, but all in due course."

"She may have been down there for a long time," Trudy said, "but she doesn't look dead to me."

"We'll see in a few minutes," Pat promised. He turned to see if Carl was on his way. He could see that Mary was speaking into the communicator that was set up under canvas at the foot of the terrain finger. Further away, vehicles were starting to move back at the camp. It wasn't long before Carl arrived on the scene with a small crew. They took over the chore of operating the release mechanism and quickly scotched the door open with wedges.

Carl lowered a drop light into the opening and handed Pat a tubular object about two meters long. "This is about as close as I can come to a periscope; we didn't bring any submarines along. It's the night vision system from a heavy construction vehicle. Don't point it at the light, or you'll blind yourself."

"No problem—it's a lot like weapons sights I'm accustomed to using." He rested the barrel of the device on the sill of the door and peered into the chamber below. It wasn't easy to aim, but he was eventually able to get a good look around. "It looks like this is some kind of anteroom to a tunnel," he announced. "It's about three and a half meters square in the vertical plane. It's a good bet that the equipment in the hangars was used in its construction. I'd say it's only eight or ten meters to a wall at the east end. There's a door in the wall, and a bunch of equipment on the floor and walls. The wall at the west end is smooth, and it's almost directly below us. There's a vertical ladder right in front of me. It doesn't go all the way to the floor. The funny thing is that there are little balls hanging all over the ceiling."

"Sounds like mushrooms," said Mary, who had returned from the runway.

"Could be," Pat said, "but I've never seen any like them, if that's what they are. The stems are extremely thin, and the bulb at the end of the stem is spherical. Hey, one of them burst when the light hit it! It looks like a handful of thistledown came out if it."

"What about Delia?" Mary asked.

Pat said nothing while he took a good, hard look at the body in the chamber. "I don't know," he finally replied. "She doesn't look like there is anything wrong with her, but it's hard to tell because she's lying face down on the floor. She isn't moving at all. Her gear is beside her, and her lantern is still in her right hand. She looks like she just fell asleep."

"Could she have gotten into a layer of oxygen deficient air and asphyxiated?" Koslovski asked. "If the tunnel is dry and there is no oxygen, decomposition wouldn't set in for a long time."

"Very possible," Pat said. "There are no signs of moisture down there. But don't mushrooms have to be in a damp place to grow, and don't they have to have something to grow in? These are hanging off of dry, solid rock."

"I think so," Koslovski said, "but I'm no expert. In any case, I would expect some desiccation and some decomposition from anaerobic organisms by now."

"For God's sake!" Mary said. "We're talking about a human being, not a bug on a pin."

Pat looked her in the eye and said, "Nobody knows that better than I. The point is that the person down there isn't moving, not even enough to stir that thistledown with her breath. I would only hope that if something happened to me, you would be as concerned as you are for Delia. But, more important, I would want you to do everything in your power to make sure that whatever happened to me didn't happen to you."

"Of course," Mary said.

"That's what we are doing now, right?" he said, understanding her urgency and trying to respect it. "We're trying to minimize the risks when we do try to get her out of there."

"Let's do it, then," Mary said, "she's lying down there, helpless, and we're getting nowhere fast."

Wade said, "Be patient, Mary. This isn't the time to blunder blindly ahead."

"I know, but it's Delia." Her face dissolved into tears, and she leaned her head into Wade's shoulder.

"Carl," Pat said, "do you have anything we can use to get Delia's body out of there?"

"Nothing built for the job," Carl said. "That hatch is too small for most of our machinery. But we can put a lifting harness on her and raise her with a hoist, or we can attach a grasper to a cherry picker. The quickest thing is to put a breathing apparatus on someone, go down there, and put a harness on her."

"I'll do it," Mary said, wiping her eyes with her sleeve.

"Thank you for volunteering, Mary," Pat said, "but what is the least risky thing to do, Carl?"

"If someone goes down there and gets hurt or trapped," Carl replied, "the problem will get a lot bigger. The problem with the maintenance machines is that they weigh three and a half tons. Do you think the rock will support one?"

"It's roughly fifteen centimeters thick," Pat said. "I would think so. But can we get one across the sand?"

"No problem. We've got crawlers that will go almost anywhere. I'll have what we need out here in a half hour or less."

Carl was as good as his word. They positioned the machine on the downhill side of the door, where the distance from solid rock was least, swung the boom around to place its grasping claw over the door, and extended the claw downward. Pat used hand signals to help Carl guide the grasper to Delia's body, gently wrap the claw around it, and raise it toward the opening.

"We're not going to be able to get her out of there this way," Pat said. "With her inside the jaws, she won't pass through the opening."

"If we can get hold of her," Wade said, "let's just lift her out by hand."

"Okay," Pat said, "but be careful."

"You'd better put surgical gloves on," Koslovski said. "She may not be as solid as she looks."

"There's no odor," Wade replied, but he and several of the workers donned gloves. They knelt around the door and jockeyed the boom until Delia's head and shoulders were accessible. Wade reached down to brush a piece of thistledown off Delia's forehead, which had a kind of greenish hue. "Hey, this thing is stuck to her skin."

"Get back!" Pat cried. "Don't touch that thing."

The men scrambled backward, but several pieces of the down wafted up out of hole, drifting about in the eddies created by the movements of the people. One of the workers stopped and said, "Shucks, captain, they're just seeds." He extended his palm to allow one to settle in it.

"Don't!" Pat commanded, but to no avail; the seed came to rest in the man's hand.

"See?" he said with a laugh. "They're harmless." He pursed his lips and puffed a little air toward his palm, causing the tuft of fluff to swing upward. The man's smile quickly changed to a look of surprise, then pain. "It stung me!" he said, grabbing his wrist. He looked in disbelief at his reddening palm; then he screamed and fell to the ground, writhing in pain.

Pat took out his weapon and began to carefully blast the motes that had escaped the chamber below. "Koslovski," he called out, "take care of this man. Carl, lower Delia back into the hole and close that hatch. If anybody sees one of these things that I don't, tell me."

"There's one on the ground," Mary said, pointing.

"Get some forceps and a bottle from Koslovski and see if you can capture it," Pat said. He kept his weapon aimed at the stinging seed while Mary went to get the bottle and forceps. When she had captured it and handed him the bottle, he glanced over at the man on the ground. The worker's hand had turned purple, and red streaks were shooting up his arm. His face was assuming the same greenish tint as Pat had seen in Delia's skin.

"Severe toxic shock," Koslovski said. "He's going to be unconscious by the time we move him. We've got to get him back to the dispensary right away."

"Let's secure here and move out smartly," Pat said. "In addition to getting treatment for this man's injury, we'll want the bio techs to investigate this organism right away."

Four men wearing gloves helped Koslovski carry the injured man back to camp. He remained comatose; his vital signs were rapidly slipping away. Once Pat was sure everything possible was being done for him in the dispensary, he took the seed to the biology lab.

Dissection of the thistledown revealed that it was made of three parts, each about a centimeter long. The top was a tuft of fibers that served to give the whole thing a high volume-to-weight ratio. Amazingly, each fiber had an articulated base that resembled a hair follicle. Evidently, the fibers not only folded up compactly during storage, but also could perform a rudimentary steering function while airborne.

The center section was thin and tubular, but it contained a cluster of complex cells that seemed to be a cortex. The bottom section was a tubercle a little more than a millimeter in diameter. It contained a stinging cell much like that in a hydra: a barbed, tubular needle, surrounded by a spiraled thrusting fiber resembling a coiled spring. At the base of the barb was a muscular vesicle full of fluid. Unlike a typical stinging cell containing poison, however, the vesicle was full of germ cells like those in plant seeds. The penetrating power of the stinger was impressive; it was effective against a typical shoe sole, for example.

Repeated scans of the workman's arm showed that fast-growing root hairs were proliferating outward from the wound site. In an hour, they were halfway up the inside of his forearm. The man's body chemistry was changing rapidly, and Koslovski decided to amputate his arm just below the elbow and attempt to detoxify him.

When Pat checked in on him again the following morning, there was good news. A complete hemolysis and heroic measures involving almost every medical tool in their arsenal had stabilized the worker and brought him back to consciousness. Pat asked about the severed limb. At first, the lab techs couldn't get the top off the specimen tray in which they had placed the arm. Finally, they were able to pry it open, and they discovered that the distal end of the arm had turned into a sheet of skin-like material that was attempting to line the tray. A mat of fibers protruded from the stump.

In talking over this development with Koslovski and the lab techs, Pat found that two schools of thought prevailed. One was that the hand should be put into a disintegrator, post haste. The other was that it should be studied, albeit under constant surveillance. The latter opinion, promoted mostly by Koslovski, won out.

After several days and the sacrifice of several laboratory animals, it evolved that the organism that had attacked the man had a simple, albeit gruesome, life cycle. It would take root in an animal and become dominant (a process that progressed only in the presence of light), and then it would somehow cause the zombie-like host to seek out a dark chamber and metamorphose into a sheet that would coat surfaces, develop the fruit that Mary and Pat mistook for mushrooms, and become dormant. When subjected to light or mechanical disturbance, the fruit burst to start the cycle anew.

Satisfying though the success of this research may have been, it did not solve any problems. Delia Brown still lay at the bottom of the chamber where the work party had found her, undoubtedly heavily infected with the parasitic organism that had felled her. The infestation of the chamber also presented a formidable obstacle to further exploration. Pat had sent off frequent reports and received many replies, but SEJS had nothing worthwhile to contribute. Pat reasoned that this was to be expected: the life forms he was reporting were hitherto unknown, and SEJS could hardly make inquiries of the aliens without endangering his mission. He was on his own and would have to do the best he could.

He called a meeting of the people who had been the most help so far. They assembled in the CP, and he stated that he wanted to develop a plan for exploring the tunnel in an organized manner. Clearly, they would have to have a system for opening the door, communicating among one another, and getting past the stinging organisms. He opened the floor for suggestions.

Carl Jensen spoke first. "The boys and I have been working on it for the past few days and we have some ideas. We rigged up a big vacuum cleaner that we think will let us collect all of the loose stingers in the chamber. We'll throw the filter into a disintegrator that we'll put by the entrance. When we get all of the loose stingers out, we'll spray the inside of the chamber with a coat of quick-setting plastic foam to keep any others from getting free. We can do all of that by remote control. The problem is that we don't know what to do with Ms. Brown's body."

"If she hasn't been exposed to too much light," Koslovski said, "there's a chance we can save her. Let's hope the stinger in her forehead hasn't grown too far. What we need to do is put her into a light-proof box that we can raise through the door, but I don't have anything like that."

"We can build what you need," Carl said, "but won't it be dangerous to take her out of the tunnel? I'd hate to think about fifty kilograms of that stinging stuff getting loose in the compound."

"So would I," Pat said. "Have we found anything that kills it?"

"The disintegrator, of course," a bio tech said, "but that's not very practical. Acids don't work, but strong caustic solutions do the job. We're testing other things, but it will take a while to be sure."

"After all this time, don't you think she's dead?" Mary asked.

"No," the tech said. "I liken it to a wasp that stings a caterpillar and lays an egg in it. The caterpillar will last a long time before the wasp larva finishes eating it, and the caterpillar isn't really dead until it's all gone. It's more like suspended animation."

"What a horrible thought!" Mary said.

"Yes, but that's the way it is," the tech said. "At least, from what Charley Goode says—he's the guy that got stung and lost his hand—the sting is pretty bad but you don't feel anything after that. Old Charley says he actually had some pretty pleasant dreams, like he was back home."

"Were they the same kind of dreams your leaders had before they went off the deep end?" Pat asked.

"Not exactly, but it wouldn't be a bad idea to have somebody watch him. I'll take care of it, and I'll be right back."

"Carl," Pat said, "I have a question for you. Rather than spray the walls with foam, couldn't we just vacuum up all of the stingers? If you put the nozzle around a cluster and tap it, they all ought to go right up to the filter, or even to the disintegrator, if you make a direct connection."

"We can, yes, but it will be much slower going because we'll have to use very thick hoses that are hard to handle."

"Why the thick hoses? The stingers don't seem to trigger on inanimate objects."

"I didn't know that," Carl said.

"Well, I'm not saying that it's a law, either," Pat confessed. "Why don't we try it with heavy hoses first, and switch if the stingers don't unload on them?"

"Okay," Carl said. "We're ready to start. What do you plan to do after the stingers are taken care of?"

"I'd like to see what is down the tunnel from the chamber," Pat replied. "How about you?"

"Frankly," Carl said, "I'd like to know more about that door mechanism. Before I do, I wouldn't want to do much exploring. It could close on us and not come open, or something."

The tech had returned and was standing in the doorway, shifting from one foot to the other. "Sir," she said, "nobody knows where Charley is. He disappeared in the direction of the hangars, right after chow."

They all looked at one another. Pat said, "There are ten of us here. Let's split into pairs and go see if we can find him."

They double-timed across the runway, each pair heading for a different building. Pat and the medic were searching the most easterly hangar when someone called from the door, "He's next door and he's all right, but you ought to come and see what he's found!"

When Pat got to Hangar 2, he saw Charley sitting in the cab of a machine that resembled a cargo pallet handler. It was essentially a wheeled platform 3 meters wide by 12 meters long. Lying along the midline of the apparatus was a row of corrugated square tubes 1.5 meters square. Unlike a pallet handler, however, the device had an odd-looking superstructure that supported a jointed boom, and it had a square hoop mounted on the end away from the cab.

"Got something to show you, cap'n," Charley said. "Are there any more coming to take a look?"

"They should all be here in a minute," Pat replied. "What do you have there?"

"Carl and I looked this gizmo over a while back," Charley answered, "but all we knew for sure was that it is a piece of materials handling equipment. I had a dream about it the other night—weird, I saw Little Peoples walking through these tubes—and suddenly it hit me, what this thing is. I've just about got it figured out. One hand ain't enough to work it though, so I'm going to need some help."

Other members of the group were coming into the hangar, Carl among them. He said, "I'll give you a hand, Charley."

Charley smiled and said, "I'll take it, boss; I miss my other one."

They all laughed, and Carl climbed up on the platform with Charley, who said, "Carl, do you remember saying that these tubes would marry up with openings in our buildings, and that they probably were above-ground tunnels to keep the Little Peoples from being blown away during storms? There are lots of these tubes stored in here, and it would work. Let me show you."

Charley raised one end of a tube and said, "These tubes are flexible, and each section has removable end caps. When you remove the caps, the tubes snap together, end to end. The boom can pick up a piece of tube and push it into that square hoop on the end of the platform. While the fixture on top of the hoop holds one section of tube, you attach the next one. Next, the boom pushes the assembly through the hoop and the operator picks up another section. Pretty clever: you could lay a tunnel from building to building during a storm. What I haven't figured out is why there are four extra winches and cables on the boom."

Carl studied the apparatus and said, "They may be a way to steer the tube assembly, Charley. Do you see the fairleads on the ends of each piece of tube? If you ran cables through to the front, I'll bet you could pull on them and bend the tubes around a corner or offset the wind."

"Way to go, Carl!" Charley gave him a slap on the back with his remaining hand. "If you're right, we can put this thing over the trap door in the tunnel and push tubing over to the doorway at the end of the room. If we leave the cap on the first section into the hole, the thistledown can't get inside."

"That'll be just ducky for getting the captain past the doorway of the tunnel," Mary said, "but it won't do Delia any good."

"Mary!" Wade said.

"I think I've got that one covered," Carl said. "We'll build a box we can lower into the chamber, use the grabber to put Delia into the box, and lift it out endwise. If the captain here will blast any stingers that float out, later we'll use Charley's contraption to get us through the entrance chamber."

A plan, thought Pat. *They've come up with a plan all on their own—and it's a damn good one!*

— CHAPTER THIRTY-TWO —

The Tunnel

During lunch on the day after the discovery of the tunnel entrance, Pat sent a sitrep aloft. It stated that although the terraformers had investigated the planet's ocean and its meager landmasses, neither the unusual biota nor the manufactured items in the hangars and the facilities east of the mountain on the main island accounted for the planet's taboo.

He further stated that because whoever had built the tunnel into the mountain had gone to considerable trouble to hide the entrance and make it difficult to open, he planned to continue his investigations there.

Pat and Carl had spent the previous afternoon and evening on plans for their next excursion into the tunnel system. The only physical resources they could use were those already on hand. Therefore, they put people to work on combining an inventory of the things in the hangars with the lists of property that the terraformers had brought with them.

The following morning, they began by investigating the door mechanism, using the expedition's geophysics instruments to develop a three-dimensional view of what lay inside the terrain surrounding the tunnel entrance. The terraformers' instruments were able to produce plan views by aiming probes downward. Lateral coverage was more of a problem, because the sand at the foot of the mountain limited the depth to which they could run cross sections.

The first thing they discovered was that the entire end of the terrain finger was monolithic. Concealed rollers allowed it to move upward and to the west to open the entry chamber for access by the heavy equipment in the hangars. Conversely, the rollers allowed gravity to return the assembly to its rest position automatically. The linkages that controlled the door positions were, for the most part, discernible. This was both a relief and a source of worry. It was nice to know how the doors worked, but everyone was amazed that the apparatus comprised large, intricate clockworks.

Opening either trap door or the massive end cap released ponderous but delicately balanced pawls that, in turn, connected to a deeply buried clock mechanism. After a fixed interval, whatever was open would slam shut and restart the cycle.

In accordance with Charley's plan, the terraformers began by removing Delia Brown's body from the chamber in a lightproof box. They were then able to cement Charley's protective tunnels in place. In so doing, they noticed a small device connected to the trap door. It turned out to be a booby trap—they had been lucky the day before. If the trap door had been blocked open long enough for the timing mechanism to run down, a box mounted on the chamber wall would have fired a volley of lethal darts, and the chamber would have filled with dry sand from a reservoir uphill.

A little experimentation showed that the trap door had approximately a two-hour duty cycle. That is, it could safely be open for one hour, after which it had to remain closed for an hour. Faint rumblings during their experiments alerted them to the possibility that the opening and closing of the hatch triggered other events in the tunnel system, so they left surveillance devices in the entrance chamber during the final cycle of the morning. From this, they learned that when the trap door closed, the wall at the east end of the room slid laterally to close the opening between the chamber and the tunnel.

After lunch, the crew pushed instruments into the tunnel by means of long poles and then closed the trap door. When it opened again, the instruments were gone. Word of this immediately started rumors of aliens hiding in the tunnels and markedly diminished the size of the crowd of bystanders at the end of the runway.

Pat began a hastily convened conference by saying, "Ladies and gentlemen, it's easy to assume that some kind of life form took the recorders, but I find that hard to believe. The only marks in the dust in the tunnel are those we made when we placed the recorders before we closed the door. There must be a physical explanation. I'm open to suggestions."

"Could there be other tunnels in there that we haven't been able to see?" Wade asked.

"Yes, but that leads back to something having taken our gear, and I'm not buying it."

"Wait, captain," Carl said. "We haven't pushed our underground survey much past the east wall of the entrance chamber, and we ought to do that. There is some funny-looking stuff where the tunnel starts, but I didn't pay any mind to it because it didn't have anything to do with the door control mechanism."

"What do you mean by 'funny-looking stuff'?" Pat asked.

"Well, like pipes and, as Wade said, maybe more tunnels under the one we're going into. I can't say for sure because we didn't carry the survey far enough."

"Let's do it, then," Pat said. "If that floor is hollow, there's no telling what could have happened."

"How far do you want us to take it?"

"How long would it take you to do 50 meters?"

"The better part of two hours, I'd say, because the farther we move away from the runway, the greater the volume of rock we have to deal with."

"Okay, let's do 20 meters and see what turns up."

They found that each of the tunnel's side walls contained an array of pipes that ended at the east end of the chamber. In addition, the floor of the tunnel was only 25 centimeters thick and was on top of a deep pit. Again, however, they found more structural elements that their instruments couldn't resolve, particularly in the east wall of the entry chamber. Pat gathered his team outside the trap door for an impromptu conference on progress so far and ideas on how to proceed. They stood around gulping water under the shade of an awning that had been set up.

"What do you want to bet," Pat said, "that our first set of recorders went into the pit through some kind of hidden trap door?"

"I can believe they went into the pit," Carl replied, "but if there is a trap door, our instruments ought to show seams in the floor. There is nothing like that where the recorders were sitting, although you can see vertical seams between the floor slabs every seven meters, as well as along the sides of the slabs."

"This is probably a dumb question," Koslovski said, "but why are the slabs' center supports round and the end supports square? And why are the end supports short, but the center supports go all the way across the tunnel?" The medic had stayed involved in the exploration; business must be slow in the dispensary, Pat surmised. This was far more exciting than upset stomachs and minor infections.

"Who knows?" Carl said. "It probably has something to do with stress relief. Stone isn't a very forgiving building material."

"It would sure make it tough to move along the tunnel," Wade observed, "if, when the door closes, the square supports retract into the walls and the slabs can pivot in the middle."

"Would it ever," Pat said, "and it would be just like the jokers who built this place to make it work that way. Whoever the builders were, they really wanted to keep people out of there."

"Or in," Carl said. "Like this whole planet."

"Why don't we cut our own entrance into the tunnel and bypass the entrance chamber?" Mary inquired. She wiped the sweat from her brow with her sleeve and chugged half a liter of water.

"If we go in from the top," Carl said, "we'll have to dig through the sand chute that empties into the chamber. It would be a lot of work, considering that we already have a door we can use. If we go in from the side, there is no telling what we will find in those pipes in the walls. It could be poison gas. Even if it's only water, it will be a hard way to go." He looked over at Pat and raised his eyebrows. "What do you think, captain? If it's worth trying, we can break out the mining equipment and have at it."

"Let's see if I understand the options, Carl," Pat said, fanning himself with a wide-brimmed hat he had borrowed. "Making our own doorway gains us unrestricted access to the tunnel. That would be nice, but isn't altogether necessary. For the moment, at least, we can explore in round trips that don't take more than an hour apiece. On the other hand, digging our own entry will take time, no matter what, and we could get hurt if we run into something unexpected. The way things have been going, we'd better expect the unexpected. Not only that, if anything goes wrong, we could scatter stingers—or who knows what—all over the landscape. Can anyone think of any important risks or benefits I haven't mentioned?"

"Yes," Mary said. "If I go into that tunnel and get hurt, or run into one of the ugly surprises we keep finding, I want to be able to get back out whenever I need to, not just when some stupid clockwork says I can."

"You're right about the need for a reliable exit," Carl said, "but it's possible that once the chamber door closes, anybody who tries to walk along the tunnel floor might be dumped into the pit underneath. For the time being, whoever goes in there had better be back out in less than an hour."

"Any other thoughts?" Pat asked.

"No, sir," Wade said, and the others shook their heads.

"Then I believe that the safest thing to do, for now, is to use the existing entrance. I'm going to send a chip up to let SEJS know what we have decided to do, and why. Then I'm going into the tunnel."

"You sure about that, captain?" Carl asked.

"I don't have a choice. The purposes of my first trip will be to test our ability to communicate, and to study the things that are immediately on the other side of the wall. Before I go in, let's see if we can figure out how to run a fiber optic cable past the wall—or through it. I have a hunch that our communicators aren't going to have much range inside the mountain, so I'd like to have hard-wired backup."

"Mary and I would like to go with you," Wade said.

"I'd welcome the company," Pat said, "but my better judgment says that the first person in there ought to be the one who is best trained for combat. Earlier, I said I didn't believe we were going to run into aliens in there, and I still don't. However, if I'm wrong, contact with aliens, especially if they are hostile, is my department." He put the hat back on his head and thought again how hot and miserable this pile of rock and sand was. He definitely wouldn't be bringing Peggy here for R&R. "By the way, if I do run into trouble and don't come out, close up the tunnel and send a report to SEJS. Do not come after me unless I tell you that it's safe to do so."

It was late afternoon when Pat climbed down to the tunnel entrance. Before he ventured out onto the sill of the tunnel, he made very sure that the workers had cleaned up all of the loose stingers in the anteroom.

He rolled over onto his back and poked his head into the tunnel opening. As far as he could tell from the dim light coming through the doorway, the tunnel walls and ceiling were bare. The floor felt solid enough, so he inched farther out and waited for his eyes to become better adapted to the dim light. The inner face of the door caught his attention. It was covered by rows of dots that were a couple of centimeters in diameter.

He took out his flashlight, held it as far up as he could reach (in case it was going to draw fire), and turned it on. Nothing bad happened, so he directed the beam toward the door. The dots turned out to be conical holes full of something translucent. "This gets curiouser and curiouser," Pat said, and explained through his comm what he had found. "I'm tempted to try to dig that stuff out and see what it is."

"That may not be a good idea," Carl said. "The ultrasound didn't reach the door too well because it is fairly loose in its track. It deserves another look before you mess with it."

"Don't worry—I'm not eager to have something spill out all over me." Pat already felt quite uncomfortable in this position; he considered himself braver than the average guy, but this place gave him the creeps.

"You may have something there, captain," Carl mused. "It looks like the door could be hollow. Oh, hell, of course it is—man, that's slick!"

"What's slick?"

"That door is built like a water-cooled blast shield, just like the ones that were used on early spacecraft launching stands. I'll bet you a month's pay to a microcredit that the pipes in the walls carry water and that the stuff in the holes is some kind of fusible plug. If a lot of heat hits the door, the plugs melt and water squirts out to cool the surface. If I'm right about what I see in the graphics, you'd play hob burning through that thing."

"How would the water get from the pipes into the door?" Pat asked. He had a pretty good view from where he was lying.

"That's what's slick—there are rotary valves at each end of the door. When it closes, they are cammed around to line the pipes up with matching holes in the door. They probably leak, but not enough to matter."

"Guess what, Carl?" Pat said. "The floor is wet in the corners, where the tunnel meets the chamber wall. You win the next Nobel Prize for technical intelligence, if there is such a thing. What bothers me, though, is what could produce the kind of heat you're talking about? I can't visualize somebody launching rockets into a mountain through a square stone tunnel."

"Maybe a weapon up the tunnel?" Carl speculated.

"On second thought," Pat said, "maybe I don't want know where the heat would come from. I suddenly have an intense desire to get out of here."

"Could it be that the heat comes from fires in the pits under the tunnel floor, or maybe even from inside the planet?" Koslovski conjectured.

"I like those ideas better than the one about a weapon, Trudy," Pat said, "and it's not impossible. Who knows?"

"While we're all letting our imaginations run away with us," Wade said, "let me throw in a thought: this planet could be an alien weapons or energy technology research site. If it is, that would explain a lot of things."

"You could be right," Pat said, getting to his feet, "but there are contraindications. For example, the planet isn't biologically hazardous, in terms of environmental contamination. However, it is an excellent question that we'll let SEJS chew on. Meanwhile, I've stood up and I'm moving around. Let's hope that if the floor drops out from under me, my safety harness holds. Carl, there are some cable or rope stubs dangling from the overhead. What do you make of them?"

"They don't show up on our charts, sir. Are they connected to fittings of some kind?"

Pat didn't answer; he was too busy investigating the overhead cables.

"Captain? Are you all right?"

"Yeah, I'm all right. I've seen this stuff before. It's Arach web that has been burned off; the ends are shriveled and balled up. There's dust all over it, so it's real old. That's why I didn't recognize it at first."

"Sir," Mary said, "you haven't been in there anything like an hour, but it's clouding up out here and getting dark."

"Okay," Pat said, "I'm coming up. I have a lot to report, and the tunnel is featureless as far as I can see with this flashlight. First thing in the morning, we'll send a robotic probe down the hall to see what we can see. Thanks, everybody—this has been a good day's work."

⋏ ⋏ ⋏

The next morning, they got off to a late start because SEJS had sent down two communications disks, and it took quite a while to go through both of them. The first item was an open message from Admiral Egan to Pat that went a long way toward explaining why there had been so little help forthcoming.

SEJS and the Federation had had to be very cautious about researching the information that Pat had sent up on alien equipment, lest the aliens discern that the humans had set up a way to penetrate the screen around the Doodlebug Planet. There was, to date, no reason to cause a confrontation. Nevertheless, quiet research of historical information about alien hardware, coupled with engineering analysis of the data Pat had collected in the hangars, had produced a wealth of useful facts about the machinery on the planet. This took up the bulk of the two chips that had come down, and Carl was not happy until he and his men had reviewed all of it. They were particularly pleased to learn that a machine for moving the terrain finger end cap was on hand, and that there was a way to energize it.

The terraformers got a lot of pleasure out of scoffing at some of the obviously erroneous conclusions SEJS's scientists and engineers had drawn about individual items of equipment, but they also were able to extrapolate solutions to some pressing problems from what they heard and saw. Charley Goode almost rolled on the floor in laughter when he heard a scientist describe a rather strange-looking contraption as a "scissoring linear platform projector of unknown function."

"Shucks, captain," Charley said, "all that thing is, is a machine for emplacing collapsible scaffolds. I tell you what, though: if you had it in the access chamber, it would let you bridge up to fifty meters of pit. That's probably what it's for. In a pinch, you could span a couple of slabs of floor and wait out a closed-door cycle."

Pat looked at Charley in amazement. For a guy who had lost a hand by ignoring the dangers of unknown flora, he had a lot of sense.

There were additional messages from Peggy and Admiral Egan at the end of the communiqués. Peggy outlined her observations of the field around the planet and indicated that both she and SEJS discounted the idea that a living organism could have brain waves as powerful as the field, but that there was intense study ongoing to determine what could. The leading theory was that a cybernetic engine under the mountain could be transmitting energy by modulating the planet's magnetic field. The flaw in this theory lay in fundamental inconsistencies between the behavior of the planet's magnetic field and the observed variations in the aliens' barrier field.

Egan commented briefly on Wade's notion about the planet being an alien research site. It was something he could neither confirm nor deny, but it would be investigated. He went on to advise that the people on the planet could do themselves more harm than good by speculating about why the planet was taboo. False conclusions could lead to their being wary of the wrong things. What was important was for them to explore with caution yet with open minds—and do it as quickly as safety measures would allow.

Counterintelligence had reported an escalation of alien information-gathering efforts and concluded that the aliens suspected that the Federation would not simply write off the terraforming expedition.

Alien patrols around the Doodlebug Planet were increasing in number; Dragonfly had had a narrow escape during a recent communications chip recovery op. The admiral expressed his sincere hope that the reasons for the taboos would soon be revealed.

To that end, Pat, Wade, and Mary began to explore the tunnel in earnest. By lunchtime, they had advanced their mapping of the underground structures to the point of no return. It was a very uninformative exercise: the tunnel went straight and level into the mountain, with no variation in construction, for as far as they could walk in half an hour.

After they set their equipment on scaffolds and started back toward the tunnel entrance, Pat said into his communicator, "Carl, how much farther do we have to go before we get to the middle of the mountain?"

"You're 3.2 kilometers in right now. It's another 2 kilometers or so to the center. The thing is, if the tunnel doesn't change direction pretty soon, you'll pass well to the south of the thickest part of the terrain."

"I see what you mean," Pat said, looking at the illuminated map displayed by his phone. "Well, that's not what I'm concerned about right now. What do we have that we can use to get us back and forth between the tunnel entrance and the instrument pallet? Even something like bicycles would extend our range a lot."

"Our shops could turn out bicycles for you overnight," Carl said, "but we have electric forklifts and tow motors available right now."

"Can you get them in here?" Pat asked.

"We can if we retract the west end of the hill," Carl replied. "The machine to do it is sitting at the end of the runway, and Charley and the boys have had it running."

"The trouble with that," Pat observed, "is that the light will arm all of the stinger pods—and who knows what else?"

"We can still plastic coat the inside of the chamber," Carl said, "and then we won't have to fool with the flexible tunnels any more. They're getting to be a bother."

"Or we could do it after dark," Pat said.

"No thank you, sir. We'd still have to use lights. Not only would they draw every doodlebug in the area—and there are some giants out here—but we'd still probably arm the stingers."

"Always the realist, aren't you, Carl?" said Pat. "I guess you're right. If you would, please ask the shops to build us some bikes. I hate to wait until tomorrow, though."

"Why not neutralize the stingers?" Carl asked. "If we do that, we can put you on wheels right away."

"I don't know—something tells me not to, and I learned a long time ago to follow my instincts," Pat said.

"Me, too," Mary piped up. "Say, Carl, you mentioned tow motors. Aren't there some cargo carts around for use with them?"

"Sure, why?"

"Would one of them fit through the trap door?"

"No, they're too wide."

"Don't the front wheels steer?"

"Yes," Carl said, "but I don't see what you're getting at."

"When Wade and I were young," she said, "we lived next door to one another on a hill. All the kids in the neighborhood used to race each other in wagons our parents bought for us. "When we were little, we just rolled down the street, but when we got older, we used the wagons like scooters. You know what I mean? With one person in the front, steering, and the other kneeling in the back, pushing, we could go like a bat out of hell. Wade and I have scars to prove it. How long would it take you to put a wagon tongue on one of those carts and narrow it enough to get it through the trap door?"

"Not more than an hour. It'll be heavy, though, and we'll probably have to take the wheels off to get it through the chute."

"The heavier it is, the farther it will coast," Mary said. "I think I'm hearing you say you could have it ready for our next trip down here."

"Yeah, but how are you going to stop the thing after you get it going?"

"That's easy: you drag your feet. Our parents used to hate the way we went through shoes, but I think it'll be worth it in this case."

"Okay," Carl said, "one wagon coming right up—but I hope you know what you're doing."

"See if you can come up with a quick release mechanism for the wheels," Pat said. "We're using the scaffolds to support the equipment we leave in the tunnel. We'll have to take the wagon in and out with us each time, or it'll fall in the pit."

"Don't worry, we'll fix you up with something," Carl said. "Charley just said he can probably rig up some brakes, too."

"Great," Pat said. "We'll see you in a few minutes. Have chow ready for us, please, and we'll try to get back in here the instant the door will open."

"The food's already on its way out, and we've already started to get your wagon fixed up." Carl said. "We'll be ready when you get here."

— CHAPTER THIRTY-THREE —

Exploration

The wagon wasn't what Pat had envisioned, but Mary and Wade said it would probably do until the bikes were ready. To make sure, they took it out on the runway and gave it a test that turned out to be fun.

The wagon was originally 2 meters wide by 3 meters long. In that form, it was relatively stable. Narrowing it to 90 centimeters to allow it to pass through the trap door made it tippy and sensitive to steering movements; Pat likened it to a dry-land canoe with a tiller on the wrong end. Unlike a canoe, it was heavy and hard to accelerate, but its pneumatic tires gave it a decent ride. As long as they didn't try to turn too sharply, it definitely would get them where they were going. More important, after they got it rolling, they could readily maintain 25 kph.

The people in the shop had done a good job on short notice; the only improvement required was the installation of some padding to save wear and tear on the operators' knees. After a lot of skylarking and a little serious experimentation, they determined that their best combination was with Mary steering and operating the brake lever, Wade pushing on the left side, and Pat pushing on the right.

The wagon wouldn't fit through the tubes they had been using to get people past the tunnel's entrance chamber. Charley come up with a way to leave the wagon in the tunnel: brackets cemented to the tunnel wall and rigged with a system of pulleys, like boat davits, to hold the wagon while the tunnel doors were closed. As soon as the trap door was open, Carl's crew lowered a set of guide rails into the entry chamber, pointed them into the tunnel, set the wagon on them, and let go. With a huge clatter, the wagon disappeared from view. They could hear it banging against the tunnel walls, but it came to rest twenty meters or so up the tunnel—none the worse for wear.

Pat, Mary, and Wade brought the wagon back to the scaffolding where they had left their exploration and mapping instruments. On a trial basis, they allowed themselves ten minutes to load their gear before setting out from the tunnel entrance. Their exploration progressed rapidly and uneventfully. At the end of their last trip of the day, they were almost two kilometers farther into the mountain than they had been at lunchtime.

The continuum of floor slabs, smooth walls, and solid ceilings was beginning to seem endless. Pat wasn't exactly discouraged, but he was beginning to wonder if they were on a wild goose chase. They were preparing to leave the tunnel for the day, putting the equipment on scaffolding, when Pat felt Mary's hand on his arm. Moderately surprised, he turned toward her and caught the glint of something golden, farther down the tunnel. Although it disappeared instantly, cold chills ran down his spine.

Mary whispered, "Did you see that? Let's get out of here."

"Let's not panic," Pat said without much conviction. He had an unexplainable but overpowering urge to leave immediately.

"Did you see something?" Wade asked.

"An eye," Mary said, "like a cat's eye. Golden. Let's go! We have no protection at all."

"I wouldn't say that," Pat said, weapon in hand, "but we're running out of time. Let's get the equipment on the wagon and head out."

It wouldn't be an exaggeration to say they set a new record for getting back to the tunnel head, but Pat felt a bit abashed by the time they got there. He really didn't know what they had seen, and whatever it was had not attacked them. Although Mary insisted that it had looked like an eye to her, Pat hadn't had a good look at it.

Their account of the incident caused a stir among the terraformers, and the number of volunteers he had for the next foray into the tunnel was encouraging. Several of the miners and construction workers were skilled with heavy lasers and were good, solid people. If the need arose, they could deploy a respectable force of skirmishers. Amid a buzz of excited conversation, they returned to camp for supper.

To Pat's surprise, when he, Mary, Wade, and Carl took seats together at a dining table, Trudy Koslovski asked to join them. Since the discovery of Delia Brown in the tunnel anteroom, Koslovski had been cordial to Pat and had been hanging around the tunnel site, but she had kept her distance otherwise.

When Pat looked questioningly at Koslovski, she said, "Captain, tomorrow is the Sabbath. It's probably a good thing. Everybody is starting to get a little uptight, and a day off will help. What I'd like to talk to you about, though, is that I'd like for you and the McClures to sleep in the dispensary tonight. There are four rooms there; three are unoccupied. You can have your privacy, but I'd like you to be where we can monitor you while you are sleeping."

"What's the problem, Trudy?" Mary inquired, and Pat noted a hint of irritation in her voice that he found strangely unlike her.

"It's probably nothing at all," Koslovski said, "but I don't want to take any chances. Visions of a golden eye were one of the things many of my catatonic patients had in common before they became unreachable, and I'd like to be able to keep you under observation for the next few nights."

"There's a big difference," Mary said, her voice rising. "This wasn't something I dreamed in my sleep—and the captain saw it too."

"I know," Koslovski said. "If Doctor Evans hadn't said she was being watched by a golden eye while she was wakeful, I'd let it go, but she did so I won't ignore it."

"Who was Doctor Evans?" Pat asked.

"Our physician," Koslovski said. "One of those who died."

"Well, it doesn't much matter to me where I sleep," Pat said, "but I can understand Mary not wanting to move into the dispensary. I just caught a glimpse of the thing in the tunnel, but whatever we saw was real. Mary saw it before I did; if she says it was an eye, I believe her."

"Was it some kind of large cat?" Koslovski asked.

"I doubt it," Pat said. "We seem to be the only mammals around, and we didn't come from this planet. But Mary didn't say it was a cat, only that it looked like one. Plenty of things have yellow eyes. To the best of my recollection, for instance, those flying reptiles up on the mountain do."

"I'm relieved to hear you say that," Koslovski said, "but I'd still feel a lot better if you'd stay in the dispensary tonight."

"You're upsetting me, Trudy." Mary's voice was unmistakably strident. "Just because I went down into that tunnel and saw something, I am *not* crazy."

"Of course not," Koslovski said, "but frankly, Mary, I have every right to be concerned about you. You aren't normally a nervous or defensive person, but you've been acting that way more and more over the past few days. We all know that increasing anxiety, accompanied by sleep disorders, are real danger signs around here. Monitoring your sleep is as easy as pie and will let us know right away if anything is wrong."

"Oh, nuts!" Mary slammed down her fork and rose to her feet. "All right, what do I have to lose but a good night's rest? I hate strange beds."

"Move your furniture into the dispensary, then," Koslovski said. "Do whatever makes you comfortable. How about you, captain?"

"Like I told you, no problem," Pat replied. "Just show me where you want me to bunk down, but do it soon. I'm tired."

▲ ▲ ▲

Pat rose the next morning feeling well rested. He vaguely remembered the thrum of rain on the roof during the night. When he went outside, the fresh smell of a storm that had just passed made him long for a tropical beach and Peggy in his arms. He saw Mary and Wade at breakfast; they too had had a good night's sleep, and Koslovski gave them all a clean bill of health.

In the absence of a chaplain, protocol called for the senior person present to lead the day's religious meeting. Pat was reviewing the scheduled passages from the Scriptures when Henry Waters brought word that a comm chip had arrived. It held a brief message from Peggy, stating that the field around the planet had been unusually active the previous afternoon. Also included was a recording of a complete service that SEJS chaplains had prepared especially for the personnel of the expedition.

The dining facility doubled as the terraformers' chapel, and it seemed to Pat that, by the end of the morning's services, it had an entirely new and pleasant aura about it. He was in an excellent mood when he walked outside to bide his time until lunch. Evidently, he wasn't the only one who felt uplifted: the small groups of people who were strolling about were smiling and chatting amiably, in noticeable contrast to the usual grim atmosphere around the camp.

Pat waved to the McClures, and they beckoned to him in return. "Hey captain," Mary said, "we're thinking about hiking up on the mountain for a picnic. Would you like to join us?"

"The traditional busman's holiday?" Pat said with a grin.

"Strictly for fun," Wade said. "The view from up there is beautiful, and there's nobody to bother you. We do it every Saturday."

"I'd feel like I was intruding," Pat said.

"You wouldn't be," Mary said. "We almost always invite several people to go along with us. It's fun, and it gives the barracks rats a different perspective on the island."

"Barracks rats!" Pat chuckled. "That's a good term for them. I have noticed that most of the expedition's people are virtual prisoners, and it's only because they won't get out and get with it. Okay, I'll go with you. Were you going to ask anybody else?"

"Henry Waters and Tiny Richardson are going with us," Wade said. "Five is about the limit; otherwise, we're likely to have stragglers or get split up, and that takes the fun out of it. And bring food."

▲ ▲ ▲

They met at the appointed time with their hats, water flasks, and food packs, and set out at a brisk pace. Henry and Tiny were puffing before they got to the end of the runway, so they took a short break by the entrance to the tunnel.

"It seems like forever since we looked at those satellite views of this place, captain," Tiny said. "Where do you think the tunnel is going to come out?"

"I really don't know," Pat said. "I'm beginning to wonder if it isn't just a straight shot through to the other side of the mountain."

"I doubt if it is," Tiny said. "If you project this tunnel straight through, it doesn't run into any of the others."

"Others? What others?" Pat asked, and Wade and Mary echoed his surprise.

"Henry, didn't you give the captain my message?" Tiny asked.

"I thought I did," Henry replied, "but maybe it slipped my mind in all the confusion when they found Delia. Captain, didn't I tell you that Tiny had given the satellite views of the rest of the island another look, and that he found several other cool spots that looked like tunnels?"

"I don't recall that, Henry," Pat said. "If it happened after we found Delia, it probably wouldn't have changed the course of events very much. Even so, I'd like to know more about it. Where are the other tunnels, Tiny?"

"Well," he said, "you know how the mountain has ridges that run off more or less to the points of the compass? Each one has a tunnel fairly close to where it meets the flat land. There are also some spots up near the top that could be holes or something. Those don't have any horizontal length to speak of. There's a big one on the west side of the saddle between the main peaks."

"For Pete's sake," Wade said. "Here we've been running back and forth in the tunnel like chickens with their heads cut off, and there may be another way in?"

"Don't jump to conclusions," Pat said. "Something tells me there's no easy way to get to whatever this place is hiding. Tomorrow we'll find out for sure. In the meantime, let's enjoy our picnic and be thankful that things have gone as well as they have."

"I feel awful," Henry said. "If Charley Goode lost his hand because I didn't pass Tiny's message along..."

"You're not to blame for that, not at all," Mary said. "We'd have gone after Delia, no matter what, and Charley would have his hand today if he'd left the stinger alone like the captain told him. Besides, if we ever get a doctor to run the equipment, Charley can regenerate a hand."

"It certainly could have been a lot worse," Pat agreed. "You're right that Henry's not to blame, but we were lucky that one hand is all we lost in finding out about the stingers."

"One hand and Delia Brown," Mary said, her voice full of regret.

"I stand corrected," Pat said, "but let's not write Delia off yet. The biotech's are working on an antidote. I bet they succeed—and when they do, they may yet save her."

"This is a terrible place," Henry said. "It's worse than the ancient Egyptian pyramids and the pharaohs' tombs."

"The aliens out there tried to tell us that, but we wouldn't listen," Tiny observed.

"That the planet was like the Egyptians' tombs?" Pat inquired.

"Not exactly," Henry said. "Have you seen the recordings of the official messages the aliens sent us?"

"Yes," Pat said.

"Well," Henry said, "evidently the Little Peoples thought we just didn't understand. They sent a special emissary aboard our ship to explain. He was the one who mentioned the Egyptian tombs."

"Baloney, Henry," Mary said. "Wade and I were there, and before we voted, we were all shown everything the aliens said about the planet. There was no mention of anything like that in what I saw."

"Not everybody saw the messenger—not even me," Henry said. "He spoke only to the expedition president. The president showed a copy of it only to holders of expedition preferred stock, and the copy had been edited by that time."

"Are you a preferred stockholder?" Wade asked. "I didn't know you had that kind of credit reserves."

"No," Henry said, "but I am the expedition clerk. I have been putting all of our records in order, so that if we get out of here there can be a proper disposition of assets. I found the president's recording of the emissary when I unlocked his secure files. Before you ask, I have the right and duty, as expedition clerk, to do that under the present circumstances."

"If this is true, why haven't you made it public?" Mary asked. "Forgive me, Henry, but this is getting to be a pretty tall tale."

"If I understand the law," Pat said, "you should at least have made these facts known to me, as senior officer present."

"I wanted to, sir," Henry said, "but civil law states that the president's private files are restricted to successors from the ranks of the expedition, unless there is an official Federation inquiry supported by subpoenas, or there are no surviving members of the expedition."

"I see," Pat said. "Well, the cat's out of the bag now, anyway."

"You mean you believe him?" Mary asked. "I think we'd better turn him over to Trudy and her midnight monitors."

Pat had a thought; he removed a napkin from his lunch, wrote something on it, folded it, and handed it to Mary. "Hold this for a minute, please," Pat said, and then he turned to Henry. "Not only do I believe you, I have a hunch about something. Now, who was the emissary of the Little Peoples? Did he give his name?"

"Yes, he made a point of it," Henry said. "I guess the Little Peoples have only one name, because he said his was Shamus."

"What's written on the napkin, Mary?" Pat said.

"Shamus Leprechaun," she said. "This is incredible."

With a grin, Pat pulled Shamus' whistle out of his tunic. "Let's climb up to your picnic spot and have lunch. I need to do some thinking, and there are some things I'd like to tell you."

They stopped at a place where the ridge they were on met the shoulder of the upper part of the mountain. There, a small, relatively flat area provided a broad westerly vista and a place to spread a ground cloth. When everyone was settled and lunch was spread before them, Pat told the story of his encounter with Shamus. He made no direct mention of the whistles being a means of tracing the movements of people who carried them (and, hence, SEJS vessels), but he related the general tenor of Egan's comments about the Leprechaun and made it plain that Shamus was due a comeuppance.

"Are you planning to use the whistle to lure Shamus in here so we can pounce on him and make him tell us the secret of this place?" Wade asked.

"That was my first impulse," Pat said, "but the more I think about it, the less I like the idea. Shamus is no fool, whatever else he may be. He'd check to see where the call was coming from before he answered it, and even if he did come without checking, he'd be in his ship. I dare say that if we duped him into coming here and he couldn't get back out, he'd be extremely angry. After what I saw him do to the head Arach, I wouldn't want to be the person he held accountable."

He dangled the whistle on its chain, so that the sun glinted off the gold. "No, I think what we'd better do is hold onto the whistle, have a meeting of all hands to let everyone know what we've learned from Tiny and Henry today, and find out whether anybody else is sitting on something important. For now, let's just enjoy our outing. I have a feeling tomorrow is going to be an interesting day."

"Didn't you say that the inscription on your whistle says that you'd want to use it long before you really should?" Henry said.

"That or something very close to it," Pat replied.

"Is Shamus clairvoyant?" Henry asked. "I mean, it sounds like he was foretelling what was going to happen here. A minute ago, you said you had the impulse to blow the whistle. Now we can all see that the wise thing to do is to wait."

"The jury is out on Shamus," Pat responded, "but in my opinion, he's mostly a tough, shrewd charlatan who knows how to sell snake oil. You've got to like the little devil, but you'd better keep an eye on him all the time. By the way, exactly what did he tell the president?"

"We may never know," Henry replied. "As I said, the recording was edited before I saw it. When we get back to camp, I'm going to activate the law computer and find out whether I can show it to you or the holders of common stock."

"Please do," Pat said, "and when you do, tell it that I am here on an official investigation. My orders are to determine why this planet is held to be taboo, and I have reason to believe that the Leprechaun's talk with the president may contain information that, by itself or in combination with other facts I have amassed, may be material in the legal sense."

"I doubt that I can state that as well as you just did, sir," Henry said. "When we get back, would you mind interacting with the computer yourself?"

"Not at all," Pat replied.

"I haven't seen you smile like that before, captain," Mary said. "Is it something Henry said?"

"The phrase 'interacting with the computer' reminded me of my ship and crew, and I'm rather fond of them."

▲ ▲ ▲

The law computer gave Pat a hard time. It would not release expedition private records to him without an access code from SEJS or the Federation, no matter how extraordinary the circumstances. Irked, Pat gave up for the moment and sent a chip skyward, reprising the day's revelations and requesting an access code.

After supper, the terraformers met in the dining hall to hear about the possibility of other tunnels. Pat didn't mention Shamus' talks with the expedition's leaders. The law computer wouldn't authorize release of that information to holders of common stock any more than it would to Pat.

Pat was up at dawn on the following day to check his mailbox, but no chip was waiting for him. He decided to go back to bed for a few minutes, but when he turned to go back into the CP, he caught sight of a huge, four-winged insect flying clumsily above the camp. This was no bumblebee: this insect was the size of a small airplane. While he watched, he saw another of the giant dragonfly-like insects emerge from the sand beyond the hangars and take to the sky.

"Amazing, aren't they?" said a voice behind him, and he almost jumped out of his skin. He spun around and saw Henry. "Sorry, captain, I didn't mean to startle you. I heard you moving around, and I thought you knew I was here."

"I didn't hear you, but it's all right. Those things make a lot of noise, don't they?"

"Yeah," Henry said, "but that's nothing. After they mate, they just

310

quit flapping their wings and crash land. The males die, and the females crawl off and lay their eggs. Every once in a while, one of them lands on the roof of a building. Talk about a racket—I guarantee nobody sleeps through that."

"What are they?"

"Adult doodlebugs," Henry answered. "They're harmless, unless you let one of them blunder into you. They come out after it rains, especially if there is a lot of moonlight." Something at the mailbox caught Henry's attention. "Oh look, a communications chip just came in for you."

"Fabulous!" Pat said. "It was worth getting up, after all."

All that was on the chip was a direct communiqué from Admiral Egan, instructing Pat to connect the recorder to the law computer and ensure that he was alone in the room with the equipment. Henry wasn't happy with this arrangement, but he didn't resist, either. Evidently, the code on the chip was an overriding one: not only did the law computer open the expedition's files, it also made the administrative computer reconstruct a complete recording of Shamus' contact with the expedition's leaders. This was a capability that Pat doubted anyone suspected was possible. He didn't, until he saw it happen.

As soon as he had viewed the reconstructed interview, confirmed that the unlocking code had been erased, and the recording of Shamus had been burned into the chip, Pat sent the chip back to Peggy and went to breakfast. While he ate, he thought over what he'd just seen.

Shamus had had three things to say. The first was an offer of rescue to the expedition's personnel in exchange for the customary rights to the salvage value of their equipment. The expedition leaders declined, explaining that they believed that the Doodlebug Planet was rich in gold.

Shamus replied that several cultures had tried to explore that possibility. Not only had all of them failed, but the planet was taboo for good and sufficient reasons. Because they had been warned, if they were to pass through the barrier around the planet, they would never reemerge.

The president pointed out that they were terraformers; thus their role was to transform unclaimed planets into fit, profitable places for humans to live, and the Doodlebug Planet appeared to be a prime candidate. Once they were settled there, they would have no desire or inclination to leave.

Shamus had sighed with a sad shake of his head. "Have ya not heard, man, that all that glitters is not gold? And that fools rush in where angels fear to tread? I'm not after callin' an honest man a fool, mind ya; I'm simply tellin' ya it's that kind of a place. Why do ya think—that a planet like that is uninhabited, and that we go to such trouble to keep it as it is? Do ya think it is fun to sit out here, tending that field?"

"We don't know what you are doing or why you are doing it," the president had said. "It doesn't help that you won't tell us. Why are you being so secretive? You must understand that it makes us suspect that you are trying to prevent us from picking a plum, as it were."

"I canna and willna speak the unspeakable," Shamus said. "All I can do is say in good faith that ye will greatly regret it if ye go through the field. That planet is a terrible, unholy place, and that's the long and the short of it."

"So be it then," the president said. "It is the will of the Creator that we shall go to terrible venues and transform them into places in which we can take just pride. We thank you for your advice and your offers of rescue, but we feel that it is providence that we and the planet are here together."

"Good luck to ye, then," Shamus replied. "We bear ye no malice, and we wish ye all success. Would that ye had the chances of a prayer in hell. Once ye go in there, there's naught we can do for ye. Seems a waste."

"Let's both hope you are wrong," the president said.

"Oh, I do," Shamus said, "I do. And if ya be the first out of there in all these years, I'll be the first in line to pat ya on the back."

"Thank you very much." The president had smiled beatifically.

— CHAPTER THIRTY-FOUR —

Dragon

At the previous evening's meeting, the terraformers had voted to put cargo lighters in service to transport scouting parties to those possible tunnel sites that lay on high terrain. A vocal minority (mostly miners and farmers) also demanded and got reversal of an earlier group decision that had grounded the dune buggies they had built shortly after arriving on the planet.

The dune buggies had been useful during the expedition's initial occupation of the island, but they had become an environmental liability when they devolved into recreational vehicles. Now the terraformers would use them for access to presumed tunnel entrances at the lower elevations of the mountain.

On his way back from the picnic, Pat had decided that he wanted to quickly check all sites that might contain tunnels, without delaying further exploration of the system they had already opened. To accomplish both of these objectives as safely as possible, he reasoned that he was going to need qualified help, and that someone would have to coordinate the help.

This presented some problems. The necessary skills were available, but the expedition's leaders had been out of action long enough that the rank and file had formed cliques. It appeared to Pat that the only thing that had kept a power struggle from developing was the widespread opinion that any new leaders would suffer the same fate as the old. Clearly, they needed leadership; it was going to be up to him to organize it. The immediate challenge was to enlist the willing support of the expedition personnel.

This proved to be easier than he had expected. When he outlined his plans, the terraformers made it plain that they were eager to expand their participation. The first group to speak up was the miners, who stated that they were fully capable of checking out tunnels. Next was Henry, who offered to set up and operate a command post. After the normally meek clerk committed himself to the effort, a flood of volunteers came forward.

Ultimately, the products of the meeting were a concept of

operations and a plan for the next day. The concept was for Pat (whom they elected to be in charge), Mary, and Wade to press onward in the first tunnel, where all agreed that important developments were most likely to occur. Charley was to take over the role Carl had played at the head of the open tunnel, while Carl, with Henry's administrative assistance, coordinated operations.

Counting Pat's group, the plan called for six parallel exploratory missions. Two of the new teams would move by cargo lighter, while the others would use dune buggies.

Excluding drivers and fliers, each party had two miners, two equipment specialists, and one person who could use a weapon effectively. The miners would control the scouting, the equipment specialists would handle communications, and the fifth person would serve as a roving sentinel.

Pat and Carl briefed the scouts on all of the hazards they had encountered to date, reminding them that anything unfamiliar was potentially a threat to life and limb. Pat assigned tightly defined objectives to the scouts. They were to determine whether the cool spots on the satellite views were tunnels; reconnoiter entrances to see if they were usable; and discover any hazards that might be present. Pat emphasized that under no circumstances were the scouts to risk injury, much less loss of life.

At this point Charley Goode stepped forward. "Carl and the captain are telling it like it is, you guys, but they ain't speaking your language." Holding his stump aloft, he continued, "The first SOB I hear of purposely doing anything stupid gets this upside the head. Get the message?"

This remark brought a burst of laughter, but it made the point more than clear.

At daybreak, the new search parties headed eastward and the McClures, with Pat, reentered tunnel number one. The cart had worked so well the day before, they had decided to not use the bicycles, which would now be available to others if there was a decision to try other tunnels. Because of the incident with the golden eye, Pat had brought a powerful spotlight along. When they stopped at the scaffolds, he shone it ahead in the tunnel. They could faintly see a transverse wall in the distance, as well as something—definitely not an eye—that glittered.

They plunged ahead, continuing to probe the walls and floor with their instruments. For four hundred meters, there was no change in the pattern, but then the pit beneath them ended and solid stone began.

From there, progress was rapid. By the time they had to return to the head of the tunnel, they were within fifty meters of the wall. They could clearly see that the flashing object was a convex mirror. Excited, they left their lighting equipment in place, put the instruments on the cart, and set out for the head of the tunnel. While they scooted along, Charley relayed reports that were coming in via Carl.

All of the sites that the scouting parties had checked out contained tunnel entrances. Apparently, a different genus of aliens had constructed each, so that no two were structurally alike. The tunnels to the north and south were open but infested with stingers and appeared to be booby-trapped. The one on the west had collapsed for a considerable distance; scrub had overgrown it, and the vegetation was thick with snakes and other vermin. The scouts there had spotted what might be the remains of a gigantic anthill and had taken their dune buggy off to explore the site.

One of the lighter-borne teams had checked out all of the smaller cool spots shown on the satellite scans. They appeared to be the mouths of ventilation shafts, but they were unusable by humans. All were bundles of thirteen glass pipes, each twenty centimeters in diameter. Air emerging from the pipes contained traces of carbon dioxide, methane, hydrogen sulfide, and sulfur dioxide. It was smelly, but breathable.

The team that was attempting to evaluate the large spot near the top of the mountain had run into difficulty. They could see an opening, but it turned out to be the rookery of the flying reptiles. The team's efforts to approach were met with savage defensive attacks. The team wanted guidance: should they kill off the reptiles and continue to explore, or should they back off?

"That's strange," Mary said, "because birds and reptiles don't normally defend their nests unless there is something around that threatens their young. What do you suppose could threaten the dinosaurs enough to make them behave that way?"

"Good question," Pat said. "Snakes, maybe? On the other hand, maybe they are cannibalistic. Some of them eyeballed me when I came in. They didn't attack, but I wasn't about to pick a fight with them. They are big, and they look fairly intelligent. They also have beaks and claws like you wouldn't believe. Anyway, Charley, ask whether the scouts can see down into the hole."

Presently the answer came back. "Not enough to matter. The sun is on the other side of the mountain, so the shadow makes the hole dark.

They say they can't even tell how steeply it slopes. Can't be too shallow an angle, though, or it would come right out on the other side."

"Tell the team to return to base," Pat said. "Makes me wish we had some of those fireflies the Marines use." He had to explain to Charley what he meant, and Charley said he might be able to fabricate something similar.

The overall plan called for everyone to meet at the end of the runway when Pat and the McClures emerged from the west tunnel. Except for the dune buggy team that had gone to the east tunnel and hadn't yet returned, they were all present. Pat and Carl conferred briefly and then set up a large map display. When each team had reported its findings and posted them to the map, it was possible to see that, if all of the tunnels ran at right angles to the doors at their ends, they wouldn't intersect in a neat cross. Rather, it appeared that the west and south tunnels would come together south of the center of the mountain, while the east and north tunnels would intersect a kilometer or so to the north.

Also, the north and south entrances were not aligned perfectly. The north entrance was a few hundred meters east of the southerly one. Therefore, if they connected, it was by a large chamber or a jog in the tunnels.

"If nothing else," Pat said, "I believe we now have an explanation of the wall we can see ahead of us in the west tunnel. It must be that we're about to join the one from the south."

"And the mirror?" Carl asked.

"A way to tell if there is any traffic coming the other way."

"That means that the south and west tunnels must have been in service at the same time," Carl concluded. "I wasn't expecting that. Their dimensions correspond to two different generations of equipment in the hangars."

"There are a number of strange things about these tunnels," said the leader of the team that had gone to the east end of the island. "I'm a hard rock miner, but I've never seen anything quite like these sites. First, where are the tailings? I'd expect to find at least some signs of spoil around the entrances, but there aren't any at the three I've seen so far."

The miner furrowed his brow, looking to Pat like he was thoroughly flummoxed. "Second, why would anybody in his right mind go to so much trouble to build facilities this elaborate in a perfectly worthless mountain? Captain, for all practical purposes, you're already at the center of the thing, but you've yet to find anything of value."

"That's for sure," Pat said. "And?"

"And third, if you wanted to get to the middle of the mountain, why would you go in the long way? Every one of these shafts goes in lengthwise of a ridge. Whoever dug these things was smart enough to build and use some ingenious equipment. They'd be smart enough to take a shorter way in, I would think."

"Anybody have answers?" Pat asked of the group. "I sure don't."

"The tailings might have been used to build the runway and our buildings," one of the technicians noted.

"Some, but certainly not all," the miner replied. "The materials from the west tunnel alone would be enough for that. What about the stuff from the pit under the west tunnel, and the stone from the other tunnels?"

"Maybe they dumped it in the ocean to provide habitat for marine life," one of the bio techs said.

"The fishermen haven't found anything like that."

"These tunnels were either built for mining, or they weren't. So far, it doesn't look like they were for mining, but it doesn't make much difference at this stage of the game." Pat heaved a deep sigh; it had been a very long day. "One question, though, out of curiosity: this island is the biggest piece of solid ground on the planet. If there is gold in the mantle, do you think maybe the mountain simply serves as a dry place from which to sink a shaft?"

"Could be," the miner replied, "but if that's the case, why didn't they dig down from here? It's a lot of extra work to go into the mountain first, not to mention the additional safety problems. Of course, if they were shooting for a basalt understory, maybe it comes nearest to sea level under the mountain. That could be it. Maybe if you dig here, you run into trouble with subsurface water. On the other hand, whoever built the camp was able to build big, glass-lined pipes below grade, so that would solve the water problem. I just don't know. This place poses one mystery on top of another, and none of it makes good sense."

"To a human," Wade observed. "Don't forget that this place was built by aliens."

"Good point," Pat said. "Maybe those big green ants just naturally like it better if they're underground."

"That reminds me," the miner said. "We didn't report it a while ago because it didn't have anything to do with the tunnels, but there definitely is a big, abandoned anthill at the far end of the island. There's also a bronze statue of a couple of ants about halfway between the tunnel and the entrance to the anthill."

"I wonder why we didn't see that when we explored the other end of the island," Mary said.

"They're pretty well hidden in a draw, and the paths haven't been used for a long time," the miner said. "If you know where the tunnel entrance is, you can't help seeing the track that's worn between it and the anthill. Otherwise, there is nothing unusual about it. The anthill is a mound with holes in the top. Brush has grown up around it, so if you weren't following the path, you wouldn't know it's there."

The miner scratched his nose; his face was covered with grime, but it looked natural on him, Pat thought. "The statue sits in sort of an alcove off the path. Funny thing is, I didn't think of it at the time, but maybe what reminded me of basalt a while ago is that that's what they used to make the base of the statue."

"Well, that's two unusual materials involved—bronze and basalt," Pat said.

"Yeah, and it's a great-looking statue, too," the miner said. "A live ant is standing over a dead one, and the live one is built so that when the wind hits it, its front legs and antennae wave."

"That's one way ants communicate," Pat said. "That, and smell, or pheromones. I'd like to make sure we send a recording of the statue and its behavior to SEJS Headquarters. Maybe, if it says something, they can figure it out. By the way, did you go into the anthill?"

"No, sir," the miner said. "There was some debris in the hole, but it didn't look like it was booby trapped or anything. We were running late, and we didn't want to take any unnecessary chances."

"You did right," Pat said. "Are the holes big enough to crawl into?"

"Yes, they are about a meter and a half in diameter. A skinny person wouldn't have any trouble getting in there, and it looked like it flared out down below. I'll be glad to check it out, if you'd like."

"I would," Pat said. "The Federation doesn't know much about those ants, so I think they'd like any information we can gather. However, I still don't want you to take any risks at all. If there's any chance of booby traps or cave-ins, get out immediately and don't go back."

"Don't worry, captain," the miner replied. "We're not about to take any chances just to crawl around in an anthill, but I don't think there's any danger. This morning I got the distinct impression that the anthill was like the camp on this end of the island: just waiting for someone to come along and move in."

"Okay, how about the other tunnel sites?" Pat asked. "Any general observations or personal opinions to add?"

"Yes, sir," the chief of the party from the north tunnel said. "Our shaft would be extremely difficult and tricky to use. We figure it must have been built by Arachs. We're guessing about how it all works, but in addition to the stingers, there's a series of banks of recessed lasers that are aimed across the tunnel from top to bottom. It's easy to get the doors open and bypass the stingers, if you know about them, but if you trip the detectors that are farther in—pow!" He smacked his hands together.

"We pitched a log in there and it disintegrated in a flash," he continued. "The power apparently comes from arrays of solar cells or something like that, mounted on rods that are camouflaged to look like cacti growing out of the ridge top. There is probably some kind of storage buffer between them and the lasers, or the system wouldn't work at night. We'll be glad to go back and try to figure out how to get past the lasers, but we don't really think it would be worth it. Anybody who goes in there will have to crawl because the ceilings are so low."

"Are you sure the entrance isn't just a bottleneck?" Pat asked.

"Fairly sure," the leader said. "We shone the dune buggy headlights in there, and with field glasses we could see for at least a kilometer. There was no change for as far as we could see."

"Doesn't sound like anything we ought to explore," Pat said, "unless you can come up with some kind of vehicle that will let you ride lying down."

"We'll look around the hangars and see what we can find," the leader said. "We'll report back no later than lunch time."

"Thank you," Pat said. "How about the south tunnel?"

"It looks like a mate to this one," the team chief said, "except that the end of the chamber doesn't come off. If you are through with the geosurvey instruments, we'll go back and check the insides of the door mechanism. It may or may not have the same duty cycle as this one."

"We're done with the instruments for now," Pat said. "I'd

appreciate it if you'd investigate it. It should be a shorter trip from the south entrance to the mirror than it is from here, and anything we can do to lengthen the working time we have below ground would help. Don't go in there without a way to install protective tubes, though."

"No sweat," the man said, smiling. "I don't want Charley to hurt his stump on my head." That brought a round of laughter, after which they set about discussing the next few hours' activity.

With a cup of coffee under their belts, the McClures and Pat set out for the junction of the west and south tunnels as soon as the door opened. When they got to their lighting equipment, they stopped the wagon and turned it around toward the entrance. Wade and Pat then began the process of applying power to the floodlights. They put two of the floods on dollies and pushed them around the corner into the south tunnel. Pat dropped back to connect another length of fiber optic cable to his communicator.

Almost immediately, he heard Mary say, "Look," and then make a choking sound. Pat whirled toward them, drawing his weapon. Wade was partially blocking his view of a huge, golden eye, the pupil of which was a narrow, vertical slit.

Just as he was bringing his weapon up to fire, Pat heard his communications implant say, "Don't! Don't shoot, and don't look straight into my eye." The voice was unfamiliar, guttural, and the tone was urgent, though not afraid. "I want to talk to you before this contact turns out like all of the others. Switch off your device for communicating with the outside and put it down. Then come into my chamber."

Pat lowered his weapon but kept it ready. "What about my friends here?" The McClures were not moving; they looked almost catatonic.

"They are not harmed, but they have temporarily lost their will to move," the voice in his implant said. "Sit them on the floor if it pleases you."

Pat holstered his weapon and put his communicator on the floor of the tunnel. Then he took Mary, and then Wade, by the hand and sat them down, side-by-side, leaning against the wall of the tunnel.

"Stay where you are for a moment," Pat heard through his implant. "It is necessary for me to demonstrate something." Orange flame, tightly concentrated in a jet about the size of a fire hose, shot past his leg and melted Pat's communicator into a glob of carbon and silicon. "I didn't want you to entertain thoughts of calling your comrades without my approval," the voice said. "Please come into my home. I am going to

320

hide my eyes from you, unless you incur my just wrath."

Pat glanced north and saw a nictitating membrane slide over the eye. He walked toward it, and the tunnel suddenly opened out into an enormous chamber, perhaps a hundred meters square and thirty high. The architecture was Gothic, unlike anything else Pat had seen on the island. Dim lights caused rich yellow glints to reflect off the walls, ceiling and vaulted arches that supported the roof. Several openings appeared to lead to other rooms and there were decorations hanging on the walls that appeared to be weapons from civilizations unknown to Pat.

"How do you like my living room?" said the voice.

"It is impressive," Pat said. "Is that real gold?"

"Yes, gold of the purest quality," the voice said. "It is the stuff of which this planet is made, woe is me. I have allowed you to come to my chamber to make it clear that I am a sentient being, the apical life form on this planet, and its sole owner. Not only do I claim the property that is rightfully mine, but the right to go where I please and do what I wish."

"That sounds reasonable and proper to me," Pat said. "Galactic law, as I know and understand it, entitles you to those rights, as long as you respect the rights of others equally."

There was a pause. Then the voice said, "Either you are lying to me, or I am surrounded by brigands."

"I am not lying, and neither I nor my people are brigands," Pat replied.

"Nor are you the ones surrounding me," said the voice. "True, your people are on my planet against my will, but I can destroy them at any time."

"We want to leave," Pat said, "but the non-humans who have stationed star bases around the planet have told us that no one and nothing that comes down here may depart. My people did not know that the planet was inhabited by a sentient being, or they would not have come here to begin with."

"So their leaders have told me," replied the voice in the implant. "Nevertheless, I am forced to remain here to protect my belongings. Those self-same non-humans you mention have coveted my gold for eons, but I have managed to protect it from them. Their repeated onslaughts have nearly filled the pits under my tunnels with their wretched, moldering remains. Now they surround my planet, keeping me from making my plight known and poised to assault again at the first

321

opportunity. Fools! Do they not know they cannot destroy a superior being?"

The lights in the ceiling and walls became brighter and Pat could begin to see the outline of the creature with whom he was talking. It looked like a dragon from a medieval legend, huge and sinuous. Pat was amazed and unwilling to believe his own eyes. The scene that unfolded reminded him of an illustration on an antique brass tray he had once seen.

The dragon was easily 50 meters long and 5 meters high at the shoulders. Its scales were a lustrous blue-green in color, and the golden walls of the chamber reflected light off the scales to give the dragon an iridescent quality that was truly beautiful. It gave itself a little shake, and Pat could see that it had bat-like wings furled along its thorax, as well as tentacle-like whiskers sprouting from its cheeks. It was virtually a montage of ancient European and Chinese representations of dragons; yet, it was unique.

"Fascinating!" Pat exclaimed. "You're really something."

"Yes," the dragon said, "am I not beautiful? But mark you, mortal, I am not of your ilk. I come from a time before, and a place beyond. Mine are powers beyond your wildest imagination, and I shall be ascendant again. Serve me well, little man, and you shall be great among the stars."

"Mark you," Pat said, "that I serve only the Creator, SEJS, and the Federation, in that order."

The great head of the dragon swung toward Pat, and the nictitating membranes started to slide away.

"You insult me in my own chamber?"

"No, I speak only the truth, lest you think me a deceiver."

"You have much to learn before you will know the truth," the dragon growled, and Pat felt himself flying through the air. He slammed against the wall and fell to the floor with the breath knocked out of him. Parallel, circular bars slid out of the floor and enclosed him in a golden cage.

"If you value your life, you will ponder what you will see and what you will hear until you have learned the rudiments of the truth." The dragon aimed a blast of warm breath toward Pat. "The first thing you need to know is that if you wish to kill yourself, all you have to do is shoot at me. Put your weapon on low power and try it. Try it, I said!"

Searing pain blasted through Pat's brain from his implant. Later he speculated that it had received a much larger signal than it could comfortably handle. Pat had no choice but to comply; he pulled himself weakly to a half-sitting position, set his weapon on stun, and fired at the dragon's head. The weapon flew out of his hand, and the dragon shot a stream of flame in his direction, controlling it so that it flared to a blossoming end centimeters short of the cage.

"Part of the truth is," the dragon said, "that my eyes and my scales are what you would call broad-band corner reflectors. What you fling at me comes right back. Now, I am hungry and I am going to go fishing—unless you'd prefer that I devour those morsels you left in the tunnel. They are foul things that I'd only eat in a pinch, or if I want a snack between meals. If you don't want that to happen soon, you'd do well to learn the truth rather more quickly than you've been doing."

Pat said nothing and the dragon disappeared down a hole at the north end of the chamber.

"Mary? Wade?" Pat called out. There was no answer.

◢◢◢

"Carl! Carl!" Charley shouted into his communicator. "Something's happened to the captain. Get over here—I'm going into the tunnel."

"Hold on!" Carl replied with authority. "Calm down. What happened to the captain? Did he call you forward?"

"No, he dropped off line to connect another length of cable. When he came back on, I heard a funny noise, kind of a squawk. A few seconds later, he said something like 'What about my friends there?' Then after less than a minute, the communicator went dead. Something's got them, and I'm going in after them."

"No, don't," Carl said. "The captain forbade that, and you know what happened the last time you did something he told you not to do."

"That's bull, Carl, this is a whole different ball game," Charley said. "It's my ass, and I'm taking it in there."

He put the communicator down, grabbed a bicycle, and said, "You heard what I said. Anybody feel like going with me? There's no time to lose."

Without saying a word, Trudy Koslovski picked up a bicycle. The miner who had headed up the scout party at the north tunnel said, "Hell, yes, let's go," and picked up his rock-cutting laser and a bike. Without further ado, the three of them slid down the chute into the tunnel and started pedaling for all they were worth.

Carl came running from the runway and hollered down the chute, "Come back here, you idiots. Wait for the captain to call you. Oh, damn! The captain's going to be mad as hell, and I don't blame him. What do I do now?"

"Just sit down and cool it, Carl," one of the miners said laconically. "They're big boys and girls, and they can answer for themselves. If I were you, I'd be figuring out what I would do if whatever's got the captain decides to come out through the tunnel."

That remark hit Carl right between the horns. He pulled himself together and said, "I'd better get word to the other parties to organize defense and rescue parties, just in case. One of you knows how to operate the machine that puts the chutes in place, right? Okay, take over Charley's job here. Check with Henry to get the time that the captain went into the tunnel, and prepare to close up one hour after that.

"One of you take a weapon and a communicator and go down to our end of the tunnel to keep an eye on things. Keep me informed. I'm going back over to the runway."

The miner who had spoken to Carl moments before picked up his gear and slid down into the tunnel.

"Remember, let me know if anything at all happens," Carl said. The technician who was manning Charley's post nodded assent, and Carl ran for the runway.

"Henry," Carl said over his comm, "that damn fool Charley went into the tunnel, and Trudy and one of the miners went with him. Things are squared away over there for the time being, but there is a chance that something has happened to the captain's party. Let's alert the other teams that something is going on and that they should be extra careful. And just in case, let's set up some kind of a defense around the tunnel head here."

"I don't know anything about defenses, Carl," Henry said, "so you'd better do that, and I'll notify the other teams. Should I send a message up to SEJS?"

"Do you know how to do that?"

"Yes, the captain showed me how, in case there was an emergency."

"The trouble is, I'm not sure there really is an emergency," Carl said. "How nearly full is the chip that he's got started?"

"I don't know, but I imagine there's a lot on it. He hasn't sent one since yesterday morning," Henry ventured.

"Damn, Henry—I wasn't bargaining for this when I agreed to coordinate the scouting parties. I don't know what I should do."

"The captain once told me," Henry said, "that pilots are trained to do something, even if it's wrong. Sounds risky to me, but apparently doing something is better than doing nothing."

"Why not send a message to the captain's contact in exactly those terms," Carl said. "Say that something may or may not have gone wrong, and that we aren't sure what to do until we know for certain. Then tell them that he told us that under such circumstances we should do something, even if it's wrong. If telling them turns out to be the wrong thing, we'll apologize later. Can you handle that?"

"Sure," Henry said. "I'll be back in a little while."

And with that, Carl turned to the task of organizing some defenses.

— CHAPTER THIRTY-FIVE —

Conversation with a Monster

It would be hours before Peggy received the chip sent by Henry, but she was extra alert that morning anyway. Prolonging the interval between chips reduced the probability that the aliens would detect Dragonfly, but it did nothing to slake her insatiable desire for complete, up-to-date information.

No amount of information could satisfy her need to have Pat back on Dragonfly with her. It was a constant ache that was both painful and pleasurable. She studied the feeling whenever she had a free moment.

She began watching the planet's electromagnetic containment field for signs of unusual activity a little after daybreak, when she judged that explorations of the tunnels would commence. After all the effort she had put into deciphering the actions of the field, she was disappointed at her lack of total success, but at least she had developed and proved several theories about what was going on. She now knew that the containment field consisted of standing spherical waves propagated at a few fixed wavelengths by the alien star bases.

Interference and absorption dynamically attenuated the electromagnetic signals emanating from the planet. What appeared on Dragonfly's displays was a mapping of local transients in the field caused by energy arriving from below.

There were several important consequences of Peggy's work. First, it was obvious that the field had very large gaps in its coverage. It stopped energy below three thousand Hertz and at a few selected higher frequencies. She was quite sure that a radio with a directional antenna, operating at frequencies that would avoid the field's primary coverage and its harmonics, could penetrate the field without being detected.

It also appeared that most of the energy absorbed by the containment field emanated from a very low frequency radio transmitter located on or near the island that Pat was on, and that this transmitter was directly coupled to the brain of a living creature. This conclusion was largely deductive, based on parallels between the signals absorbed by the containment field and those propagated by SEJS's system for communicating over great distances or through dense matter.

Third, and most important, Peggy was getting good enough at deciphering the containment field's local variations that she had been able to detect and read radio signals used by the terraformers for local transmissions. For example, she had been able to follow the conversations among the dune buggies that had gone out to the various tunnel entrances, unless two or more individuals were transmitting at the same time.

Thus, when the dragon began to talk to Pat through Pat's implant, Peggy was a very surprised and interested eavesdropper. Of course, Pat's implant had very little power, so she was able to hear only the dragon's side of the conversation, and she had no idea what sort of being was doing the talking.

As soon as it was clear that the dragon's conversation was temporarily at an end, Peggy popped Dragonfly up to CX-26, dumped what she had decoded into the cruiser's mass storage, and requested permission to go down to the planet. Bud Moore told her to return to station and prepare to go to the planet on order, but not to jump the gun. True, it seemed reasonable that the taboo had been based on the presence of some type of evil being on the planet—and possibly a great quantity of naturally occurring gold. Barring a clear emergency, however, it was SEJS's prerogative to determine the next step.

"Aye, aye, sir," she said. Feeling the very human emotions of anxiety and frustration, she returned Dragonfly to station.

🔺 🔺 🔺

While Charley Goode's group was speeding toward the south tunnel intersection on a rescue mission, Pat was trying to free himself from the cage (gold may be soft, but the bars were too thick for him to bend). Exhausted from his efforts, he slumped to the floor and leaned his head back. He looked upward and saw several small spots of light playing about on the north wall of the dragon's chamber.

What now? He thought.

There was enough dust in the air of the chamber that he eventually saw that the light was coming from the south tunnel. "Whoever is there, don't come down here," he called out.

No answer. *Probably can't hear me yet,* Pat thought. *Let's hope and pray the dragon doesn't come back.* In a few minutes, the lights went out in the tunnel. *Must have reached the intersection,* he thought, and he called out another warning. Still no answer.

Soon, faint noises came from the south tunnel and Pat heard Charley's voice. "Anybody in there?"

"Yes, I'm here!" he hollered. "Get the hell out of here as fast as you can go, and take Wade and Mary with you. Don't come back until I call you."

"I'll leave you a new communicator," Charley called to him from across the dragon's lair. "What is this place?"

"Damn it, Charley," Pat said, "are you writing a book or something? Get out of here while you still can."

"The others have already started back," Charley said, his voice coming closer now, "and I need to have something to report. What happened?"

"This place belongs to a dragon, and it isn't a nice one. Look it in the eye and you're catatonic. Shoot it with a laser and it's reflective. Make it mad and it squirts fire at you—or locks you up in a cage."

"Are you sure? I thought dragons were mythical."

"No, I'm putting you on. You know what a compulsive liar I am. Damn it, Charley, look at that communicator over there if you don't believe me."

"I did. It's melted, and it's still hot." Charley's voice was very close. "Well, I'll be damned—you really are in a cage, aren't you?"

"Yes, but the dragon seems to want me alive for the time being. It would kill you or anybody else on sight, and that's all I know. Get out fast, before it comes back and finds you."

"Let me get you out of that cage first." Charley peered through the bars, his white teeth evidence of a grin even in the semi-darkness of the dragon's lair.

"No, damn it! Gold conducts heat too well. It would take your laser forever to cut these bars. Please, *get out!* As long as it's dealing with me on its own terms, the dragon will talk to me."

"Okay, we're gone, but we'll be back with a saw."

"Please, no, or I'll have to shoot you," Pat said. "Just ask Henry to send a chip up to Peggy. He'll know what you're talking about. Hurry—I hear sloshing in the dragon's exit. It's coming back."

Actually, Pat didn't hear sloshing yet, but Charley didn't linger. It was a good thing; in a matter of minutes after his departure, the dragon emerged wetly from its tube.

"How was the fishing?" Pat asked.

"Good enough for a morning snack," the dragon transmitted, but then its whiskers flared and swept through the air. "Aha, more uninvited guests have arrived," it said, and it plunged its head into the south tunnel. "Where are your friends?"

"I don't know," Pat said. "Chances are, they left with your other uninvited guests."

"Bother," replied the dragon, and it disappeared into the tunnel. Pat was amazed that such a large creature could squeeze through such a small aperture, especially with wings folded along its body.

Presently, the dragon emerged from the tunnel, backing out tail first. Pat noted that it had a dorsal fin that ran from the tip of its tail to just aft of its hind legs. The tip of its tail had a pair of spines that projected slightly downward, and it used them to probe its path and to brace itself for turning around. "They're all out and the doors are closed," the dragon said. "It's just as well. We need to talk, and no nonsense."

"May I ask some questions?" Pat said.

"No, I will tell you everything you need to know. You are beginning to try my patience, little man, and you have not yet performed your function. Best you keep your counsel."

Pat said nothing, and the dragon continued. "I have emptied the minds of the other leaders of your people, and I have learned all there is to know about your state of knowledge, your patterns of behavior, and your motives. *You* are a special case. Your implant prevents my reading your thoughts, but it provides a way to communicate directly. Your language limits my ability to express my thoughts, but it will suffice.

"In knowledge and intelligence, you lie well below the Little Peoples, somewhere between the ants and the Arachs, as you call them. Remember that I have defeated all of them, singly and in combination. Because of those defeats and their abominable pride, they have collectively aligned themselves against me. This conspiracy consists of their attempts to block me from communicating with other beings at my plane of existence, and they seek to pilfer my riches. In the natural order of things, they will eventually desist from bothering me, much as lice fall from one's hide when winter comes.

"The charter of your SEJS has two clauses that interest me. One is its mandate to enforce laws that make my claim to this planet incontestable. The other is the directive that allows it to exercise its power to support colonization of the galaxy by members of your species.

Are these not in conflict? One implies that SEJS must, upon discovering the unlawful assaults being perpetrated against me and my property, come to my aid. The other indicates that your species might join in trying to steal my planet as a place for colonization. Which is it to be? Are you my allies, or are you my enemies?"

"At this point," Pat replied, "we are neutral. My mission is to find out why our terraformers were told that if they came here, they could not leave. If I discovered that they wanted to leave, I was to try to facilitate that. Until now, none of us had any inkling of why this planet was held taboo, and I am not yet sure why there is a blockade against departures. I am sure that SEJS will not adopt a position until the facts are fully known."

"Humph!" the dragon snorted. "It should be obvious that the aliens, as you call them, want no one to leave here lest my riches and their dastardly crimes become common knowledge. It would tarnish their false reputations, and it would pull in scoundrels from all over the galaxy. Believe me, sharing is not one of their behaviors. I suppose you want me to release you so you can make a report? Tell me, how long do you estimate that it would take SEJS to come to my assistance?"

"They could be here instantly."

"That is not what I asked. Do not bandy words with me."

"All right, then," Pat said, "if they are going to do it at all, it will take not less than one day and not more than fourteen."

"Not good enough," the dragon said. "The non-humans will have reinforcements here long before then."

"Why? They don't know I'm down here, and they certainly have no way to gauge SEJS's intentions."

"Bad assumptions, captain," the dragon replied. "The Little Peoples, in particular, will have been tracking you for weeks. Even now you are carrying one of their tattletales around your neck."

"It has been disabled. But how did you know about the whistle?"

"I have forgotten more about the Little Peoples than you will ever know, but I am gratified to find that I underestimated your technical knowledge. Perhaps a day will be enough. I shall think about it until the tunnel doors can be opened. Meanwhile, I am going to get some lunch. Don't go anywhere until I come back."

Fat chance, Pat thought, eyeing the bars of his cage. He settled down for a wait. What else was there to do?

— CHAPTER THIRTY-SIX —

In the Dragon's Lair

Just when Peggy despaired of receiving the all clear to take Dragonfly on a rescue mission, CX-26 popped down, scooped up Dragonfly, and journeyed through hyperspace to a remote site in the sector. Bud Moore came up on Dragonfly's displays and said, "Peggy, there has been a major change in the situation. SEJS wishes to brief you fully before giving you new orders. Stand by for encrypted download."

Peggy listened to the download with growing interest and excitement. SEJS related that, following receipt of Peggy's report and the information sent up by Henry, they had confronted the Little Peoples' representative to the Federation.

The representative, to SEJS's surprise, had read a prepared statement in return:

It reflects favorably on your technical development that you have arrived at this point within two weeks of the time you placed an agent on the Doodlebug Planet. However, we regret to inform you that your information is grievously incomplete and erroneous.

Our continued presence in the vicinity of the planet is not voluntary. It is in your best interests to disengage. Nothing and no one that goes to the Doodlebug Planet may leave it. Spare yourselves; desist while you can. May peace be with you.

A recording of Admiral Egan then said, "Commander Varner, the message from the Little Peoples has effectively paralyzed the Command Group here. It will take them days, if not longer, to realize that that is its purpose. As I am sure you are astute enough to see, it tells us nothing really useful and neither confirms nor denies that our understanding of the taboo is correct.

"I don't give two whoops and a holler about any gold that may be down there, but I would like to get the terraformers out. Most of all, Captain Callen is obviously in need of help. I am releasing you to do as you see fit. CX-26 will assume Dragonfly's station if you vacate it and will remain—either until we arrive in force, or until it is clear that nothing will be coming up from below.

331

"If you go to the planet, which I am guessing you will, do not bother to send communications chips back and forth. CX-26 has confirmed that he is able to decipher modulations in the barrier field the same way you did. If necessary, he will communicate directly with you by X-band burst transmissions, which will blow right past the field. God bless you, Peggy, and good luck."

Peggy felt a lump in her throat and a strange feeling in her chest. She did not hesitate; she immediately told Bud that she wanted to go to the planet.

Bud said, "Just between you, me, and the lamp post, Peggy, if you can use some help from a CX, all you have to do is ask."

The hyperspace jump followed, quick as a wink. A few minutes later, Dragonfly was hovering at the end of the runway on the Doodlebug Planet, and Peggy was introducing herself to Carl, Charley, and Henry. As soon as she learned that nothing had happened since Charley had emerged from the tunnel, Peggy gave Dragonfly a thumbs-up signal, and the ship darted away to the top of the mountain. Once there, she asked for and received a lesson from the search team on how to ride a bicycle.

When Peggy had done a quick preliminary investigation at the site, she returned Dragonfly to the runway and reconnoitered with the men. "The ship was able to interrogate the captain's implant by transmitting down the tunnel that comes out of the top of the mountain," she told Charley, Carl, and Henry. "We can send messages to him that way, but when the dragon is in its chamber, its brain waves drown out his implant. At least we know he is alive.

"Now, I'm going to go in there alone, carrying some tools, food, and water. Initially, I will drop the tools off in the south tunnel, where the dragon will not expect them to be. If anything happens to me and you want to try to rescue the captain, then you can sneak in there, cut the bars of his cage, and get out as quickly as you can. A plasma or hydro cutter will work much quicker than a saw.

"I think there's a fairly safe way to get in and out. I am quite sure that all of the obstacles in the tunnel are there to keep the dragon in, or at a safe distance, not to keep us out. I also believe that the dragon's feeding cycle determined the duty cycle of the tunnel doors, and that the mirror is a way to observe it without being paralyzed by looking it directly in the eyes. You'll need to send teams in through two tunnels at the same time, going backwards and using a mirror to look over your shoulder. You'll be able to see it safely and stay out of his range.

"Once you've caught it at home, keep its attention as long as the doors are open. Chances are, by the time the doors are open again, it will have to be away, feeding."

"Lady," Charley said, "anybody ever tell you you're as smart as you are good looking?"

"Not in so many words, Charley," she said, "and please don't count on my being absolutely right about all that. We know almost nothing reliable about dragons. By the way, I'd like you to try something: take all of the catatonic people, starting with the McClures, and put them inside a metal enclosure."

"What, like a radio frequency energy shield?" Carl asked.

"Exactly," Peggy said. "Ten Hertz to one kilohertz."

"Will do," Carl said, "if I can get anybody to come out of hiding. They're all afraid that the dragon is going to come over the beach or fly in here and attack."

"We can't rule that out," Peggy said, "but I have the feeling it would have already done that, if it could. Its wings are probably vulnerable when it's flying. Maybe the doodlebugs and the animals in the shallows are deterrents, too."

"Hey, Carl," Charley said, "you know that thing in the hangar you said looked like a humongous blunderbuss? That's what it was! Don't you know that thing would play hell with a dragon's wings? Thanks, commander—I'll have it set up in no time."

"First," Peggy said, "how about opening the tunnel for me? Close it after twelve minutes, no more."

"How will we know when to open it?" Carl asked.

"I'll be transmitting to the ship when I get to the dragon's chamber, and the ship will relay all traffic back to you. In the absence of Captain Callen or me, the ship can give you a lot of information and guidance. She can talk to you by radio or by a loudspeaker, and she can deploy when she doesn't have to move too fast. She's also being monitored by SEJS, so please do keep the ship informed."

"Treat her like a person?" Carl asked.

"Yes, please," Peggy said. "Her name is Dragonfly. Now that's ironic, isn't it?"

Peggy parked her bicycle just short of the intersection, went into the south tunnel a few meters, and quietly deposited the tools she had brought. Then she walked to the mouth of the central chamber. She found the dragon sitting on its haunches at the foot of the opposite wall; it caught sight of her and watched her intently.

"Greetings from SEJS," she said. "I am Lieutenant Commander Varner." She glanced at Pat's enclosure and saw him rise quickly to his feet; he was staring at her with a broad grin. She felt that odd feeling in her chest again, as if her heart had swelled, and she smiled at him reassuringly. "I have brought rations and water for your prisoner, and I seek to determine your intentions with respect to him and the terraforming expedition on the surface."

The dragon dropped to the floor and slid menacingly forward, its quivering barbels extended to the sides, until its face was less than half a meter from hers. It bowed its neck, turning toward Pat, until its eye was directly before her. A rumble sounded within it and, contemptuously, it drew the nictitating membrane away from the surface of its eye.

Peggy stared impassively into the dragon's eye and said, "Well?"

The dragon recoiled in surprise. "Well, indeed—and greetings! Your arrival is the most interesting development in quite a while. Can you explain why SEJS does not deign to send a member of their own species, much less a delegate of stature appropriate to the master of the galaxy's richest planet?"

"I submit," Peggy replied, "that SEJS has already done so. Captain Callen is clearly a member of the human species, and well-established diplomatic protocols underlie selection of someone of his stature for this particular mission."

"I will agree that Captain Callen is a human," the dragon acknowledged, "but the sovereign of a planet merits at least an ambassador. A captain is, at best, equivalent to a chargé d'affaires."

"Quite right, on the face of the matter," Peggy replied. "However, SEJS perceives an equilibrium between the powers that control this planet and those surrounding it. SEJS stands to gain the freedom of fewer than two hundred people, and little else, by disturbing that equilibrium. They could lose much more by offending either side without a more complete understanding of the situation. Therefore, they sent a representative in the form of Captain Callen, who is considered to be capable of collecting essential information without exciting suspicion by his mere presence."

"SEJS's perceptions are in error," the dragon retorted. "It should be obvious that the star bases around my planet are no more than jackals following a lion. I can destroy them at any time with one swipe of my paw, but there are always more of them to come crawling back and gnaw away at what is rightfully mine."

The dragon drew itself up and stared down its nose at Peggy. "Does that misperception account for SEJS's failure to abide by its lawful charter? If what I have learned from the minds of the terraformers is correct, having discovered the extent and nature of the wrongs being perpetrated against me and my property, SEJS should have immediately helped me set things right. They shall regret their failure to act in a timely manner."

"From what I have personally seen in other sectors of the galaxy," Peggy responded, "and from facts that are a matter of public record in non-human historical accounts, I can assure you that when SEJS begins to extend its sphere of influence into this sector, any wrongdoing here will be rectified. Meanwhile, SEJS will undoubtedly conduct itself judiciously. I must say, however, that you have done little to convince SEJS that it should side with you. You have not presented evidence of your prior claim to this planet, nor have you established the credibility of your description of the situation.

"You should not find either of these matters difficult to accomplish. The non-humans who are blockading this planet have themselves been exceedingly uncooperative. However, even as we converse, SEJS's duly appointed delegate lies imprisoned in your chambers for no apparent reason. I am confident that SEJS will not intercede on your behalf as long as this situation persists."

The dragon snorted and waved a claw at her. "If SEJS had sent an unarmed, diplomatic envoy, the present situation would not prevail. To date, I have done only what I believe to be reasonable and proper to protect my sovereign interests."

"SEJS is understandably curious about the situation here," Peggy said, "but its only established objectives are to understand the prevailing taboo, ascertain whether the terraformers wish to leave, and, if they do, facilitate their departure. I infer that you would like to see them gone."

"Yes—they are trespassing on my planet." The dragon let out a long, slow hiss. "Moreover, they are a complication I could do without. I bear them no malice, however; it has been clear to me for some time now that they would not have come if they had known what they were getting into. I believe that they would depart if they could. Nevertheless, the blockaders are unlikely to allow them to pass, and I am concerned that if they do manage to leave, they will spread tales that will bring more vermin to my door."

"The non-humans have stated that nothing may leave this planet," Peggy said. "On the other hand, if they can be temporarily dispersed, the humans can escape, and you will have a respite. It would be unrealistic to suggest that SEJS could preclude the spread of rumors that might interest fortune hunters, but we may be able to offer satisfactory arrangements for your security. Little can be done about the non-humans' prior knowledge, but SEJS can impose and enforce an off-limits sanction that will keep humans away."

"There are always risks," the dragon observed. "Am I to take those risks for nothing?"

"Not at all," Peggy said. "You stand to benefit in a number of ways. SEJS will be grateful, and that body can be useful in a number of ways. For example, a shift in expansion priorities in favor of this sector would bring you friendly neighbors and would undoubtedly reduce the non-humans' freedom to harass you. Such matters are certainly negotiable."

"We shall see," the dragon replied. "You may leave now. When you are out of the tunnels, I shall allow the captain to come out and partake of the sustenance you have provided. When it is possible for you to return, I shall have a final answer for you."

Peggy set down the canteens and rucksack she was carrying.

"Hold," the dragon commanded. Peggy stopped and looked questioningly at it. The lights became much brighter, and the dragon scrutinized her carefully. Suddenly, the lights went out altogether, and the dragon said, "Go."

Peggy's recollection of the path she had taken on the way in was total and, counting steps in the manner of an unsighted person, she walked back to her bicycle and started riding westward. The light on the bicycle illuminated the tunnel ahead of her. She glanced back over her shoulder and saw the eye of the dragon, watching her in the mirror.

△ △ △

When Peggy was out of the tunnel, the dragon turned the lights up and let Pat out of his cage. Pat was more than ready to be free; he had a desperate need to relieve himself, and his hunger and thirst had become almost maddening.

The dragon spoke to him in his implant. "Your automaton performed admirably, captain. She could be of use to me under certain circumstances. Perhaps, in exchange for your freedom and that of the terraformers, we could arrange for the one named Varner to join a permanent legation here."

"Perhaps," Pat said, "or we might be able to provide a legate with equal abilities but fewer logistic requirements. Shall I contact SEJS to advance such a request?"

"Not just yet," the dragon replied. "I am going to go out for a while. Please remain here. There are hidden dangers in the tunnels, and I would not want anything to happen to you. Feel free to look around this room, if you wish, but do not touch unfamiliar things. I have some souvenirs that could be as dangerous as the tunnels."

"Where may I relieve myself? I do not want to soil your residence."

"Very good," the dragon responded. "I take care of such functions when I am out in the ocean, but you can use my garbage disposal pit. It is in that corner of the chamber." The dragon pointed with one extended claw. "I will open the lid for you, but it will close in a few minutes to keep the creature that eats my scraps from getting out. Don't stay near the edge too long, or it may eat you too. It moves slowly, but if you let it get close enough to put a tentacle on you, you'll never get loose."

Once the dragon had gone, Pat wolfed down the rations Peggy had brought, used the bag to relieve himself, and went to the waste disposal pit in the corner of the room. He tossed the bag inside; then, curious, he peered into the pit. It was a cube about three meters on a side with a small stream of water flowing across the bottom. Clinging to the side was a colorful Molluscan that was virtually identical to the one he had seen when Shamus had mediated discussions. The opening of the lid must have frightened the creature: Pat glimpsed the flesh of its mantle retracting rapidly, revealing a glossy pink and white shell. It resembled a cowry—one as big as a fifty-five-gallon drum.

It shrank back into a corner as far as it could go and pulled itself tightly against the wall. Presently, it haltingly extended an eyestalk and, after exposing the eye briefly once or twice, looked around. When it saw Pat, it slid its mantle back out, changed colors in a rapid series of waves, frantically wriggled a row of fringes around its gills, and extended short tentacles that it twisted together in writhing motions.

All Pat could do was shrug. From his first contact with this species, he knew the animal was trying to communicate with him, but he had no way of knowing what it was trying to say. It looked pathetic, and scars crisscrossed its flesh. Yet, if the thickness of its tentacles was any indication of the creature's strength, the dragon's warning was valid.

Its captivity troubled him, but he set that concern aside for the time being. The lid to the pit closed, and Pat strolled slowly around the chamber, thinking about the dragon and about Peggy. Her presence indicated that the overall situation had deteriorated badly and that, one way or the other, things were soon going to move off top dead center. He must find a way to talk privately with her.

ᛉ ᛉ ᛉ

Peggy was working at a prodigious pace. She had conscripted all of Carl's technicians and organized them into fabrication teams. As fast as they could weld lengths of steel cable to form a huge elliptical net, she and Carl were attaching powerful electrical assemblies to the edges and testing them. When they finished, they collapsed the net along its major axis, lifted it onto dollies, and rolled it down to the end of the runway. Dragonfly met them there.

While Peggy replenished her energy in the ship, she briefed Charley on what he was to do with the net. When she was sure that he understood fully and would not attempt to improvise if things didn't go the way she had planned, she had him reopen the tunnel door, and she returned to the dragon's chamber.

The dragon wasn't there, but Peggy was sure that it was observing. Therefore, she chose her words and her tone carefully. "Captain, has the dragon made its plans known to you?"

Pat quickly inferred her suspicions from her formality. "No, he simply told me I could look around if I made sure not to touch anything unfamiliar. This is an interesting place. The floors are stone, but the rest of it seems to be gold. There must be tons of it in here."

"A gold floor would be extremely cold to the touch," Peggy explained. "I believe a dragon, being reptilian, requires more warmth."

"I guess you're right," Pat agreed. "The dragon seems to be a souvenir collector, though. There are all sorts of gadgets in here, most of which I don't recognize. The most intriguing thing I've seen, however, is the garbage disposal system. It consists of a Molluscan that lives in a covered pit in the corner."

"Well, at least we know one thing they're good for."

They were interrupted by the return of the dragon. It looked at Peggy and said, "Very astute observation. The more I see of you, the better I like you."

"Before you give us your decision," Peggy said, "I would like to know something: Who are you?"

The dragon made a snorting noise that could have passed for a laugh. "I have many names. Why do you ask?"

"When I find myself playing a game," Peggy replied, "I like to know the rules, and I like to know something about the other players. Are you a player, the rule maker, or both?"

Both Pat and the dragon were surprised, but the dragon spoke first: "One of the things that make this game interesting is that it is up to you to discover the rules as you go along. It is not my job to spell it out for you."

"Just like life, eh?" Peggy observed.

"Just like life, and death," the dragon answered. "This is a high-stakes game."

"You claimed to be a superior being," Peggy said. "Did you lie, or am I correct in surmising that you are the being who presides over games of chance?"

"Peggy, that is blasphemy," Pat warned her, wondering how she could not know. She still had a lot to learn. "Ultimately, only the Creator controls such things."

"Can you support that assertion by scriptural reference?" Peggy challenged.

"Not off hand," Pat said, "but you are talking about natural laws, and those are established only by the Creator."

"It strikes me," Peggy said, "that what little has been revealed to the human race by the Creator is full of references to angels, seraphim, cherubim, and all sorts of beings, large and small, about which humans know precious little. I quote:

When men began to multiply on earth and daughters were born to them, the sons of heaven saw how beautiful the daughters of man were, and so they took for their wives as many as they chose…

"Scripture goes on to say,

At that time the Nephilim appeared on earth (as well as later),

339

after the sons of heaven had intercourse with the daughters of man, who bore them sons. They were the heroes of old, the men of renown.

"Those words can be taken as legends to account for the ancient giants," Peggy continued, "and to use the constantly increasing wickedness of mankind as the moral basis for the Biblical flood. But who can say with certainty that the legends are not true?"

"Before you get carried away," the dragon said, "let me assure you that I am not the serpent who was in the Garden of Eden, much less Satan. I neither crawl on my belly nor eat dirt."

"So you say—but would you tell us if you were Satan?"

"Why would I not? Satan is quite pleased with himself and his accomplishments. If he were bashful, why would he continue to hope to overthrow the Creator?"

"How do you know so much about things that are written in the Bible?" Pat asked.

"The terraformers' chaplain has excellent recall of such things. All I have to do is interrogate his mind. Besides, I have my own knowledge of the deeds of the Creator."

"You have not answered my question," Peggy reminded the dragon. "Who or what are you—and what is the purpose of this enormous game?"

"Those are not your original questions," the dragon pointed out, "but this I will tell you: I control the game in which we are all now players, and it would take years to tell you its many purposes."

"The only way to emerge from the game alive, then," Peggy concluded, "is to either join you or fight you and win."

"Quite right. I must say that in some respects you have already progressed further than any of my previous opponents. That is not true of the humans with whom you are currently allied. They can't win this game without finding a way to defeat me in open combat. You, however, may ally yourself with me. I offer you undreamt-of knowledge and power. You could become a consort of the pantheon."

"I am afraid you are in for a fight," Pat said, watching the dragon closely. "Miss Varner is a loyal SEJS officer. We would much prefer an amicable solution, but if you insist on a battle, you will get more than you are bargaining for."

"I believe you will find that SEJS doesn't carry much weight here, captain," the dragon replied. "For the first time in her existence, Miss Varner is free do as she chooses. I am confident that she will see the wisdom of accepting my offer—but in either case, I look forward to playing the Doodlebug Planet game with you. The fighting is half the fun."

The dragon turned his attention back to Peggy, and so did Pat—and what he saw blew his mind. Before Pat's very eyes, Peggy's face was transforming into the visage of a dragon. And not just her face: her skin took on a scaly iridescence that made her look like a miniature of the dragon before them.

"Ah, you see, Miss Varner is as intelligent as I thought," the dragon said, and it released a cloud of steam in her direction. "Marvelous, my dear—ours shall be an intellectual and physical union from which legends will be spun."

Peggy-the-dragon's scaly lips parted, and she blasted a jet of liquid hydrogen squarely in the center of the dragon's left eye. It screamed and dived into its exit tunnel, as if seeking to do something—anything—that would relieve its pain.

"Thus begins the legend of the one-eyed dragon," Peggy said ironically. Pat was amazed to see she had already morphed back to human form. Don't worry, captain," she said, "I never had any yearnings for that evil worm; I just needed a way to get it out of here and let it know it's in for a fight. Let's move! The dragon controls this chamber completely, and when its pain subsides, it's going to let us have it with everything it's got. There is much to do before then."

— CHAPTER THIRTY-SEVEN —

Dragonfly's Fate

Pat followed Peggy at a sprint, heading out of the dragon's lair toward the tunnels. "How are we going to get out of here?" Pat called to her back; she was a lot faster than he was.

"We're not," she said. "The tunnels are the safest place on the planet right now. The terraformers are on their way in through the west and south doors, and Dragonfly is depth charging the dragon to keep it busy. If she doesn't hit it, we have only a couple of minutes to render the main chamber safe. Come on." She had grabbed Pat's arm as he started to turn into the west tunnel, and they almost fell as they lurched southward.

After a few strides, she said, "Grab a tool bag and let's get back to the chamber. First, I want to let that Molluscan out of its pit."

"But it's dangerous," Pat said.

"Yes, especially to the dragon. After years of eating unnatural offal to survive, it has a very big grudge to settle. I hope it's as tough as I think it is." Peggy purposefully manipulated a small cloth sack she took out of her tool bag and yelled, "Duck!" She lobbed the sack into the far corner, and they hit the deck. An explosion blew open the lid of the garbage pit.

Peggy came up firing a laser at sensors that were affixed to the walls. When the last of them fell in gobbets to the floor, Peggy said, "Okay, here's the plan. It isn't much, but it's all we've got, so we have to make it work. If I run out of energy, it's all in your hands."

"Ready for orders, ma'am."

"The grandfather of all supercomputers is buried in this mountain somewhere, probably straight down from here. I'm pretty sure the dragon is now the only eyes, ears, hands, and legs it has left. The dragon may be a droid—I'm not sure. In some ways it acts like one, but in others, it doesn't. Maybe it's something in between."

A droid! Pat thought, shocked. *I never would've thought of that.*

"I am sure that if you knock out the computer, the dragon will be a lot easier to beat. The trouble is, I don't know how to get to where it is.

342

There has to be a way, but we'll have to find it after the dragon is subdued."

"This room is full of hidden doors," Pat said. "One of them may be it, but how are we going to going to neutralize the dragon? Lasers won't work, and he's tough."

"Charley is bringing a net that we'll hang on the ceiling to drop on it. The trick will be to get a noose over its nose so it can't squirt fire."

"Talk about having a tiger by the tail!" Pat exclaimed. "Suppose we get him lassoed and wrapped up in the net. What then?"

"The net will be electrified," Peggy said, "to keep the dragon from communicating with the computer and to zap it into submission. If that doesn't work, all we've got left is a cannon Carl found in the hangars."

"I love you, Peggy," Pat said, "but remind me not to cross you."

She smiled and kissed him quickly. "Dragonfly reports that the terraformers entered the tunnels ten minutes ago and that she has already used up half of the charges we built. The dragon is definitely trying to get back in here. I'm going to try to communicate with the Molluscan. It's coming up out of the pit. Don't worry, I'll be careful. See if you can hurry Carl and Charley—and if you can, look for the doors you mentioned."

"Good luck," Pat said. "Old slimy over there isn't easy to read." He headed into the tunnels and was surprised to almost immediately encounter Henry. The expedition clerk was walking carefully but quickly and was holding onto a mesh bag containing several items that were floating above his head.

"You're a welcome sight," Pat said. "I wasn't expecting to see you in here. What are you doing with those antigravity capsules?"

"I'm not a total wimp, captain," Henry said, "and after I forgot to tell you about Tiny's message, I felt I owed you one. Anyway, here I am. We have a couple of bottles of nitroglycerin that commander Varner asked us to bring, and we plan to use the capsules to hang the net."

"Holy cow—you're not kidding that you aren't a wimp. That stuff could blow the whole mountain apart if you bumped it."

"Yes, sir," Henry said, "that's why she picked me to bring it in. She said I was the most careful person available."

"I don't know what she's planning to do with the nitro, but I don't think the dragon will like it. Be careful; you'll have to change direction up ahead."

"No problem, I have it covered." Henry gave him a grin and a mock salute and took off around the corner, leaving Pat shaking his head. Charley and Carl weren't far behind with the net, but their progress slowed markedly at the intersection of the tunnels. The cable was inherently stiff; they had to manually haul a bight of cable around the corner, pull the slack northward, haul another bight, and so forth. Even with Pat's help, they were bleeding and battered by the time they dragged it around the last corner. It was a bedraggled group of people that ended up in the chamber with the net.

While the terraformers wrestled the net forward, Pat and Peggy used the anti-gravity capsules to float up to where they could shoot studs into the ceiling and attach rings to them. They passed lines through the rings and winched the net into place. Finally, and none too soon, the net was hung from the rings by explosive bolts and the lines were cast off. The trap was set.

The terraformers pulled all of their gear back into the tunnels and placed the cannon in the chamber's south doorway. They bore sighted it on the ocean tunnel, chambered a round, and waited.

"Dragonfly reports she is out of depth charges and the dragon is headed this way," Peggy announced. She and Pat were waiting at mouth of the ocean tunnel with the noose.

"I watched the first part of the fight, and Dragonfly did great," Charley called out from the south tunnel. "One time, she brought the dragon to the surface and it shot fire at her. She dodged it and hit it with another depth charge. That dragon must be hurtin'."

"Good for Dragonfly," Pat said, relieved that his little ship had done so well. "Where's the Molluscan?"

"I don't know," Peggy said. "The last time I saw it, it was sliding into the exit that leads to the ocean, right here. See the trail of slime it left?"

"Uh-oh," Pat said. "I hope it doesn't warn the dragon."

"Don't worry," Peggy said. "It hates the dragon's guts."

"You were able to talk to it?"

"Sort of," Peggy said. "It understands Federation sign language. I don't know exactly what it plans to do, but it is going to try to help us."

This quickly became moot. A slightly punch-drunk dragon burst suddenly from the ocean tunnel. As soon as its snout and barbels were visible, Peggy toggled a switch that dropped a forklift truck into the pit in the south tunnel. Cable ran from the forklift through pulleys to the noose that was draped around the tunnel opening. In an instant, the noose had closed on the bulge at the end of the dragon's snout, the cable cutting all the way to the bone. It snatched the huge beast off its feet and dragged it into the chamber. The net dropped from overhead, and another falling forklift closed the net's purse-like opening violently, knocking the dragon to the floor and dumping it on its side. Ground cables that connected the net to the wall glowed hotly, heated by the dragon's attempts to transmit signals through the steel mesh.

The beast fought until it was exhausted, but it couldn't escape the net. When the dragon's writhing had slowed, Peggy darted in and threw a tarp over its head to hide its eyes.

"Oh, no!" she cried. "The Molluscan is in the net with the dragon. It's being burned alive."

Pat looked where she was pointing and saw that the colorful organism was adhering to the underside of the dragon's tail, near its rear legs. The net was frying its way into the mollusk's mantle; yet, it inched implacably toward the dragon's body. Amid clouds of steam and the stink of burning flesh, it stopped just short of the dragon's vent and extended what looked like a copulatory organ.

"I don't believe this." Charley had come out of the tunnel and was staring at the Molluscan. "I mean, revenge is one thing, but—"

Suddenly they saw a pointed black organ emerge from a slit alongside the copulatory organ. It lanced into the dragon's anal vent, and then retracted. Almost immediately, a paroxysm seized the dragon. Whatever the mollusk had done, it had hurt.

"A stinger?" Charley said. "I didn't know snails had stingers."

"Some marine snails are extremely poisonous," Peggy said. "I have a hunch the dragon is not long for this world."

"Miss Varner," Charley said, "I think the snail is trying to get your attention."

The mollusk was as good as dead, but it was moving the tips of its tentacles slowly. "It is repeating something," Peggy said. "It looks like 'My work is done. The dragon is had by a bad life. Get help.' That's a strange deathbed pronouncement."

"Why do you say that?" Pat asked. "The Molluscan seems to have done what it set out to do, and the dragon certainly led an evil life. Now it wants help. It's hurting."

"No," Peggy said, "that's not what it is saying. The part about the bad life is the other way around, definitely. It is saying, literally, 'A bad life has it,' or 'owns it,' or something like that."

"Possesses it?" said Henry, who had also come forward. "Maybe it is saying that the dragon is possessed, like by an evil spirit. I wouldn't argue with that."

"Neither would I," Pat said, "but what can we do about it? Is anybody here an exorcist?"

"Captain, what happens when something that is possessed dies?" Peggy asked.

"I suppose the spirit that possessed it goes somewhere else," Pat said. "Why?"

"That's it!" Peggy said. "That's why the aliens are blockading the planet. They don't want the evil spirit to get out."

"Oh, no—now we've done it. When the dragon dies, all hell could break loose down here." Pat could hardly believe what he was saying, but it seemed to be reality. "There's no telling which of us the spirit will try to possess next."

"Call the aliens for help," Charley said. "That's what the snail was saying. Hurry up! The dragon isn't going to last forever."

"What can the aliens do about an evil spirit?" Pat asked.

"They've had this one bottled up on the planet for a long time," Peggy said. "I believe they can collapse their field into a smaller region if they want to."

"How can we call them when our signals can't escape that damned field up there?" Pat said.

"Blow Shamus' whistle," Peggy said, "and I'll also have Dragonfly send a message that CX-26 can't miss."

Pat took the stopper out of his whistle and blew. Nothing happened. "No good," he said.

"And I couldn't reach Dragonfly," Peggy said. "She must not have returned to her station above the tunnel up there. Damn it!"

The dragon was almost completely still now.

"How can we get out of here?" Pat said. "The doors are closed at the ends of the tunnels."

"Never fear," said a squeaky voice. Pat spun around and there behind him stood Shamus. "Is SEJS willing to pay me a billion credits to take care of this?"

"To hell with you and your money," Pat said. "May the spirit that possesses that dragon seize you and all of your descendants until the end of time. Now, be off with you, you sorry excuse for a Leprechaun!"

"I'll soon have ya talkin' out the other side o' yer face, Patrick Callen," Shamus replied.

"Not so," said another voice. "'Twas ugly of him to say it that way, Shamus Leprechaun, but you've long been a disgrace to the good name of the Little Peoples. I'll deal with ya later."

The voice came from a regally clad elf who was standing in the center of the chamber. "Stand aside, all of you—there is no time for talk. We must get the dragon out to where our fields can reach him."

Two enormous green ants suddenly dashed in from the north tunnel, seized the net in their jaws, and pulled the dragon to the mouth of the tunnel from whence they had come. There they stopped, turned, and waved their antennae and forelegs frantically.

"The dragon must cooperate by flattening his body, or they won't be after gettin' him through the tunnels," the elf said. "Quick, who has an idea?"

"Cut him up," said Charley.

"Sure, and that'll let the cat out o' the bag," the elf said.

"The underwater tunnel," Peggy said.

"Aye, he'll go through there," the elf said, "but who's to pull him? The Molluscans and crustaceans have the strength, but they're slow and the dragon is near death. What happened to him?"

Pat quickly outlined the events of the past few minutes. "How much time do we have?"

"No more than ten minutes, probably fewer," the elf said. "We must do something now, or abandon the planet and start over again later."

"Can you get the captain to our ship, the Dragonfly, quickly?" Peggy asked.

"Aye, in a wink," the elf said.

"Captain," Peggy said, "meet me to seaward. I'll pull the net's cable through the tunnel, and Dragonfly can take it from there. Charley, can you rig it for us? We don't want anyone hurt. When we cut the forklifts loose, the cables are going to lash around. Make sure everybody is clear of them. And Carl, before you release the tension, weld the noose so it can't come off the dragon's snout."

They complied quickly. Carl severed the noose cable close to the dragon's nose, and the cable flew into the tunnel. The sound of a forklift hitting the bottom of the pit reverberated loudly. Carl then severed the main cable, leaving ten meters or so of it attached to the net. It whipped back and forth, but as soon as it stopped, Peggy bent a towline onto the cable.

"Sir Elf," she said, "can you have the ants place the dragon where—"

"Done," said the elf, "and the name, fair lady, is Oberon. Stay clear of the bottom when you are coming out of the tunnel. There are fearsome grasping things living there that even the dragon avoided."

"Thank you." Peggy wrapped two full turns of the towline around her waist. "I shall. And what about the free-swimming animals? They could tear me apart."

"We'll keep them away, with pleasure," Oberon said. "Hurry now—we've no time to waste."

Taking a powerful lantern in one hand and the tag end of the towline in the other hand, Peggy dashed down into the water. Oberon beckoned to Pat and said, "Take me by the hand, boyo, and hang on tight."

The next thing Pat knew, he and Oberon were suspended in midair over the mountain, hanging above the vertical tunnel that ventilated the dragon's lair. The flying reptiles that lived there raised a fearsome clamor and took wing as if to attack, but a gesture from Oberon froze them in place. It probably wouldn't have mattered anyway, for Dragonfly popped into place before them and opened her boarding hatch. Pat half flew and half fell in, having difficulty shaking off an attack of vertigo.

"Talk to me on the subspace emergency frequency," Oberon said. Then he disappeared into a small ship that had materialized alongside Dragonfly. Four strange-looking ships also appeared just above the ocean's surface immediately north of the mountain, formed a rectangular pattern, and began dropping lumps of something into the water.

Pat put his helmet on, slid into the pilot's seat, and closed the hatches. Oberon's voice came into his earphones, saying "…Molluscans dropping toxin into the water that will stun anything with gills. Do you read me, Dragonfly?"

"Affirmative," Pat said, "but what about the air breathers? Our fishermen told me that there are some really mean ones out there. Our depth charging of the dragon has probably killed a lot of fish, and that could touch off a feeding frenzy."

"Let me see what the Molluscans can do," Oberon said. "Meanwhile, Commander Varner should emerge about 100 meters west of a line due north of the dragon's cave, 50 meters offshore and 15 meters down. Why don't you stand by there?"

"Will do," Pat said, and Dragonfly popped into position above the specified point. He noticed that he was now among the Molluscans' ships, but not centered on them. Then he realized that they were making allowance for the current while they were discharging their poison.

Several anxious minutes passed before Oberon spoke again. "Captain Callen," he said, "the Molluscans have an idea that isn't all bad, if we can make it work. Are you in contact with Commander Varner?"

"Not yet," Pat replied, "but it won't be long. We're starting to detect traces of her signals."

"Good," Oberon said. "I don't know quite how this all works, but the Molluscans have some kind of a machine they want to emplace around the mouth of the tunnel. They call it a siphon and filter system, but it sounds like a pump to me. What it will do is geyser everything in the tunnel up into the air. We'll have to catch Commander Varner and get her out of the way before a Molluscan tug seizes the other solids in the siphon's stream and hauls them out into planetary orbit. It's something they put together during their last turn at trying to defeat the taboo, when the dragon captured their chieftain."

"You mean this kind of thing has happened before?" Pat said.

"Aye," Oberon replied, "many times. We probably aren't going to win this time either, but you've come as close as anyone since the beginning. You've acquitted yourselves well, far better than we expected. The main thing is, if we fail, stand off from the dragon's body at least five kilometers until we can drive the evil one back to the planet. Ya don't want to be his next host. We'll explain it all to ya later."

"I'm glad to hear that. In the meantime, how are we going to extract Peggy from the column of water?"

"I'll tell the Molluscans to get ready, but to tell ya the truth, I don't know. As long as she's in contact with the water, my powers are no good. They'd just dissipate."

"How were the Molluscans going to do it?" Pat asked.

"They were only going to paralyze the dragon with a small dose of poison and bring him out nice and easy. Then, they were going to snag him out of the siphon with a net. They are not sure they can catch something as small as Miss Varner, get reset, and bring the dragon out in time. We need to get her out of the way immediately."

"I can always try to grab her by hand," Pat said, "but I don't like the odds of doing it right the first time. Let me see if she has any ideas. She's just about in comm range."

Pat watched while the Molluscans brought a toroidal object from the hangar area and lowered it into place, and then he held a brief conversation with Peggy. "Oberon," Pat said, "she has an idea that may work. I'm going to back Dragonfly into the tunnel as far as I can. She'll grab my engine shrouds, and I'll pull her out. Can you cut the line and take care of getting the dragon out?"

"Won't the water pressure crush your hull?" Oberon asked.

"It may, but Peggy doesn't think so and she's usually right about such things. Besides, this will save some time. Nothing ventured, nothing gained."

"You won't think that if the dragon dies while you're down there and the demon possesses one of you."

"If it does," Pat said, "you'd better hope it gets me and not her."

"Aye, she's a clever one. Well, I have no better idea."

"By the way," Pat said, "she pointed out that she built the net to contain the dragon's electromagnetic emissions, and that it worked in the cavern. Doesn't that mean that it will hold the demon?"

"I wish I knew," Oberon replied. "Let us hope so. In any case, I must warn the Molluscans that the tow cable may become electrically hot."

"Okay," Pat said, "we're going down below. This is going to be strange. I'm not checked out on submarines."

He checked to make sure that all hull openings were closed, and eased the boat into the water. She wouldn't sink; instead, she bobbed around in the heavy ground swell, leaving Pat feeling nauseated. "Nuts to this," he said to himself, and he applied power and negative pitch. This forced her below the surface and, as long as he kept her moving, she was stable—but it was like trying to ride on top of a balloon.

"Let me do it," Peggy's voice said.

Pat almost jumped out of his skin. He instantly felt stupid; after all, he knew as well as anyone that much of Peggy was resident in the ship's dynamic memory. Nevertheless, he said, "You just about gave me a heart attack. All right then—you have the helm."

Previously he hadn't been any closer to the planet's ocean than several hundred meters. He was surprised to see that the water was gin clear. Dragonfly executed a diving spiral, and her hull began to creak and groan. The palms of Pat's hands started to sweat, and he became even more alarmed when Dragonfly almost collided with the bottom and one of the huge, anemone-like organisms that populated it. "Stop!" he cried.

"Why?" Dragonfly asked, but, fortunately, she did stop.

"Can't you see where you're going?" he said. "You're about to hit bottom, or one of those creatures on it."

"I have meters to spare," the ship said.

"No you don't," Pat said. "The water must be confusing your sensors. You've overshot the tunnel opening, and you have us only centimeters from some kind of animal that is trying to grab us."

"We have a problem," the ship said. "Apparently the salt water is confusing me, and you have trouble handling the ship underwater. Do you want the con?"

"You handle the ship," Pat said, "and I will give you verbal instructions."

"Aye, aye, sir."

"Take her up three meters and level off," Pat said.

"Up three and level," she replied. In this mode, they backed Dragonfly down the dragon's tunnel almost 20 meters before the ship's lights revealed Peggy approaching.

Nine minutes after Oberon had appeared in the chamber, Dragonfly broke surface, passed the net cable to a waiting Molluscan vessel, flew over to the runway, and set Peggy down. Dripping and looking a mess, she dived through the opening hatch into her cockpit and said, "I think we've made it. Let's go see."

The Molluscan tow vessel was accelerating toward a geosynchronous orbit around the planet. They had not quite made it when the dragon gave a dying spasm. Fire spat from the net and ran up the tow cable. The Molluscans dropped the cable in the nick of time and moved quickly away from their tow, which began to glow with a blue radiance.

"Good try, but not good enough," they heard Oberon say. "We can't envelop him in time. Evacuate all sentients from the planet! Anyone still there in two minutes stays permanently."

Suddenly CX-26, her screens down, popped into view less than a hundred meters from the dragon's corpse. "Get out of there, you fool!" Oberon said, but the cruiser projected a field from her bows that fanned out conically and closed around the dragon.

"Where do you want this thing?" Bud Moore inquired. "I'm not sure how long we can hold it, but we've got it for now."

"Any permanent orbit," Oberon said. "Star bases, stand by to redeploy field."

The cruiser began to gain velocity, and Oberon asked, "How long will your field hold up after you break away, unidentified SEJS cruiser?"

"Don't know," Bud said, "never tried this before. Ship's computers don't like it at all. It's draining power like you won't believe!"

All they could do was follow and watch. When CX-26 was almost at orbital conditions, Bud said, "We are at engine meltdown. I'm going to put all we have left into giving the payload a nudge. We won't have enough power to get away. So long everybody, it's been nice knowing you."

"Shake it loose now, CX-26, and we'll push you away as far as we can," Pat said. "Is that all right with you, Peggy?"

"Yes, sir!" she said.

The sparking, writhing ball of energy slowly separated from the bow of the cruiser. "Orbital conditions met," Oberon said. "Redeploy field."

Peggy and Pat pressed Dragonfly's bow against the cruiser's side and began to apply power. They slipped and slid, denting Dragonfly's bows and scattering small pieces of debris.

"Get out of here," Bud said. "Dragonfly's going to rupture and kill you."

Pat was already sealing the helmet of a space suit he had grabbed out of a locker and quickly donned.

"So rupture her, Peggy!" he said.

She applied full power. The little ship crumpled against the cruiser. Vapors and pieces scattered far and wide, but her engines continued to produce thrust. Slowly at first, CX-26 moved farther and farther away from the encapsulated dragon.

Bud saw a blinding flash alongside his ship, and his heart sank into his boots. When his vision began to return, Dragonfly was gone. Nearby were two alien star bases, holding between them a force field that pulsated like an electroencephalogram.

Tears of sorrow welled in his eyes, and he said, "Give me emergency battery power to the comm systems. Activate subspace distress signals and notify SEJS that Dragonfly is a total loss."

In the distance, the cruiser's bridge illuminated faintly from the glow of her emergency survival system's indicators, and Oberon's voice came through on the subspace channels.

"Captain Moore," he said, "the Little Peoples will not countenance your distress in the face of such gallantry. Permission to replenish your energy."

"At what price?" Bud said. "We are not derelict, and we shall destroy the ship if there are any attempts at boarding."

"Are ye daft, man?" Oberon said. "There is no charge. We have recovered your energy from the field over there, and even if we had not, I would give it back to ye ten times over for naught but a draught of whatever you have that'll pass for a libation. It's been a long, hard day and we'd lift a tankard with ye, if ye'll have us aboard."

"Forgive me, sir," Bud said. "We shall gladly accept the return of our energy, and I'll be only too happy to open a bottle of our best, if only to toast our lost compatriots."

"My humble apologies," said Oberon, "I saw no damage to your ship and I assumed you sustained no casualties. With your kind permission, we shall join you in rendering full honors."

"We had no losses aboard CX-26," Bud said, "but I am surprised you did not see the explosion of Dragonfly. No one could have survived that."

"Well now," Oberon said, "I'd not be giving ya much for what's left of Dragonfly, but I have two very wealthy young SEJS officers aboard my ship who might wish to talk to ya about who did or didn't survive what.

"And they may or may not be wanting to beg a ride home with ye. Not everyone owns two full shares of the Doodlebug Planet and all that's in her. Who knows, maybe they'd like to trade a part of that for one of my boats. I must ask them."

The End

— ABOUT WILLIAM A. KEEFE —

Bill Keefe was born in Monterey Park, California, in 1938. His father was US naval officer from 1937 through 1959. This led to Bill attending 12 primary and secondary schools in California, Virginia, Massachusetts and Rhode Island. His first full-time job was as a sailor aboard a 68-foot square-rigged ketch. Sailing dinghies and radio-controlled Lasers continues to be one of his hobbies.

Bill graduated from the Virginia Military Institute (VMI) in 1958 with a BS in physics and a US Army commission in Artillery. While a cadet at VMI, he enjoyed two summers in Japan. After graduation, he taught math and biological drawing at VMI for a year and came on active duty as an Ordnance officer in 1959. He retired in 1979 as a Lieutenant Colonel, having had command and staff duties in air defense artillery, missile systems maintenance, inventory management, special weapons, logistics, and operations research/ systems analysis. He served in the US at Aberdeen Proving Ground, MD, Ft. Bliss, TX, White Sands Missile Range, NM, and Redstone Arsenal, AL. He had overseas tours in South Korea, France, Germany, and South Vietnam. His awards and decorations include a Legion of Merit, a Bronze Star with Oak Leaf Cluster, a Meritorious Service Medal with Oak Leaf Cluster, and an Army Commendation Medal. While at Aberdeen in 1969 – 1972, he taught logistic subjects at the Ordnance School, became a Master Instructor, and earned an MS in Management Engineering from The George Washington University. Toward the end of his Army career, he became active in hunting and the shooting sports. He earned "Gross Gold" pins in hunting-style shooting in Germany and Luxembourg, hunted big game in Germany, and took up trap and skeet shooting upon returning to the States.

After retiring from the Army, Bill got an MS in Computer Science from the University of Alabama in Huntsville in 1982 and worked in computer systems engineering, computer simulation modeling, software engineering and software development. His employers ranged from "beltway bandits" in Virginia and Alabama to the Bank of America's consumer lending systems development organization in Jacksonville, Florida. He retired for the second time in 2003.

He now lives at St. Augustine Beach, FL., where he is close to his son, daughter and granddaughter. His wife of 49 years, Carolyn, passed away in July 2013. His interest in animals seems to have affected his daughter, who is a Veterinarian with an exclusively feline practice. He enjoys all forms of rifle and shotgun shooting, and is the only National Skeet Shooting Association Level 3 instructor in Florida.